NEW YORK REVIEW BOOKS
CLASSICS

T0014005

MOTLEY STONES

ADALBERT STIFTER (1805–1868), the son of a provincial
linen weaver and flax merchant, was born in the rural Bohemian
market town of Oberplan, then part of the Austrian Empire
but today in the Czech Republic. When Stifter was still a child,
his father was crushed under an overturned cart; the family
was left poor, but Stifter's grandfather sent him to school at
the Benedictine monastery of Kremsmünster and he proved
a brilliant student. Stifter attended the University of Vienna,
where he studied law but failed to obtain a degree. Instead he
supported himself as a much sought-after tutor to the children
of the high Viennese aristocracy while also acquiring a small
reputation as a landscape painter. For a number of years Stifter
eagerly courted the daughter of a rich businessman, but his lack
of worldly position turned her family against him, and in 1835 he
married Amalia Mohaupt, a milliner. In 1840, he published his
first story, the success of which started him on a career as a writer,
and in 1850, after working as an editor on two newspapers, he was
appointed supervisor of elementary schools for Upper Austria.
Stifter's works include numerous stories and novellas, as well as
Witiko, a historical novel, and *Indian Summer*, considered one
of the finest examples of the German bildungsroman. Stifter's
mental and physical health deteriorated in his final years. In 1868,
suffering from cirrhosis of the liver, he committed suicide.

ISABEL FARGO COLE is a writer and a translator of such authors
as Annemarie Schwarzenbach, Franz Fühmann, Wolfgang Hilbig,
and Klaus Hoffer. She lives in Berlin, Germany.

MOTLEY STONES

ADALBERT STIFTER

Translated from the German by
ISABEL FARGO COLE

NEW YORK REVIEW BOOKS

New York

THIS IS A NEW YORK REVIEW BOOK
PUBLISHED BY THE NEW YORK REVIEW OF BOOKS
435 Hudson Street, New York, NY 10014
www.nyrb.com

Translation and foreword copyright © 2021 by Isabel Fargo Cole
All rights reserved.

This translation has been published with support from the Austrian Federal
Ministry for Art, Culture, Public Services, and Sports.

First published as a New York Review Books Classic in 2021.

Library of Congress Cataloging-in-Publication Data
Names: Stifter, Adalbert, 1805–1868, author. | Cole, Isabel Fargo, 1973– translator.
Title: Motley stones / Adalbert Stifter; translated from the German by
    Isabel Fargo Cole.
Other titles: Bunte Steine. English
Description: New York City: New York Review Books, 2021. | Series: New York
    Review Books classics
Identifiers: LCCN 2020015769 (print) | LCCN 2020015770 (ebook) |
    ISBN 9781681375205 (paperback) | ISBN 9781681375212 (ebook)
Subjects: LCSH: Stifter, Adalbert, 1805–1868—Translations into English.
Classification: LCC PT2525 .A15 2020 (print) | LCC PT2525 (ebook) |
    DDC 833/.7—dc23
LC record available at https://lccn.loc.gov/2020015769
LC ebook record available at https://lccn.loc.gov/2020015770

ISBN 978-1-68137-520-5
Available as an electronic book; ISBN 978-1-68137-521-2

Printed in the United States of America on acid-free paper.
10 9 8 7 6 5 4 3 2

CONTENTS

Translator's Foreword · vii

MOTLEY STONES

Preface · 3

Introduction · 9

Granite · 11

Limestone · 41

Tourmaline · 93

Rock Crystal · 127

Cat-Silver · 173

Rock Milk · 229

TRANSLATOR'S FOREWORD

The wafting of the air the trickling of the water the growing of the grain the surging of the sea the budding of the earth the shining of the sky the glimmering of the stars is what I deem great; the thunderstorm that looms in splendor, the lightning that cleaves houses, the storm that drives the breakers, the fire-spewing mountain, the earthquake that buries whole lands, these I do not deem greater than those first phenomena, indeed I deem them smaller, for they are the mere effects of much higher laws.

—Adalbert Stifter, preface to *Motley Stones*

"WE SEEK to glimpse the gentle law that guides the human race," Stifter concludes, both modestly and grandly. His "gentle law" reflects the aspirations of the Biedermeier period between the Napoleonic Wars and the Revolutions of 1848, a time when peace came at the price of a stifling conservatism. Today, Biedermeier is a scornful by-word for bourgeois piety, the retreat into private idylls; Stifter is regarded as a paradigmatic writer of the period and popularly misunderstood as a stodgy sentimentalist. Yet Thomas Mann called him "one of the most peculiar, enigmatic, secretly audacious and strangely gripping storytellers in world literature," and for Franz Kafka he was "my obese brother." With a sensibility too idiosyncratic for his contemporaries to grasp, Stifter explored the abyss in the idyll.

Adalbert Stifter was born in 1805 to a family of small tradesmen in the village of Oberplan in the Bohemian Forest (now Horní Planá, in the Czech Republic). A bright child, but prone to self-destructive mood swings, Adalbert was mentored by the village schoolteacher, and in 1818, a year after his father's accidental death, was admitted to the prestigious school at the Benedictine abbey in Kremsmünster. A country bumpkin among children of privilege, he was homesick but thrived academically.

It was a pivotal moment in European history: In 1814, on the eve of Napoleon's defeat, Europe's great powers met at the Congress of Vienna to negotiate a new, reactionary order, stamping out the liberal aspirations that had sparked the French Revolution and the Napoleonic Wars. The congress was chaired by Prince Klemens von Metternich, who would maneuver the Austrian Empire to dominance and turn it into the first modern surveillance state.

In 1826, Stifter enrolled as a law student at the University of Vienna, but he became sidetracked by science and literature courses and a growing interest in painting. Meanwhile, he earned his way as a private tutor for wealthy families. With a talent for teaching, he found himself in demand, but it was a precarious job, marked by the social gulf between himself and his employers. Unprepossessing in appearance, smallpox-scarred, socially awkward, and plagued by depression, the young man struggled with the anonymity of the big city, yet found solace in its cultural offerings. Vienna's sparkling artistic life was the sugar on the pill of Europe's most repressive regime.

During a summer visit to Oberplan, Stifter fell in love with Fanny Greipl, the daughter of an affluent merchant family in a neighboring town. From 1827 to 1835 he would pursue a conflicted, largely epistolary romance with the woman he saw as his soul mate and a "saint." She appears to have reciprocated his feelings, but their relationship was thwarted by opposition from Fanny's parents—a student moonlighting as a tutor was hardly a desirable match—and by Stifter's own insecurities. He vacillated between his artistic pursuits and his studies, quitting the university in 1830. And in 1832 he began a relationship with a beautiful demimondaine called Amalia Mohaupt, the daughter of an impoverished military family. The two had little in common; unlike Fanny, Amalia was uneducated and uncultured. Stifter went on pining after Fanny and dithering until she stopped answering his letters and married another man in 1836. She died giving birth to her first child. Her death, and the lost chance at true love, left a deep mark on Stifter and his work.

Meanwhile, in 1837, he had married Amalia. He was at a professional dead end and had committed to an incompatible relationship. But amid personal crisis, he forged ahead with his writing, achieving his first publication in 1840: the novella "Der Condor." Written with the surreal intensity of Romantic writers such as Jean Paul and E.T.A. Hoffmann, it featured a young woman who accompanies scientists on a balloon flight beyond the stratosphere. Bold in form and touching on cutting-edge issues of science and women's emancipation, "Der Condor" was a sensation. Overnight, Stifter found himself a sought-after writer.

For years, he would produce short stories and novellas, along with several longer works marked by an episodic or assemblage-like quality: the epistolary *Feldblumen* (Flowers of the Field, 1841); *Die Mappe meines Urgroßvaters* (My Great-Grandfather's Portfolio, 1841); and *Bunte Steine* (*Motley Stones*, 1853), a cycle of six thematically related novellas. Later Stifter would produce two novels of truly epic dimensions—*Nachsommer* (*Indian Summer*, 1857) and *Witiko* (1865–1867)—but as his recent biographer Wolfgang Matz points out, both were modestly subtitled *Erzählung* (story or tale). For Matz, this reveals "something very significant about his entire oeuvre: its rootedness in *storytelling* as the transmission of lived experience." Stifter braids acts of storytelling into the rhythms of daily life, not as flights of fancy but as his characters' homely, often groping efforts to tell the truths of their and others' lives. Stifter was celebrated (and attacked) for the realism with which he detailed everyday tasks alongside spectacular natural panoramas. His characters often seem sketchier by contrast. But the lacunae and gray zones of their perspectives lend his writing a more challenging realism—realism as the insight into the difficulty of truly grasping reality.

Stifter thwarts expectations of clear-cut dramatic arcs, with an open-ended quality that is often startlingly modern. His tales lend themselves to nested and assembled narratives, inviting readers to trace connections. Many are rooted in the Oberplan region, so that landscapes, villages, castles, historic incidents, and legends recur, forming one vast web that he obsessively wove and rewove.

Stifter had quickly been picked up by the book publisher Gustav Heckenast, based in Pest, who would become one of his closest friends, providing him with financial and moral support all his life. In 1842, Stifter proposed a collection of his short stories, which ultimately swelled to six volumes under the typically modest title *Studien* (Studies). While writing new stories, he was revising and often completely rewriting his old work; for instance, five of the six novellas in *Motley Stones* are reworkings of earlier stories.

Despite his newfound success, Stifter struggled financially. Though Amalia was a skilled housekeeper, they had a tendency to live beyond their means, suggesting a shared hunger for the trappings of bourgeois prosperity. Quite a literal hunger—their meals were known for their opulence. Stifter lapsed into a habit of binge eating, a contrast to his credo of moderation, which disturbed his contemporaries and has plausibly been tied to his lifelong depression and to the tensions of his marriage. His relationship with Amalia lacked intellectual and emotional rapport, and remained childless, failing to live up to the familial idyll that Stifter so desperately strove for. As a pedagogue and a writer, Stifter had a strong affinity to children, a keen awareness of their aspirations and vulnerabilities. However, he never successfully assumed the role of father, and that failure haunted him and his oeuvre. In 1845, when Amalia's widowed brother Philipp asked for help bringing up his four children, Stifter initially hedged, citing his financial insecurity. Ultimately, in 1847 he and Amalia agreed to take in Philipp's daughter Juliane—a decision that would end in tragedy.

As a tutor, Stifter was now working for Austria's most powerful families, foremost that of Prince Klemens von Metternich himself, whose son Stifter instructed in math and physics. Now that his literary talent had been recognized, he was able to use these connections as an entrée to Vienna's influential intellectual salons. However, his relationships with the elite remained marked by subservience. His bent toward liberal humanism and social reform was counterbalanced by an emotional need for order and authority—a stance that grew increasingly conflicted as political rebellion brewed and finally broke out in 1848.

Beginning in Paris that February, a wave of uprisings swept Europe, releasing tensions that had been bottled up since Napoleon's defeat. Diverse coalitions of rebels demanded constitutional monarchies, freedom of speech, ethnic self-determination, and better conditions for peasants and the proletariat. In Austria under the Habsburg monarchy, forms of serfdom still prevailed, and Metternich kept the lid on nationalist aspirations within the multiethnic empire. In March, uprisings in Vienna led to Metternich's resignation and the promise of a constitution.

Initially, Stifter was eager to contribute to a freer society. In April he helped select Viennese delegates to the Frankfurt Parliament, the revolutionaries' momentous (but ultimately failed) attempt to unite German-speaking lands as a federal state with a liberal constitution. Soon, however, he felt overwhelmed by the political turmoil and retreated to the provincial town of Linz; intended as a brief respite, the stay would become permanent. By mid-May the situation in Vienna grew so tense that the Imperial family fled to Innsbruck. For Stifter, this symbolized a dangerous slide into chaos. Horrified by the violence on both sides and the nationalist movements tearing apart the empire, Stifter began to long for peace and order at all costs. Ultimately the Hapsburgs' absolutist monarchy emerged victorious but made a few concessions such as ending serfdom and instituting bureaucratic and educational reforms.

Seeing an opportunity to put his reformist pedagogy into action—and earn a desperately needed steady income—Stifter sought a position in the educational ministry. In 1850 he was appointed inspector of schools for Upper Austria. Drawing on his own experience to address the difficulties of hardscrabble rural communities, he pushed to move away from rote learning and toward a more individualized focus on children's needs and aptitudes. He embraced the new task at first, but found that it left little time or energy for writing—in the decade after 1848 he would produce just two significant works. Soon he felt crushed by the grind of travel and paperwork and frustrated as his reform proposals were regularly rejected. Meanwhile, a family tragedy was brewing: in 1851, Juliane, now eleven, ran away for two weeks. It is unclear whether Stifter ever developed a close relationship with her, as he rarely mentions her in his letters or papers. Meanwhile, Amalia's relationship with Juliane was outright abusive; there is ample testimony that she treated the girl like a servant and even beat her.

Motley Stones reflects Stifter's conflicted relationship toward children. It proclaims itself to be "an assortment of fancies for young hearts," tales of unassuming goodness not "meant to preach virtue and morals, as the custom is, but rather to work solely by what they are." Yet he gave Juliane a copy for her twelfth birthday with a moralizing dedication:

> Receive here for the first time a book your father has written, for the first time read in print the words you have hitherto heard only from his lips, be good like the children in this book; keep it as a keepsake; if ever you should desire to deviate from the Good, let these pages plead with you not to do so.

This reads as an admonishment of the rebellious Juliane, who, according to Stifter's biographer Alois Hein, was described by family acquaintances as having "something Gypsy-like despite her golden hair and violet eyes, an innate flightiness and lack of restraint." Yet a different note is conveyed by the story "Cat-Silver," in *Motley Stones*. Its protagonist is a Gypsy-like "brown girl," vibrant and keenly intelligent, whose inability to find a place in bourgeois society is described with profound sympathy. This story—the only one written specifically for the collection—reads as a veiled attempt to connect with Juliane, or at least to grapple with their relationship. The preachy birthday dedication, by contrast, rings false on many levels. The children in *Motley Stones* are not "good" in a Goody-Two-shoes sense—they are mainly good at surviving. They are constantly endangered by the recklessness, neglect, abuse, or clueless good intentions of the adults, most shockingly in the warped father-daughter relationship of "Tourmaline." Far from "fancies for young hearts," the tales in *Motley Stones* suggest an adult heart's unarticulated self-recriminations.

In other ways, too, *Motley Stones* suggests a reckoning with certain tensions of the preceding years. Not only was Stifter politically homeless, stranded between revolution and reaction, but he was becoming passé as a writer, especially among liberal intellectuals. In 1849, Friedrich Hebbel, a writer who grappled dramatically with social issues, had satirized the "new nature writers" such as Stifter who, according to him, rhapsodized about beetles and buttercups while ignoring the cosmos and the depths of the human heart. Stifter's preface to *Motley Stones* was a direct rejoinder to Hebbel, an apologia for "small things," for harmony and balance as an alternative to the strife of 1848. At the same time, the stories themselves belie Hebbel's critique, riven by glimpses of peril and psychological extremis and illuminated by flashes of cosmic consciousness.

Needled by his reputation as a "miniaturist," Stifter had long toyed with ideas for a sweeping, dramatic epic (on the life of Robespierre, for instance). At last, in 1857 he published the novel *Indian Summer*—nearly a thousand pages long but almost entirely devoid of drama, conflict, and, indeed, plot. Stifter had produced a bildungsroman, a novel of education, in a radically literal sense. The affluent young narrator, Heinrich, rambles across the country, engaging in scientific pursuits at whim. One day he seeks shelter from a thunderstorm in the country villa of Baron von Risach, a haven for the arts and sciences. Over the years, the kindly baron becomes Heinrich's mentor, and through him Heinrich meets the woman he will marry. The narrative consists of descriptions of the characters' intellectual pursuits, their philosophical conversations, and the serene spaces of Risach's house and garden. Risach's home is a utopian vision of Stifter's humanist ideals and his "gentle law." All is dreamlike harmony— Heinrich's sentimental and scientific education unfolds smoothly; love is restrained tenderness, free from doubt or passion. Only the end reveals what is held at bay: romantic tragedy and political strife. We learn that Risach was forced out of government service by intrigues and lost the love of his life through misunderstandings, finding reconciliation only in old age. The idyll of *Indian Summer* is indeed too good to be true. It expresses the yearning for an unattainable tranquility, a phantasm captured only in words. Striving for a language of utter objectivity that would set his vision in marble, Stifter went to an extreme that alienated even his supporters.

His detractor Hebbel now excoriated the "ponderous Adalbert Stifter" as the epitome of a trend for an "obtuse realism" obsessed with trivial details—"evidently he took Adam and Eve as his presumptive readers, for only they could fail to be familiar with the things he describes with such rambling breadth." Elsewhere he jeered: "[Stifter] has finally lost all sense of proportion.... All that is missing is the contemplation of the words one is using to describe things, and the description of the hand writing down that contemplation." For him, Stifter epitomized the "crossing of a boundary": "the overrated talent for the diminutive proceeds naturally from unravelling the form to fragmenting and crumbling the material."

It is ironic, and telling, that the progressive Hebbel should fall back on conservative catchwords, speaking of boundaries and proportion and expressing a fear of disintegration. Provoked by Stifter's peculiar poetics, Hebbel unwittingly touches on his subversiveness: the radical naivete, the Adamic perspective with which Stifter defamiliarized the mundane. Hebbel's Escher-like image of a hand writing its own description likewise suggests how far Stifter was ahead of his time. Only in the twentieth century, with an ever-keener focus placed on language itself, would his literary experiments be appreciated.

Stifter was deeply wounded by the widespread rejection of the opus he had intended as an expression of his ideals. And in March 1859, tragedy struck. Juliane disappeared again, leaving an enigmatic note: "I am going to join my mother in the great service." Uncannily, her parting words echo those of the "brown girl" in "Cat-Silver." In April, her corpse was found in the Danube. Her motives for ending her life remained unclear, but Stifter was haunted by a sense of guilt. Meanwhile, years of excess had taken their toll on his liver. After a breakdown in early 1864 and a severe diet that left him gaunt, he was pensioned off from his position in the school system. Increasingly, he withdrew into his work on another massive novel, *Witiko*.

Even longer than *Indian Summer*, *Witiko* appeared in three volumes between 1865 and 1867, telling the tale of the eponymous founder of a Bohemian dynasty that had fascinated Stifter since childhood. It was his bid to follow in the footsteps of the wildly popular Walter Scott—but rather than drama and grand passions, *Witiko* offered a static pageant of minutely described knights and fair maidens, castles and landscapes. Though action-packed compared with *Indian Summer*, *Witiko* negates its plot with a still more extreme strategy of narrative flattening and protraction. Meanwhile, the subtle psychology that flickers between the lines of *Indian Summer* is now snuffed out entirely. The characters in *Witiko* lack interiority and communicate in ritualized dialogues driven by austere rhythms. Stifter had purged language to a point of ultimate objectivity, reducing it to basic building blocks, exhaustive in painterly detail but scrupulously free of metaphor.

Cautious praise of the first volume—on the surface, at least, Stifter had finally produced a proper novel—gave way to incomprehension. *Witiko* remains one of the famously inaccessible peaks of German literature. However, over the decades it has found admirers as a bold experiment that synthesizes archaisms with strikingly modern language techniques.

The ailing, embittered Stifter would spend his final years reworking *Die Mappe meines Urgroßvaters* (My Great-Grandfather's Portfolio) and producing several shorter works that in different ways explored the outermost bounds of the speakable. These stories, "Der Kuss von Sentze" (The Kiss of Sentze) and "Der fromme Spruch" (The Pious Words) honed the minimalist language of *Witiko*, limning mental pathologies with a sense of the absurd that suggests his kinship with Kafka. His final work, the autobiographical essay "Aus dem Bairischen Walde" (From the Bavarian Forest) from 1867, describes an incident the year before when, fearing a cholera outbreak, he fled to a beloved vacation spot in the Bavarian Forest and became trapped by a blizzard. Gazing out his window at the whirling snow, Stifter experienced the grandeur of nature as an annihilating force, the utter negation of any "gentle law." The "white darkness" described in "Rock Crystal" overcame the psyche of the man describing it.

Most poignant is the autobiographical fragment "Mein Leben" (My Life), which Stifter began in the fall of 1866 in Oberplan on a final visit to his family home. It begins:

> The smallest grain of sand is a wonder we are unable to fathom.... And then there are the planets that float like our Earth as other earths in the vastness of space that is first revealed to us through them. Then there are the fixed stars farther beyond them.

Only then does Stifter zoom in on himself, a tiny speck in this cosmos:

> The phenomena of my life, which was simple, like a blade of grass growing, have often filled me with wonderment.

Sitting in the parlor of his childhood home, he gropes his way back to his earliest impressions, a time before language:

> Far back in the empty void is a thing like delight and bliss that reached in and seized almost obliterated my being and that nothing in my future life would compare to. The traits noted are these: It was splendor, it was commotion, it was below.... Then there was something wretched, intolerable, then something sweet, assuaging. I recall strivings that achieved nothing, and the cessation of something awful and annihilating.

Later, the intimations of destructiveness take concrete form:

> Once again I found myself amid the awful, annihilating thing I spoke of above. There was crashing, chaos, pain in my hand and blood on it, my mother bound my wound, and then there was an image that I see before me now as clearly as though

painted on porcelain in the purest of colors. I was standing in the garden, which first enters my imagination then, my mother was there, then the other grandmother, whose form also came into my memory for the first time at that moment, I felt the relief that followed each time the awful and annihilating thing left, and I said, "Mother, there's a blade of wheat growing."

My grandmother replied, "We don't talk to boys who break windows." I didn't understand the connection, but the extraordinary thing that had just left me came back at once; indeed my mother said not a word, and I recall something great and terrible weighing on my soul, which may be why that event still lives on within me. I see the tall slender stalk of wheat as clearly as though it were standing by my desk; I see the figures of my mother and grandmother, pottering about in the garden; I see the plants of the garden as a mere indistinct green luster, but the sunshine that surrounded us is present quite clearly.

After that incident there is darkness once again.

This vignette encapsulates the light and darkness of Stifter's life: the self-inflicted pain, the child's vulnerability, the adults' emotional cruelty, the "small thing," the stalk of grass, that offers something to cling to.

Increasingly weakened by cirrhosis of the liver, in the winter of 1867, Stifter caught a flu that sapped his remaining strength. On the night of January 25, 1868, when Amalia stepped away from his bedside for a moment, he cut his throat with a razor. He lived on in a coma for two days, dying on January 28. The circumstances of his death remain controversial to this day: accident, act of delirium, or suicide attempt? In its very ambiguity, his final act echoes that long-ago childhood trauma. Did little Adalbert shatter the window by accident or on purpose? Did he mean to harm himself? One way or the other, he was forced to bear the blame.

Stifter's death was officially put down to his liver trouble; rumors of suicide were suppressed. He was canonized in the image of the conservative miniaturist that had sat so uneasily with him. The dark, challenging, and innovative sides of his work were glossed over. The novella "Rock Crystal" was touted as a Christmas classic—despite its descriptions of an icy void that overshadows the tale's religious symbolism. For new generations of writers, veering between realism and radical experiment to find a language for modernity, Stifter was irrelevant or anathema. But the twentieth century brought more admirers of his writing: Thomas Mann, Franz Kafka, Karl Kraus, Friedrich Nietzsche, Martin Heidegger, Hannah Arendt, Walter Benjamin, Hermann Hesse, Peter Handke, W. G. Sebald.

And in the twenty-first century, his work resonates in unexpected ways with the disruptions of our times and the search for new ways to narrate them. In his incisive 2016 book-length essay *The Great Derangement: Climate Change and the Unthinkable*, Amitav Ghosh argues that modern Western thought, which posits that the world is predictable and subject to rational ordering, has been unable to grasp the radical instability of our environment in the Anthropocene. He traces this failure of imagination back to the nineteenth-century tradition of "realist" literature: "Probability and the modern novel are in fact twins...vessels for the containment of the same kind of experience. Before the birth of the modern novel, wherever stories were told, fiction delighted in the unheard-of and the unlikely."

Ghosh suggests that traditional narratives such as folk epics condense vast spans of experience, operating with a scale that can accommodate rare and catastrophic events. For instance, knowledge about hurricanes or tsunamis that recur at long intervals is passed down in the form of myths. But then (here he cites Franco Moretti) "the novel takes its modern form, through 'the relocation of the unheard-of toward the background...while the everyday moves into the foreground.'" This construction fails, however, in times of climate change, when the unheard-of intrudes with increasing regularity. Our "realism" takes as its yardstick a cozy daily life that is actually a historical anomaly, while refusing to face the "abnormal" developments that, ironically, our consumerist comforts make increasingly probable.

A friction-filled but illuminating dialogue emerges between Ghosh's arguments and Stifter's form of "realism." At first, Ghosh's insights seem to back up the criticisms raised against Stifter. The small routines of daily life are, after all, an obsessive, almost ritual presence in Stifter's work. But another more recent writer can be brought into the fray in Stifter's defense: Ursula K. Le Guin and *The Carrier Bag Theory of Fiction*. Her witty Paleolithic parable contrasts the violent adventure tales of the (male) hunters with the explorative, nonlinear narratives of the (female) gatherers. Unlike Ghosh, she argues for modern fiction as a form that lends itself to subversion:

> The novel is a fundamentally unheroic kind of story. Of course the Hero has frequently taken it over.... So the Hero has decreed ... first, that the proper shape of the narrative is that of the arrow or spear, starting *here* and going straight *there* and THOK! hitting its mark (which drops dead); second, that the central concern of narrative, including the novel, is conflict; and third, that the story isn't any good if he isn't in it.
>
> I differ with all of this. I would go so far as to say that the natural, proper, fitting shape of the novel might be that of a sack, a bag.... A novel is a medicine bundle, holding things in a particular, powerful relation to one another and to us.

A narrative, she writes, might be "a leaf a gourd shell a net a bag a sling a sack a bottle a pot a box a container."

Le Guin's evocation of *thingness* uncannily echoes Stifter's distinctive attitude toward commas—and a key aspect of his sensibility. Squeamish about weaponry, his narratives foreground the modest tools of household chores, women's and men's daily work. That, for him, is the heart of the matter, not merely the background against which the Hero performs the Action (to borrow Le Guin's ironic capitalization). Indeed, in Stifter's "Tourmaline," "great men" and their deeds are literally reduced to the status of wallpaper, while most of the Action happens offstage.

"It is always in people's ordinary everyday infinitely recurring actions that [the gentle] law most surely forms the fulcrum, for these actions are the lasting the underlying ones, like the millions of fibrils of the tree of life," Stifter writes. At the same time, Stifter embeds these actions within vast cycles of destruction and renewal, hinting at the deep-time perspective that Ghosh sees as an antidote to modern shortsightedness. By detailing the efforts needed to maintain everyday life through centuries of hardship and turmoil, Stifter underscores its precariousness.

Four of the six novellas in *Motley Stones* revolve around the very catastrophes he belittles in his preface: plagues, storms, floods, fires, unprecedented blizzards, and hailstorms. His characters face a natural world whose signs constantly elude interpretation. The blizzard in "Rock Crystal," the hailstorm in "Cat-Silver" that shatters all that is solid—these phenomena defy traditional weather lore. Yet the scrupulously described catastrophes never seem like literary contrivances. They are not symbolic tempests, projections of the protagonists' inner dramas. The storms themselves are the dramas. However anomalous, they seem to follow a greater logic that would be revealed from the right point of view. Devastating storms can be imagined as mere ripples of the electric force that is "gently and ceaselessly altering shaping and life-giving."

At the same time such a stratospheric "gentleness" shades unnervingly into indifference, indeed implacability. Sebald writes that Stifter takes the Romantic era's evocations of "indifferent, destructive force[s]" to the point of an unprecedented "radical indifferentism." Behind Stifter's facade of faith, he sees a "profound agnosticism and a pessimism that stretches to cosmic dimensions."

Stifter, a profoundly insecure man, set out to seek firm ground—but wherever he looked, his gaze undermined it. In startling fashion, he anticipated the "derangement" described by Ghosh. His language seems at first to flow like a calm river; up close, it is a tide of ice grinding its way onward, fissured by powerful strains. As Sebald and other modern commentators note, Stifter did not grapple openly with the disturbing implications of his work. But they are all the more powerful for being conveyed as though unconsciously, without explanation or resolution. His peculiar gift calls to mind an image from his preface: a magnetic needle blindly recording invisible storms.

A NOTE ON THE TRANSLATION

I have aimed to convey both the transparency and the strangeness of Stifter's language. One of his most striking idiosyncrasies is his usage of commas: in places they are unexpectedly omitted to create subtle rhythmic effects, convey shifts of tone in spoken dialogue, or allow the items in a list to merge in one unbroken flow; elsewhere, they are used liberally to create different rhythms. Another is his use of repetition. For instance, Stifter exhaustively describes his characters' paths through the landscape—often the same path taken over and over like a theme with subtle or sometimes dramatic variations. In these passages, the verbs *gehen* (to walk or go) and *sehen* (to see or look) are repeated to mantra-like effect.

When translating from German into English, there is always a temptation to seek solutions in the thesaurus. English has a richer vocabulary, while German offers more modular freedom to form new words and juggle their order. German's flexible sentence structure means that semantic repetitions can be enlivened by varied syntax. In Stifter's writing, the structure and propulsion often stems from these repetitions, or from the contrast between austere diction and jarring or piercingly lyrical turns of phrase. I have made every effort to convey repetition without monotony and retain Stifter's inimitable interplay of delicacy and bluntness.

MOTLEY STONES

PREFACE

IT WAS once said against me that I fashion only small things, and that my people are always ordinary people. If that is true, I am now in the position of offering readers something smaller and more insignificant still, namely an assortment of fancies for young hearts. Nor are they even meant to preach virtue and morals, as the custom is, but rather to work solely by what they are. If there is anything noble and good in me, it will exist in my writings on its own; but if it is not in my nature, I will strive in vain to depict the sublime and the beautiful, for baseness and ignobility will always show through. Fashioning great or small things was never the aim of my writings; I was guided by other laws entirely. Art is so high and exalted for me; for me, as I have said elsewhere, it is the highest thing on earth after religion, and so I have never regarded my writings as poetical, nor shall I presume to regard them so. The world has but a very few poets, who are the high priests, the benefactors of humanity; but it has a great many false prophets. Yet if not all spoken words can be poetry, they may be something else whose existence is not utterly unjustified. To give kindred spirits an hour of pleasure, to send forth greetings to all of them known or unknown, and add a grain of good to the edifice of the eternal, that was my writings' aim, and that it shall remain. I would be very glad to know for certain that I had achieved even this aim alone. But so long as we are speaking of great and small things, I shall put forth my views, which are likely to differ from those of many people. The wafting of the air the trickling of the water the growing of the grain the surging of the sea the budding of the earth the shining of the sky the glimmering of the stars is what

3

I deem great; the thunderstorm that looms in splendor, the lightning that cleaves houses, the storm that drives the breakers, the fire-spewing mountain, the earthquake that buries whole lands, these I do not deem greater than those first phenomena, indeed I deem them smaller, for they are the mere effects of much higher laws. They occur in isolation, and are the results of one-sided causes. The force that makes the milk in the poor woman's pot swell and boil over is the same that thrusts the lava upward in the fire-spewing mountain and makes it flow down the mountain slopes. These phenomena are merely more striking, more apt to draw the gaze of the ignorant and inattentive, while the scientist's mind tends chiefly toward what is whole and universal, and can find grandeur in it alone, for it alone is what sustains the world. The particulars pass, and a short time later their effects are barely seen. We shall illustrate our words with an example. Suppose a man spent years observing the magnetic needle whose one end always points North, recording in a book at fixed times each day the shifts as the needle points now plainly now less plainly northward; an uninformed person would surely regard this endeavor as a small thing and a mere game; but what awe is inspired by this small thing, and what enthusiasm by this game, when we learn that these observations are in fact made across the earth's entire surface, and the charts compiled from them show that certain small shifts in the magnetic needle often occur simultaneously and to the same degree in all parts of the world; that, then, a magnetic storm is passing over all the earth, that all the earth's surface at once is sensing a sort of magnetic shiver. If, just as we have eyes for light, we had a sense organ for electricity and the magnetism arising from it, what a great world what a wealth of immeasurable phenomena would open up before us. But though we lack this physical eye, we possess the mental eye of science, and it teaches us that the electric and magnetic force acts upon a vast stage, that it is diffused across all the earth and throughout all the sky, that its flow engulfs everything, and that it manifests itself by gently and ceaselessly altering shaping and life-giving. Lightning is but a small feature of this force; the force itself is a great thing in Nature. But since science grasps only grain upon grain, makes only observation upon observation, amasses the universal only from particulars, and finally since the multitude of phenomena and the field of facts is infinitely great, so that God has made the joy and felicity of inquiry inexhaustible, and we in our workshops can represent only the particular and never the universal, for that would be Creation—thus the history of what is great in Nature consists in a perpetual metamorphosis of views about this greatness. When human beings were in their childhood, their mind's eye as yet untouched by science, they were enthralled by what was close at hand and striking, and were compelled to fear and admiration: but when their minds were opened, when their eyes turned toward the greater context, the particular phenomena fell away, and law rose higher and higher, the marvels ceased, and wonder increased.

As is outward Nature, so too is inward nature, the nature of the human race. A whole life filled with righteousness simplicity self-mastery rationality efficacy within one's sphere admiration of beauty joined with a cheerful serene death is what I deem great: powerful stirrings of passion wrath's rumbling emergence the thirst for vengeance the inflamed spirit striving for action, tearing down, altering, destroying, and in this excitation often casting away its own life, these things I deem smaller, not greater, for they are but the product of isolated and one-sided forces, like storms fire-spewing mountains earthquakes. We seek to glimpse the gentle law that guides the human race. There are forces whose aim is the endurance of the individual. They take and use all that is necessary for that individual to stand and evolve. They ensure the endurance of the one, and thus of all. But when someone is bent on seizing everything his nature needs, when he destroys the conditions for another's existence, it angers some higher thing within us, we help the weak and the oppressed, we restore the balance so that he may stand as one human being beside the other, and walk his human path, and when we have done this, we feel gratified, we feel far more exalted and inwardly moved than we feel as individuals, we feel ourselves as the whole of humanity. And so there exist forces working toward the endurance of all humanity that must not be curtailed by individual forces, but, on the contrary, work to curtail them. The law of these forces is the law of justice the law of morals, the law decreeing that each should stand respected honored unmolested beside the others, that he may walk his higher human path, and gain the love and admiration of his fellows, that he be cherished as a gem, as each person is a gem for all other people. This law is found wherever people live alongside others, and is shown whenever people act upon others. It lies in the love of husband and wife the love of parents for their children of children for their parents in the mutual love of siblings of friends in the sweet affinity of the sexes in the industry that sustains us, in the works we perform for our own sphere for distant spheres for humanity, and at last in the order and form with which whole societies and states compass and complete their existence. For that reason poets old and new have drawn on these subjects to commend their works to the sympathy of peoples near and far. For that reason the student of humankind, wherever he sets foot, sees this law alone, for it is the only universal the only sustaining and never-ending one. He sees it in the lowest hut as well as in the highest palace, he sees it in a poor woman's devotion and in the hero's calm defiance of death for his fatherland and humanity. Certain movements within the human race have imbued souls with a direction toward a goal, ultimately lending a different shape to entire spans of time. When the law of justice and morals is seen in these movements, when it has ushered them in and carried them onward, we as all humanity feel elevated, we feel humanly universalized, we sense the sublime that penetrates the soul wherever immeasurably great forces work together in time or space upon a distinct rational whole. But when the law of right and morals is not apparent in these movements, when they struggle toward one-sided and selfish goals, the student of humankind turns away in disgust, however tremendous and terrible they may be, and regards them as a small thing as a thing unworthy of humanity. So powerful is this law of right and morals that wherever and whenever it has been opposed, in the end it has emerged from the battle triumphant and glorious. Indeed, even when individuals or entire peoples have perished for the cause of right and morals, we do not feel that they are vanquished, we feel they are triumphant, our pity is mingled with exultation and rapture, for the whole is higher than the part, goodness is greater than death; we say then that we feel the sense of the Tragic, and are lifted with shivers of awe into the moral law's purer ether. When we see mankind move through history like a serene silver river toward a great eternal goal, we sense the Sublime and particularly the Epic. But however powerfully the Tragic and the Epic may work, however broad their strokes, however superb they are as artistic devices, it is always in people's ordinary everyday infinitely recurring actions that this law most surely forms the fulcrum, for these actions are the lasting the underlying ones, like the millions of fibrils of the tree of life. Just as in Nature the universal laws work, quiet and ceaseless, and striking phenomena are merely isolated expressions of these laws, so too does the law of morals work, quiet and soul-quickening, through the unending dealings of people with people, and the momentary wonders of deeds performed are merely small signs of this universal force. Thus, just as the law of Nature sustains the world, this law sustains humanity.

Just as in natural history views of what is great have constantly changed, so too has it been in people's moral history. First they were moved by the most obvious things, physical strength and wrestling victories were praised, then courage and military valor aimed to express and act out violent emotions and passions toward hostile bands and alliances, then the sovereignty of the tribe and the authority of the family were extolled, and meanwhile beauty and love, like friendship and sacrifice, were celebrated too; but then a vista opened up to something greater: order was imposed on entire spheres of humanity and human relations, the right of the whole joined with that of the part, and magnanimity toward foes and the suppression of one's emotions and passions for the sake of justice was exalted and glorified, as even the ancients held moderation to be the prime manly virtue; and at last a bond embracing the peoples was conceived as a thing to be desired, a bond that gives one people's gifts in exchange for the other's, that advances science, sets forth its treasures for all humanity, and in art and religion leads to simplicity in what is exalted and divine.

As it is with humanity's ascent, so it is with its decline. Declining peoples first lose their sense of moderation. They strive for isolated particulars, they fling themselves shortsightedly on narrow and trifling things, they raise the conditional above the universal; then they pursue pleasure and sensuality, they seek to gratify their hatred and envy of their neighbor, their art depicts what is one-sided what is valid from one perspective only, then what is disjointed dissonant bizarre, eventually what excites and tantalizes the senses, and at last immorality and vice; in religion what is innermost degenerates to mere form or to opulent effusions, the distinction between good and evil fades, the individual scorns the whole, pursuing his pleasure and his ruin, and so this people falls victim to its inner disarray or to an external foe more savage but stronger. ——

Having in this preface taken my views of great and small things thus far, let me say too that I have sought to glean certain experiences from the history of humankind, and have worked aspects of these experiences into poetic efforts; but these very views and the events of recent years have taught me to mistrust my powers, and so these attempts shall rest until they can be better executed or else destroyed as futile.

But those who have followed me through this preface, by no means suitable for young listeners, may, I hope, deign to enjoy what more modest efforts have produced, and pass on with me to the innocent things that follow.

—ADALBERT STIFTER
Autumn 1852

INTRODUCTION

As a boy I took home twigs plants and flowers that caught my fancy, and other things too that pleased me almost better still because they did not lose their color and vitality as quickly as the plants did, namely all kinds of stones and things of the earth. On fields on marges on heaths and pastures and even on meadows where nothing grows but high grass these things lie about in profusion. As I was allowed to roam far and wide, I inevitably discovered the places to find these things, and took home what I found.

On the road from Oberplan to Hossenreuth there is a wide stretch of turf that reaches into the fields, enclosed by a wall of unmortared stones. In these stones little flakes glitter like silver and diamonds, and can be pried out with a knife or an awl. We children called these flakes cat-silver, and took great pleasure in them.

There is a stone on Altrichter's Hill so fine and soft that you can cut it with a knife. The local people call it soapstone. Out of that stone I made bars cubes rings and signets, and then a man who made clocks barometers and ancestral charts, and also varnished pictures, showed me how to paint the stone with a fine layer of varnish to make the prettiest blue green and reddish lines come to light.

When I had time, I laid out my treasures in a row to contemplate and delight in them. And there was no end of wonderment when a stone had so enigmatic a gleam and shine and twinkling gaze that it was impossible to fathom where it came from. Of course now and then they included a piece of glass I had found in the fields, shimmering in all the colors of the rainbow. When I was told that it was just broken glass, and weathered at that, which was how it had picked up those shimmering colors, I thought: My, that might be just a piece of glass, but it has the prettiest colors, and it's a marvel how it managed to take on those colors in the cool damp earth, and I left it there among the stones.

I have never yet lost the spirit of collecting. To this very day I literally carry home stones in my satchel to draw them or paint them, and make further use of their images, and not only that, here I am starting a collection of diverse odds and ends and fancies for young people, for them to take pleasure in, arrange to their liking and contemplate. True, for this collection my young friends must be much older than I was when I brought home my odd stones of the field to admire. There is no chance that the collection will contain a gem, no more than there is any danger that I might have had an uncut diamond or ruby among my stones, thus having been immeasurably rich without knowing it. But should these things include some bits of broken glass, I beg my friends to think as I thought of my glass back then: But it has all kinds of colors, and so let it stay here with the stones.

Could one dedicate a collection to someone who has died, I would dedicate this to my deceased young friend Gustav. I met him by chance and came to love him, and he trusted me like a father. He enjoyed fancies, and like a girl took pleasure in the occasional sweetmeat, and always got them when he ate at my table. In his brighter home let him think now and then of his older friend who is in this world still, and wishes to linger there a while longer.

As more stones exist than can be counted, I cannot say in advance how long this collection shall be.

—THE AUTHOR
Autumn 1852

GRANITE

Outside the house where I and my fathers were born right next to the entrance lies a great eight-cornered stone shaped like a much-elongated block. Its sides are rough-hewn, but its top surface, so often sat upon, is as fine and smooth as though coated by the most artful of glazes. The stone is very old, and no one has heard tell of the time when it was laid there. Our house's most ancient graybeards sat on that stone, as did those who perished in tender youth and now slumber in the churchyard alongside all the others. The hollows trodden in the sandstone slabs serving as the stone's base also show its age, as do the deep holes worn by falling drops where the slabs project under the gutter.

One of the most recent members of our house to sit upon that stone was I, in my boyhood. I liked to sit on the stone because, at least back then, it afforded a sweeping view. Now that view is somewhat obstructed by buildings. I liked to sit there in the first days of spring, when the sun's balmier rays brought forth the first warmth along the house wall. I looked out upon the fields, plowed but not yet sown, sometimes I saw a glass shard glimmer and gleam like a white fiery spark, or I saw a vulture fly past, or I gazed at the far bluish forest that stretches its jagged edge along the sky where the thunderstorms and cloudbursts come down, so high up that I thought you could seize the sky by climbing its tallest tree. Other times I gazed out at the road that runs close to the house, now watching a harvest wagon now a herd now a peddler pass by.

In the summer evenings my grandfather liked to sit on the stone too, smoking his pipe, and sometimes, when I had long since gone to sleep, or in my commencing slumber took in only the fragments of sounds, young lads and girls sat there as well on the stone or on the wooden bench beside it or on the stack of planks, and sang out sweet songs into the gloomy night.

One of the things I saw often from that stone was a man of a most peculiar sort. From time to time he would come up Hossenreuth Road pushing a gleaming black wheelbarrow. On that wheelbarrow he had a gleaming black cask. His clothes had not been black at first, but with time they had grown quite dark, and gleamed as well. When the sun shone down on him, he looked as though he had been greased with oil. He wore a wide-brimmed hat under which his long hair spilled down his neck. He had a brown face and kindly eyes, and his hair had already turned a yellowish-white hue, as it tends to in people of low station who have to work hard for a living. Approaching the houses, he would cry out words I did not understand. Following this cry our neighbors would emerge from their homes with vessels in their hands, usually black wooden pots, and come out onto our lane. Meanwhile the man had drawn near, pushing his wheelbarrow up to our lane. There he stopped, turned the tap on the spigot of his cask, and let a brown viscous liquid flow into the vessels the people held under it, a liquid I clearly recognized as wagon grease, for which they paid him a number of kreuzer or groschen. When it was all over, and the neighbors had departed with their purchases, he closed the cask up again, carefully scraping back whatever had oozed out, and went on his way. I must have been there almost every time this took place, for if I happened not to be out on the lane when the man came, I heard his cry just as well as the neighbors did, and was sure to be on the spot sooner than any of them.

One day, when the spring sun shone cheerfully, making everyone jovial and roguish, I saw him coming up Hossenreuth Road again. Approaching the houses he cried out his usual chant, the neighbors came up, he gave them what they needed, and they went away. After that was done, he tidied up his cask just as he always did. To scrape back what had collected on the spigot or, when the tap was opened, on the lower barrel staves, he had a long flat narrow short-handled spoon. With this spoon he skillfully removed every residue of liquid hiding in joints or corners and scraped it back in on the bunghole's sharp rim. I sat on the stone while he did this, and watched him. By chance my feet were bare, as they often were, and I was wearing hose that had grown too short. Suddenly he looked over at me from his work and said, "Would you like to have your feet greased?"

Having always regarded the man as a great curiosity, I felt honored by his familiar manner, and held out both my feet. He dipped his spoon into the hole and went to work, laying one slow stroke on each of my feet. The liquid spread beautifully on the skin, extraordinarily clear and golden brown, and sent up its pleasant resinous fragrance. Following its nature, it gradually spread down my feet and around their curves. Meanwhile the man went on with his business, smiling over at me a few times, then slipped his spoon into a sheath next to the cask, pounded the bung back into the bunghole, slung the wheelbarrow's carrying straps around his back, picked it up and pushed it onward. Now that I was alone, with a feeling that was half pleasant, but still not entirely reassuring, I decided to go and show my mother. Carefully holding up my hose, I went into the parlor. It was Saturday, and every Saturday the parlor had to be mopped and scoured spick and span, which had been done that morning, just as the wagon-grease man liked to come to town on Saturdays to stay on till Sunday and go to church. The grain of the wooden floor, well scrubbed and then dried, thirstily drank up the wagon grease from my feet, so that each step I took left a bold print on the floor. My mother was sitting at the table by the front window, sewing. As she saw me coming, marching forward, she leapt to her feet. For a moment she hovered there, either struck by admiration, or looking about for an instrument to greet me with. At last she cried, "What has this unholy son of my flesh gotten up to this time?"

And to keep me from going any farther forward, she ran toward me, picked me up, and, heedless of my fright and her apron, carried me out into the hallway. There she set me down, went to the attic stairs—under which, this being the only place it was allowed, we had to leave all the switches and branches we brought home, of which I had amassed a large collection in the past few days—took out whatever she could lay hands on and lashed my feet long and hard until the leaves of the switches, my hose, her apron, the flagstones and all the surroundings were covered with pitch. Then she let me go, and went back into the parlor.

Though from the outset I had not been quite easy in my mind about the whole affair, this appalling turn things had taken, and this rift between me and my dearest relation in the world, now virtually obliterated me. In a corner of the hallway there stands a big stone block on which the yarn used for household weaving is pounded with a wooden mallet. I stumbled toward this stone and sank down upon it. I could not even weep, my heart was cramped, and my throat seemed laced shut. Inside I heard my mother and the maid discussing what to do, and I feared that if the pitch stains could not be removed, they would come back out and punish me some more.

At that moment my grandfather walked in through the back door which leads to the well and the garden, and came toward me. He had always been the kindhearted one, and whatever misfortune descended on us children he would never ask who was to blame, he simply helped. Having come to the place where I sat, he stopped and looked at me. Grasping the state I was in, he asked what had happened, and how I had come to this pass. I wanted to unburden myself, but even now I could tell him nothing, for at the sight of his kind, benevolent eyes all the tears that had failed to come before emerged now with a vengeance, and ran down in streams, so that for weeping and sobbing I could only utter broken and garbled sounds, and lift up my little feet on which the ugly red of punishment was showing through the pitch.

But he smiled and said, "Now, now, come to me, come along."

As he spoke he took me by the hand, gently tugged me down from the stone, and led me, so stricken that I could barely follow him, down the length of the hallway and out into the yard. A broad flagstone porch runs about the yard along the buildings. On the porch various footstools and the like are usually standing under the eaves so that the maids can sit safe from the weather while hackling flax or doing similar chores. He led me to one of those footstools and said, "Sit there, and wait a bit, I'll be back in a moment."

With these words he went inside, and once I had waited a while, he came back out again carrying a great, green-glazed bowl, a pot of water, soap and cloths. He set these things down on the flagstones next to me, pulled off my hose as I sat there on the footstool, tossed them aside, filled the bowl with warm water, lowered my feet in, and washed them with soap and water until a great white and brown mound of foam rose up from the bowl, the wagon grease, being still fresh, was washed away completely, and not a trace of pitch could be seen on my skin. Then he dried my feet with the cloths and asked, "Is it better now?"

I nearly laughed through my tears; weight after weight had been lifted from my mind as he washed, and while already my weeping had abated, now just a few stray tears seeped from my eyes. Now he brought another pair of hose and put them on me. Then he took the dry ends of the cloths, wiped my tearstained face, and said, "Now go across the yard and through the big entrance gate and out onto the lane, and make sure no one sees you and no one gets their hands on you. Wait for me on the lane, I'll bring you new clothes, and change clothes myself. I'm going to Melm today; you can come along and tell me how this misfortune came about, and how you got into that wagon grease. We'll leave your things there, someone is sure to put them away."

With these words he nudged me toward the yard and went back into the house. I tiptoed across the yard and hurried out the entrance gate. Out on the lane I walked a long way from the big stone and the front door, to be safe, and stopped at a place where I could see into the front door from a distance. Where I had been birched, I saw two maids at work, kneeling on the floor and moving their hands back and forth across it. They were probably trying to remove the pitch stains left by my birching. The house martin flew shrieking in and out the door because of the constant commotion beneath its nest today, first my birching and now the busy maids. At the farthest end of our lane, a long way from the front door, where the little hill on which our house stands begins to slope toward the passing road, there lay several logs intended for a building or some work of that kind. I sat down on them, and waited.

At last my grandfather emerged. He had his wide-brimmed hat on his head, he had on the long coat he liked to wear on Sundays, and in one hand he carried his walking stick. In the other he had my blue-striped jacket, white socks, black laced boots and my gray felt hat. He helped me into these things and said, "So, off we go now."

We walked down the narrow footpath through the greenery of our hill to the road and continued along it, first between our neighbors' houses, which stood in the spring sun, with people greeting us from them, and then out into the open. Before us stretched a wide field with beautiful green grass, and bright kind sunshine flooded all the things of the world. We walked down a white path through the greensward. My pain and my anguish had already nearly vanished, I knew things were bound to turn out well, now that my grandfather had taken the matter into his hands as my protector; the open air and the shining sun had a calming effect, I enjoyed the feel of the jacket on my shoulders and the boots on my feet, and the air ran gently through my hair.

After we had walked for a while through the meadow, the way we usually walked when he took me along, meaning that he curbed his long strides, but took them all the same, so that at times I had to scurry along beside him, my grandfather said, "Now tell me how you came to get into so much wagon grease that your hose were covered with pitch, and not only that, your feet were covered too, there's a patch of pitch in the hallway, and pitch-stained switches lying about, and throughout the house wherever you go you see patches of wagon grease. I told your mother you're coming with me, you don't need to worry now, you won't be punished any more."

Now I told him how I had been sitting on the stone, how the wagon-grease man had come by, how he'd asked me if I wanted my feet greased, how I'd held them out to him, how he'd laid a stroke on each of them, how I'd gone into the parlor to show my mother, how she'd jumped up, how she'd grabbed me, carried me into the hallway and birched me with my own switches, and how after that I'd been left sitting on the stone.

"You're a fine little fool," my grandfather said, "and old Andreas is an awful rascal, he's always played those kinds of tricks, and now he'll be laughing to himself in secret for coming up with the idea. That it happened this way helps your case a great deal. But you see, even old Andreas, however dim a view we might take of his actions, is not as guilty as we others think; for how should old Andreas know that wagon grease seems such a frightful thing for people and that it can make such a mess in the house? For him it's a ware that he's constantly handling, that he lives from, that he loves, and that he gets a fresh supply of whenever it runs out on him. And how should he know about scoured floors when he's on the road with his cask rain or shine year after year, when he sleeps in barns at night or on the Sabbath, and has hay or straw sticking to his clothes. But your mother is right as well; she had to think that you'd rashly smeared your feet with all that wagon grease yourself, and that you'd gone into the parlor so as to dirty the beautiful floor. Just give her time, she'll come around, she'll understand everything, and all will be well. When we get up to that hill there, where we'll have a view all around, I'll tell you a story about pitch-men like old Andreas, a story that took place long before you were born, and before I was born, and that will show you the marvelous fates that people can have on God's earth. And when you're strong enough, and can walk, next week I'll let you come along to Spitzenberg and the Stag Mountains, and along the way in the spruce glen you'll see a distillery where they make the wagon grease, where old Andreas always gets his supplies, where the pitch that greased your feet today came from."

"Yes, Grandfather," I said, "I'll be quite strong."

"That will be fine, then," he replied, "and you can come along."

With these words we had come to a wall of unmortared stones, beyond it a green meadow with its white footpath. Grandfather climbed up over the stepping-stone, pulling his stick and coat over after him, and, as I was too small, helped me across; and we walked onward along the neat clean path. About midway across the meadow he stopped, and pointed to the ground, where a clear stream welled up beneath a flat stone, and trickled onward through the meadow.

"That's the Behring Springlet," he said, "which has the best water in these parts, excepting the wonder-working water from the roofed-over spring on Spring Mountain, near the Chapel of Mercy by the Good Water. People fetch their drinking water from this springlet here, field hands come a long way to drink from it, and sick men from distant parts have sent people with jugs to bring them water. Mark this springlet well."

"Yes, Grandfather," I said.

After these words we walked onward. We walked down the foot-path through the meadow, we walked up a path between fields, and came to a hollow covered with short dense near-gray grass, where spruce trees stood at various intervals in all directions.

"What we're walking on now," my grandfather said, "is the Dry-beaks, a funny name, either it comes from the arid barren ground, or from the weedy little plant that covers the ground by the thousands, whose blossom has a white beak with a little yellow tongue inside. Look, the mighty spruce trees belong to the people of Oberplan, allotted according to their tax status; their needles don't grow in two rows, they grow in sheaths like tufts of green bristles, they have supple resinous wood, they have yellow pitch, they give sparse shade, and when a soft breeze comes, you hear the calm slow rustling of the needles."

As we walked on I was able to observe the truth of my grandfather's words. I saw hosts of the little white-yellow flowers on the ground, I saw the grayish turf, I saw the pitch like drops of gold on the trunks, I saw the countless tufts of needles on countless branches sprouting as though from tiny dark boot shafts, and though there was barely a breeze to be felt, I heard the calm rustle in the needles.

We walked on and on, and the path became quite steep.

At a somewhat higher, more open spot, my grandfather stopped and said, "So, here we'll wait a bit."

He turned around, and once we had caught our breath from the exertion of climbing, he raised his stick, pointed to a remote massive forest ridge in the direction we had come, and asked, "Can you tell me what that is?"

"Yes, Grandfather," I replied, "that's the alp where a cattle herd grazes in the summer and is driven back down in the fall."

"And what is that in front of the alp?" came his next question.

"That is the Hütten Forest," I replied.

"And to the right of the alp and the Hütten Forest?"

"That's Philippgeorg Mountain."

"And to the right of Philippgeorg Mountain?"

"That's the Lake Forest, where the dark deep lake waters are."

"And to the right of the Lake Forest?"

"That's the Plöckenstein and the Throne Forest."

"And to the right of that?"

"That's the Tusset Forest."

"And after that you cannot name them; but there are many more forest ridges with many names, stretching on for many miles across the lands. Once, the forests were ever vaster than they are today. When I was a boy they reached all the way to Spitzenberg and the Abbey Crofts, there were wolves in them still, and at night, at the right time of year, we could hear the stags bellowing even in our beds. Do you see the smoke column rising from the Hütten Forest?"

"Yes, Grandfather, I see it."

"And farther back another one rising from the forest by the alp?"

"Yes, Grandfather."

"And another from the glens of Philippgeorg Mountain?"

"I see it, Grandfather."

"And far back in the basin of the Lake Forest, which you can hardly see at all, another one faint as a little blue cloud?"

"I see it too, Grandfather."

"You see, those smoke columns all come from the people who make their living in the forest. First there are the woodcutters, who saw down the trees of the forest here and there, leaving nothing behind but stumps and brush. They light fires to cook their food on, and to burn the branches and brushwood they don't need. Then there are the charcoal burners, who make a great kiln covered with earth and brushwood, and in it burn the billets to make the coals you often see them carting past our house in great sacks, off to distant parts that have no fuel to burn. Then there are the haymakers who dry hay on the little meadows or in the forest clearings or cut it from between the stones with their sickles. They also make fires to cook on, or so that their draft animals can lie down in the smoke to get relief from the flies. Then there are the gatherers who look for tree fungus, medicinal herbs, berries, and other things, and like to make a fire to refresh themselves. Finally there are the pitch burners, who build furnaces from the forest soil, or make clay vaults over pits, and alongside them build huts from forest trees to live in them and distill wagon grease in these furnaces and pits, or tar, turpentine and other spirits. Where you see a thin little thread of smoke rising, it might be a hunter, roasting his bit of meat, or having a rest. These people have no lasting place in the forest, for they go here and then there, according as their work is done, or they cease to find what they seek. So too the smoke columns have no lasting place, and today you see them here, and another time elsewhere."

"Yes, Grandfather."

"That is the life of the forests. But now let us look at what lies outside them. Can you tell me what those white buildings are that we see through the double-trunked spruce?"

"Yes, Grandfather, those are the Pranghofer Crofts."

"And over to the left of the Pranghofer Crofts?"

"Those are the houses of Vorderstift and Hinterstift."

"And farther to the left of that?"

"That's Glöckelberg."

"And farther toward us, by the water?"

"That's the hammer mill and David's Croft."

"And all the houses quite near us, with the church rising in their midst, and behind them a mountain with another chapel on it?"

"But Grandfather, that's our own market town Oberplan, and the chapel on the mountain is the Chapel by the Good Water."

"And if it weren't for the mountains and the ridges around us, you'd see many more houses and villages still: the Karl Crofts, Stuben,

Blackbrook, Longbridge, Melm, Honnetschlag, and in the opposite direction Pichlern, Perneck, Salnau and several others. You'll come to see how much life there is in those villages, how many people labor there day and night for their living, and enjoy the happiness granted us here below. I showed you the woods and the villages because that is where the story took place, the one I promised to tell you as we climb. But let us go on, so that we'll soon get where we're going; I'll tell you the story as we walk."

My grandfather turned, and so did I, he planted the tip of his walking stick in the barren turfy ground, we walked on, and he told his story: "All these woods and all these villages were once the scene of a strange but true event, and a great misfortune descended upon them. My grandfather, your great-great-grandfather, who lived at that time, told us about it often. Once upon a time in the spring, when the trees had just come into leaf, when the petals had just fallen, a terrible sickness descended on this region, and broke out in all the villages you saw, and in those you couldn't see because of the mountains rising in front of them, and even in the forests you showed me. Long before that it had been in distant lands, and carried off staggering numbers of people. Suddenly it came into our land. No one knows how it came—whether people brought it, or it came in the mild spring air, or the wind and the rain clouds carried it with them—no matter, it came, and spread through all the towns that lie about us. The white petals still lay on the road, and the dead were carried out over them; the spring leaves peeped into a chamber, and a sick man would be lying there, tended by one who was falling sick himself. The pestilence was called the plague, and in the space of five to six hours a person was both healthy and dead, and even those who recovered from the malady were never quite healthy and never quite sick, and could pursue their occupations no longer. Before that tales had been told in winter evenings of a sickness in other lands, of people perishing as though by divine judgment; but no one had believed it would come into our woods, for nothing foreign ever came, until it did come. First it broke out in Ratschlag, and all who caught it died at once. The news got around, the people took fright and ran about pell-mell. Some waited to see if it would spread, others fled, and met the sickness in the regions they turned to. In just a few days they were bringing the dead to the Oberplan churchyard to be buried, and soon from villages near and far and from the market town itself. Almost all day long the passing bell was heard, and the knell could no longer be rung for each death, but was rung instead for all in common. Soon they could not all be buried in the churchyard; instead great pits were dug in the open fields, and the dead were put in and covered up with earth. There were houses where no smoke rose, there were houses where the livestock bellowed because people had forgotten to feed them, and there were cattle that ran wild because there was no one to bring them from the pastures to the stalls. Children stopped loving their parents and parents stopped loving their children, people threw the dead into the pit and walked away, that was all. The red cherries ripened, but no one thought of them, and no one plucked them from the trees, the grain ripened, but it was not harvested in the usual neat orderly manner, indeed much would not have been harvested at all had not some man taken pity on a little boy or granny who was the only soul spared in the house, and helped them to bring it in. One Sunday when the priest of Oberplan mounted the pulpit to hold the sermon, there were seven people with him in the church; the others were dead, or sick or tending the sick, or confusion or obduracy kept them from coming. When the people saw this, they burst out in loud sobbing, and the priest could not give a sermon, but read a Low Mass instead, and they went their separate ways. When the sickness had reached its height, when people no longer knew whether to seek succor from heaven or on earth, a farmer from the Amisch house happened to walk from Melm to Oberplan. On the triple spruce sat a little bird, singing:

> Eat gentian and pimpinell',
> Rise up and stave off the knell,
> Eat gentian and pimpinell',
> Rise up and stave off the knell.

"The farmer fled, he ran to the priest in Oberplan and told him these words, and the priest told them to the people. They did as the little bird had sung, and the sickness abated more and more, and before the oats had been harvested, and before the brown hazelnuts ripened on the bushes by the fences, it had gone. People ventured out again, smoke rose in the villages as the beds and other belongings of the sick were burned, for the sickness had been highly infectious; many houses were freshly whitewashed and scoured, and the church bells tolled peaceful chimes once more, calling to prayer or to feast days in the church."

At that very moment as though summoned by his words the great bell from the steeple in Oberplan pealed clear bright and pure with its deep distinct chimes, and the sounds rose up to us under the spruces.

"See," my grandfather said, "it's already four o'clock, and the evening bell is chiming to end the day's work; you see, child, that tongue is telling us, as though we could almost make out the words, how good and how happy and how peaceful everything is in this region again."

With these words we had turned, and gazed back at the church. It loomed up with its dark tiled roof and the dark steeple from which the chimes came, and the houses thronged around it like a gray flock of pigeons.

"Evening has come," said my grandfather, "and so we must say a short prayer."

He took his hat from his head, crossed himself, and prayed. I doffed my hat and prayed as well. Once we had finished, crossed ourselves, and covered our heads again, my grandfather said, "It's a fine custom, on Saturday afternoons that bell gives the sign that the eve of the Lord's Day has begun, and all that is strictly earthly must rest. On Saturday afternoons I do no serious work, at most I take a walk to a neighboring village. The custom comes from the heathens who used to live in these parts; all days were the same to them, and once they had converted to Christianity, they needed a sign that the Lord's Day was approaching. At one time this sign was strictly observed; when the bell rang, people prayed, and ceased their hard work at home or in the fields. When she was a young girl, your grandmother would kneel down whenever the evening bell rang, and say a short prayer. Just as I go walking these days, though to different places, back then I'd walk to Glöckelberg on Saturday evenings, because your grandmother lived there, and at the sound of the village bell she'd often kneel by the garden fence in her red bodice and her snow-white skirt, and the flowers of the garden were just as white and red as her clothes."

"Grandfather, she always prays even now when the evening bell rings, in the chamber, by the blue shrine with the red flowers on it," I said.

"Yes, that she does," he replied, "but the others don't heed the sign, they work on in the fields, and work on in the house, just as our neighbor the weaver's picking stick clatters away even on Saturday evenings, until night falls and the stars are in the sky."

"Yes, Grandfather."

"But here's something you won't know, that Oberplan has the loveliest chimes in all the region. The bells are tuned as the strings of a violin are tuned, so that they ring in harmony. That's why no new ones could be made if a bell broke, or got a crack, and then the beauty of the chimes would be no more. Back when your uncle Simon was on the battlefield fighting the enemy, and took sick, I visited him, and he said, 'Father, if only I could hear Oberplan's bell ring once more!' But he never heard it again, and he died."

At that moment the bell stopped ringing, and once more there was nothing but the sun's kind light above the fields.

"Come, let's go on," my grandfather said.

We walked on upon the grayish turf between the tree trunks, from one trunk to the next. There was a well-worn path as well, but the turf was softer and more pleasant to walk on. Only, the soles of my boots had turned so smooth from the short grass that I could hardly take a step now, and slipped every which way as I walked. Noticing this, my grandfather said, "You shouldn't drag your feet so; on this grass you need to plant each step so it holds, otherwise your soles get polished smooth, and you can't find your footing. You see, everything has to be learned, even walking. But come and give me your hand, I'll guide you so that you can get on without trouble."

He reached out his hand, I took it, and walked on supported and secured.

After a while my grandfather pointed at a tree and said, "That is the triple spruce."

A great trunk rose up, bearing three slender trees that mingled their branches and twigs in the air. Many fallen needles lay at its feet.

"I don't know," my grandfather said, "if the little bird sang the words, or if God put them in the man's heart, but the triple spruce must not be cut down, nor may its trunk and its branches be harmed."

I took a good look at the tree, and then we walked on, and after some time we gradually emerged from the Drybeaks. The trunks grew thinner, they grew sparser, at last they ceased entirely, and we were walking up a very rocky path, with fields around us again. Here my grandfather showed me another tree, and said, "See, this is the Macht Beech, the most notable tree in these parts, growing from the rockiest soil there is. See, that's why its wood is hard as stone, that's why its trunk is so short, why its branches are set so close and hold fast to their leaves, so that the crown forms a sort of orb through which not a single little eye of the sky can peer. When winter draws near, people look at this tree and say: When the autumn winds sing in the Macht Beech's dry leaves, and those leaves drift across the ground, winter shall soon come. And indeed, a short while later the hills and fields are swathed in the snow's white blanket. Mark that tree well, and in later years, when I'm long in my grave, remember it was your grandfather who showed it to you first."

From this beech we walked uphill for a short time and came to the crest of the ridge, from which we looked down on the regions beyond, and saw the village of Melm in a mass of trees at our feet.

Here my grandfather stopped, pointed to a distant forest with his stick and said, "See, there on the right, that dark forest is Rindles Mountain, and behind it is the town of Rindles which we can't make out. Farther to the left, if it weren't for the woods, you'd see the great

Alsch Manor. At the time of the plague, everyone in Alsch Manor
perished but for one single maid who had to tend the cattle, two rows
of stalls with the cows that gave the milk for the cheese made at the
manor, and then the bulls and the young stock. For weeks she had to
feed them and wait, for the pestilence did the livestock no harm, and
they stayed feisty and content until the lord of the manor learned
what had happened, and sent some of the survivors to help her. In
the big hammer mill you showed me on our way up, all the people
died too, but for one hunchback who had to do all the work, serving
the people who brought their grain when the plague was gone and
wanted their flour; which is why they say to this day: 'I've got more
work than the hunchback at the hammer mill.' Of Oberplan's priests,
only the old pastor was left to minister to the souls; the two assistant
priests died, and the sexton died, and his son, who had already taken
holy orders. Of the households on the curved lane next to the short
row of houses where the market is, three were utterly wiped out."

After these words we went downhill by the hollow-way, in all the
lovely play of light and color the sun caused in the thickets' green
leaves, down to the village of Melm.

My grandfather had an errand in the first house there, at Macht
Croft, and so we went in through its arched entrance gate. The farmer
was standing in the yard in his shirtsleeves and a vest with many
peaked metal buttons. When he saw my grandfather, he greeted him,
and took him into the parlor; but they let me sit out in the yard on a
little wooden bench by the door, and sent me bread and butter to eat.
I rested, and looked at the things that were there: the unloaded carts
that stood nested together beneath the shed roof, the plows and har-
rows crowded in a corner to make space, the farmhands and maidservants going back and forth, doing their Saturday chores and
preparing for the Sabbath; and they joined the things that already
filled my head, triple spruces the dead and the dying and little singing
birds.

After a while my grandfather came back out again and said, "So,
I'm done, and we'll head back home now."

I got up from my bench and we walked over to the entry arch, accompanied thus far by the farmer and his wife, who took their leave there, and wished us a good journey home.

When we were alone once more, striding homeward up the hollow-way, my grandfather went on: "In the depths of fall, when the lingon-berries ripen, and the mists rise on the mossy meadows, the people returned to the ground where the dead had been buried without consecration or ceremony. Many people went out to gaze at the fresh mounds of earth, others asked the names of those who were buried there, and when the ministry in Oberplan had been fully reestablished, the place was consecrated like a proper cemetery, a solemn service was held beneath the heavens, and all the prayers and blessings that had been neglected were made up for. Then the place was surrounded by a fence and strewn with quicklime. From that time onward, the memory of the past was preserved in many things. Surely you know that many places in these parts still have *Plague* as their byname, for instance Plague Meadow, Plague Path, Plague Slope; and if you weren't so young, you'd have seen the column that's no longer there, that stood on the marketplace in Oberplan, saying when the plague came, and when it ended, and bearing a prayer of thanks to Christ on the cross, who adorned the top of the column."

"Grandmother told us about the Plague Column," I said.

"Since then, though, other generations have come," he went on, "unaware of what happened and despising the past; the fences are gone, and ordinary grass has covered the sites. People are glad to forget old calamities, taking health for a good that God owes them and that they squander in days of blossoming. They pay no heed to the places where the dead lie, and say the byname 'Plague' carelessly, like 'Hawthorn' or 'Yew.'"

Meanwhile the hollow-way had taken us back up to the crest of the hill, and the forests which we'd had to turn to see on our way out were now before us, and above them the sun was setting in great splendor.

"If it weren't for the evening sun shining in our eyes so," said my grandfather, "and everything floating in a fiery haze, I could show you the place that I'm going to speak of and that belongs to our tale.

It's many hours' travel from here, it's straight across from us, where the sun is setting, and that is where the true forests begin. There the firs and spruce, the alders and maples, the beeches and other trees stand like kings, at their feet the multitudes of the bushes and the dense throng of the grasses and herbs the flowers the berries and mosses. The springs flow down from all the heights, rushing, and murmuring, and telling what they've always told, they flow over pebbles like bright glass, and merge into brooks to go out into the lands, the birds sing above, the white clouds gleam, the rains beat down, and when night comes, the moon shines upon it all, like a woven cloth of silver threads. In this forest there is a dark, dark lake, behind it is a gray cliff that is mirrored on its surface, along its sides dark trees stand gazing into the water, and at its foot is a tangle of raspberries and brambles. At the foot of the cliff lies a white jumble of fallen trees, white trunks shattered by lightning loom from the brambles and gaze out at the lake, gray stones have lain there for a hundred years, and the birds and the wild beasts come to the lake to drink."

"That's the lake I meant, Grandfather, when we were coming up," I said, "Grandmother told us about its water, and the strange fish in it, and when a little white cloud floats over it, a thunderstorm is coming."

"And when a little white cloud floats over it," my grandfather went on, "while the rest of the sky is clear, more and more come to join it, becoming a whole host of clouds, and this host lifts up from the forest and moves out toward us with the storm that brings us heavy rain, and oftentimes hail. At the edge of this forest, where now there are fields that back then were still dense groves, there stood a pitch burner's cottage at the time of the plague. In this cottage lived the man whose story I shall tell you. My grandfather knew that cottage, and he said that now and then its smoke was seen rising from the forest, just as you saw the threads of smoke rising as we came up this way today."

"Yes, Grandfather," I said.

"At the time of the plague," he went on, "this pitch burner meant to escape the universal scourge that God had called down upon humanity. He meant to go up into the highest forest where no human ever ventures, where no breath of humans ever comes, where nothing is as it is down below, and where he thought he could stay healthy. But if someone did manage to find him, he meant to slay him with a poker rather than let him come close and bring the pestilence. But when the sickness was well over, he meant to return, and go on with his life. And so when the black-grimed wheelbarrow men who bought their wagon grease from him brought news that the plague had appeared in the bordering lands, he set forth, and went up into the high forest. But he went farther than the lake, he went where the forest is still just as it was at the Creation, where no people have ever worked, where no tree falls unless struck by lightning, or toppled by the wind; and then it lies where it is, and new saplings and plants grow up from its body; the trunks loom high, and between them are the unseen, untouched flowers and grasses and herbs."

While my grandfather was speaking, the sun had gone down. The fiery haze had suddenly vanished, the sky, where not a cloud stood, had become a golden gulf, as in an old painting, and in this gulf the forest stretched dark blue and distinct.

"See, child, now we can see the place I'm speaking of," my grandfather said, "look straight ahead at the forest, and you'll see a darker blue, that's the basin where the lake is. I don't know if you can see it."

"I see it," I replied, "and I see the faint gray stripes of the cliff by the lake."

"Then you have sharper eyes than I," my grandfather replied, "and now move your eyes from the cliff to the right and up toward the edge, there you'll see those higher, greater woods. There should be a rock there with a projecting brim like a hat, showing like a little hump on the edge of the woods."

"Grandfather, I see the little hump."

"It's called Hat Rock, and it stands far above the lake in the high forest, where hardly anyone has ever been. But a wooden dwelling is said to have stood by the lake at one time. The Knight of Wittinghausen built it in the Swedish wars as a refuge for his two daughters.

His castle was burned down, and its ruins still loom from the Thomas Woods like a blue block."

"I know the ruin, grandfather."

"The house stood behind the lake, where it was protected by the cliff, and an old huntsman watched over the girls. Today all these things are gone without a trace. From this lake the pitch burner climbed up to the Hat Rock, and looked about for a suitable place. But he wasn't by himself, his wife and his children were with him, his brothers, cousins, aunts, and farmhands were with him, and he had taken his livestock and his household effects. And he had brought all kinds of seeds and grain, so that he could break up the ground and plant it, and lay in provisions for the future. Now they built huts for the people and the animals, they built furnaces for distilling the pitch, and they sowed the seeds in the dug-up fields. One of the people in the forest was a brother of the pitch burner's who decided not to remain, but to return to his cottage. So the pitch burner said he should give them a sign when the plague had broken out. On the town hill, at noon, he should send up a column of smoke, let it rise steady for an hour, and then smother the fire. To make absolutely sure, he should do this three days in a row, so that the forest dwellers would know it was a sign that had been given them. But when the pestilence had passed, he should give them a sign that they could come back down and not be taken sick. At noon from the town hill he should send up a column of smoke, keep it steady for an hour, and then extinguish the fire. He should do this for four days in a row, but an hour later each day; by these special proceedings they would know that all danger had passed. But if he fell sick, he should leave the task as his last testament to a friend or acquaintance, and that person to a friend or acquaintance in turn, so that one day one of them would raise a column of smoke, and could expect a reward from the pitch burner. Do you know the town hill?"

"Yes, Grandfather," I replied, "it's the black jagged forest that rises behind Perneck, with a chunk of rock at its peak."

"Yes," said my grandfather, "that's it. It's said there were once three brothers, one on the alp, one on the town hill, and one high up in the Thomas Woods. They'd give each other a sign when one was in danger, smoke by day and fire by night, so that it could be seen, and the others would come to help. I don't know whether the brothers survived. Now the people who had fled lived on in the high forest, and once the plague had broken out in our parts, a column of smoke rose at noon from the town hill, rose steady for an hour, and then ceased. This happened three days in a row, and the people in the forest knew what had come to pass. —But look, it's getting cool, and the dew is already falling on the grass, come, I'll button up your jacket so you don't catch cold, and then I'll tell you the rest of the story."

While my grandfather was telling his story, we had entered the Drybeaks, we had passed the triple spruce, and walked between the dark trunks on the almost colorless grass to reach the fields of Oberplan. My grandfather laid his stick on the ground, bent down to me, tightened my scarf, adjusted my vest, and buttoned up my jacket. Then he buttoned up his own coat, took his walking stick, and we walked on again.

"But you see, my dear child," he went on, "it was all for naught, they had only been tempting the Lord. Once the forest shrubs had blossomed, white and red, as nature wills it, once the blossoms had turned into berries, once the things the pitch burner had planted in the forest soil had sprouted and grown, once the barley's golden whiskers had come, once the rye was whitening, once the oats hung on their little threads, and the potato plants bore their green balls and bluish flowers—all the pitch burner's people he himself and his wife all but one single little boy, the pitch burner's son, had died. The pitch burner and his wife were the last, and as the survivors had always buried the dead, but the pitch burner and his wife had no one left after them, and the boy was too weak to bury them, they went on lying in their hut as corpses. Now the boy was alone in the tremendous awful forest. He freed the animals from the stalls because he could not feed them, thinking that they could graze on the forest grasses, and then he ran away from the hut, for he was terrified by the dead man and woman. He went to a clearing in the forest, and now there was nobody anywhere, nobody but Death. When he knelt down amid blossoms and bushes and prayed, or when he wept and wailed for Father and Mother and all the other people, and then got to his feet again, there was nothing around him but blossoms and bushes, and the livestock moving under the trees of the forest as they grazed and jingling their bells. See, so it was with that little boy, who might have been just about as big as you. But you see, the pitch burner boys aren't like the ones in the market town or the cities, they've been taught the ways of nature, they know how to make a fire, they aren't afraid of storms, and have little clothing, no shoes in summer and no hats on their heads, just sooty hair. In the evening the boy took steel flint and tinder from his satchel, and made himself a fire; the fire in the pitch burner's furnace had long since gone out and died. When he was hungry, he used his hands to dig potatoes from under the upward-striving vines, and baked them in the embers of the fire. Springs and brooks quenched his thirst. The next day he sought a way out of the forest. He had forgotten how they'd come up into it. He went to the mountain's highest point, he climbed a tree and gazed around, but all he saw was forest, sheer forest. Now he decided to go to higher and higher places in the forest, until one day he could look out and see the forest's end. To eat he also took the grains of the barley and rye, which he had roasted in the ear on a stone over the fire, to burn away the hairs and husks, or he worked the tender raw grains from their husks, or he peeled the turnips that grew in the cabbage patches. At night he buried himself in leaves and twigs and covered himself with brush. The animals he'd freed had gone away; either they had lost their way in the woods, or they also feared the hut of the dead, and fled from it; he no longer heard the jingling, and they did not appear. One day, looking for the animals, on a hill with brambles and rocks he found a little girl lying in the middle of a bramble bush. The boy's heart pounded madly, he came closer, the girl was alive, but she had the sickness, and lay there unconscious. He came closer still, the girl had on white clothes and a little black coat, her hair was in a tangle, and she lay in the thicket as awkwardly as though she had been thrown there. He called, but got no reply, he took the girl's hand, but the hand had no grasp, and was lifeless. He ran down into the valley, scooped up water with his old hat, which he'd taken with him from the hut, brought it back to the girl, and moistened her lips. He did this over and over. He didn't know what might have helped the child, and even had he known, he would have had nothing to give her. It was hard to crawl through the tangled thicket to the place where the girl lay, so he took a big stone, laid it on the brambles' creeping tendrils, and repeated this until he had covered the brambles, until they were held down and the stones formed a pavement. On this pavement he knelt down, moved the child, gazed at her, tidied her hair, and having no comb he brushed the damp locks clean with his hands, so that they once again resembled fine pretty human hair. But he couldn't lift the girl to carry her to a better place, so he went up the hill, tore out the dry grass, tore out the stalks that grow high up on the rocks, gathered the dry leaves that were left over from the fall, clinging to the undersides of bushes, or blown by the wind into cracks in the rocks, and piled it all in a heap. When there was enough, he carried it to the girl, and made her a softer bed. He laid these things under her body in the places where they were most needed. Then he used his knife to cut twigs from the bushes, stuck them in the ground around the child, tied their tips together with grass and plant stalks, and laid light branches on top to make a roof. He laid twigs across the girl's body, and covered them with broad-leaved plants like colts-foot to make a coverlet. For himself he fetched food from his dead father's fields. At night he made a fire of wood and dead leaves he'd gathered. And so by day he sat by the unconscious child, tended to her and protected her from animals and flies, and by night he kept a blazing fire. But see the child did not die, her state improved more and more, her cheeks grew softer and lovelier, her lips took on a rosy hue and were no longer so pale and yellow, and her eyes opened, and gazed about. She began to eat too, she ate the strawberries, still to be found, she ate raspberries, already ripening, she ate the kernels of the hazelnuts, not yet ripe but sweet and soft, at last she ate the white mealy flesh of the roasted potatoes and the tender grain kernels, all of which the boy brought to her, and lifted to her lips; and when she slept, he went up the hill and climbed up a crag to look all around, and searched for the livestock again, for now it would have been good to have milk. But he could see nothing, nor could he find the animals. When the girl was stronger, and able to help out, he took her to a place where overhanging branches sheltered her, but thinking that a storm might come, and the rain might beat through the branches, he looked for a cave, where it was dry, and made a bed, and brought the girl there. Above this cave was a stone slab, where they had a fine view over the forest. I told you that the sickness was very severe, that in the space of five to six hours a person was both healthy and dead; but I am telling you too: whoever came through the sickness was healthy very quickly, only for a long time they were feeble, and had to be tended. The children stayed in this cave now, and the boy fed the girl, and did every good thing she needed. Now the girl told him how she had come to the forest. Her father and mother and several other people had left their distant home when the sickness approached, and sought higher ground where the pestilence wouldn't reach them. In the great forest they had lost their way, the father and mother had died, and the girl was left behind all alone. Where her father and mother had died, where the other people had gone, how she had ended up in the brambles, that she did not know. Nor could she say where her home was. And the boy told the girl how they had left their cottage, how they had all gone into the woods, and how they had died, and he was the only one left alive. And so, you see, the children sat in the cave when the day passed over the woods and lit up the greenery, the birds sang, the trees glistened, and the mountain peaks gleamed; or they slept when it was night, when it was dark and still, or the cry of a wild beast rang out, or the moon hung in the sky, and poured its beams out over the treetops. You can imagine what it was like when you see how the night is even here, how eerily the moon floats in the clouds, though we're already so close to the houses, and how it shines down on our neighbor's black rowans."

As my grandfather told his story we had passed down through the fields of Oberplan, we had crossed the meadow with the Behring Springlet, we had climbed over the stone wall, we had crossed the soft turf, and were already approaching the houses of Oberplan. In the meantime night had fallen, the half-moon hung in the sky, a mass of clouds had piled up in its light, and its beams fell straight onto the rowan trees that stood in our neighbor's garden.

"Once the girl had grown quite strong," my grandfather went on, "the children thought about leaving the forest. They conferred on how best to do this. The girl had no idea at all; but the boy said that all streams flow downhill, that they flow on and on without stopping, that the forest was high up, while human habitations stand on very low ground, that a broad flowing stream had passed their very own cottage, that they had climbed from this cottage into the forest, they had climbed up and up and met several streams flowing down; so if they kept to a flowing stream heading downhill, they would come out of the woods and find their way back to humankind. The girl saw the sense of this, and joyfully they resolved to take that course. They prepared for their departure. They took potatoes from the fields, as many as they could carry, and many sheaves of grain on the stalk. The boy made his jacket into a bag, and for strawberries and raspberries he made pretty little pouches out of birch bark. Then they set out. First they sought the brook in the valley which they had always drunk from, and walked on beside its waters. You see, the boy guided the girl because she was weak, and because he was wiser in the ways of the forest; he showed her the stones to step on, he showed her the thorns and spiky branches to avoid, he led her when the path grew narrow, and when they came to great crags or thickets and swamps, they skirted them, and cleverly found their way back to the brook. In this way they walked on and on. When they were weary they sat down and rested, and when they had rested they walked onward. At noon he made a fire, and they baked potatoes, and roasted their ears of grain. He found water in springs or cold brooks that flowed in little trickles over white sand from the black forest ground or from thickets and stones. When they found patches of berries and nuts, they gathered them. At night he made a fire, made a bed for the girl, and made his own bed just as he had in his first days in the forest. And so they wandered on. They passed many trees, the fir with its hanging beards of moss, the fissured spruce, the long-armed maple, the white-dappled beech trunks with their light-green leaves, they passed flowers plants and stones, they passed beneath the singing of the birds, they passed frisking squirrels and grazing deer. The stream went around hills, or it went straight, or it wound around the trunks of the trees. It grew and grew, countless little tributaries came from the glens, and flowed with it, from the leaves of the trees and from the grasses drops dripped in, and flowed with it. It babbled over the pebbles as though telling the children a story. By and by came other trees, from which the boy could clearly tell that they were gradually emerging: the spiky fir, the spruce with its rough trunk, the maple with its great boughs, and the knobbly beech all ceased, the trees were smaller fresher pristine and graceful. By the water stood alder shrubs, there stood willows, the crab apple tree showed its fruits, and the wild cherry tree gave them its small black sweet cherries. By and by there came meadows, there came pastures, the trees thinned out, standing in scattered copses, and all at once, with the brook already flowing as a broad calm stream, they saw the fields and dwellings of people. The children rejoiced, and went up to a house. They hadn't come out into the boy's home town, they didn't know where they had come to, but they were received with great kindness, and cared for. Meanwhile a column of smoke rose once more from the town hill in the boy's home, it rose up at noon, remained steady for one hour and then ceased. This happened four days in a row, an hour later each day, but there was no one to understand the signal."

As my grandfather reached this point in the story, we arrived at our house.

He said, "We're tired, and it's so warm; let us sit on the stone for a bit, and I'll tell you the end of the story."

We sat down on the stone, and my grandfather went on: "When the people learned who the boy was and where he had come from, he and the girl were taken to his uncle in the pitch burner's hut. His uncle went up into the forest and in horror burned the forest hut where the dead pitch burner lay with his wife. And the girl's whereabouts were found out by her relatives, and they came to the pitch burner's cottage to fetch her. You see, in those days the plague broke out in other parts of the forest as well, and many people died of it; but different times came, and health returned to our lands. Now the boy stayed with his uncle in the cottage, where he grew and grew, and they went about the business of distilling wagon grease turpentine and other things. When many years had passed, and the boy was nearly a man, one day a little carriage pulled up outside the pitch burner's cottage. In the carriage sat a lovely maiden, dressed in a white frock and a little black coat, and wearing a bramble bouquet on her breast. She had the cheeks, the eyes, and the fine hair of the forest girl. She had come to see the boy who had saved her and guided her out of the forest. She and the old kinsman who'd come with her asked the boy to come along to the girl's castle, and live there. The boy, who loved the girl too, went with them. There he learned all kinds of things, grew more and more accomplished, and at last became the husband of the girl he'd found in the forest during the plague. There, you see, he gained a castle, he gained fields, meadows, woods, farms, and farmhands, and as he'd been wise and attentive even as a boy, he increased and improved it all, and was loved by his underlings, his neighbors and friends, and his wife. He died as a distinguished man, respected throughout the land. How different are people's fates! He often invited his uncle to come dwell there and spend his life with him, but his uncle remained in the pitch burner's hut, and went on and on with the business of distilling, and as the forest dwindled and dwindled, as the fields and meadows advanced to his hut, he went deeper into the woods, and there he went on distilling the wagon grease. The children from his marriage kept to the same occupation, and old Andreas is his descendant, he too nothing but a wagon-grease carter, doing nothing but roaming the land with his black cask, and smearing wagon grease on the feet of foolish little boys who don't know any better."

With these words my grandfather finished his story. But still we stayed sitting on the stone. All the while the moon had shone brighter and brighter, the clouds had stretched out longer and longer, and I gazed at the neighbor's black rowan tree.

Then my grandmother's face peeked out the door, and she asked whether we wouldn't come to supper. We went into my grandparents' parlor, my grandmother folded a pretty little table of brown- and white-streaked plumwood out from the wall, covered it with white linen, gave us plates and silverware, and served us a chicken with rice. As we ate she said, looking angry, that the grandfather was even sillier and more careless than the grandson, for he'd taken a green-glazed bowl to wash wagon-greasy feet, and now it was too disgusting to be used.

My grandfather smiled and said, "Then let's smash the bowl, so it won't be used by mistake, and buy a new one; it was better than letting the rascal go on living in fear. After all, you're looking out for him too."

As he spoke he pointed toward the heating stove, where my pitchy hose were soaking in a little tub.

Once we had eaten, my grandfather said that I should go to bed now, and he took me to my bedroom himself. As we passed through the hallway where I had come by my punishment, the young swallows twittered softly in their nests as though drunk with sleep, in the parlor a little lamp burned on the table, as it did all through every Saturday night in honor of the Virgin, and in my parents' bedroom my father lay in bed with a lamp beside him, reading as usual; my mother was not at home, as she was visiting a sick aunt. We greeted my father, he gave a friendly reply, and we went into the children's room. My sister and my little brother were already asleep. My grandfather helped me undress, and stayed by my side until I had said my prayers and pulled up the blanket. Then he went away. But I couldn't sleep, thinking of the story my grandfather had told me, I remembered this detail and that, and thought of questions I needed to ask. At last weariness claimed its due, and sleep closed my eyes. As I drifted away, in the light shining in from my parents' room I saw my mother come in, but could not rouse myself to full consciousness. She went to the vessel of holy water, moistened her fingers, came up, besprinkled me, and made the sign of the cross on my brow, mouth, and breast, and I knew that all was forgiven, and at once I fell asleep, blissful, I can truly say, with the joy of reconciliation.

But my first sleep was not a peaceful one. Many things dwelled with me, the dead, the dying, the victims of the plague, triple spruces, the forest girl, the farmer of Macht Croft, the neighbor's rowan tree, and already old Andreas was smearing my feet again. But my sleep must have run a good course, for when I was woken the sun was shining through the windows, it was a lovely Sunday, everything was festive, after prayers we had our Sunday breakfast and put on our Sunday clothes, and when I went out onto the road, everything was pure fresh and clear, the things of the night had passed, and the neighbor's rowan tree was not half as big as yesterday. We were given our prayer books and went to the church, where we saw our father and grandfather sitting in the pew reserved for the burghers.

Many years have passed since then, the stone is still lying outside the house of my fathers, but now my sister's children play on it, and my old mother must sit there often, gazing out into the wide world where her sons are scattered.

But the ways of the world are strange, for I recall the whole story my grandfather told, indeed for long years when there was talk of pretty girls I always thought of the forest girl's fine hair; but I know nothing more about the pitch stains that commenced it all, whether they were washed away or planed off, and often, when I planned a trip home, I meant to ask my mother about it, but that, too, I forgot every time.

LIMESTONE

HERE I shall tell a tale a friend once told us, a tale in which nothing unusual occurs, but which all the same I have never forgotten. Of ten listeners, nine will find fault with the man in the story, while the tenth will remember him often. The story was prompted by a dispute that developed in a gathering of my friends about the way in which a person might be endowed with various of the talents. Some, pointing to the so-called virtuosos, maintained that a person could be extraordinarily favored with a certain gift, while possessing the others only to a small degree. Others said that the gifts of the soul are always present to the same degree, all equally great or equally mediocre or equally small, but fate determines which one takes preeminence, and that creates an apparent disparity. With different youthful impressions, and in different times, Raphael might have become a great general rather than a great painter. Others again held that wherever reason—as that ability that transcends the senses, indeed as that most exalted of all human abilities—is present in great abundance, so are the other, subordinate abilities. The reverse, they said, was not true; one baser ability might stand out in particular while the higher ones did not. But when there was a significant gift of whatever kind, exalted or base, those subordinate to it had to be significant as well. The reason they gave was that the baser ability is always the servant of the higher, and that it would be nonsensical to possess the higher gift that commands, but not the baser gift that serves. Finally there were some who said that God had created human beings as he created them, we could never know how he had distributed his gifts, nor could we debate the question, it being uncertain what might yet come to light in future. At that my friend told his story.

As all of you know, he said, for years now I have been working as a land surveyor in the civil service; the government sends me here and there on surveying assignments. I have come to know different parts of the country and different kinds of people. Once I was in the town of Wengen, with the prospect of staying there for quite some time, as my duties dragged on, and kept increasing. I often passed through the nearby village of Schauendorf, and became acquainted with its pastor, an admirable man who had established its first orchards and caused the village, once surrounded by hedges, brush, and thickets, to resemble a garden nestled amid an abundance of gracious fruit trees. One day he invited me to a church festival, and I said that I would come late, as I had some crucial work to finish. When I had finished my work, I set out on the road to Schauendorf. I walked across the high-lying fields, I walked through the orchards, and as I approached the parsonage, I saw that the midday meal must already have begun. In the garden, which, as was typical of Catholic parsonages, lay in front of the house, there was no one to be seen; the windows onto the garden were open, I could peek into the kitchen, where the maids were busy about the fire, and from the parlor rang the occasional clatter of plates and the clink of silverware. Stepping inside, I saw the guests sitting around the table, and one place left untouched for me. The pastor led me to it and urged me to sit. He said he would not introduce me to those present, nor name me their names; some I knew already, others I would come to know during the meal, and he would tell me the names of the rest once we had risen from the table. So I sat down, and it happened as the pastor had said. With some I grew acquainted, from some I learned their names and circumstances, and as dish succeeded dish and wine loosened the tongues, many a new acquaintance was already like an old one. There was one guest alone who could not be made out. He sat smiling and amiable, listening attentively to everything, always turning his face in the direction of the liveliest conversation, as though he had a duty to do so, his expressions showing agreement with each speaker, and when conversation livened up elsewhere, he turned that way and listened. But he himself spoke not a word. He sat quite far down the table, his black figure looming over the white linen tablecloth, and though he was not tall, he never straightened up to his full height, as though he thought that unseemly. He wore the clothes of a country priest. His jacket was quite worn and threadbare; it gleamed in some spots, and in others it had lost its black color and was reddish or bleached out. Its buttons were of thick bone. His black vest was very long, and also had buttons of bone. Two tiny white lappets—the only white thing on his person—hung down over his black cravat as a badge of dignity. As he sat there, some sort of ruffle would sometimes emerge ever so slightly from his sleeves, and he was always covertly tucking them back. Perhaps they were in a state that embarrassed him. I saw that he never took much of any dish, and always courteously thanked the steward who served them. When dessert was served, he barely sipped at the fine wine, took only tiny pieces of confectionary, and set nothing aside on his plate, the way the others did, as a customary memento to bring back to their families.

These idiosyncrasies made me notice the man.

When the meal was over, and the guests had risen from the table, I was able to observe the rest of his body. His breeches were of the same cloth and in the same state as his jacket, reaching down below his knees and fastened there by buckles. Then came stockings, black but nearly gray. His feet were shod in wide shoes with large buckles. They were of sturdy leather and had thick soles. Thus clad, the man stood there nearly all alone as groups formed to converse, his back almost touching the pier between the windows. His bodily appearance matched his clothing. He had a long gentle almost timid face with beautiful clear blue eyes. His brown hair was tied back simply, already shot with white strands that showed he was already approaching fifty, or had known sorrow and tribulation.

After a short while he retrieved from a corner a rattan walking stick with a black bone knob like the buttons on his clothes, and went up to the host to take his leave. The host asked if he was really going so soon, at which he replied that it was time he left, he had a four hours' walk to his parsonage, and his feet weren't what they'd been in his younger days. The pastor did not detain him. He made his farewells and went out the door, and a moment later we saw him walk through the grain fields, climb the hill that bounded the village to the west, and seemingly vanish in the radiant afternoon air.

I asked who the man was, and learned that he was a pastor in a poor district, that he had been there for a very long time, made no request to be transferred away, and rarely left the house except on very urgent business. —

Many years had passed since that luncheon, and I had completely forgotten the man, when my work called me to a dreadful region. Not that there were wilds gorges chasms cliffs and plunging waters—in fact all those things entice me—rather there was nothing but many little hills, each hill made of bare gray limestone, not fissured, as so often with this kind of rock, or dropping off steeply, but separating into broad rounded forms, each surrounded by a long sandbank at its foot. Through these hills a little river called the Zirder wound in great bends. The water of the river, which the reflection of the sky often tinged dark blue amid the gray and yellow of the rock and sand; the narrow bands of green that often edged the water; and the other patches of turf scattered amid the outcroppings were all that relieved and refreshed the eye in this landscape.

I was living at an inn in a part of the region that was somewhat better and accordingly far away. There a road passed over a rise, called, as is typical of some regions, the High Road, and the inn was named after it. So as not to lose time by going back and forth, I always brought along cold provisions and wine to the place where I was working, and took my main meal in the evening. Some of my men lived in the inn as well, while the rest housed as best as they could, building wooden huts in the stony land.

The region called the Corrie Rocks, though in truth not so very remote, is one that few will know, for there is no reason to travel there.

One evening, returning from work alone, having sent my men on ahead, I saw my poor pastor sitting on a heap of sand. He had burrowed his big shoes nearly all the way into the sand, and sand covered the tails of his jacket. I recognized him instantly. He was dressed more or less as he was when I first saw him. His hair was much grayer now, as though it had hastened to take on this hue, his long face had grown distinctly wrinkled, and only his eyes were blue and clear as before. The walking stick with the black bone knob was propped at his side.

I stopped in my tracks, came closer, and greeted him.

Not having expected a greeting, he got up hastily and thanked me. There was no trace of recognition in his face; nor could there be, for at that luncheon he must have observed me far less than I him. He simply stood there looking at me. And so, to start a conversation, I said, "Your Reverence, no doubt you don't know who I am."

"I do not have that honor," he answered.

"But I have had the honor," I said, echoing his courteous tone, "of dining at the same table with Your Reverence."

"I do not remember," he replied.

"Your Reverence, you are the same man, are you not," I said, "who attended a church festival given by the pastor of Schauendorf, and who was the first to leave after dining, saying that he had a four hours' walk to his parsonage?"

"Yes, I am the same man," he responded, "eight years ago I went to Schauendorf for the hundredth jubilee of the church's dedication, as was proper, I stayed for luncheon because the pastor invited me, and afterward I was the first to leave, because I had a four hours' journey home. I haven't been to Schauendorf since."

"Well, I was at that table too," I said, "and just now I recognized Your Reverence at once."

"That's astonishing—after so many years," he said.

"It is part of my profession," I replied, "to meet many different people, and remember them, and I have gained such skill in remembering that I recognize people I saw years ago and one time only. And so we meet again in this abominable region."

"It is as God created it," he responded, "fewer trees grow here than in Schauendorf, but sometimes it's beautiful too, and every so often it's more beautiful than anything else in the world."

I asked him if he lived in the region, and he replied that he had been a pastor in the Corrie for seven and twenty years. I told him that I had been sent to map out the region, that I was surveying the hills and valleys so as to set them down in miniature on paper, and that I lived out on the High Road. When I asked him if he came here often, he answered, "I like to go out to exercise my feet, and then sit on a rock to contemplate the things around me."

As we conversed, we had started walking; he walked by my side, and we spoke of various inconsequential matters, the weather, the season, the way these rocks were peculiarly suited to soaking up the sun's rays, and other things.

However shabby his clothes had been at that luncheon, now, if possible, they were shabbier still. I could not recall having seen his hat then, but now I kept looking at it; not a single tiny hair remained of the nap.

When we had reached the place where his path diverged from mine, leading down into the Corrie to his parsonage, we took our leave, expressing the hope of meeting again often.

I walked along my path to the High Road, still thinking of the pastor. His extraordinary poverty, such as I had never encountered in a person above the state of beggary, and certainly not in those who must shine out before others as a model of cleanliness and order, lingered on in my mind. To be sure, the pastor kept himself almost vigilantly clean, but this very cleanliness threw his poverty all the more painfully into relief, showing the looseness of his clothes' weave, their flimsiness and insubstantiality. I gazed back at the hills covered only with rock, I gazed back at the valleys where only the long sandbanks stretched, and went inside my inn to dine on the roast goat they were wont to serve me.

I did not ask about the pastor, so as not to receive an uncouth reply.

From then on I met the pastor often. As I spent the entire day in the Corrie Rocks, and often strolled through them in the evening to explore different ends and sections of them, and as he sometimes came out that way himself, we could not fail to meet. Several times we fell into conversation. He did not seem averse to meeting me, and I was glad to run into him too. Later on we often walked about together in the rocks, or sat on one rock and contemplated the others. He showed me many a small creature, many a plant peculiar to the region, he showed me its singularities, and pointed out the differences between certain rocky hills which even the most meticulous observer would have thought to have exactly the same shape. I told him about my trips, showed him my tools, and, when we happened to be working, explained their use to him.

In time I would sometimes go down with him to his parsonage. Where the most massive rock breaks up somewhat, we walked down a gentler slope toward the Corrie. At the edge of the rocks was a meadow where several trees stood, one of them a fine tall linden, and behind the linden was the parsonage. At that time it was a white, one-story building that stood out beautifully against the more inviting green of the meadow, against the trees and the gray of the rocks. The roof was covered with shingles. The garret windows had little doors, and the windows of the house could be closed with green shutters. Farther back, where the terrain formed an alcove, the church with its red-roofed steeple stood tucked away in the rocks. In another part of the Corrie stood the school amid its meager garden. These three solitary buildings made up the entire community known as the Corrie. Other dwellings were scattered throughout the area. Here and there huts perched on rocks as though affixed there, with little garden plots of potatoes or goat fodder. Far out toward the open country was more fertile ground belonging to the parish, with plowlands, pasture, and clover fields.

Within sight of the parsonage windows, the Zirder flowed by on the edge of the meadow, and a high bridge crossed the river and descended toward the meadow. The meadow was little higher than the riverbed. Apart from the rocks, this tableau of the high bridge across the lonely river was all that could be seen from the parsonage.

When I accompanied the parson into his house, he never took me to the upper floor, but always led me through a spacious vestibule into a small chamber. The vestibule was completely empty, except that in a niche, quite wide but shallow, there stood a long wooden bench. Whenever I visited the parsonage, a Bible lay on that bench, a large book bound in sturdy leather. The small chamber held a table of soft unpainted wood, around it several chairs of the same type, and against the wall a wooden bench and two yellow-painted chests. Otherwise there was nothing, excepting a small medieval crucifix beautifully carved of pearwood that hung above the equally small holy water stoup on the doorjamb.

On these visits I made a strange discovery. Even back in Schauendorf I had noticed how the poor parson kept furtively tucking his ruffled shirt cuffs back into his jacket sleeves, as though he were ashamed of them. Now he kept doing the same thing. I observed him more closely, and found that he had no reason whatsoever to be ashamed of his cuffs; in fact, as other glimpses of his clothing told me, he wore the finest, most beautiful underlinen I had ever seen in the world. And these linens were of an impeccable whiteness and cleanliness one would never have suspected from the state of his outer garments. He must have taken great pains in caring for them. As he never spoke of it I, too, was silent on the matter; surely that goes without saying.

Amid this companionship part of the summer passed.

One day an unusual heat prevailed among the rocks. All day long the sun had failed to shine through, but it suffused the dull shroud veiling all the sky so that one could always see its pale image, so that all objects in this rocky terrain were cloaked in an unsubstantial light unaccompanied by shadows, and the leaves of the few visible plants hung limp; for though barely a half-sunlight filtered through the dome of haze, there was a heat as if three tropical suns were all blazing down from a clear sky. We had such a hard time of it that I sent my men home shortly after two. I sat under a rocky overhang that formed a sort of cave, where it was much cooler than out in the open. There I ate my midday meal, drank my cooled wine, and read. Toward evening the cloud layer did not break, as it often does on such days, nor did it grow denser; it covered the sky just as evenly as it had all day. And so I was very late leaving the cave, for just as the shroud blanketed the sky unchanged, the heat had barely diminished, and no dew could be expected that night. I walked very slowly through the hills, and saw the pastor coming across the sandy slopes, contemplating the sky. We approached each other and exchanged greetings. He asked me where we had worked that day, and I told him. And I told him that I had been reading in the cave, and showed him my book. After that we walked on together across the sand.

After a while he said, "You won't be able to reach the High Road now."

"Why is that?" I asked.

"Because the thunderstorm will break," he replied.

I looked at the sky. The cloud cover had grown denser, if anything, and all the bare rock surfaces we could see were cloaked in the strangest lead-colored light.

"The thunderstorm," I said, "has been brewing all day long, but how soon the layer of haze will condense, cool down, produce wind and electricity and pour itself forth, that, I believe, cannot be gauged."

"It may be impossible to say precisely," he replied, "but I've lived in this area for twenty-seven years, I've made certain observations, and they suggest that the storm will break sooner than one might think, and will be quite severe. And so I think it best that you come with me to my parsonage and spend the night there. The parsonage is so close that we'll be able to reach it easily, even though we see the storm plainly in the sky; you'll be safe there, and tomorrow you can go about your work as soon as you please."

I responded that despite what I had said it was not impossible that a steady rain, at least, might develop out of the haze. In that event I would be protected; I had along a coat of oiled silk, I need only take it out of my bag and put it on, and the rain would do me no harm. And even if I had lacked this protection, I had been soaked by rain so often in the line of duty that I had no desire to impose on someone and bring disorder into his home just to avoid such a thing. But if there really were a storm impending that might bring a hard rain or hail or even a cloudburst, then I would gladly accept his offer and ask shelter for the night, but on the condition that it truly be nothing but shelter, that he should not disrupt his household nor go to any trouble beyond giving me a place beneath his roof; for such a place was all I needed. Besides, I pointed out, we had a ways to go along the same path, we could postpone the question, keep observing the sky, and finally make our decision accordingly.

He agreed, and said that if I stayed with him, I need not fear that he would go to any trouble, I knew that his was a simple home, and he would make no arrangements but those required for me to spend the night.

Having sealed this agreement, we went on our way. We walked very slowly, in part because of the heat, and in part because it was always our custom.

Suddenly a faint light fluttered about us, turning the rocks red.

That was the first flash of lighting, but it was mute, and no thunder followed.

We walked onward. After a while the lightning flashed several times, and as the evening had already grown quite dark, and the cloud cover had a muffling effect, with each flash the limestone loomed rose-red before us.

When we came to the place where our paths parted, the parson stopped and looked at me. I admitted that a storm was coming, and said I would go with him to his parsonage.

And so we took the path into the Corrie, passing down the gentle stony slope to the meadow.

When we had reached the parsonage, we sat down for a bit on the wooden bench that stood outside the house. Now the storm was full-blown, a dark wall looming in the sky. After a while, white trailing mists emerged on the unbroken dark storm wall, fringing the belly of the cloud bank with long, swelling bands. There the storm might already be raging, though not a blade of grass nor a leaf stirred where we were. In storms such trailing, bloated mists are often bad omens, always heralding gusts of wind, often hail and downpours. And now the lightning was followed by distinct claps of thunder.

At last we went into the house.

The pastor said that it was his custom, when storms came at night, to set a candle on the table and sit quietly in its light as long as the storm should last. By day he would sit at the table without a light. He asked me whether he might stay true to his practice today. I reminded him of his promise not to go to the slightest trouble for my sake. And so he led me across the vestibule into the familiar chamber, and told me to set down my things.

On a leather strap over my shoulder I generally carried a case containing drawing instruments drawings and also some surveying tools. Next to the case was a bag containing my cold provisions, my wine, my drinking glass, and my contrivance for cooling the wine. Removing these things, I hung them over the back of a chair that stood in the corner. I leaned my long measuring stick against one of the yellow chests.

Meanwhile the parson had gone out, and now came back holding a light. It was a tallow candle in a brass candlestick. He set the candlestick on the table and laid a brass wick-trimmer next to it. Then we sat down at the table, and stayed where we were, waiting for the storm.

It seemed it would not be long in coming. When the pastor brought the candle, the scant brightness coming in through the windows had vanished, the panes loomed like black panels, and total night had descended. The lightning was more intense; despite the candlelight, each flare lit up the corners of the chamber. The thunder grew more solemn and urgent. This went on for some time. At last came the first gust of the storm. The tree in front of the house trembled faintly for a moment, as though struck by an abruptly dying breeze, then all was still again. Presently the tremor returned, but now longer and deeper. A short time later came a powerful gust, all the leaves rustled, the branches shuddered, judging by what we heard from indoors, and from then on the noise never ceased. The tree belonging to the house, the hedges around it, and all the bushes and trees nearby were caught up in one great surge that kept subsiding and swelling. In between the thunder clapped. But the storm had not yet come. Between the lightning and the thunder an interval remained, and the flashes of lightning, bright though they were, were not yet snaking lines, but merely diffuse flares.

At last the first drops struck the window. They struck the glass, hard and separate, but their comrades soon came, and in a short while the rain was pouring down profusely. It quickly swelled, rushing and racing, until at last it seemed as though whole masses of water were descending on the house, as though the house were groaning under its weight and the groaning and creaking could be heard from within. The rumble of the thunder was barely heard through the coursing of the water; the coursing of the water became a second thunder. The storm was overhead at last. The lightning darted down like threads of fire, and its flashes were followed, quick and hoarse, by the thunder, which now vanquished all other roars, and made the windowpanes jitter and ring in its deepest finishes and fadings.

Now I was glad I had taken the parson's advice. Rarely had I seen such a storm. The pastor sat simply and quietly at the table in the little chamber, and the light of the tallow candle lit his form.

At last there was a thunderclap fit to jolt the whole house out of joint and cast it down, and right after that another. Then came a brief lull, as there often does with such phenomena, the rain flinched back for a moment as though alarmed, and even the wind paused. But soon it went on as before, only that its main force was broken, and it all continued more smoothly and steadily. Little by little the storm quieted down to a mere steady wind, the rain was lighter, the lightning flashed more feebly, and the thunder rumbled more dully, as though moving out into the open countryside.

When at last the rain was nothing but a drizzle, and the lightning an afterglow, the parson stood up and said, "It is over."

He lit a candle stub and went out. After a while he came back in, carrying a serving board with several things for the evening meal. He took a little jug of milk from the board, set it on the table, and filled two glasses from it. Then he brought strawberries in a green-glazed bowl and several chunks of black bread on a plate. For cutlery he laid a knife and a little spoon at each place, and then he carried the serving board back out.

When he came back in, he said, "This is our evening meal; may it satisfy you."

He stepped up to the table, folded his hands, and murmured a blessing to himself, I did the same, and we sat down for our evening meal. We drank the milk from the glasses, we cut pieces from the black bread with our knives and ate the strawberries with our spoons. When we were finished, he folded his hands again, said a prayer of thanksgiving, fetched the serving board, and carried away the leavings.

In my bag I still had leftovers from my midday meal and in my bottle I still had wine. And so I said, "If Your Reverence permits, I will take the leftovers of my midday meal from my satchel, for otherwise they will spoil."

"Of course, you may do as you please," he said.

I took my bag and said, "Then you can also see, Your Reverence, how I dine as a wandering man, and what sort of utensils I use.

"You must understand," I went on, "that however highly we praise water, particularly mountain water, and however valuable and splendid a role this substance may play in nature's great balance, all the same, when a man spends days working in the open fields in the sunshine, or walking amid hot rocks and hot sand, or climbing crags, a drink of wine and water is infinitely more refreshing, and gives more strength, than the purest choicest water in the world. My duties soon taught me this, and so I always supply myself with wine on all my journeys. But only good wine does good service. And so I had a pure good wine delivered to me up on the High Road, and every day I take some of it with me into my rocky hills."

The poor parson watched me unpack my utensils. He regarded the little tin plates, several of which could be stacked together to form a flat disk of modest size. I set the plates on the table. Next to them I placed knives and forks from my case. Then I cut slices of fine white bread that I sent for twice a week, then slices of ham of cold roast meat and cheese. All this I arranged on the plates. After that I asked him for a flask of water; that alone, I said, I did not take with me, for out in nature I could count on finding it everywhere. When he had brought water in a pitcher, I unpacked my drinking utensils. I took out the bottle, still half filled with wine, I set the two glasses—I always have one in reserve—on the table, and then I showed him how I cooled my wine. The glass is wrapped in a rag of loosely woven cloth, the cloth is moistened with a highly volatile liquid called ether, which I always carry with me in a bottle, a liquid that evaporates very quickly and forcefully, causing a chill that makes the wine fresher than if it had just come up from the cellar, indeed as though it had been put on ice. Having freshened two glasses of wine in this manner, mixed them with water and set one at his place, I invited him to eat with me.

He took a little taste of these things, as though to honor my invitation, sipped from his glass, and could not be persuaded to take any more.

Now I, too, ate but a small amount of the victuals I had set out, and packed it all away again, ashamed of the discourtesy I had committed in my hastiness.

I glanced at the parson's face, but it expressed not the slightest trace of rancor.

Now that the table was cleared, we talked for a while by the light of the tallow candle. Then the parson went about making my bed. He brought in a large wool blanket, folded it four times, and laid it on the bench by the wall. From a similar blanket he made a pillow. Then he opened one of the yellow chests, took out a sheet of extraordinary beauty delicacy and whiteness, unfolded it and spread it over my bed. When I saw the superb quality of the linen in the candle's faint light, and involuntarily glanced at him, he blushed.

To wrap my body he laid a third blanket on the bed.

"That is your bed, as well as I can make it," he said. "When you're ready to take your rest, you need only say the word."

"I will leave that to Your Reverence," I replied. "If you have a certain bedtime, please observe it. I am bound to no particular hour; in my way of life, my sleep is now brief and now long, I take to my bed now earlier and now later."

"Neither am I at the mercy of time," he rejoined. "And I can arrange to sleep according to my duties; but as the storm has kept us up later than usual, as you are sure to get up quite early tomorrow morning and may well have to go up to the High Road to fetch some of your things, I think rest would be the best thing now, and we should seek it."

"I am quite in agreement, Parson," I said.

After this conversation he left the chamber, and I thought he had gone to his bedroom. And so I undressed as far as I ever do, and lay down on the bed. I was just about to extinguish the candle, which I had set on a chair beside my bed, when the parson came back in. He had changed his clothes, now wearing gray wool stockings gray wool hose and a gray wool jacket. He was unshod, in his stocking feet. Thus dressed he stepped into the room.

"You have already retired," he said, "I have come to wish you a good night, and then go to bed myself. Sleep well, then, as well as you can on that bed."

"I will sleep well," I replied, "and wish you the same."

After these words he went to the holy water stoup that hung beneath the beautifully carved little crucifix, sprinkled himself with the water, and left the room.

By the light of my candle I saw him lie down on the wooden bench in the shallow niche in the spacious vestibule, and place the Bible under his head as a pillow.

As soon as I saw this, I jumped up from my bed, went out into the vestibule in my nightclothes, and said, "I object, Your Reverence, this is not what I intended, you can't sleep on this bare bench while leaving me the better bed. I'm used to sleeping in all kinds of places, even outside under a tree; let me sleep on this bench, and you take the bed that you meant to leave to me."

"No, my dear sir," he said, "I haven't left a bed to you; where yours is, no bed is ever made otherwise, and where I'm lying now, I sleep every night."

"You sleep every night on this hard bench and with this book as your pillow?" I asked.

"Just as you, through your vocation, are accustomed to all beds, even in the open air," he rejoined, "I am accustomed through my vocation to sleep on this bench and use this book as my pillow."

"Is that really possible?" I asked.

"Yes, it is so," he replied, "I am telling you no lie. I could have made myself a bed on this bench, just as I made you one on yours; but a very long time ago I took to sleeping in these clothes on this bench here, just as you see me, and I do so to this day." As I still hesitated, skeptical, he said, "You can set your mind at rest, quite at rest."

I made no more objections; the argument that he could have made himself a bed was a persuasive one.

After standing there a while longer, I said, "If it's an old custom of yours, esteemed sir, then naturally I have no more objections to make; but you must understand why at first I spoke against it, for usually people everywhere have proper beds."

"Yes, they do," he said, "and they grow accustomed to them, and believe it must be so. But it can also be otherwise. People grow accustomed to everything, and habit comes very easy then, very easy."

After his words I went back into my room, bidding him good night a second time, and lay down on my bed again. And now I recalled that however many times I had been in the parson's home, I had in fact never seen a bed. I thought about the matter a while longer, and could not fail to feel, most soothingly, the extraordinary delicacy of the parson's fine linen on my body. After a short while the parson provided actual proof that he was accustomed to his sleeping place; for I heard from his steady gentle breaths that he had already lapsed into a deep slumber.

Now that I, too, was at peace, now that the parsonage was deathly still, now that the wind had ceased, the rain was only faintly heard, and the lightning flashes, as though they had lost their way, cast but a rare feeble light at the windowpane, my eyes closed in slumber; after snuffing out the candle, I heard a few more drops strike the window, then it was as though a faint glow flared up on the pane, and then there was nothing more. —

I slept beautifully, woke late and opened my eyes to broad daylight. It was as though some gentle noise had fully awakened me. When I opened my eyes all the way, and looked around, I saw the parson in the vestibule, dressed in his gray nightclothes, cleaning the dust from my clothes with a brush. Quickly I rose from my bed, went out, and interrupted his efforts, saying that this must not be, I could not accept such a thing from him, it was not his duty, the dust did not bother me, and if I wanted it gone, I could easily brush it off myself.

"It is not my duty as a priest, but it is my duty as a host," he said, "I have but one old maidservant, who doesn't live in the house; she comes at certain times to perform my little chores, but today she hasn't arrived yet."

"No, no, that makes no difference," I said, "let me remind you of your promise not to go to any trouble."

"It is no trouble," he rejoined, "and I am almost done."

With these words he gave the jacket a few more strokes with the brush and then let me take both brush and jacket. He left the vestibule and went into a different room I had not yet seen. In the meantime I got dressed. After a while he came back in, fully dressed himself. He was wearing the old black garments he had worn the day before and all the other days. We went to the window. The scene had changed completely. It was a beautiful day, and the sun rose resplendent in measureless blue. What a thing a thunderstorm is! The subtlest the softest thing in nature is what causes this cataclysm. The sky's fine invisible vapors, that in the heat of the day or several days are innocuously suspended in measureless space, increase until the air above the ground is so heated and rarefied that its uppermost freight sinks down, so that the lower vapors are cooled, or another cold breath stirs them, making them instantly form masses of fog, generate electrical fire, and unleash the storm, causing new cold, stirring up new fog, masses that coalesce as ice or as droplets, sweep along with the storm and pour down upon the earth. And once they have poured down, and the layers of air have mingled, the very next day that air is often revived in all its purity and clarity, ready once again to absorb the vapors caused by the heat, again to gradually begin the same game, thus causing the cycle of rain and sunshine that delights and sustains humans animals and plants.

The limestone hills had been washed smooth by the night's measureless rain, and stood white and gleaming beneath the blue of the sky and the rays of the sun. Receding one behind the other, they displayed their brilliant refracted colors in delicate shades of gray, yellow, red, rose, and in between lay long shadows blue as air, the lovelier the farther back they stretched. The meadow by the parsonage was fresh and green, the linden, having lost its older and feebler leaves in the storm, stood newborn, and the other trees and bushes around the parsonage raised their gleaming wet branches and twigs toward the sun. Only near the bridge had the storm caused a less pleasant spectacle. The Zirder had overflowed its banks and flooded the part of the meadow which, as I said, lay not much higher than the riverbed. The high bridge, as it descended, led straight into the water. Yet disregarding the damage the flood must have caused by washing sand onto the meadow, even this was a beautiful phenomenon. The great expanse of water gleamed in the rays of the sun, adding to the green of the meadow and the gray of the rocks a third chiming, shimmering note, and the bridge stood out bizarrely like a dark line over the silvery mirror.

The parson showed me several glimpses of very remote regions that otherwise could not be seen, but that today, in the cleansed air, were distinct as clear-cut pictures.

After a brief contemplation of the morning spectacle to which our eyes instinctively turned, the parson brought cold milk and black bread for breakfast. We ate, and I prepared to set out. Over my shoulder I slung my case and the satchel with the leather strap, I took my walking stick from the corner beside the yellow chest, took my white walking hat, and thanked the parson from my heart for sheltering me in the heavy storm.

"Not too humble a shelter, I hope," he said.

"No, no, Your Reverence," I rejoined, "it was all so kind and good of you, I only regret causing you disruption and disturbance; in future I'll take good heed of the weather and the sky, so that no one else need atone for my carelessness again."

"I gave what I had," he said.

"And I desire greatly to do a service in return," I replied.

"People live side by side, and can do one another many good turns," he said.

With these words we had come out into the vestibule.

"I must show you the third room," he said, "here I have a chamber where I dress and undress, where no one can see me, and where I store various things."

With these words he led me from the vestibule into a side room or rather a vault whose door I had not noticed earlier. In this vault too stood very inferior furniture. A large cabinet of soft wood holding clothing and other such things, probably also the wool blankets used for my bed, a few chairs, and a board with loaves of black bread and a pot of milk: that was all. Once we had left the room again, he shut it, we took our leave, and promised to meet again soon.

I stepped out into the cool clean air and onto the damp meadow. It occurred to me how odd it was that we had only ever been on the ground floor, yet in the night and in the morning I had clearly heard footsteps in the house above us; but I strode onward without letting the thought distract me.

I did not take my usual path; instead I struck out toward the Zirder. When you survey a land, when you spend many years drawing landscapes and their formations on paper, you take a sympathetic interest in the character of these lands, and you come to love them. I walked toward the Zirder to see what effects its flooding had brought, and what changes it had wrought in its immediate surroundings. Having stood a while by the water, and watched it at work, without observing any effects but the flood itself, I suddenly experienced a spectacle I had never seen before, and had company I had not yet been granted in this rocky country. Apart from my men, who were so familiar to me, as I was to them, that we must have seemed mere tools to one another, I had seen only a few people in my inn many a wanderer on the path and the poor parson among the rocks. Now this was to change. As I looked, I saw a jaunty merry boy crossing the bridge from the far bank, which was higher and not flooded. Approaching the end of the bridge, which sloped down into the flood-waters of the Zirder, he knelt and, as far as I could see through my spyglass, untied his shoelaces and took off his shoes and socks. But having taken them off, he did not go down into the water, as I had expected; instead he stayed where he was. A moment later a second boy came and did the same. Then came a barefoot boy, who stopped as well, and then several more. At last a whole flock of children came walking across the bridge, and when they reached the end of it, they ducked down, just as a flock of birds comes flying through the air and descends upon some small patch of ground, and I could clearly see that they were all busy taking off their shoes and socks.

When they had finished, one boy walked down the bridge and gingerly into the water. The others followed him. Not sparing their hose, they waded deep into the water, and the girls' skirts swirled in the water about their feet. To my surprise I now saw a tall black figure in the middle of the water, none other than the poor parson of the Corrie. He stood in it nearly up to his hips. I had not noticed him earlier, nor had I seen him wade in, for my eyes had been fixed on the bridge the whole time, and only as the children moved in my direction had I shifted my gaze to the foreground. The children all waded toward the pastor, and after pausing beside him and talking to him a while, they set out toward the bank where I stood. As they picked their way with more or less care, they scattered across the water as they came, standing out like black dots on the gleaming surface, and reached me one by one. Seeing that the shallow flood-waters posed no danger, I stayed where I was, and let them come. The children came up and stopped in front of me. At first they gazed at me with shy and truculent faces; but from youth I have been a great friend of children, I have always loved children dearly as budding blossoms of humanity, and have been blessed since my marriage with a number of them myself; finally no creatures detect kindness more rapidly than children, whose trust is thus gained with equal rapidity: and so I was soon surrounded by a circle of chattering, bustling children trying to ask questions and answer questions. It was easy to tell where they were headed, for all of them had their school satchels slung over their shoulders on leather or cloth straps. As I also carried my satchel and case on a leather strap over my shoulders, it must have been a comical sight to see me standing like a large schoolboy among the little ones. Some bent down, busy putting their shoes and socks back on, while others, still holding them in their hands, looked up and talked to me.

I asked where they came from, and was told that they came from the Corrie Crofts and the Rock Crofts, and that they were going to school in the Corrie.

When I asked why they had waited together on the bridge rather than wading into the water one by one as they came, they said that their parents had ordered them to be very careful, and if there was water flooding the meadow by the Zirder, to go into it all together, not one by one.

"But what if the water were deep enough to go past a tall person's head?" I asked.

"Then we would turn back," they replied.

"But what if the water came on in a rush when you'd already crossed the bridge and reached the meadow, what would you do then?"

"We don't know."

I asked how long it took them to get here from the Corrie Crofts and the Rock Crofts and was told: one hour. And their homes must indeed have been that remote. They lie on the far side of the Zirder on ground just as barren as the Corrie, but their inhabitants are very industrious, mainly burning lime from their rocks and transporting it far away.

I asked whether their parents had also instructed them to spare their shoes and socks, which they affirmed, and I marveled at the inconsistency with which they held their dry shoes and socks in their hands while standing before me with wretchedly wet hose and skirts.

I asked what they did in the winter.

"We cross then too," they said.

"But what if there's snowmelt on the meadow?"

"Then we don't take our shoes off, we keep them on and walk through."

"And what if the bridge is icy?"

"Then we have to be careful."

"And what if there's a blizzard?"

"That doesn't matter."

"And what if the snow is awfully deep, and there's no path?"

"Then we stay home."

At that moment the parson came toward me with the last of the children. It was time too; for the children had already grown so confiding that a tiny little boy, carrying the basis and beginning of all the sciences on a square of cardboard, was about to recite the alphabet to me.

Seeing me in the children's midst, the parson greeted me warmly, saying how good it was of me to rush to their assistance too.

Taken aback by the suggestion, I said at once that I had not come to assist them, for I had not known that any children were going to cross the bridge, but if assistance had been necessary, I surely would have been glad to provide it.

Now, as he stood there in the children's midst, I saw that he must have been far deeper in the water than they, for he was wet to the hips and beyond, a depth that would have reached up to some of the children's necks. Not understanding the discrepancy, I asked him about it. He said that it was easy to explain. The Wenn farmer, who owned the flooded meadow where he had been standing in the water just now, had dug rocks out of the meadow the day before yesterday, and carted them away. A pit was left behind. Today, seeing the meadow by the Zirder covered with water, he had thought that the children's path might pass close to this pit, and one of them might come to harm. And so he thought to stand next to the pit to avert any danger. But as its sides were steep, he had slipped in himself, and once standing in it he had remained there. One of the smaller children might even have drowned in the pit, deep as it was dug. The meadow would have to be leveled again; for the water was murky when it flooded, and concealed the depth and the irregularity of the ground underfoot.

The wet children crowded around the wet parson, they kissed his hand, they talked to him, he talked to them, or they stood there and gazed up at him confidingly.

But at last he said that they should wring out their wet skirts now and squeeze or brush the water from all their clothes, and whoever had shoes and socks should put them on; then they should get moving, so as not to catch cold, they should go stand in the sun to dry more quickly, and then go to school, and behave themselves.

"Yes, we'll do that," they said.

And at once they did as instructed, they bent or crouched down, they wrung out their skirts, they squeezed the water from the feet of their hose, or they pressed and wiped it from folds and flaps, and I saw that they did so adroitly. It was no grave matter either; they all wore linen shifts, unbleached or striped with red or blue, which would soon dry and barely show that they had been wet, and as far as their health went, I thought, their young bodies would easily withstand the damp. Once they finished wringing out the water, they proceeded to put on their shoes and socks. When they had finished this too, the parson bade me farewell again, thanked me once more for coming, and headed with the children down the path into the Corrie.

I called to the children to work hard at school, they called back "Yes, yes," and went off with the parson.

I saw the figure of the parson, amid the throng of children, crossing the damp meadow to the Corrie school, and then I turned and took the path that led to my rocks. I had decided not to go up to the High Road, but return at once to my men and the place where I was working, because I had no time to lose, and still had the provisions the parson had spurned the night before. And I wanted to put my men's minds at rest, for they had surely learned that I had not returned to the High Road that night, and might be worried about me.

Climbing toward the heights of the limestone hills, I thought about the children. How great a thing is inexperience and innocence. Obeying their parents they go where they might find death; for when the Zirder floods the danger is very great, and the children's ignorance can make it incalculably great. But they know nothing of death. Though its name may cross their lips, they do not know its nature, and their upward-striving life has no perception of extinction. If they themselves slipped into death, they would not know, and would die before they realized it.

As I thought these things, I heard the little bell in the Corrie's church belfry ringing out into my rocks, a summons to the early Mass to be held by the parson and attended by the children.

I went deeper into the rocks and found my men, who were glad to see me and had brought me provisions. —

What with the length of my stay in the region, I could not help hearing things about the parson from other people's lips. I heard it was really true—after his words I had no longer doubted it anyway—that for many years now he had slept on the wooden bench in his vestibule, with the Bible under his head, wearing only his gray woolens in summer, and using a blanket in winter. He had worn his clothes so long, and kept them in such good repair, that no one could remember when he had ever bought new ones. He rented out the upper floor of his parsonage. A man had come along who had held an office and then retired, and was now living off his income in the place of his birth. He had availed himself of the parson's rented room to take up lodgings there with his daughter, so that he could look out on the setting in which he had spent his childhood. That a man would seek out, as the balm and delight of his old age, a region anyone else would seek to escape, was renewed proof for me of—as the poet said—the sweet attraction that our birthplace exerts upon us, never letting us forget it. The parson was said to eat nothing but a piece of black bread for breakfast and supper, while his midday meal was prepared by his servant Sabine, who cooked it at home and brought it to the parsonage. It often consisted of warm milk or a soup, or even cold dishes in the summer. When he was sick, he did not send for the doctor or for medicine, but went to bed and fasted until he recovered. With the income from the rent and his salary he did good deeds for people he selected with care. He had no relatives and no friends. In all the years he had lived here, no one had ever come to visit him. All his predecessors had been pastors in the Corrie for a short time only, and then moved on, but he had already been here a long while, and it seemed he would stay till the end of his life. He never went visiting in the neighborhood; indeed he had few dealings with people, and when he was not busy with his official duties or at the school, he would read in his chamber, or he would walk across the meadow to the Corrie Rocks and walk about in the sand there, or sit there alone with his thoughts.

There was a widespread rumor in the area that because of how he lived, he had money saved, and he had been robbed three times already.

I could not know which of these things were true and which were untrue. Each time I met him I saw his calm clear blue eyes, his simple nature, and his bitter unfeigned poverty. Whatever his past had been, I did not probe, nor did I wish to.

I had heard several of his sermons too. They were Christian in a simple way, and though their oratory left something to be desired, they were clear and serene, and there was such goodness in them that they entered the heart.

My assignment in the district drew on and on. The rocky recesses of that forbidding landscape posed such obstacles that we seemed likely to require twice as much time as for an equal expense of tamed, fertile land. As though that were not enough, the authorities effectively set us a time limit by instructing us to take up work in a different part of the realm at a certain date. Not wanting to disgrace myself by falling behind, I did all that I could to pick up the pace of our work. I left the High Road, I had a shack built in the part of the Corrie Rocks where we were working, I lived in the shack and shared the common meals cooked over the campfire. I had all the men move close to me, living in shacks in or near the site of our work, and I hired several new men for odd jobs to expedite the proceedings.

Now we got down to hammering surveying driving stakes chaining setting up plane tables sighting through theodolites constructing lines goniometry computation and the like. We advanced through the rocky hills, and our markings spread through the limestone terrain. It was an honor to survey this tricky patch of ground, and I was proud to do a fine and handsome job of it, often working deep into the night in my shack. I drew some sheets twice over, and discarded the inferior ones. All the material was properly sorted.

Understandably, amid these activities the parson faded into the background. But once, not having seen him in the Corrie Rocks for some time, I grew uneasy. I was used to seeing his black figure among the rocks, visible from afar as the only dark spot in the limestone expanse that stretched gray in the twilight or glowed red in the setting sun's rays. Thus I asked about him, and learned that he was ill. At once I resolved to visit him. I used my first free moment to do so, or rather, I freed myself the very next evening, and went to him.

I found him not in his usual bed in the vestibule, but in the chamber, on the wooden bench where he had made my bed that stormy night. Under his body they had spread the wool blankets I had used, and he had let them, because he was ill. They had given him a blanket to cover himself as well, and had moved the spruce table next to his bed so that he could put his book and other things there.

Thus I found him.

He lay there quietly, and even now could not be persuaded to admit a doctor or take medicine, not even the simplest remedies that were brought to him in his room. His reason was a strange one: that to seek treatment would be to tempt God, for God had sent the illness, and God would take it away, or would let it be followed by the death he decreed. Finally, too, he had little faith in the beneficial effects of the medicines or the skill of the doctors.

When he saw me, his expression turned quite cheerful; he was clearly delighted that I had come. I asked him to forgive me for not coming sooner, I had not known that he was ill, because of all my work I had not left my shack to go out into the Corrie Rocks, but I had missed him, had asked about him, and now I had come.

"That's a fine thing, that's very fine," he said.

I promised to come more often now.

Questioning him more closely about his state, I gathered that his illness was not serious, though likely to linger, and so I went away with my mind put at rest. All the same, one day I called for post-horses and rode to the city to consult a doctor I knew, setting forth all the symptoms I had learned of by questioning the pastor on several visits. He assured me that I had seen things rightly, that the malady was not a grave one, that nature could do more than human hands, and that the parson would recover, though it would take some time.

As I came to see the pastor more often, I grew so used to sitting on the chair at his bedside for a spell in the evening and chatting, that I began to do so every day. I left the Corrie Rocks after my day's work was done and crossed the meadows to the parsonage, and afterward worked by candlelight in my shack. I could visit more easily now that I was living quite close to the parsonage, which had been far from the case on the High Road. I was not the only person looking after the parson, though. Old Sabine, his maidservant, not only came to the parson's house more often than duty required, she spent most of the time she could spare from her own household, which consisted only of her, in the parsonage, performing the little services a sick man required. Apart from the old woman there also came a girl, the daughter of the man who rented the room on the upper floor of the parsonage. The girl, strikingly beautiful, would bring the parson soup or some other dish, or inquire about his health, or ask on her father's behalf whether he could help the parson in any way. The parson always held quite still when the girl came into his room, he pulled the blanket up to his chin and never stirred beneath it.

The schoolteacher also came by often, and several fellow clergymen from the area dropped in to inquire about his health.

Whether it was the illness that unbent the man, or the daily visit that brought us closer together, we grew much better acquainted now that the parson was ill. He spoke more, and revealed more of himself. I sat at the spruce table that stood by his bed, arriving punctually every day. As he could not leave the house, and could not go into the Corrie Rocks, he made me report the changes taking place there. He asked me if the blackberries in Kulter Hollow were already starting to ripen, if the grass by the Zirder Heights, which in spring turned such a pretty green, was already yellowing and withering, if the limestone was continuing to weather, if the fallen chunks in the Zirder were accumulating and the sand was proliferating, and other things of that sort. I told him these things, and other things as well, I told him where we had worked, how far we had advanced, and where we would start in the morning. As I did, I explained certain things about our work that had been obscure to him. Sometimes I read to him from the newspapers which I had delivered by messenger to the Corrie Rocks twice a week.

One day, his illness having taken a definite turn for the better, he said that he had a request for me.

When I replied that I would be very glad to do him any service at all in my power, that he need only say what he wanted and I would do it without fail, he said, "I must tell you something first, before I state my request. Mind you, I'm not telling the story because it's important, but so that you'll see how things came to be as they are, and so that you may be more inclined to fulfill my request. You've always been very good to me, and recently, I've heard, you even rode out to the city to question a doctor about my symptoms. This gives me the courage to turn to you.

"I am the son of a prosperous tanner in the capital. My great-grandfather was a Swabian foundling who came to the city on foot, staff in hand. He learned the tanning trade through the kindness of benefactors, he sought out several workshops to work in, he went to different countries to earn his bread with his hands, and to learn how the trade is plied everywhere. With this knowledge he returned to our city and worked in a reputable tannery. He distinguished himself by his skills; at last he was made foreman, and the proprietor entrusted him with various responsibilities, and assigned him to conduct experiments developing new preparations. At the same time my great-grandfather tried his hand at small commercial transactions, purchasing raw materials for modest sums and reselling them. In this way he amassed a small amount of capital. Finding himself growing older, he bought a large garden in a remote suburb with unused land adjoining it. He built a workshop and a small house on this land, married a poor girl, and, now his own master, pursued his craft and his commercial dealings. He thrived, and died as a respected man esteemed among tradespeople. He had one son, my grandfather.

"My grandfather carried on his father's business. He expanded it still further. He built a large house on the edge of the garden, its windows facing what one day would be a street lined with buildings. Behind the house he built workshops and storerooms. Altogether my grandfather was a great one for building. Aside from the house he built a large compound used for additional workshops and other parts of our business. He sold the vacant land next to our garden, which was worth a great deal, as the city was entering a great boom. He surrounded the garden with a wall that had cast-iron gates at regular intervals. He greatly advanced the business, and constructed great vaults where our own merchandise and the merchandise we traded was displayed for sale. My grandfather in turn had just one son to carry on the business: my and my brother's father.

"Our father merely built the drying lofts atop the workshops, added a small wing to the house, facing the garden, and a hothouse. In his day a street had already sprung up outside the main building's windows, lined with houses, paved with cobblestones, and filled with pedestrians and vehicles. I recall from my childhood that our house was very large and spacious, that it had many yards and rooms used for our business operations. My favorite memory is of the beautiful garden where trees and flowers herbs and vegetables grew. In the buildings' rooms and yards the journeymen went about dyed almost yellow-brown from working in linen clothes, stacks of leather bundles towered in the great ground-floor vault and the two smaller ones adjoining it, hides hung from the racks in the drying loft, and were sorted in other large rooms. In the sales vault they were stacked neatly on the shelves. There were cows in the cowshed, six horses in the stable, and carriages and wagons in the coach house. I even remember the big black dog Hassan who lived in the big yard, allowing all to come through its gate, but none to go out.

"Our father was a big strong man who would walk through the spacious rooms of the house, inspecting everything and giving directions. He hardly ever left the house except on business, or to go to church; and when he was at home but not overseeing operations, he would sit at his desk and write. Often he was seen in the garden as well, strolling with his hands behind his back, or standing and gazing up at a tree, or contemplating the clouds. He took pleasure in cultivating fruit trees, hiring a gardener especially for that purpose, and sending for grafts from all over Europe. He was very kind to his men, he provided for them adequately, and saw that each got his due, but also that each did his duty. If one of his men took sick, he would go to his bedside, ask how he was, and often administer the medicine himself. In the house he was known only as Father. He avoided ostentation, going about, if anything, too modestly and too plainly rather than too imposingly, his quarters were simple, and when he rode out in a carriage it had to be one that looked very middle-class.

"We were two brothers, twins, and our mother had lost her life giving birth to us. Father revered her, and never took another wife, for he could not forget her. As the street was too noisy, we were put in the back wing, facing the garden, which our father had added to the house. We had a large room, with windows that looked out on the garden and a long hallway between it and the other living quarters, and so that we would not have to pass through the front rooms each time we went out, our father had stairs built in the garden wing allowing us to go straight to the garden and from there to the street.

"After our mother's death, our father had entrusted the management of the household to a maidservant who had served mother even before her marriage, and had been a sort of governess to her. Our mother had commended her to Father on her deathbed. Her name was Luise. She managed and supervised everything concerning food and drink, regarding the linens the china the furniture in the house the cleaning of the stairs and rooms the heating and airing, in short all that pertained to the house's inner workings. She was in charge of the maids, and she took care of the needs of us boys.

"When we grew older, we were given a tutor who lived in the house with us. Two fine rooms were put in order for him, adjoining our room, and together with it making up the entire back of the wing known as the garden wing. From him we learned what all children must begin their learning with: the alphabet reading writing arithmetic. My brother was much cleverer than I, he could memorize the letters, he could join them to form syllables, he could read distinctly and in paragraphs, his sums always came out right, and when he wrote his letters they were always even and on the line. With me it was different. The names of the letters escaped me, and then I couldn't say the syllables they formed, and when I read I had great trouble with the long words, and it was a torment to go a long time without a comma. In arithmetic I followed the rules, but I generally ended up with very different sums from the ones we were supposed to arrive at. When I wrote I held the pen just right, kept a close eye on the line and moved my hand smoothly up and down, yet the letters were never even, they dipped below the line, they pointed in different directions, and my pen failed to produce the hairline strokes. Our tutor was very dedicated, and my brother showed me many things until I could do them myself. In our room we had a large wooden desk to study at. Each of the table's long sides had several drawers, one row for my brother to put his school things in, the other for me. A bed stood in each of the back corners, and next to each bed was a night table. At night our door was opened to our tutor's room.

"We went into the garden quite often, and passed our time there. Often we took drives through the city with our gray horses, or we drove out into the countryside, or elsewhere, and our tutor always sat with us in the carriage. We walked with him too, strolling on the bastions of the city wall or along an avenue, and whenever some special spectacle came to the city, and our father permitted it, we went with him to see it.

"Once we had been well instructed in the primary-school subjects, it was time for the Latin school subjects, and our tutor told us that we would be examined on them by the director and the professors. We learned Latin and Greek, we learned natural history and geography mathematics composition and other things. We received religious instruction at home from the worthy chaplain of our parish church, and in matters of religion and morals our father led by example. But as it had been in our earlier lessons, so it was here. My brother learned everything well, he did his exercises well, he could say Latin and Greek things in German, he could solve algebraic equations, and his letters and compositions seemed written by a grown man. I could do none of this. I also worked quite hard, and when I started each subject I didn't do badly, I understood it, and could say and do things; but as we moved further confusion arose, things became mixed up, I lost

my bearings, and could not see clearly. When translating from German, I followed all the rules closely, but each word always had several
contradictory rules, and when my translation was finished, it was full
of mistakes. It was the same when I translated into German. Each
Latin or Greek book always had the strangest words that refused to
fall in line, and when I looked them up in the dictionary, they weren't
there, and the Latin and Greek books failed to follow the rules we
learned in our grammars. I was best at two secondary subjects which
our father had us learn because they could be of use to us in the future,
French and Italian, for which a tutor visited us at home each week.
My brother and our tutor encouraged me greatly, and sought to assist
me. But when it came time for the exams, I fell short, and my grades
were poor.

"Several years passed this way. When the time our father had set
for learning these things was over, he said that now we must learn
the business he would pass on to us after his death, and that the two
of us must carry on as honorably and respectably as his and our forebears had done. He said we must be instructed in the same way as
our forefathers so that we would know to do business in the same
way as they had. We must learn all the tricks and skills of our trade
from the ground up; first we must be able to work like any good
worker, like the best worker in our trade, so that we could judge the
workers and the work, so that we would know how to treat the workers, and so that the workers would respect us. Only then should we
proceed to learn the other things the business required.

"Our father wished us to live like our workers too, so that we
would understand their situation, and not be strangers to them. And
so he wished us to eat live and sleep with them. Our tutor left us,
leaving each of us a book in remembrance, we moved out of our study
and into the workers' quarters.

"Our father appointed our business's best journeyman, who was
also the foreman, as our mentor, and committed us to his supervision.
Each of us was given a place in his workshop, we were equipped with
tools, and had to begin like any apprentice. When we ate we went to

the same table where all our workers sat, but we went to the places at the lower end, where the apprentices were. We slept in the apprentices' dormitory, which adjoined the bedroom of the foreman, the only one who could sleep in a room of his own. For that reason he had to be more than a highly skilled worker, he had to stand out for his rectitude morals and conduct. In our house no other kind of person was hired for that position. He had special supervision over the apprentices because they still required training and discipline. To sleep in we were given beds like the apprentices, and to wear we were given the outfit of all our workers.

"So it began. But this went just as all previous things had gone. My brother worked quickly, and produced fine pieces of work. I did just as our master instructed, but my pieces didn't come out as they were supposed to, and weren't as fine as my brother's. I worked extraordinarily hard, though. In the evening we often sat in the workers' common room and listened to them talk. They would mention examples of wicked workers too, but these were not meant to tempt us, rather to fortify us, and fill us with revulsion. Our father said that whoever wishes to live must know life, the good and the evil of it, yet the latter must not assail but rather strengthen him. On such evenings I liked to fetch what the workers sent me for, wine cheese and other things. For that they were very fond of me.

"Once we had been trained in one workshop, and could do those things, we moved on to another, until at last we were discharged, and entered the trading operations as apprentices. When we were finished there too, we moved on to the office and the clerical work of our business.

"When, after a considerable time, our years of apprenticeship were over, we moved into the room where the sons of the house lived, and were given the simple clothing our father was wont to wear.

"A short time after we had finished our apprenticeship, when my brother was already being consulted on all the aspects of the business, our father took ill. He wasn't so seriously ill that there was any danger to be feared, nor did he have to take to his bed, but his sturdy form dwindled, he grew lighter, he wandered about in the house and the garden, and no longer devoted himself to our business dealings as had once been his habit and his pleasure.

"My brother took over the management of the business, I had no need to get involved, and in the end our father spent most of the day in his sitting room, when he wasn't in the garden.

"Around this time I asked permission to move back into our old study to live there. My request was granted, and I moved my belongings down the long hallway into the study. As our father gave no instructions and no commands regarding the business, and my brother assigned me no work, I had the leisure to do as I pleased. No one had reproached me for failing to get adequate marks in our academic subjects, and so I resolved to go over them once more, and learn everything properly. I took a book from the shelf, sat down, and read the beginning. I understood everything, and studied it, and memorized it. The next day I repeated what I'd learned the previous day, tested myself to see if I still knew it, and studied a new section as well. I assigned myself very little material, but I tried to understand it, and retain it thoroughly in my memory. I assigned myself exercises to work through, and succeeded at them. I looked for the exercises we had been given by our tutor, did them over, and this time I made no mistakes. What I had done with one book, I did with the others. I studied hard, and little by little I was spending all day in the study. When I had some free time, I liked to sit and take up the book my tutor had given me in remembrance, and think of the man who had lived with us back then.

"In the study all had been left as it was. The big oak desk still stood in the middle, still bearing the marks we had made in its wood, intentionally with our knives or by chance with other instruments, still showing the dried rivulets of ink that were left when an accident happened with the inkstand and no amount of washing or sanding would help. I pulled out the drawers. Mine held my schoolbooks still, with the red chalk or pencil strokes showing how far we had to read; they still held the notebooks in which we had worked out our exercises, and the tutor's red ink strokes shone out, showing our mistakes; they still held the old dusty pencils and pens. It was the same with my brother's drawers. They, too, held his old learning materials in immaculate order. Now I learned at the very same table the lessons I'd learned years before. I slept in the same bed, next to it the night table with the candle. But my brother's bed was empty, and was always covered up. In the two rooms the tutor had occupied I kept several chests of clothes and other things, but other than that they, too, were unused, with nothing but the same old furniture. Thus I was the sole occupant in the back of the garden wing, and this went on for several years.

"Suddenly our father died. My shock was tremendous. No one had thought that death was so near, that indeed there was any danger at all. To be sure, lately he had withdrawn more and more, his figure was stooped, and often he spent days at a time in bed; but we had grown so used to this state of affairs that in the end it seemed routine, all who lived in the house saw him as their father, who belonged so essentially to the house that no one could imagine his passing, and I really never thought that he could die, and that he was so ill. At first all was thrown into confusion, but then his body was prepared for the funeral. Behind his coffin went all the poor people of the district, there went the men from his business his friends many strangers his house staff and his two sons. Many tears were wept, such as are wept for few of our countrymen, and folks said that an outstanding man an excellent citizen and an honorable businessman had been laid to rest. Several days later his will was opened, and it said that we two brothers had been appointed heirs and had inherited the business jointly.

"After some time had passed my brother said to me that the entire burden of the business now rested on our shoulders, and at that I disclosed to him that I had relearned the Latin Greek natural history geology and arithmetic in which I had made so little progress back when we were being tutored, and that now I was almost fully conversant in these things. But he replied that Latin Greek and the other subjects were not exactly essential to our trade, and that I had made these efforts too late. I rejoined that just as I had relearned these academic subjects, I would gradually relearn all the operations and skills that were directly required for our business. At this he repeated that if the business were forced to wait for me, by the time I was ready it would already have gone under. But he promised to shoulder all that lay in his power, and leave me to do as I pleased, I could observe, I could help, I could go on studying, but one way or the other my share would be preserved for me undiminished.

"I went back to my study and did not interfere with the business affairs, for it seemed I did not understand them, and he left me there. In fact, he even sent me better furniture and provided me with various amenities so that I would not be uncomfortable. After some time had passed he appeared with our family's lawyer with court officials and with witnesses who had been friends of our father, and gave me a legal document stating my hereditary claims, my share of the inheritance, and what was due to me in future. My brother the witnesses and I signed the document.

"I went on studying; my brother managed the full scope of the business. After a quarter of a year he brought me a sum of money and said that this was the interest due to me from my share of the inheritance that was invested in the business. He said that he would hand over this sum to me every quarter. He asked me whether I was content and I replied that I was very content.

"After another such interval had passed, he put it to me that my studies did, after all, have to lead somewhere, and asked whether I wouldn't be inclined to work toward becoming a member of the learned professions for which the things now occupying me were the prerequisites. When I replied that I had never considered the matter, and that I didn't know what profession might befit me, he said that was not necessary now, I should merely use the knowledge I had gained to begin taking the examinations, so that I would have certificates of my qualifications; I should seek to master the missing subjects and take those examinations as well, and when the time had come for me to decide on a profession, I would have more experience and be in a better position to decide which direction to take.

"Very pleased with the suggestion, I consented. After some time

I took the first examinations in the lower disciplines, and did exceptionally well. This emboldened me, and with great zeal I went about acquiring the remaining knowledge. My heart stirred joyfully within me at the thought of someday belonging to one of the professions that I had always regarded with such awe, that serve the world with their scholarship and their skill. I worked very hard, I scraped the time together, I rarely set foot in the rest of the house, and after another interval had elapsed, I was able to pass another examination with good results.

"And so I had wholly become the garden wing's denizen, I was allowed to remain so, and with a clear conscience could devote myself to my endeavors.

"The back of our garden adjoined another garden, though it was really more of a meadow, with a tree here and there that no one tended. The path through that other garden passed just outside one of our cast-iron gates. In that garden I always saw beautiful white sheets and other linens hung up on long lines. I often gazed over at them, sometimes from my windows sometimes through the gate when I happened to be in the garden. When they were dry they were gathered up in a basket, while a woman stood by giving instructions. Then the woman took a cloth to wipe off the lines strung between the posts, and wet sheets were hung up. This woman was a widow. Her husband had held a position that earned him a good living. Shortly after his death his kind old employer died as well, whose son had such a hard heart that he gave the widow just enough to keep her from starving. And so she rented the garden that adjoined ours, and she rented the little house that stood in the garden. With the money her husband had left her she fit out the house and garden so that she could do the washing for people who entrusted her with linens of all kinds, delicate and otherwise. She had cauldrons installed in the little house, as well as other equipment for boiling the laundry and preparing the lye. She set up washing rooms, and places where the laundry could be ironed and folded, and for the winter and spells of bad weather she built a drying loft. In the garden she had posts driven into the ground at regular intervals, with rings attached to the poles and lines that were drawn through the rings and frequently changed. A brook ran behind the house, which was what had prompted the widow to establish her laundry here. There were channels for pumping water from the brook to the cauldrons, and a washhouse was built over the water of the brook. The woman had hired many maids who had to do the work properly while she stood by, gave instructions, and showed the right way to do everything; as she did not have the laundry treated with brushes and crude instruments, and as she made sure that it was very white, and that worn spots were mended, she had a great many customers, she had to expand her establishment and hire more workers, and not infrequently a fine lady would come and sit with her under the tall pear tree in the garden.

"This woman had a little daughter, a child, no she was a child no longer—I didn't rightly know whether she was still a child or not. The daughter had delicate red cheeks, she had delicate red lips and innocent brown eyes that gazed about kindly. Over these eyes her lids were big and gentle, and from them drooped long lashes, dainty and demure. Her dark hair lay beautifully on her head, parted smoothly and neatly by her mother. At times the girl carried a long basket of fine wicker; a very fine white cloth was spread over the basket, and it must have held exquisite linens which the child had to take to some woman or other.

"I so loved to look at her. Sometimes I stood at the window and looked over at the garden where washing always hung on the lines, except when night fell, or bad weather came, and I was very fond of those white things. Then sometimes the girl would come out, cross the meadow hither and thither on various tasks, or, though the little house was quite hidden behind the branches, I would see her standing by the window and learning her lessons. Soon I knew the time when she carried out the washing, and I would sometimes go down into the garden then and stand by the cast-iron gate. The path went by the gate, and so the girl had to pass me. She knew quite well that I was standing there; for she always blushed, and walked with more restraint.

"One day, seeing her come from afar with the washing, I quickly reached through the bars of the gate, laid in her path a beautiful peach I had picked beforehand for that very purpose, and went into the bushes. I went in too deep to see her. When so much time had gone by that she must long since have passed, I came out again, but the peach was still lying on the path. Now I waited for the time of her return. But when she had returned, and I went to look, the peach was still lying on the path. I took it back in. The same thing happened again a while later. The third time I stood where I was, the peach lying with its soft red cheek in the sand, and said as she approached: 'Take it.' She looked at me, hesitated for a moment, then bent down and took the fruit. I no longer know where she tucked it away, but I know for certain that she took it. After some time had passed I did the same thing again, and once again she took the fruit. This happened several times, and at last I handed her the peach through the bars.

"Finally we also spoke. What we spoke of, I no longer recall. They must have been ordinary things. We also held hands.

"In time I could hardly wait for her to come with her basket. I was standing at the gate every time. She stopped when she reached me, and we spoke to each other. Once I asked her to show me the things in the basket. She parted the linen cover with little strings and showed them to me. Inside lay ruffs fine sleeves and other things that had been ironed. She told me what they were called, and when I said how beautiful they were, she replied: 'The linens belong to an old countess, I always have to take them to her myself, so that nothing happens to them, because they're so fine.' When I said again, 'Yes, they're fine, they're extraordinarily fine,' she replied: 'Indeed they are fine, my mother says that linens are a home's highest good next to silver, they are fine white silver themselves, and if they are sullied, they can always be cleansed to fine white silver again. They are our noblest and closest garments. That's why Mother collected so much linen that we had plenty after my father's death, and that's why she has taken on the task of cleaning other people's linens, and won't let them be touched with rough, unfitting things. Gold is precious too, but it's not a household good, it's mere adornment.' At these words I recalled indeed that on her body, at her neck or at her sleeves, I had always seen the finest white linen, and that her mother always wore a snow-white bonnet with a fine ruffle surrounding her face.

"From that moment on I took some of the money my brother gave me every quarter and purchased very fine linens like those of the genteel countess, and all sorts of silver housewares.

"Once, as we stood there together, her mother passed nearby and cried: 'Johanna, for shame.' We were ashamed of ourselves indeed, and ran away from each other. My cheeks burned with shame, and I would have been horrified if anyone had seen me in the garden.

"From then on we never met at the gate again. I went into the garden whenever she passed, but I stayed in the bushes so that she couldn't see me. She walked past with flushed cheeks and downcast eyes.

"Now I had dressers put in the two rooms that adjoined my sitting room, with narrow top drawers in which I placed the silver and wide bottom drawers in which I laid the linens. I stacked together what belonged together, and tied it up with red silk ribbons.

"When for some time I had not seen the girl pass the gate, I didn't dare to ask, and when at last I did ask, I learned that she had been sent to another city, and would become a distant kinsman's bride.

"I cried so hard then, I thought my soul would leave my body.

"But some time later a terrible thing happened. My brother had one main money-dealer who always lent him, on trust, up to a certain sum of money for running expenses, to be squared as circumstances allowed. I don't know whether other people undermined my brother's credit or whether the money-dealer himself grew apprehensive after two businesses that owed us considerable amounts failed and cost us our fortune: from then on he refused to pay our bills of exchange. My brother had to cover several with large sums, and lacked the cash to do so. The friends he turned to grew apprehensive themselves, and so it came that the bill creditors sued, and that our house our other properties and our goods were assessed to see whether they would suffice without seizing outstanding monies owed to us. When this became known, all those with demands upon us came and wanted them fulfilled; but those who owed us money did not come. My brother meant not to tell me, so as not to grieve me, believing that he could pull through. But when our house was ordered to be sold for the immediate payment of our bill debts, he could keep it from me no longer. He came to my room and told me everything. I gave him the money I had; my needs were very modest, and I had saved a large share of my income. I opened the narrow top drawers of my dressers and laid out all my silver on our oaken desk and offered it to him. He said it was not enough to save the house and the business, and refused to take it. Nor did the court make any demands of me, but I could not stand to see my brother leave claims unfulfilled, thus burdening his conscience, and so I added it all to the other assets. Taken together it was enough to pay all the creditors' claims, satisfying them in every particular. But our beautiful house with its back wing and our beautiful garden were lost.

"I've forgotten all the other blows that followed; but even the prospect of using the remaining money to establish a small business and gradually build ourselves up again was soon thwarted.

"My brother, who was unmarried, was so deeply grieved that he came down with a fever and died. His coffin was followed by no one but myself and several people to whom he had done good turns. Ever since my great-grandfather's generation there had been nothing but only children, sons, down to myself and my brother, and our housekeeper Luise had passed away long before, and so I had no relatives and no friends left.

"I had seized on the idea of becoming a preacher of the Word of God, a priest. Even if I was unworthy, I thought, God through His mercy might still let me strive to become an unobjectionable servant and representative of His Word and His works.

"I gathered up my certificates and papers, went to the seminary and anxiously requested admittance. It was granted me. At the set time I moved into a room there and began my studies. They went well, and when I was finished, I was consecrated as a servant of God. At first I served by assisting old parsons with their ministry. That brought me into different situations, and I got to know people. From the parsons I learned spiritual and worldly qualities. When enough years had passed that no one could take it amiss if I applied for a parish, I asked for this one, and received it. I have spent more than twenty-seven years here, and now I shall never leave. People say it's a bad parish, but it yields enough for a preacher of the gospel to live on. They say its countryside is ugly, but that's not true either, if only you look at it properly. My predecessors were transferred to other parsonages. But my living colleagues who are my age or somewhat younger distinguished themselves greatly during their training, and are superior to me in all their qualities, and so I will never request to be promoted and moved elsewhere. My parishioners are good, they have opened their hearts to many an instructive word of mine, and will open them in future.

"And then I have a worldly, more personal reason for staying in this place. You'll learn it later on, when you hear the request I have to make of you. I'm coming to that request, but there is one more thing I must say before I make it. In this parsonage I've begun to save money for a certain purpose, not a bad purpose, concerning not just worldly well-being, but another kind as well. I won't mention that purpose now, it shall become known at some point, but it was the reason why I began to save. I brought no savings with me from my father's house; the remaining money that came in was used for various things, and for years no more has come. My only legacy from my father is that one single crucifix that hangs on my door above the stoup. My grandfather bought it in Nuremberg, and as I was always fond of it, my father gave it to me. And so I began to put away money from the income of my parsonage. I wore simple clothes and kept them as long as possible in good repair, I disposed of the bed, and lay on the bench in the vestibule with the Bible under my head as my witness and succor. I stopped keeping servants, and hired old Sabine's services, which suffice for me. I eat what is good and beneficial for the human body. I've rented out the upper floor of the parsonage. I've been reprimanded twice for that by the honorable episcopal consistory, but now they tolerate it. Because people supposed I kept money in my house, which was true, I was robbed of it three times, but always started over from the beginning. As the thieves took only the money, I sought to remove it from their grasp. I have invested it in absolutely safe securities, and when interest accrues, I reinvest it. And so I have not been troubled for many years. Over this long span of time my way of life has become a habit, and I love it. But there is one sin against this frugality that weighs upon my conscience: I still have the fine linens that I laid up in my room in our garden wing. It is a grave error, but I have sought to atone for it by skimping still more on my physical needs and other things. I am too weak to do without them. It would be so sad if I had to give away the linens. After I die they'll bring in some money, after all, and I don't even use the bulk of them."

Now I knew why he was ashamed of his splendid linens.

"I am sorry," he went on, "that I cannot help the people here as much I would wish to; but I can use the linens for no other purpose, and not everyone can do all the good they might wish to; the greatest fortune would not suffice for that.

"You see, now I have told you everything, how it has been with me, and how it is still. Now I come to my request. Perhaps, when you consider all the things I have told you, you will grant it. It will be burdensome to fulfill, though, and it's only your kindness and goodness that permits me to put it forth. I have deposited my will with the court in Karsberg, in the castle. I presume that it is secure there, and I have the receipt here in my house. But all human things are subject to change, fire devastation an enemy invasion could come and imperil my will. And so I have prepared two identical copies to keep as securely as possible, so that after my death they may come to light and their purpose be fulfilled. That is my request, that you take one copy into your hands, and keep it safe. The other I will keep here, or I will give it to someone else to keep in order to fulfill its purpose. Of course then you must allow me, when you leave this place, to write you a note from time to time, telling you that I am still alive. When the letters cease, you will know that I am dead. Then you must send the testament through reliable hands, and against receipt, to Karsberg, or to whichever authorities can execute it. All this is only a precaution in case the one deposited with the court should be lost. The will is sealed, and you shall learn its contents after my death, if you are not averse to fulfilling my request."

I told the parson that I would be delighted to comply with his wish, that I would keep the document with as much care as my own most precious things that would be irreplaceable if destroyed, and that I would gladly follow all his instructions. And I hoped that the time was yet distant when his testament and its two copies would be unsealed.

"We are all in God's hands," he said, "it may be today, it may be tomorrow, it may take many years yet. For the sake of the purpose I'm pursuing alongside my pastoral duties, I hope it may not be so soon; but God knows what is best, and to bring even this one work to fruition he does not require me."

"But as I might die before you," I rejoined, "for good measure I shall keep written instructions with the will, passing my obligation into other hands."

"You are very good," he replied, "I knew you would be so kind, I was sure of it. Here is the document."

With these words he drew a document out from under his pillow. It was folded and sealed with three seals. He placed it in my hands. I examined the seals; they were clean and intact and displayed a simple cross. On the outside were the words THE LAST WILL AND TESTAMENT OF THE PARSON IN THE CORRIE. I went to the table, took a sheet of paper from my letter case, wrote that on that day I had received from the parson a paper sealed with three seals bearing a cross and marked with the words LAST WILL AND TES-TAMENT OF THE PARSON IN THE CORRIE. I handed him this attestation, and he slipped it under his pillow. For the moment I put the will in the satchel that carried my drawings and other work.

After this discussion I stayed with the pastor for quite a while, and our conversation turned to other, more trivial matters. Sabine came in with his meal, the girl from the upper floor came down to ask how he was feeling. When the stars showed high in the sky, I walked to my hut through the pale rocks and the soft sand, thinking of the parson. For the time being I put the will in the case where I kept my valuables, so that later, at home, I could store it safely.

In my rocky maze I passed the time that followed the parson's story just as I had passed the previous time. We surveyed, and worked, and drew; by day I gathered material, toward evening I visited the parson, spent a few hours at his bedside, and then worked at night in my shack while one of my men fried me a scanty steak at the makeshift stove.

Little by little the parson got better, finally leaving his bed, just as the doctor in the city had said he would, then he went outside, he went back to church, and at last he went back out into the Corrie Rocks, wandering about in the hills or standing by and watching us work.

But everything comes to an end, and so did our long sojourn in the Corrie Rocks. We had advanced farther and farther, we had come closer and closer to the boundary of the district assigned to us, at last the posts were set up along it, everything had been surveyed up to that point, and after a little bit of paperwork the Corrie Rocks, in their entire likeness, were stored away on many sheets in our portfolio. The rods the posts the workshops were cleared away at once, the shacks were dismantled, my men went their separate ways, and the Corrie Rocks were as they had been, free and empty of these inhabitants.

I packed my suitcase, took my leave from the parson from the schoolteacher from Sabine from the tenant and his daughter and from other people, had my trunk taken to the High Road, went there on foot, sent for post-horses, and when they had come, I rode forth from the scene of my work hitherto.

I must mention a very strange feeling I had then. Something approaching profound melancholy seized me as I parted from the region which, when I first set foot there, had seemed so repellent. As I emerged into more inhabited parts, I was compelled to turn around in my carriage and gaze back at the rocks where the lights glimmered, so gentle and faint, and whose recesses held the lovely blue shadows where I had long lingered, while now I rode forth to green meadows to marked-off fields and tall upward-striving trees.

Five years later chance took me back to the vicinity, and I seized the opportunity to visit the Corrie Rocks. I found the parson walking about in it as before, or occasionally sitting on one of the rocks to look around. His clear blue eyes were just as they had been.

I showed him the letters that I had received from him, and had kept. He thanked me very warmly for having sent a reply to each letter, he said that they were a joy to him and that he read them often. He showed my letters to me as we sat together again at the spruce table in his chamber.

The Zirder, a sky-blue ribbon, flowed through the rocks, the rocks had their gray hue, and the sand lay at their feet. The strips of green and the few shrubs were unchanged. On the High Road the innkeeper and his wife were as before, even their children were almost as before, indeed the old guests seemed to be sitting at the tables, so great is the resemblance among the people who travel over that ridge.

After that visit to the area my business did not take me there again, nor did I find time to visit the Corrie on my own. Many years passed, and the parson's wish that God might grant him a long life on account of his purpose seemed to be fulfilled. Every year I received several letters from him, which I answered regularly, and which resumed regularly the next year. I seemed to notice just one thing: that the letters revealed something like a tremor in his hand.

After long years a letter came from the schoolteacher. In it he wrote that the parson had fallen ill, that he spoke of me, and that he had said, "If only he knew I was ill." So he had taken the liberty of informing me, not knowing whether it might not do some good, and he asked my forgiveness for being so intrusive.

I replied that I could not regard his letter as an intrusion, that in fact he did me a great service, for I took a great interest in the parson in the Corrie. I begged him to write me often about the parson's condition, and if it should worsen, to inform me at once. And if, contrary to expectations, God should swiftly subject him to his mortal fate, he should tell me that, too, without the slightest delay.

To reassure the parson I wrote to him as well, saying that I had heard of his illness, and had asked the schoolteacher to write me frequently about his condition; I begged him not to exert himself to write me, and to have himself a bed made in the chamber, and told him that, as in previous years, his indisposition would soon pass. At the moment my work did not permit me to visit.

He wrote me a few lines nonetheless, replying that he was very very old, that he was waiting patiently and was not afraid.

After the schoolteacher had written two letters saying that no change in the parson's state had occurred, there came a third, reporting that he had passed away after receiving the last rites.

Reproaching myself, I now set everything aside and prepared for the journey. I took the sealed paper from my cabinet, I took the parson's letters too, which could help identify his handwriting, and I set out for Karsberg.

When I arrived, I was told that the parson's will had been officially deposited at the castle, that a second one had been found in his belongings, and that I should report at the castle in two days to present my will, after which the wills would be opened and verified.

I spent those two days in the Corrie. The schoolteacher told me about the parson's last days. He had lain quietly in his illness, as in the illness during which I had so often visited him. Again he had taken no medicine, until the parson from the Wenn, a neighbor of the Corrie parson's and the same man who administered the last rites, had put it to him that he must use earthly remedies as well, and leave it to God whether they would work or not. From that moment on he took everything he was given, and submitted to all that was done with him. He lay in his chamber again, where once more they had made him a bed from woolen blankets. Sabine was always with him. When it came time to die, he made no special preparations, but lay as he had every day. No one could tell whether he knew he was dying. He was as usual, and spoke his usual words. At last he fell into a gentle slumber, and it was over.

He was undressed so as to be clothed for the bier. The finest of his linens were put on him. Then he was dressed in his threadbare coat, and over his coat came his surplice. Like this he was laid out on the bier. The people came in great numbers to view his body, for they had never seen such a thing; he was the first parson who had died in the Corrie. He lay there with his white hair, and his face was mild, only much paler than it had been, and his blue eyes were covered by their lids. Several of his colleagues came to inter him. When his coffin was lowered into the ground, many of the people who had gathered began to weep.

Now I inquired about his tenant on the upper floor. He came down himself to the parsonage vestibule where I was, and spoke to me. He had hardly any hair left, and so he wore a black skull cap on his head. I asked about his lovely daughter, who had been a quick young girl back then, when she often came into the parson's sickroom on my visits. She had gotten married in the capital, and was the mother of almost grown children. She had not been with the parson in his last days either. The tenant told me that he would probably have to move to his daughter's; he would surely lose his apartment when the new parson came, and would not find another one in the Corrie.

Old Sabine was the only one who had not changed; she looked exactly as she had back when she tended the ailing parson on my first visit. No one knew how old she was, and she did not know herself.

I had to stand in the vestibule of the parsonage because the little chamber and the vault adjoining the vestibule had been sealed. The single wooden bench, the parson's bed, stood in its usual place, and no one had paid it any thought. But the Bible no longer lay on the bench; I was told that it had been put in the chamber.

After the two days that had been set as a waiting period before opening the will, I went to Karsberg and appeared in the courtroom at the appointed hour. A number of people had gathered, and the heads of the parish council and the witnesses had been summoned. The two wills and the catalog of the parson's estate lay on the table. I was presented with my attestation, which had been found among the parson's belongings, confirming receipt of his will and was requested to show it. I handed the will over. The handwriting and seals were examined, and the validity of the will was acknowledged.

In the usual manner, the will deposited with the court was now opened and read, followed by the one I had submitted. It matched the first one word for word. Finally the one found in the parson's home was opened, and it, too, matched the others word for word. The date and the signature were the same in all three documents. All three wills were immediately declared to be one single will existing in three copies.

But the contents of the will surprised everyone.

The parson's words, leaving off the beginning in which he invokes God's assistance, commends the document to His protection, and declares that he is in perfect command of his reason and will, go as follows: "Just as every person finds, or should seek, something apart from his position and his profession that he must achieve so as to do all he must in this life, so have I found something to achieve aside from my pastoral duties: I must remove the danger to the children of the Corrie Crofts and the Rock Crofts. The Zirder often floods, and can then become a raging torrent that rapidly sweeps onward; in the first years of my tenure cloudbursts twice caused it to wash away all the crossings and bridges. The banks are low, and the bank on the Corrie side is even lower than the Rock Crofts bank. Three things can happen then: either the Corrie bank is flooded, or the Rock Crofts bank is flooded as well, or even the bridge is swept away. But the children from the Corrie Crofts and the Rock Crofts must cross the bridge to the Corrie to go to school. If the Corrie bank is flooded and they go down from the bridge into the water, some might stray into a pit or a hollow, and be killed; for the muddy water of the flood hides the ground from sight; or while the children are wading through the water it might rise so quickly that they cannot reach dry ground; or they might come from the Rock Crofts bank and go onto the bridge, but find the water over the Corrie bank to be too deep, they might linger, deliberating or wavering, so long that in the meantime the water covering the Rock Crofts bank would be too deep as well; then the bridge is an island, and the children standing upon it can be swept off along with it. And even if none of these things should happen, in winter they walk with their little feet in water filled with snow and ice floes, and do great harm to their health.

"To put an end to this danger in future, I have begun to save my money, and my instructions are as follows: using the sum of money found to be my property following my death, and adding to it the proceeds from the sale of the possessions I leave behind, a schoolhouse shall be built for the schoolchildren of the Corrie Crofts and the Rock Crofts in their midst, and then part of the sum shall be invested such that the interest can pay the teachers' salaries, and furthermore another part shall be put to profitable use so that the schoolteacher in the Corrie can be paid an annual compensation for the loss suffered by the children's absence, and finally, if anything is left, it shall go to my maidservant Sabine.

"I have written three identical wills, so that they will be safer, and should any other instructions or statements be found in my papers that do not match the content and date of these wills, they shall be invalid.

"But so that even now the danger may be diminished, I go to the meadow on the Corrie bank every day to look for ditches pits and hollows, and mark them with sticks. I have asked the owner of the meadow to level any pits and hollows as soon as possible, and he has always complied with my requests. When the meadow is flooded, I go out and seek to help the children. I learn the ways of the weather so as to predict floods, and warn the children. I do not stray far from the Corrie, so as not to neglect my duty. And I shall always do so in future."

Deposited with the wills were the parson's accounts up to the date of their drafting. The accounts from that point to the parson's death were found in his papers. They had been kept with great rigor. From them, too, one saw how diligently the parson had saved. The very smallest amounts, even pennies, were included; new sources of money, however insignificant, were tapped, and little trickles flowed forth from them.

The auction of the parson's belongings was set for the fifth day after the opening of the will.

As we left the court, the parson's tenant said to me, weeping, "Oh, how I misjudged the man, I almost took him for a miser; my daughter knew him better than that, she always loved the parson dearly. I must write her about this at once."

The schoolteacher from the Corrie blessed the parson, who had always been so good to him, and had so liked to visit the school.

The other people learned the will's contents as well.

Only those whom it concerned most closely, the children in the Corrie Crofts and the Rock Crofts, knew nothing of it, or if they learned of it, they did not understand it, and did not know what it was that had been intended for them.

Wishing to be present at the auction, I returned to the Corrie, and decided to spend the four days visiting various spots in the Corrie Rocks and other areas where I had once worked. It was all unchanged, as though, besides its simplicity, it had also been imbued with immutability.

When the fifth day had come, the seals were removed from the doors of the parson's dwelling, and the belongings he had left were auctioned off. Many people had come, and in light of the will the auction took a remarkable course, filled with noteworthy incidents. A coat found among the dead man's possessions, in the worst conceivable state for a piece of clothing not in tatters, was bought by a parson for a pretty penny. The Corrie parish purchased the Bible to donate it to the church. Even the wooden bench, which had not even been locked away, found a buyer.

I bought something at the auction as well, namely the little carved wooden crucifix from Nuremberg and all the remaining sheets and tablecloths of that fine and beautiful linen. My wife and I own the linens to this day, and have used them very rarely. We keep them to commemorate the fact that the parson saved these things out of a profound abiding and tender emotion and never used them. Now and then my wife has the linens washed and ironed, delighting in their indescribable immaculate beauty, and then the folded things are tied with the old faded red silk ribbons, which have survived, and are put back in the closet. —

Now one might ask what the outcome of all this was.

The sum that the parson had saved and the sum accruing from the auction of his belongings were, taken together, much too small to set up a school. They were too small even to build a medium-sized house of the type common to the area, much less a schoolhouse with classrooms and accommodations for the teachers, and furthermore to cover the teacher's salary and compensate the former schoolteacher.

That was like the parson, who did not grasp worldly things, and had to be robbed three times before investing his savings for interest.

But as evil is always futile in itself, and has no effect in the great scheme of things, whereas good bears fruit, even when begun with inadequate means, so it was here: "To bring this work to fruition God did not require the parson." When the matter of the will and its shortcomings became known, the rich and prosperous people of the surrounding area came together at once and soon underwrote a sum that seemed adequate to carry out all the parson's intentions. And each declared that, should any more be necessary, he would be willing to pay it. I, too, contributed my mite.

I had parted from this district the first time with a sense of melancholy; now tears flowed from my eyes as I left the lonely rocks. —

Now, as I speak, the schoolhouse has long been standing amid the Corrie Crofts and the Rock Crofts; it stands in a wholesome, airy location in the schoolchildren's midst. The teacher lives in the building with his family and his assistant, the schoolteacher in the Corrie receives an annual compensation, and a share was even intended for Sabine. But she did not want it, and from the outset allotted it to the schoolteacher's daughter, of whom she had always been fond.

The Corrie cemetery's only cross ever erected for a parson stands on the grave mound of the man who established these things. At times, perhaps, a prayer will be said there, and many a one will stand before it with an emotion that was not felt for the parson while he was yet alive.

TOURMALINE

TOURMALINE is dark, and what is told here is very dark. It took place in past times, as what was told in the first two pieces took place in past times. Here can be seen, as in a melancholy letter, how far a man may go when he clouds the light of his reason, understanding the world no longer, abandoning the inner law that unfailingly leads him to do what is right, surrendering absolutely to the fervor of his joys and torments, losing hold and slipping into states we barely know how to unriddle.

In the city of Vienna, some years ago, there lived an odd fellow; such big cities have many sorts of people, engaged in all sorts of things. The fellow we speak of here was a man about forty years of age who lived on the fourth floor of a building on St. Peter's Square. The gallery leading to his apartment was closed off by a cast-iron gate, on which hung a bell pull that could be rung, whereupon an elderly maid came to unlock the door and show the way in to her master. When one had passed through the gate, the gallery continued; on the right was a door to the kitchen, where the maid was, with a single window looking out onto the gallery, and on the left a long iron balustrade and the open courtyard. The gallery ended at the door to the apartment. Opening the brown door, one entered an antechamber, rather dark, where the great wardrobes holding the clothes stood. It was also used for dining. From this antechamber one entered the master's room. Strictly speaking it was a very large room with a small side room. In this room all the walls were completely papered over with portraits of famous men. There was not a single patch, not the size of a hand, where the original wall could be seen. So that he, or sometimes a friend, when one came, could contemplate the men quite near or right next to the floor, he had had leather-padded lounges made, of varying heights and on rollers. The lowest was a hand's breadth high. One could roll a lounge to whichever men one liked, recline upon it and contemplate them. For those higher and highest up, he had double-sided rolling ladders, their wheels covered in green felt, which could be rolled to all parts of the room and from whose steps one gained different perspectives. In fact, all the things in the room had rollers so that one could easily move them from place to place and not be impeded in one's inspection of the portraits. As far as the fame of these men was concerned, it was all the same to the owner what their life pursuits had been and what pursuits had brought them fame; quite possibly he had them all.

This room had an enormous grand piano whose note stand held many music books and which he liked to play. There were also two stands with two cases holding violins, which he also played. On a table was a case with two flutes, which he used for his own pleasure and to perfect himself in that art. By one window stood an easel with a paint box, at which he painted in oils. In the adjoining room he had a large desk where he piled many papers and composed poems and wrote stories, and beside which stood his bookcase, in case he wished to take out a book and amuse himself by reading. His bed stood in this room as well, and in the back there was a contraption for working in cardboard, where he made boxes receptacles screens and other decorative objects.

The neighbors in the house referred to this man as the pension man; but few could say whether he was called that because he lived on a pension or because he worked in a pension office. It could not have been the latter, though, for then he ought to have gone to his office at certain times, but in fact he was home at all hours of the day and often for days at a time, pottering away at the manifold occupations he had taken upon himself. Aside from that he would go to the coffeehouse to watch the chess players, or walk about in the city to observe all the things to be seen there, or join a circle of friends who

met at an inn on certain days. So it seemed he must have a small
pension enabling him to lead this life.

This man had a lovely wife, about thirty years old, who had borne
him a child, a little girl. His wife occupied a chamber adjoining her
husband's large room, just as large and also with a smaller side room.
One could enter the wife's room from the husband's, or one could
enter it from the antechamber by a little secret passageway, as the
apartment's four rooms were lined up in a row perpendicular to the
outside gallery. The little passageway was useful as it allowed the wife,
when her husband was receiving friends, to reach the antechamber
easily and without disturbing the men, and from there to proceed to
the kitchen.

The wife's rooms were furnished in her fashion. The larger room
had dark curtains at the windows, and in it stood soft couches of the
same material, and a fine large table, always dust-free and gleaming
to a high sheen, with a few books or drawings or the occasional other
thing resting upon it. Mirrors hung on the piers between the windows,
with slender pier tables below them holding a few pretty things made
of silver or porcelain. At one window stood an exquisite little sewing
table with fine linens delicate fabrics and other things for working
with, and a small chair in front of it that fit into the window bay. At
the second window stood the embroidery frame with an identical
little chair, and against the short side wall of the third window bay
stood the writing desk, with the writing case the inkstand and an
array of writing utensils upon its clean green surface. In a sort of
semicircle around the desk stood tall dark plants, some broad of leaf.
The large wall clock had no chime, and ticked so softly that it was
barely to be heard. Besides these things, in the back of the room stood
a curio cabinet with glass panes and silk curtains, so that the wife
could place different things in the compartments, and draw shut the
silk in front of them.

The second, smaller room had snow-white curtains that fell in
dense folds; near the window stood a table, not for displaying pretty
things, but for household purposes. Then came a large chaise longue
various chairs and footstools. In the back stood the wife's white bed

draped in white curtains, next to it a night table with a candlestick with a bell with books a tinderbox and other things. Near the bed on a pedestal stood a gilded angel, its wings folded about its shoulders, supporting itself with one hand and gently stretching out the other to hold the tip of a white drape whose lavish folds parted and fell in the shape of a tent. Beneath this tent a dainty basket rested on a table, in the basket a white bed was made up, and in this bed was the couple's child, the little girl by whose side they often stood to gaze upon the tiny red lips and the rosy cheeks and the little closed eyes. And finally the room held a very fine large painting depicting the Holy Mother with the Infant. It was framed in folds of dark velvet.

In her rooms the wife presided, she looked after all the child's needs, and occupied herself with work with reading with embroidery with the management of the household and other things of the kind. She had few dealings with the outside world, nor did women often come to visit her.

At the time when this couple lived on St. Peter's Square, another man living in Vienna was causing a great stir. He was a scintillating artist, an actor, and back then the whole world was under his spell. Old men of our day who knew him in his prime go into raptures when they speak of him, telling how he interpreted and performed this role or that, and these speeches generally end by concluding that we have such artists no longer, and nothing the new time brings forth can stand comparison with what our fathers saw. Those of us now getting on in years may have known the actor, and may have seen him perform, yet probably never knew him in the midst of his fame, but only when he was declining from its zenith, albeit he maintained his luster for a very long time, almost into his dotage. This man, named Dall, was chiefly famed for tragedy, though he appeared in other genres, especially dramas, with extraordinary success. Stories have survived of certain moments in which he carried spectators to the utmost extremes, extreme rapture or extreme horror, until they felt they were in reality, not in the theater, and waited anxiously to see how events should unfold. In particular his portrayal of august per-

sonages is said to have had such dignity and majesty that nothing of
the kind has since been seen on stage. A profound authority on such
matters once said that Dall did not devise his roles through contrived
contemplation or preparations and exercises; rather, when they spoke
to his own nature, he inhabited them, trusting to his personality,
which inspired him to the right action at the right moment, and in
this way, rather than play the roles, he really was what they depicted.
This explains why it was that when surrendering absolutely to the
situation, he did things on the spur of the moment that astonished
both himself and the audience, leading to remarkable tours de force.
But it explains, too, why he could not play a role at all, even badly,
unless he could inhabit it. For that reason he never took on such roles,
and no cajoling and no arguments, however forceful, could persuade
him.

All this explains Dall's character and his way of life outside the
theater too. His outward appearance was captivating, he moved lightly
and pleasingly and carried his body as the expression of a lively, agile
spirit which voiced itself very clearly through that instrument. A
cheerful man, he sought his friends where he found them and was so
convivial that when he sat among chatting friends over a glass of fine
wine, chatting away himself, it was impossible to believe he was the
same man whose magnificent performances excited our souls to the
most profound convulsions to fear and horror and to joy and ecstasy.
But precisely because he was what he played, and because he found
within his body the most apt expression for it, the emotions that
arose in his fiery spirit took fiery form on the surface of his body, be
it in movement in expression in voice, and they were ravishing. For
this he was the darling of society, he stimulated it, and gave it sensa-
tions. People sought him out and strove to captivate him. He moved
in the most diverse circles, thus acquiring the light smooth freedom
of his comportment, but none of these circles had a hold on him: just
as his spirit guided him on stage, so too it led him among people, to
live with them and feel emotions, it led him out into nature to behold
it and feel it; but it drew him away from people again when his spirit

was given nothing more to move it, and it drew him away from nature when its gentle speech ceased to excite him and he sought more powerful impressions and more profound contrasts. And so he lived in emotional states, abandoning each as he pleased.

This man was acquainted with the pension man, and one might say that he was in nothing so constant as in this acquaintance. Whichever circles he had just left, he liked to go to St. Peter's Square, climb the four flights of stairs, ring the bell at the cast-iron gate, have the elderly maid admit him, and pass through the antechamber into the pension man's chamber of heroes. There he sat, chatting about all the pension man's diverse occupations. In fact, perhaps he sought out the company of the pension man because there were so many different things there. It was art, in particular, that attracted Dall in all its forms indeed its deformations. And so they discussed the pension man's poems, he had to play one of his two violins, he had to blow his flute, had to perform some piece of music or other on the piano, or they would sit by his easel, discussing the colors of a painting or the lines of a drawing. Dall was most experienced in the latter; he was an outstanding draftsman himself. For the pension man's cardboard constructions he spelled out the length and breadth the connections and relationships.

As for the portraits of famous men pasted to the walls, he would recline upon the lowest of the lounges and examine the bottom row one by one. The pension man had to say what he knew about each one, and if neither of them had anything sufficient to say of a man except that he was famous, they got out books which they studied until they found something to satisfy them. Then he reclined on the higher lounges, then he sat on the next higher, then he stood up, and at last he stood on the various steps of the ladder. This way he came to appreciate the convenience of such lounges, and the pension man had to have a large rolling armchair made for him, with an upholstered back and well-made arms.

He liked to sit in this armchair when he came, and they would fall to chatting.

In this manner considerable time passed.

At last Dall began a love affair with the pension man's wife, and continued it a while. The wife herself, in her fear, confessed it at last to her husband.

Dall must have known of it, or must have sensed from the wife's pangs of conscience that she would confess to her husband the affair with his friend. For now he no longer came, though lately he had visited the apartment on St. Peter's Square more often than in earlier days.

The pension man's rage was extraordinary, he wanted to run to Dall, reproach him, murder him; but Dall could not be found at his home either, nor was he performing in the theater at that time, and no one knew where he was. The pension man made every effort to track down Dall, he went to his home every day at different hours, but never found him, and people said Dall had taken a little trip to get some rest. The same thing was heard in all the city's circles, and it was said the artist would surely return soon to delight the world with his brilliance. But the pension man would not be put off, and went on looking for Dall. He sought him in all parts of the city, he sought him in public squares in the church in places of amusement and on promenades, and yet again he sought him at home. The man he sought was nowhere to be found.

The pension man went on in this way for a considerable time. Suddenly, though, he became very still. His friends saw that the unrest lately afflicting him had gone. He sat there calm and pensive. Then he went to his wife and said that Dall had been bound to claim her, why had he brought him into his home, she'd given him her heart just as he took the hearts of thousands from their bodies in a single evening of theater.

Toward friends, who learned of the matter in a general way from hushed conjectures circulating in the city, he expressed himself consciously or unconsciously such that they had to suppose his emotional state to be as described.

Dall, from his remove, must also have learned how things stood, and he must have known that the pension man was now calm; for when nothing out of the ordinary occurred and everything seemed to be going along as usual, Dall came back to town, and was seen on stage once more.

One day the wife of the pension man vanished. She had gone out, just as she usually went out, and she had not returned.

The pension man waited, he waited until night came; when she failed to appear, he thought she might have had an accident, and he drove in a rented carriage to all his acquaintances and friends and asked if they had seen his wife, but no one could tell him anything. The next day he reported the matter to the authorities, he demanded official action, and looked into all the accident victims and vagrants. But the authorities found nothing either, and she was not among the accident victims, nor was she among the vagrants without a fixed abode.

Then the pension man thought that perhaps Dall had taken her somewhere and was keeping her in concealment. He went to Dall and demanded that he say where his wife was, and give her back to him. Dall declared that he knew nothing about the wife, he had not seen her since his last visit to the apartment on St. Peter's Square, he rarely left the house, and then only to go to the theater and back.

The pension man went home.

After some time he came to Dall again, knelt down in front of him, clasped his hands and begged Dall for his wife. Dall replied once again that he knew nothing whatsoever about his wife, she had not gone away at his bidding, he did not know her whereabouts and could not give her back.

The pension man withdrew.

After a few days he came again, knelt down again and begged for his wife with clasped hands. Dall swore that he didn't know where the woman was and that he couldn't give her back.

The pension man came yet again a few days later, did the same thing, and received the same answer. Then he came no more. He sent away the maid, he took the child from her bed, took her in his arms, left his home, locked the door behind him and went away.

When friends came to visit him, they learned from the neighbors that the pension man was gone, that he must have set out on a journey, for he had taken the child with him, and though it was summer, he had been wearing his coat.

And so the apartment on the fourth floor of the building on St. Peter's Square stood empty, and the cast-iron gate leading to the gallery was locked.

When half a year had passed, and the pension man had not returned, nor had anyone paid the rent for the apartment, the landlord reported the case to the authorities. Friends of the missing man were sent for, and were asked whether they knew his whereabouts; but no one did know. One by one, all the people were sent for who were known to have had relations with the pension man; but not one could provide information. On the court's recommendation, and moved by his own goodwill toward the pension man, the landlord decided to wait a while longer to see whether the pension man might return of his own accord. According to the neighbors and the porter, the pension man had not had the least thing moved out of his apartment; in fact, no one could even recall whether he had carried a suitcase when he left. As the apartment was known to contain many and valuable things, they thought it probable that the pension man had merely gone off on a trip, that some chance circumstance had prevented him from returning or sending word, and that he was sure to return again.

But when two years had passed, and the pension man had not come back, nor sent any news of himself, an official announcement was put in the papers demanding that he send word, and declare whether he would keep his apartment on St. Peter's Square, and settle the rent as required by law. If no word came within a certain period of time, his lease would be considered terminated, his belongings would be auctioned off, the back rent would be paid from the proceeds, and any remaining sum would be placed in the custody of the court.

But that time elapsed without the pension man returning, or any word coming, or anyone appearing to take care of the apartment.

At that the authorities prepared to force entry.

A locksmith had to open the lock of the cast-iron gate. The elderly maid was not there to take the people into the antechamber and the pension man's room, her kitchen window was not smooth and clean as it had been, it was covered with dust and draped in cobwebs. In the kitchen all was as usual, the maid had cleaned everything before going away, and put it in its place, but each thing was covered with dust, and the wooden tubs had fallen to pieces within their metal hoops. In the antechamber the wardrobes were filled with clothes; from the woolens a cloud of moths flew up, the others were undamaged. The wife's clothes hung there as well, with beautiful silk dresses among them. The china and silver was in the cupboard.

When they opened the pension man's room, they found everything as it had been. The lid of the grand piano was open, there were the two violins, the cases with the flutes, but one of the flutes was missing. An unfinished painting was on the easel, books and papers lay on the desk, and the bed was covered with its delicate coverlet. The famous men were dusty and yellowed from the pent-up air. The lounges stood about, but it was a long time since they had rolled. The actor's big armchair stood in the middle of the room.

In the wife's rooms nothing seemed changed at all, the furniture stood in its old arrangement, with the same old things on its surfaces; but the tiny alterations that had in fact occurred showed how things had changed here. The heavy curtains hung still, when once they had moved slightly alongside the open windows, the flowers and plants were withered stalks, the clock with the soft tick no longer ticked at all, its pendulum was still, and it showed the same unchanging hour. The linens and the other needlework lay upon the tables, but they showed no touch of a hand, and grieved beneath the dust. In the side room the white curtains hung in their many folds, but in those folds was light quick-sifting dust, the Holy Mother gazed down from the painting, the red draperies were gray, the gilded angel held the tip of the linen tent, but dust covered the linen drapes, and beneath them was the empty basket, and the child's rosy face was no longer there.

The authorities took possession of all these items by listing them in a book. Then they were moved together into two rooms, to take stock of them and guard them more easily. At that the apartment was closed again, and sealed.

None of the things that were found suggested the whereabouts and present circumstances of the pension man. Nor was any money found; it was assumed that he had taken all his cash along on his trip.

The day of the auction was appointed, and once it had been carried out, part of the proceeds went to the landlord to cover the back rent with interest, and the authorities took the rest into custody for the missing pension man. All the heroes had been taken down from the walls, the apartment on the fourth floor of the building on St. Peter's Square stood empty, and a sign posted on the door declared that it was available for rent.

The whole affair had caused a great stir in Vienna; people guessed more or less at the true circumstances, and discussed the matter for quite some time. At one point the tale went about that the pension man was in the Bohemian forest, living in a cave where he hid his child, going out by day to earn his living and returning to the cave at night. But other city affairs intervened, as events always come thick and fast in such places, people spoke of other things, and soon the pension man and his story were forgotten.

Since the time of the events related above, a number of years had passed. This story comes from a friend who knew the actor quite well, and had learned from his friends the precise nature of his relationship with the pension man's family. She herself, at the time the incident occurred, had been so young that it made little impression on her.

We shall now let the rest follow in her words.

Quite some time ago, she said, when I had been married for just a few years, we had a very pleasant, inviting apartment in the suburbs. My husband could easily travel the short distance into the city, where official duties called him each day; I did not go in often, because the household kept me quite busy, because the children were small and gave me plenty to do, because I devoted myself gladly to their care; but if I did need to go into town, it was merely a stroll when the weather was fine, and in bad weather it did not cost much to take a carriage. For the children the open and airy apartment, which came with a spacious garden, was quite a boon, and when my husband once thought of giving it up, a friend of his, a distinguished doctor, urgently advised against it. One side of the apartment looked out over the garden and beyond it to more gardens and the nearby vineyards and wooded hills that surrounded the city. It was I who spent the most time there, with the children. The front windows faced the suburb's broad straight beautiful main road, filled with pleasing, not too hectic activity, with merchants' stalls and stands, and carriages driving past, and people strolling. This side of the apartment had our drawing room another fine room and my husband's study. The stretch of road between the city and the countryside was so smooth and so short that it never took long to reach one or the other.

Once, on a fine mild morning, I believe it was just as spring was arriving, with my husband already in town and the children at school, the balmy breeze inspired me to open the windows to air the apartment and, as always, take that opportunity to do a bit of dusting, tidying up, and so on. From our apartment we were apt to hear the bell of the hospital chapel calling people to Mass, and often, when I was properly dressed, I would go over to do my devotions. That bell was pealing through the air just as I looked out onto the street from the window of our best room, shaking out a dust cloth. But apart from the chiming of the bell, another thing made me linger at the window for a moment. When I looked down to see what sorts of people were passing, I caught sight of a strange pair. A man, quite aged—judging by his back, which was turned to me—dressed in a coat of thin yellow baize pale-blue breeches big shoes and a little round hat, walked down the street leading a girl dressed just as oddly in a brown cloak that lay about her shoulders rather like a toga. The girl had a head so big that it gave you a turn, and you kept looking at it. The two went their way at a fairly quick pace, but both were so awkward and clumsy that you saw at once they weren't used to Vienna, and didn't know how to move as other people did. But for all his awkwardness and clumsiness, the man took pains to help the girl sidestep the passing carriages and keep her from bumping into people. They were heading for the church where the bell was pealing.

Driven by curiosity, and thinking that the man might be taking the girl to Mass, I decided to go there as well, to do my devotions and learn more about the pair or observe them. I dressed quickly, wrapped myself in a shawl, put on my hat and went forth. I turned onto the lane that led from the main road around the corner of the school of military medicine in the direction of the chapel, where I had seen the two people turn; but I didn't see them on the lane. I walked along it, passed under the arch which, at that time, marked its end, turned the corner, and walked up to the church; but I saw them nowhere. Nor did I see them among the few people in the church. Now I did my usual devotions, immersed myself in them, and when Mass was over and I prepared to leave, I looked around once again to offer them my assistance, if they needed it; but I had been mistaken, the pair was not in fact in the church. And now I betook myself home again.

Quite some time had passed since this incident, and I had long since forgotten it, when one very fine night my husband and I strolled home from the city. We had gone to the Hofburg Theater, and the night being so fine and clear, we decided to accept the suggestion of a friend who had attended the performance with us to visit with his family before going home. As usual, we discussed the play, we argued about this and that, refreshments were brought, and it was midnight by the time we went on our way. We declined our friend's offer of his carriage, saying that it would be robbing this beautiful night to sit in the carriage and fly across the clear space between the city and the suburb rather than stroll through it and savor its open illuminated loveliness. No objections were made, and we set out on foot.

Emerging from the gates and leaving the city behind, the wide serene greensward with its many trees met us, and over all this space was a moonlit night of real splendor. A tremendous sky, seeming molded from a gemstone, was suspended above the great panorama of the suburbs; there was not a single cloud, and from the zenith the circle of the moon spilled down its light. We strolled down the row of trees that lined the road, passing a few solitary walkers and couples. Because it was such a fragrant, almost southern night, we walked back across the open space and crossed it once again, so that finally we were almost the last people there. Now we turned to head home too. As we walked down our suburban blocks without ever meeting a soul, we perceived that we were not, after all, the only ones who had felt the appeal of this lovely moonlit night, that someone else's heart had been moved by its radiance; for in the universal stillness, broken only by our steps and the distant calls of nightingales, we heard the strange playing of a flute. We heard it faintly at first, then louder as we walked onward. We stopped for a while to listen. Had it been ordinary flute-playing, no doubt we would soon have moved on again, for in our city it is not uncommon to hear music from some house or other, even late at night, but the playing was so strange that we lingered. It was not outstanding, it was not entirely amateurish; what compelled the attention was that it was unlike anything one describes and learns as music. The theme was no tune that was known to us; no doubt the musician was expressing his own thoughts, and even if they were not his own, he put so much more into them that they could be seen as such. The most tantalizing thing was that once he had begun a passage and enticed the ear to follow, there always came something other than you expected and had the right to expect, so that you had to keep starting from the beginning, and following along, ending up in a confusion that verged on madness. And yet despite its incoherence there was a grief and a lament and some other alien thing in this playing, as though the musician were using clumsy means to tell of his woe. It was almost touching.

"Strange," my husband said, "he must have had an odd way of learning the flute, he strikes up the melody right, but he doesn't keep it up, he takes things too quickly, he can't make the breath last, he hurries it, and it breaks off, and yet there's a kind of heart in his playing."

We couldn't make out where the music was coming from; we almost thought it came from the old Perron House, which was nearby; but the house was about to be demolished, there were very few people still living there, and the notes did not sound at all as though they were floating down from some window.

After lingering a while longer, we walked on, the strange flute music faded behind us, until at last we heard it no more, we came home and laid ourselves to rest alongside our children, who had already slept more than half their rejuvenating sleep.

After this incident another stretch of time passed.

Those who have lived in our city a long while will recall the old Perron House. Those who have known Vienna for even fifteen or twenty years are aware that this city is in a constant process of transformation, and that despite its age it is a new city; the buildings are always being renovated in new ways and for various uses, old immutable monuments such as St. Stephen's Cathedral are too few and far between to lend the city a uniform appearance, and so it always looks like something built yesterday. The old Perron House stood on the main road of our suburb, not far at all from our home. It had the peculiarity, one unknown to today's younger residents of our capital, of having underground chambers. The windows of these chambers were generally set just above the pavement of the street. They were not very large, and had sturdy iron bars, usually backed by a dense mesh of iron wire which, when the occupant was not especially tidy, were covered by the dried muck that spattered in from the street, and presented a sorry sight. The Perron House was already a very old building at the time, black in appearance, with ornaments from ancient times. Only its narrow end faced the street; the larger rooms looked out on a garden in the back. It had a little door painted in dark-red paint gone nearly black and studded with many metal nails whose material was unrecognizable because a black film covered their heads. Next to the little door there was a big entryway, but it had not been used since time out of mind; it was locked, covered with the muck and dust of the road, and had two crossbars fixed to the walls with iron clamps.

We had a friend back then who has remained our friend in all the times that followed. Professor Andorf was unmarried, a genial friendly man full of intellectual gifts, possessing a warm feeling heart and responsive to all that was good and beautiful. He came to visit us quite frequently and shared scholarly pursuits with my husband; often beautiful writing would be read aloud, or music would be played, or various things would be discussed with cordial intimacy. This Professor Andorf lived in the Perron House, and had actually chosen not the street side but the courtyard. He had taken the apartment voluntarily because it was very quiet, and his occupations consisted of reading writing and a bit of piano-playing; though he was a genial sociable man, he had chosen this apartment in particular because it appealed to his poetic powers—which expressed themselves less in creation than in reception—to observe the gradual subsiding fading decaying, and to watch as, little by little, birds and other animals took possession of the walls from which the people had withdrawn; there was nothing he loved more in the world, he would say, than to stand at his window on a rainy day and watch as the water trickled down from the thistles the coltsfoot and the other plants in the yard and the moisture crept down the old walls.

One day, already dressed and about to go to his office, my husband said, "Here is a book that belongs to Professor Andorf; it's very important and I'm anxious to keep it from falling into strange hands; would you be so good as to wrap it in paper, seal it, and have some reliable person take it to the professor? I didn't have time to do it myself, and so I am asking you."

He laid the book on my sewing table, I told him that I would perform the errand for him, and he went out on his official duties.

But as it occurred to me later that afternoon that I had to go into town anyway, and would pass the Perron House, I thought I might take the opportunity to deliver the book myself, so that it could not possibly fall into the wrong hands. And so I decided to do just that. When the time came, I dressed, put the book in my workbag, which I like to carry with me, and set out. Reaching the Perron House, I pressed down the handle of the little red door. I had never been inside the building. The handle yielded easily, and the door opened. But standing in the passageway that opened up behind the door, I looked about in vain for a lodge or apartment with a porter or someone else who could assist me. And so I walked down the passageway, finding no stairway leading to the upper floors, and came out into the court-yard. It was paved with flagstones, large but in part already in pieces.

I saw Professor Andorf's plants, the ones that enthralled him with their trickling water when it rained, and I saw the grass sprouting up in all the gaps, flourishing untrodden. In the walls surrounding the courtyard I saw several doors that must have led to stables or carriage sheds, but the doors were never opened, as shown by their weathered desiccated somewhat dilapidated appearance the tall grass at their feet and the rusty brown hinges. There were also three openings leading to stairways, but the openings looked uninviting, and the stairs seemed unused. Among the windows, blind or with a bluish glitter or shut with wooden shutters, I saw several with clean glass and white curtains inside. I concluded that they must belong to the professor's apartment, but I did not know how to reach it.

At that moment I heard soft footsteps behind me and heard a not unpleasant rather refined male voice saying, "What is it that you wish?"

I turned and saw a little man standing behind me, with sparse gray hair on his head and an artless expression on his face. He hadn't really dressed; he was wearing only linen breeches and a jacket of similar material, with nothing on his head, and slippers on his feet.

"I'm looking for Professor Andorf," I said.

"What do you wish from Professor Andorf?" he asked. "Do you have a message or something I could give him? Herr Professor is not at home."

I looked at the man more closely. He had a longish face and blue eyes. There was nothing repellent about his countenance.

"I have a book to give him," I said, "which belongs in his hands alone, but since he isn't home, the book can wait, my husband can send it to him some other time."

"I'm the porter of the house," he responded, "you can entrust the book to me; but if you prefer to bring it to him yourself, or have it brought by one of your servants, you'll find the professor at home every day until nine in the morning, and usually between four and six in the evening."

As I looked at him, wavering doubtfully, he said, "My dear lady, give me the book, I'll handle it carefully so that it won't get dirty, I won't peek inside, and I'll hand it over to Herr Professor Andorf as soon as he comes home."

I took another look at him, struck by the propriety of his demeanor. In the few remarks he made to me, his words had been carefully chosen, as in refined society, only there was something unsteady about his blue eyes, as though they were constantly glancing back and forth. Lacking the courage to wound him with my mistrust, I fumbled open my workbag, pulled out the book, and placed it in his hands. I hadn't wrapped it up after all, as I had intended to hand it over myself. He noticed this at once, and said, "I'll wrap the book in paper, set it aside until the Professor returns, and hand it over to him."

"Yes, please do that," I said, and with these words I left the house.

But no sooner had I reached the street than anxiety seized me. A fruit seller tended to sit about twenty steps from the little red door, by the wall of the next building. She sat there every day, as long as the weather wasn't too nasty; on ordinary rainy days she unfurled a broad canopy over her merchandise. I knew the woman well, and had often bought fruit from her for the children. I went to this woman and asked whether she knew the porter of the Perron House. She said that she did know him, that he was a respectable man, that when he went out he was sure to come home before darkness fell. There were no tales to tell about him, she said; he was very quiet. It was high time the Perron House was renovated, incidentally, there weren't many people still living there, much less genteel folk, excepting Herr Professor Andorf, as I knew quite well myself, and in a few years no one at all would want to live there anymore. If Herr Perron weren't always traveling in foreign parts, he'd know how things stood with the house, how little money it earned him, and how much better he'd do to tear it down and build another in its place.

I bought some fruit from the woman, put it in my bag, and went on my way into town.

When my husband had come home, and we were having lunch, my conscience troubled me, and I told him what I had done; but with the goodness and indulgence that had always dwelled within him, he reassured me, and said that I had done quite rightly, that he himself, if he had taken the book there and the same had happened to him, would have done no differently. The book would end up in the right hands sure enough. Nevertheless, the next time the professor visited us after this incident, I told him I had given the book to the porter of the Perron House and asked whether he had received it.

"I received the book," said the professor, "but I thought you'd sent it by way of that old man. I had no idea we had a porter in the Perron House, and if we have one, he must be the quietest porter in the world, for I've never heard a thing from him. I have a key to open the little door when I come home late and it's already locked. By the way, I'm sorry I wasn't home when you dropped by; I could have had you in and shown you the building's various oddities."

Another long while had passed since this incident when a new portent occurred. One day our oldest son Alfred came home from school, hurried up the stairs, burst into the parlor and cried, "Mother, I didn't hurt him, Mother I didn't hurt him."

"Alfred," I said, "whatever is the matter?"

"Mother, you know the Perron House," he replied, "I was walking along the wide sidewalk, and I saw a raven sitting on the pavement. He wasn't afraid, it seemed he couldn't fly, and he walked along ahead of me when I followed him. I bent down, talked to him, reached for him, and he let me pick him up. Mother, I didn't hurt him, I only petted him. Then a horribly big face looked out of the basement window of the Perron House and cried: 'Stop, stop.'

"I looked over at the head, its eyes stared, it was very pale, and terribly big. I let the raven go, stood up, and ran home. Mother, I really didn't hurt him, I only wanted to pet him."

"I know, Alfred, I know," I said, "put down your school bag and go to the nursery, there you'll get your lunch, and forget about the raven, he doesn't matter."

The boy kissed my hand and went to the nursery with a light heart.

But my heart was not so light, I had grown pensive. I recalled the pair I had seen long ago and followed toward the hospital chapel.

That girl had also had, in the boy's words, a horribly big head. Now I began to connect the incidents. If the head Alfred had seen was the same one I had noticed on that girl, she had to be living in an underground chamber in the Perron House. When I recalled the porter of the Perron House, to whom I had given the book for Professor Andorf, it seemed to me that he had approximately the figure and stature of the man I had seen walking down the street with the girl. Perhaps, then, the porter was the girl's father.

It occurred to me once more how respectably indeed agreeably the porter had behaved when he induced me to hand over Professor Andorf's book, how choice and fine his speech had been, suggesting that something unusual was at work here, and I resolved to inquire after the porter of the Perron House on occasion, and should any assistance be required, to provide it according to the modest means at my disposal.

When Alfred encountered the raven, it was late fall. In the very mild winter that followed, I often went into town with my husband. Sometimes we visited friends, sometimes we went to the theater, of which I was quite fond at the time. Returning home in the evening, on several further occasions we heard the strange flute music we had heard that moonlit night, and now could clearly tell that it was coming from the underground rooms of the Perron House.

But an opportunity to make the acquaintance of the Perron House porter was hard to find. First of all, I didn't want to impose, and then Professor Andorf was so little acquainted with the porter of the house that he hadn't even known it had a porter, and finally there was no one else who went into the Perron House and could have made an introduction. Part of the winter passed without my managing to act on my intentions.

One day I was busy tidying up our nicer rooms. We had had company the day before, and there was a bit of a mess. Then I heard a hum and hubbub from the street, and when I opened the window and looked out, I saw several people standing at the little door of the Perron House, and more and more coming to join them. I called one of my maidservants and sent her down to ask what the matter was.

After a while the girl came back and said that the porter of the Perron House had struck himself dead. At once I put on a cloak, went downstairs, and headed toward the Perron House. But rather than get drawn into a discussion with the people standing outside the little red door, I went to the fruit seller I knew, who was sitting at her stand, and asked, "What on earth has happened here, and how can a person strike himself dead?"

"No one has struck himself dead," the woman replied, "it's just that the porter of the Perron House has died. A quarter of an hour ago, when no one happened to be passing on this side of the street, the girl his daughter came out to me and told me in secret that her father was dead. Then she went straight back to the Perron House. I called over the shoemaker's apprentice, and told him to go to the town hall and report what the girl had told me. The apprentice must have told people on his way, and that's why they've already come. But soon there should be someone from the town hall too, a bailiff a doctor an inspector a councilor or whoever it may be."

While the woman was speaking, still more people had gathered, but none of them went through the little red door, either out of respect for the dead man who lay within, or from fear of the strange Perron House.

At last the officials who had been sent to investigate arrived.

"This is the woman who told me," said the apprentice, pointing to the fruit seller.

The fruit seller had to go with the officials, which she did readily, after spreading a big white cloth over her wares. I introduced myself to the officials and asked them to take me along to the chamber, saying that I wished to help if there was anything that needed to be done. They were happy to let me. The apprentice, as the one who had reported the incident, had to come along as well.

When we reached the door, all the people crowded toward it, but the men from the town hall said that no one who was not an official, or did not have an official invitation, could go inside the house. Then two police officers were posted on either side of the little door, we went in, and the officers stepped into the doorway and let no one else inside.

Past the little door we walked down the passageway to the court-yard, and from the courtyard back into the main entryway with the locked portal, and found a door in its side wall. The door was opened. Behind it a stairway went down into the depths, where the porter's chamber was said to be.

When we had gone down the stairs and entered the chamber, we saw that it consisted of one single room. A ladder reached up to the window and next to it lay the old dead man. He was wearing a yellow baize coat and pale-blue breeches. When the men lifted him up and laid him on what appeared to be his bed, I saw from his face that he was indeed the man to whom I had given the book. At first they had meant to try to revive him, but the moment they touched him they had felt that he was cold, and closer examination showed that he was unquestionably dead.

When could he have died?

There was no one else in the room but the girl with the big head. She sat far back on a chair of pale unpainted wood and watched from a distance to see what they would do with the man. On a screen in front of a bed that I took to be the girl's, perched the jackdaw, for it was a jackdaw not a raven that Alfred had tried to catch. The bird nodded its head and uttered all sorts of noises, but they were garbled beyond comprehension and hardly human-sounding. I saw the flute lying on a table not far from where the girl sat.

While the men were inspecting the body and trying to arrange it decently on the bed, I meant to speak to the girl, gain her trust, and then take her with me to remove her from this unhappy place. I approached, and spoke to her, trying to use the most courteous but simplest possible language. To my surprise, the girl replied in words that seemed to come straight from a book, but what she said was barely intelligible. Her thoughts were so strange, so unlike anything expressed in our everyday intercourse, that one might have thought them weak-minded, had they not in part been extremely sagacious.

I happened to have a few confections and some fruit in my cloak. I took out a bit of pastry and offered it to the girl. She reached for it, ate it, and the features of her big face glowed with visible joy. I tried to use the opportunity to discern from her features how old she might be, but the unusual shape of her head and face made this impossible. She might have been sixteen, or she might have been twenty.

Now I gave her a second piece, then a third, then several at once.

As for her words, I shall convey the approximate sense in our speech or manner of speaking, because the girl's train of thought would not be understood otherwise, and because I am unable to repeat things from memory exactly as she said them.

I asked her whether she liked to eat such things when she had them, whether they were good.

"Yes, good," she said, "give me more."

"I'll give you more," I replied, "if you come with me, and stay in a different room until night has come, and day has come. Then I will take you back to this room that is yours. I have no more of those sweet things here, but there are lots of them in the room where you shall go with me."

"I'll go with you," she said, "but when day comes, we'll come back to our house."

"Yes, then we'll come back to this room," I said.

I now gave the girl a special kind of apple. She ate it with signs of enjoyment.

I also asked the girl whether she had a mother, or living siblings.

She had no mother, she replied, and she had only ever been alone with her father. The concept of siblings seemed to be utterly foreign to her.

I then asked how her father had died.

"He climbed up the ladder," she said, "that goes up to our window. I don't know what he wanted to do, and then he fell down, and lay there. I waited for him to get better again, but he didn't get better. He was dead. When one night and one day had passed, I told it to the woman who always sits close by our little door. After that the people came."

I told the men what I had learned, and said that I would bring the girl to my home and take care of her myself for now. The authorities in charge of the case could always find the girl with me if they wanted to ask for her back. And I would tell my friends and acquaintances of the matter, so that we could collect money to give the man a proper burial. The men had no objection to this.

Meanwhile they had finished with the body. It had been found that the poor man had fallen for some reason or another from the ladder propped against the window, as appearances indicated and as the girl had said, and that in his fall he must have injured his neck vertebrae, resulting in instantaneous death. I was told that the law would require an autopsy, which made it seem all the more desirable that the girl should be taken away from the chamber. The statements of the fruit seller and the apprentice had been taken down, and they were told that they were free to go.

I went to stand by the body for a while. Now it lay on the bed in its clothes. The features of the face were little altered, and were almost as they had been on the morning when the man stood before me in the courtyard of the Perron House, and convinced me to give him the book. The blue eyes were closed, and with the lids covering their conspicuous restlessness, his face even had a gentle look. The others must have sensed it too; for a moment they stood around the bed in silence, gazing at the man. At last the apprentice and the fruit seller left the room. I, too, stepped away from the sight.

I approached the girl and told her that I would take her with me now, and that she should follow me as she had said she would.

The girl replied that she would indeed go with me, and that when the next day had come, we should go back to the room again.

I replied that by all means this should be so.

Now she followed me quite willingly. We climbed the stairs, I took her by the hand, we went across the courtyard and down the corridor and onto the street through the little red door. On the street the people were still standing about, and if anything the crowd had grown. A dense throng surrounded the fruit seller and the apprentice, who were telling what they had seen and learned inside the house. I quickened my step so that I and the girl could escape the crowd and the scrutiny and astonishment provoked by the sight of the girl's unusual head.

I took her to my home.

There I gave her a proper meal, presuming that since yesterday she could not have eaten regularly. That must indeed have been so; for the girl ate with evident pleasure, and seemed quite revived. She told me later that she had eaten all the bread that was in the house.

We had a room facing the garden where an old nurse, who had served with my parents and then taken care of my children, had lived until at last her daughter married and she went to live with her and if need be do for her daughter's children what she had done so long for the children of strangers. Since that time the room had stood empty, but the furniture remained. I now had it fixed up for the girl I had brought. I had the bed made, and had the room heated cozily. Then I took the girl there. I had made sure that none of my servants should catch sight of her, so that they should not frighten her with stupid stares, much less with exclamations. Thus I myself had brought the meal to her in our dining room, where she was before she could be taken to the back room, and I had ordered that no one should come into the dining room.

We had an elderly housemaid who had been with us since our marriage, who was greatly devoted to us and our children and enjoyed certain privileges, having a say in family affairs and other crucial matters. I called this maid, explained the case of the strange girl, and asked her to stay in the room with her, speak to her kindly, assist her, and make her stay as pleasant as possible. She promised to do all these things. I provided underclothes too, in case the strange girl should need anything. And I brought more confections and fruit to her room, to fulfill the promise I had given.

I told the girl that I had to go now because I had other things to do, that the maid would stay with her, and that I would come back and see how she was.

The girl seemed to understand all this perfectly.

I went and sat down in my study to write to several friends and acquaintances and ask them for assistance.

When my husband came home in the evening, I told him everything that had happened and what I had done, and asked him if it was all right.

He said it was all quite right, he approved of everything, and took up the matter himself. He wrote some letters too, and then he took a carriage to pay a personal visit to several of his friends. When he came home late that night, he brought assurances of help, and kind replies to several letters had arrived that very same evening. We went to bed satisfied.

The next morning my husband went with me to the underground room. The autopsy had taken place. The spinal cord had been crushed by the vertebrae in a place where life's most delicate seat seems to be, and this had caused his death. The body was already in a coffin, and had been prepared for burial. We sent word to the church to make arrangements for the funeral. While my husband made further arrangements, I went home to persuade the strange girl to stay in my home until the funeral was over.

She was already awake, and dressed. She asked to go home. I told her that I had no time right now, that several things had to be taken care of, and that once they were done I would by all means return and take her back to her home myself. She consented to these things, was given her breakfast, and the maid I had provided remained with her.

Professor Andorf had come over, having learned of the matter. Other friends we had written to came to witness the case with their own eyes. Once again many people had gathered at the red door. They were mostly people from the lower classes, brought by curiosity and a kind of visceral sympathy typical of their kind; and then, as they tend to in the city, passersby had stopped, had asked what had happened, and after hearing the answer had joined the people waiting, if their time at all permitted it.

As the morning drew to a close, the priest appeared, and the body was consecrated and brought to the church, where it received the usual prayers and was taken to the graveyard. We had arranged for a simple funeral so that some of the money collected could be set aside for the orphaned girl. Once the corpse had been taken away, all the people had withdrawn from the little red door.

I felt it was now time to take the girl back to her underground home. I saw clearly that I could gain her trust only by scrupulously keeping my word; for among her other peculiar qualities, the girl had a blind faith in the words of other people. And so I went to the back room, said that I had finished the things that had been keeping me, and that I would now take the girl back to her home. She rose happily from her chair and followed me.

When we had entered the underground room, she asked about her father. I was at a loss, for I had thought that she knew her father was dead, having used the word herself; and that she would thus know where he had been taken when she failed to find him in the chamber. So I said that she knew her father had died, she had said herself that he had not gotten better, but was dead, and so he had been buried according to the rites of our religion.

She was perplexed for a while, then said, "He won't come back at all?"

I lacked the courage to say yes, and I lacked the courage to comfort the girl with deceptions, trapped instead in admission by halves.

After a while she asked again, "He won't come back at all?"

Now I no longer had the courage to be untruthful; I told the girl that her father was dead, that he would never move again, that we had put him under the ground, as was done with all dead people, and that there he would go on lying in peace.

At that she began to cry bitterly; I tried to comfort her, but my words had no effect, she went on crying until little by little she calmed herself somewhat. When she had grown quieter, I asked whether she would come back home with me; whenever she wished I would take her here again. As the chamber was empty, the girl offered little resistance, and I took her to the room where she had slept. After a while we went back to the underground chamber. And so I repeated the procedure several times over the course of the day, in part to keep the girl occupied, in part to accustom her to the change in her situation, and to give her the illusion of freedom, so that no sense of compulsion would make her grow refractory and impossible to handle.

I also gave her food that I thought might appeal to her.

Toward evening, when we were back in the underground chamber, I suggested that she could sleep once more in the room where she had slept the night before; it was warm there, a good bed was there, the friendly maid was there, and supper had been prepared.

She said she would come along if she could bring the jackdaw with her.

I was happy to oblige.

She moved toward the jackdaw, calling it strange unintelligible names, and tried to catch it. The jackdaw huddled atop the screen and let the girl take it in her two hands. Like that she took it away, and like that we returned to my back room. I sat the girl down in a capacious armchair near the heating stove, arranged for supper, and retired after the day's exertions.

The porter's things had been sealed in his chamber, and the movable property had been impounded. But the key to the door had been left with me so that I could visit the room often with the orphaned daughter. My husband had been asked if he would take custody of the girl, and he had consented.

I did not know what best to do with the girl. Thus we decided to keep her with us until my husband had been given all the dead man's papers and any other items that might clarify the dead man's circumstances and show what should become of her.

It was very hard to wean the girl from the underground vault. She clung to the chamber with a tenacity that was incomprehensible. Only through our frequent visits to the underground room, through confiding chats about unimportant matters, and last but not least through attentive care on which she thrived, could I gradually accustom her to her new room. I gave her good underclothes, and had our maidservants make her dresses that suited her well and in which she felt comfortable and attracted less attention. More than anything she seemed to shy away from the fresh air, and when I took her down to the wintery garden for a while, she moved awkwardly, staring at the leafless branches. For the first few days no one visited her but me and the elderly maid, but little by little she grew used to the sight of other family members, who were all urged to treat her kindly and not alarm her, for instance by obvious scrutiny.

Little by little I ascertained what things she had learned. However choice and perfect were the words she spoke, however well ordered—though the thoughts were often hard to divine—she had no notion or knowledge of the simplest womanly work. Even the washing of a rag or the sewing together of two patches was beyond her comprehension. Her father must have had all that done outside their home. But she often spoke with the jackdaw, unintelligibly to us, sometimes we found her singing softly, and she could play a little on her father's flute, which we had had to bring her.

Once she had become quite attached to me, I induced her to speak of her past. But either she had forgotten all that had happened earlier, or the events that had happened just recently exerted such power over her memory that she no longer remembered what had gone before. All she ever spoke of was the underground chamber.

"Father went forth," she said, "took the flute with him, and often returned only by the time the lights were burning. He would bring a pot with food which we heated in the little stove and ate. Often I'd put wood chips in the stove when he was gone and heat up food that was kept in a pot on the shelf, for sometimes a great deal was left over. Another time I had nothing but bread, and ate that. Sometimes he stayed home too. He taught me things, and told me many stories. He always locked the door when he went away. When I asked what lesson I should do while he was gone, he'd reply: Describe the moment when I'll lie dead on the bier, and they'll bury me; and when I said: Father, I've described that lots of times, he'd reply: Then describe your mother in the torment of her heart, how she wanders about the world because she doesn't dare come back, and how she puts an end to her life in despair. When I said: Father, I've described that lots of times too, he'd reply: Then describe it again. When I was finished with the lesson of Father lying dead on the bier and Mother wandering about the world and putting an end to her life in despair, I'd climb up the ladder and look through the mesh of the window. There I saw the hems of women's dresses pass, saw the boots of the men, saw pretty coattails or the four paws of a dog. What went on by the houses across the street was unclear."

When I asked the girl where she had the drafts of her lessons, she replied that her father had collected them all and that they were stored somewhere. A few bits and pieces were here. With these words she went to a closet where she kept her clothing, took a few crumpled papers out of the pocket of an old discarded coat and handed them to me. I unfolded them. They bore writing, part in ink and part in pencil, often crossed out with Xs and other symbols. Little could be made of them.

I asked her about God about the creation of the world and other religious subjects. She recited the proper passages from the catechism quite fluently, gazing about with her calm, expressionless eyes. I tried to discover whether she had attended our church's religious services, and learned that she had repeatedly gone to church with her father, but had never heard music—or flute-playing, as she put it—nor had she spoken with anyone. Thus she could at most have gone to Low Mass.

At last my husband was given custody of the girl, and received and signed for the dead man's estate as cataloged by the court officials. From the dead man's papers, which he immediately examined in detail, it emerged that he was none other than that pension man who had gone away one day and vanished without a trace. We had known the man's story only in a general way, and had long since forgotten it. Now it was called up from memory anew, and details were inquired from those who might know them.

And so the girl with the big head and the broad features was the rosy infant, she had slept beneath the tent whose tip the gilded angel held in its fingers, whose folds parted around the little bed, and her parents had gazed at her in delight.

The only belongings found were a few shoddy utensils some old clothing and the beds. The only cash was a little sack filled with copper coins. Nothing more.

My husband searched the papers for some indication of the dead man's assets; he must have had some, as none who had been questioned could recall that the pension man had held any office at the time he had lived in the house on St. Peter's Square, nor had he pursued any business, and yet he had lived respectably and comfortably. Thus he must have had earnings from some piece of property. But not the least thing could be found in all his papers, not even the tiniest note. My husband went to all the bureaus in Vienna that had anything remotely to do with money or any other assets, and made inquiries, but nowhere was any information to be had. Now one by one he visited all the business managers deputies solicitors and whatever else such men are called; but he could learn nothing from any of them. At last he seized on the expedient of announcing the case in the newspapers, as far as the question of the assets was concerned, and requesting anyone with information to come forward; but no answer came. And so the poor girl's fortune, if any still existed, had to be given up for lost.

The sum that remained after auctioning off the furniture and other things that the pension man had left in his apartment on St. Peter's Square and after paying the debt to the landlord, and that had been taken into custody by the courts, was handed over to my husband to use for the girl. It had grown considerably with the interest that had accrued over the years.

My husband could find out nothing for certain about the vicissitudes of the dead man's fate after his departure from Vienna. But when he tried by every means possible to ascertain the particulars of the dead man's life and consequently the fate of the girl's fortune, one thing came to his attention, namely that a man whose description closely fit that of the deceased had often been seen in the suburbs far from the dead man's home, appearing with his flute in inns in gardens and in public places and playing there for handouts. In his pot he often took away gifts of food from people's kitchens. It could not be determined whether he had played near his home as well.

From the custodian of the Perron House my husband learned that at some point, even the custodian was no longer quite sure when, the dead man had been allowed to live in the underground chamber free of charge in order to perform the duties of a porter, though the occupants had always kept keys for the little red door, and kept them still. But little could be learned from the custodian, for due to the dilapidated state of the Perron House he took little care of it, nor did the owner urge him to do more.

One day my husband brought a great sheaf of papers into my room and handed them to me. I looked at them, leafed through them, and saw that they were the girl's drafts and written exercises. I made the effort, when I had time, to read through the greater part of these papers. What could I possibly say about them? I would call them literature if there had been thoughts in them, or if one could have unraveled the cause origin and course of what was told there. An understanding of what it meant to die to wander about in the world and take your life in despair was utterly absent, and yet these things were the dismal subject of the exercises. The locution was clear and succinct, the sentence construction was right and good, and the words though senseless were lofty.

This circumstance inspired me to recite passages from the works of poets and other writers that possessed a certain elevated tone. The girl took keen notice. Soon she declaimed similar things herself, and later she delivered, with a certain theatrical air, passages from our people's best and most glorious works. But if you delved more deeply into the work from which she had recited, inquiring as to its substance sense and form, she could not understand what you were after. And not one of those books had been found among the dead man's belongings. The recitation of such passages was a pleasure to which the girl yielded ecstatically. We discovered that the soft words she spoke to the jackdaw were filled with similar things, and the tunes she sought to coax from her father's flute seemed to have the same spirit.

My husband also searched for the girl's mother. His intent was to restore to the girl her first, natural relation and mainstay, but also to learn particulars from the mother, if she were found, that might suggest the whereabouts of the fortune. At first my husband cautiously investigated by way of official channels then with the greatest discretion through individual persons and through the newspapers; but however rigorously these investigations were pursued, however many letters were written, however many instructions were given, however many replies were received: no news came of the woman, to this day no one has had word of her, nor has she returned.

Nothing the girl said told us anything about her earlier life.

We had summoned our family doctor, a friend of my husband's, to examine the girl's physical state, as her strikingly large head indicated some anomaly. His opinion was that this abnormal growth had been induced by fusty dwelling places and perhaps by the father's madness, that swelling and glandular trouble had set in. A visit to the iodine baths might do good on both counts. As I had already planned a spring trip to the region of the baths to spend several weeks with my husband's brother, I decided to take the girl with me. I placed as much hope in the beneficial effects of the fine air and the journey as in the baths themselves. Indeed, after two months in the countryside and the prescribed visit to the baths, her head did become somewhat smaller and better formed, and the features of her face became suppler clearer and more expressive.

We also instructed the girl in everyday things, and encouraged her to perform the essential tasks of daily life. We sought to give her a taste for all kinds of womanly handiwork, and at last through conversation and through reading simple books but mainly through personal dealings to transform her wild and disjointed indeed almost uncanny learning into simple harmonious and comprehended thoughts, and initiate an understanding of the things of this world. How difficult this was is shown already by the fact that months passed before she could tolerate Alfred speaking to the jackdaw or playing with it, or occasionally picking up her father's flute.

When at last we could venture it, we rented a room nearby for the girl to live in. The woman renting out the room looked after the girl, a priest instructed her in religion, we went over quite often to visit her, and thus she grew gentler, and her physical state continued to improve, so that in the course of events, when she came of age, my husband was able to hand over to her the documents regarding the money held by the court and what had been left from her father's funeral, and finally she was able to produce carpets coverlets and things of that sort which, together with the interest from her small fortune, provided her with a living, all the more so as people, touched by her fate, were always happy to buy the pieces she produced. —

Thus the woman's story, and thus the girl lived in the years to come.

The great actor is long since dead, Professor Andorf is dead, the woman has long since moved away from the suburb, the Perron House no longer exists, a gleaming row of houses now stands where it and its neighbors were, and the young generation does not know what once stood there, and what happened in that place.

ROCK CRYSTAL

OUR CHURCH celebrates many different festivals that strike us to the heart. One can hardly conceive of a sweeter thing than Pentecost, or a thing more earnest and holy than Easter. The sorrow and melancholy of Holy Week and the solemnity of the Sunday that follows accompany us throughout our lives. One of the loveliest festivals is observed almost at the midpoint of winter, when the nights approach their longest and the days their shortest, when the sun shines most slantingly on our land and snow covers all the fields, the festival of Christmas. While many countries speak of the day before the feast of the Lord's nativity as Christmas Eve, we call it the Holy Eve, the next day the Holy Day, and the night in between the Hallowed Night. The Catholic church marks Christmas Day, as the day of our Savior's birth, with its greatest celebration; in most regions midnight itself, as the hour of the Lord's birth, is hallowed with a splendorous night Mass, to which the bells send their summons through the pitch-dark wintry still midnight air, and the people hasten with lamps or on dark familiar paths from snowy mountains past rimy woods and through creaking orchards to reach the church from which the solemn sounds emerge and which looms with its long lit windows in the middle of the village girded by ice-sheathed trees.

The church festival is coupled with a festival of the home. In nearly every Christian land, children are shown the advent of the Holy Christ Child—a child like them, the most wondrous child that was ever in the world—as a joyful shining festive thing that works upon you all your life and sometimes, in old age, amid dim somber or poignant memories, appears as a glimpse of times gone by, flitting on bright shimmering wings across the bleak, sad, emptied night sky. The children are given the presents brought by the Holy Child for their delight, usually on Christmas Eve, when the deep dusk has fallen. Lights are lit, usually a great many of them, often little candles poised on the handsome green boughs of a fir or spruce tree in the middle of the room. The children are not allowed to come until the sign is given that the Holy Child has been there, and has left behind the presents he brought with him. Then the door is opened, the little ones are let inside, and in the lights' marvelous glimmering splendor they see, hanging from the tree or arrayed on the table, things that far surpass all the visions of their imagination, things which they dare not touch and which at last, once they have received them, they carry about in their little arms all evening, and take to bed with them. When now and then they hear in their dreams the chimes of midnight calling the grown-ups to Mass, it may seem to them that the angels are flying through the sky, or that the Holy Child is going home, having visited all the children and brought each a splendid present.

When the next day comes, Christmas Day, it seems so festive to them when they stand in the warm parlor attired in their finest clothes, when their father and mother dress up to go to church, when there's a festive midday meal, better than on any other day of the year, and when friends and acquaintances come that afternoon or toward evening, sitting about on the chairs and benches, chatting and gazing cozily out the windows into the winter landscape, where slow snow-flakes are falling, or fog veils the mountains, or the cold blood-red sun is sinking. Scattered throughout the parlor, on a little chair or on the bench or on the windowsill, lie the presents of the evening before, magical but already more familiar.

After that the long winter passes, the spring comes and the never-ending summer—and when the mother tells of the Holy Child once again, that his festival will soon come, and he will descend this time too, the children feel that since his last appearance an eternity has passed, and that the joy they felt then lies far away in a fog-gray region.

Because this festival has such a long echo, because the reflection of its splendor reaches so far into old age, we dearly love to watch as children celebrate and rejoice in it. ——

In the high mountains of our fatherland there is a village with a small but sharply pointed church steeple that stands out from the green of all the fruit trees with the red paint of its shingles, visible from afar in the mountains' dusky blue haze. The village lies right in the middle of quite a wide valley shaped almost like an elongated circle. Apart from the church it has a school, a town hall, and several imposing houses that form a square where four lindens stand with a stone cross in the middle. These houses are not just farmhouses, they harbor the trades that are essential to humanity and provide all the handicrafts the mountain dwellers require. In the valley and up in the surrounding mountains there are a great many more scattered cottages, as is so often the case in mountainous regions, whose inhabitants all attend the church and the school, and support the abovementioned trades by purchasing their products. In fact, still more cottages belong to the village that cannot even be seen from the valley, that lie still deeper in the mountains, whose inhabitants rarely come out to see their fellow villagers, whose dead must often be kept over the winter and brought to burial after the snow has melted. The greatest man the villagers see in the course of the year is the pastor. They revere him, and usually these pastors, after staying a while in the village, become accustomed to solitude, and do not mind staying, and simply go on living there. At least within living memory the village pastor has never been a man who hankered for the outside world or was unworthy of his position.

No roads pass through the valley, they have their two-track paths to bring the harvest home in little one-horse wagons, and thus few people come into the valley, among them the occasional solitary wayfarer, a nature lover who stays a while in the innkeeper's prettily painted upstairs room, contemplating the mountains, or even a painter who draws the little pointed steeple and the splendid crests of the crags in his sketchbook. And so the inhabitants make a world of their own, they know everyone by name and by their stories, going back to their grandfathers and great-grandfathers, they all mourn when someone dies, when someone is born they know his name, they have a language unlike that of the lowlands outside, they have their disputes, which they arbitrate, they stand by each other, and come together when anything extraordinary happens.

They are very steady-going, and the old ways persist. If a stone falls out of a wall, the same stone is put back in, the new houses are built like the old ones, and if a house has brindle cows, it always raises brindle calves, and the color stays with the house.

The village looks out to the south upon a snowy mountain whose gleaming horns seem to loom just above the roofs, though in fact it is not so close at all. All year long, summer and winter, it stares down into the valley with its projecting crags and its white expanses. As the most striking thing in their vicinity, the mountain is the object of the inhabitants' study, and has become the centerpiece of many stories. There is not a man in the village, young or old, who doesn't have something to tell about the mountain's peaks and jagged ridges, its caves and ice crevasses, its waters and rockslides, something he has experienced himself or heard others relate. And this mountain is the pride of the village, as though they had made it themselves, and it is not entirely certain—however highly one must rate the valley dwellers' upright, truthful character—that they don't tell the occasional lie for the mountain's honor and glory. Aside from being their landmark, the mountain is a real boon for the inhabitants, for when a group of mountaineers comes to climb it from the valley, the villagers serve as guides, and to have been a guide, to have experienced this and that, to know this and that spot, is a distinction all are eager to claim. They often speak of it when they sit together in the inn, telling of their adventures and their marvelous experiences, and never neglecting to relate the words of this traveler or that, and what he gave them in reward for their efforts. And then, too, the mountain sends down from its snowfields the waters that feed a lake in its high-up forests and create the brook that flows merrily down the valley, driving the sawmill the gristmill and other contraptions, cleansing the village and watering the livestock. The mountain forests provide wood, and they hold back the avalanches. Hidden passages and fissures up in the heights filter the water that flows in veins down the valley, emerging in wells and springs from which the people drink and offer their superb, oft-praised water to strangers. But they enjoy this last benefit unthinkingly, believing that it has always been so.

Regarding the mountain's yearly chronicle, in the winter the two prongs of its summit, which they call horns, are snow-white, and when visible on bright clear days loom blindingly in the air's dark blue; then all the alpine fields surrounding the summit are white; all the slopes are white; even the perpendicular cliffs which the locals call walls are covered with white wind-blown hoarfrost, and with delicate ice, like a varnish, so that the whole great mass rises like a magic palace from the rimy gray of the forest freight spread heavily about its foot. In the summer, when sun and warm wind clear the snow from their steep sides, the horns rear up black—so the locals say—in the sky, only with exquisite white veins and speckles on their ridges; in fact, though, they are a tender distant blue, and what they call veins and speckles are not white, but the lovely milky blue of distant snow against the rock's darker blue. Even when it is hot, the uppermost parts of the alpine fields around the horns never lose their firn, the solid snow of years past that gleams down then all the whiter against the green of the trees in the valley, but the winter's snow, a mere down, vanishes from their lower reaches, and the indistinct shimmer of blue and green grows visible, the shifting ice that then lies bare, and greets the valley dwellers from above. At the edge of this shimmer, what looks from afar like a fringe of splintered gems is, seen close-up, a jumble of gigantic rugged blocks, slabs and rubble, jostling and interlocked in chaos. When a long, hot summer comes, the ice fields are exposed far up into the heights, and a much greater expanse of green and blue looks down into the valley, crests and cavities are denuded that otherwise were seen only in white, the dirty hem of the ice grows visible, pushing along rocks, dirt, and mud, and the waters flow more profusely to the valley. This continues until little by little autumn returns, the water abates, and one day a steady gray rain covers the entire floor of the valley, after which, once the mists have dissolved from the heights, the mountain is clad in its soft cloak again, and all the cliffs cones and crags stand clothed in white. So it unfolds, year after year, with small variations, and will continue to unfold so long as nature remains as it is, and snow is on the mountains and people in the valleys. The valley dwellers call the small changes great, note them well, and use them to reckon the progress of the year. In the exposed rock they note the heat and the anomalies of the summer.

As to climbing the mountain, the approach is from the valley. You head eastward along a fine track that leads over a saddle into another valley. "Saddle" is what they call a moderately high mountain ridge that joins two taller, more eminent peaks, over which you can cross between the peaks from one valley to another. This saddle, which joins the snowy mountain to a tall mountain ridge across from it, is covered with fir woods. At about its highest point, where the path gradually begins to descend to the valley on the other side, there stands what is known as a "misfortune column." Once a baker, carrying bread in the basket that hung from his neck, was found dead in that spot. A sign was painted showing the dead baker with his basket and with the circle of fir trees around him, and underneath an explanation and an entreaty for a prayer; the sign was put on a red-painted wooden column, and the column was erected at the site of the misfortune. At this column you turn off from the path and walk along the length of the saddle rather than crossing its breadth into the valley beyond. Here the firs form a passage, as though a road ran between them. Sometimes, too, a path leads in this direction, used for bringing wood from the higher slopes down to the misfortune column, but then grass covers it over again. When you continue along this path, which gradually leads uphill, you end up at last in a place free of trees. It is barren heath, without even a shrub, covered with straggling heather, dry mosses, and plants that take to barren soil. The ground grows steeper and steeper, and for a long stretch you walk uphill, but always in a gully that resembles a rounded trench, with the advantage that it keeps you from losing your way in the vast treeless ever-same expanse. After a while outcroppings appear, rising straight from the grassy ground like churches, between whose walls you can walk uphill a long while. Then bald ridges nearly bare of vegetation appear once more, now looming into the air of the higher regions and leading straight to the ice. Steep rock faces drop off on both sides of the path, and this causeway joins the snowy mountain to the saddle. To surmount the ice, you walk for some time along its edge, where the outcroppings hem it, to reach the older firn that has built up over the glacial crevasses and at most times of the year will bear the wanderer's weight. At the firn's highest point the two horns loom up from the snow, the tallest of which is the mountain's summit. These peaks are very hard to climb; as they are surrounded by a trench of snow—the Firn Fissure—now broader, now narrower, which you must leap over, and as their perpendicular walls offer only tiny ledges to lodge the foot, most mountain climbers content themselves with reaching the Firn Fissure and enjoying the panorama, so far as the horn does not obscure it. Those who wish to climb to the summit must use crampons, ropes, and iron rungs.

There are other mountains on the southern side of the valley, but none so high, though they, too, are covered with snow in early fall, and keep it until late in spring. But the summer always takes the snow away, and the cliffs have a friendly sheen in the sunshine, and the gentle green of the woods lower down is cleaved by broad blue shadows so lovely that if you looked all your life, you could never look your fill.

On the other sides of the valley, from north and east and west, the mountains stretch out, longer and lower, with some fields and meadows reaching quite high up their slopes, above which you see clearings alpine huts and the like, until they stretch along the sky edged by fine-toothed forest, serrations that show their low elevation, while the southern mountains, though harboring forests still more magnificent, sweep a perfectly smooth edge across the brilliant sky.

When you stand in the middle of the valley, you have the sensation that no path leads into this basin and no path leads forth from it; indeed, those who are often in the mountains know this illusion well. In fact, not only do various paths lead out to the northern plains, some on almost level ground and following the mountain rifts; toward the south, where the valley seems almost utterly closed off by perpendicular walls, a path even crosses the saddle mentioned above.

The village is called Gschaid, and the snowy mountain that gazes down upon its houses is called Gars.

Beyond the saddle lies a much lovelier and lusher valley than that of Gschaid, and a beaten path leads down from the misfortune column. At the entrance to the valley is the imposing market town of Millsdorf, very large, with various workshops, and several buildings housing urban trades and professions. The inhabitants are far more prosperous than those of Gschaid, and though the valleys lie just a three hours' walk apart, an insignificant trifle for mountain dwellers accustomed to great distances and fond of travail, the customs and habits of the two valleys are as different, even their external appearance is as dissimilar, as though many miles lay between them. This is often the case in the mountains, due not only to the valleys' differing exposure to the sun, which favors them to a greater or lesser degree, but also to the character of the inhabitants, whose occupations pull them in one direction or another. But all concur in embracing tradition and the ways of their fathers, in having little use for great comings and goings, and in their extraordinary love of their native valley, without which they can barely live.

Months may pass a year may pass before an inhabitant of Gschaid crosses over to the valley on the other side and visits the big market town of Millsdorf. It is just the same with the Millsdorfers, though for their part they do have dealings with the outside world, and thus are not as isolated as the Gschaiders. There is even a track that one might call a road running down their valley, and many a traveler and many a wanderer passes through without the slightest suspicion that north of his path, beyond the snowy mountain gazing down from on high, there is another valley with many houses scattered throughout it, where the village with the pointed steeple stands.

The village tradesmen who satisfy the valley's needs include a shoemaker, that trade being indispensable wherever people have risen above their primitive state. The Gschaiders are so far above that state that they require fine, sound mountain footgear. But for one minor exception, their shoemaker is the only one in the valley. His house stands on the square in Gschaid where all the better houses stand, its gray walls, white sills, and green shutters looking out upon the four linden trees. On the ground floor is the workshop the journeymen's room a large and a small sitting room a little shop as well as a kitchen a pantry and all the adjoining closets; on the upper floor, or strictly speaking under the gable, is the attic room, the best room in the house. In it stand two canopy beds and fine polished wardrobes, as well as a cupboard with dishes a table with inlays upholstered armchairs a wall-mounted safe-box with the family savings, on the walls hang pictures of the saints two fine pocket watches prizes from shooting competitions, and finally target and shooting rifles and their paraphernalia are mounted in a special cabinet with glass panels. Adjoining the shoemaker's house is a smaller cottage separated from it only by the arched gateway, built in the same manner, and belonging to the shoemaker's house like a part to the whole. It has just one room with all the amenities. It is meant to serve the owner of the house, once he has handed over the property to his son or heir, to dwell with his wife until both have died and the cottage, vacant once more, awaits a new occupant. In the back the shoemaker's house has a stable and a barn, for all the valley dwellers, even if they pursue a trade, are farmers as well, deriving good and lasting sustenance thereby. Behind these buildings, finally, is the garden lacked by few of Gschaid's better homes, yielding vegetables, fruit, and flowers for festive occasions. In Gschaid, typically of mountain villages, bees are often kept in these gardens.

The minor exception mentioned above, the rival to the shoemaker's hegemony, is old Tobias the cobbler, though really he is no rival at all because he merely mends shoes, has his hands full with that, and has not the remotest notion of competing with the town's distinguished shoemaker on the square, especially as the town shoemaker often provides him with leather scraps soles and other such things free of charge. In the summer old Tobias sits under elder bushes at the end of the village to do his work. He is surrounded by shoes and low laced boots, all of them old gray muddy and torn. There are no boots with long shafts, for those are not worn in the village and the surrounding area; only two people own them, the pastor and the schoolteacher, but they have their mending and their new boots done by the town shoemaker. In the winter old Tobias sits in his little room behind the elder bushes, which he keeps toasty warm, for wood comes cheap in Gschaid.

Before inheriting the house, the town shoemaker poached chamois, and in general, as the Gschaiders say, was up to no good in his youth. Always one of the school's best pupils, he learned cobbling from his father, then went on the road as a journeyman, and returned at long last. Rather than do the proper thing for a tradesman and wear a black hat as his father had done all his life, he donned a green one, stuck it with all the kinds of feathers there were, and strutted around wearing it with the shortest loden coat to be found in the valley, whereas his father had always worn a dark coat, black if possible, which, as befitting a tradesman, had to be cut very long. The young shoemaker was seen wherever there was dancing or ninepins. If ever someone gave him advice, he would whistle a little tune. He took his target rifle to all the shooting contests nearby, and sometimes brought home a prize, which he took for a great triumph. The prizes generally consisted of artfully mounted coins, to win which the shoemaker, spendthrift that he was, had to spend more of those coins than made up the prize. He went on all the hunts that were held in the region, and gained the reputation of a fine marksman. But sometimes he went off alone with his double rifle and with crampons, and once was said to have suffered a serious head wound.

In Millsdorf lived a dyer whose dyeworks were at the very start of town when you came down the path from Gschaid, quite sizable, employing many workers and even—an unheard-of thing in the valley—machines. He also owned a large swath of farmland. The shoemaker went over the mountains to win this dyer's daughter. She was known far and wide for her beauty, but also for her reclusion modesty and domestic virtue. Yet still, or so they said, the shoemaker had caught her eye. The dyer would not let him into the house; and the lovely daughter, who even before had never visited public places or festivities, and had rarely been seen outside her parents' house, now went nowhere at all but to church, or walked in their garden or through the rooms of their house.

Some time after the death of his parents, when their house had fallen to him and he lived there all alone, the shoemaker changed completely. Whereas earlier he had reveled, now he sat in his workshop and hammered away at his soles night and day. Boastfully he offered a prize for anyone who could make better shoes and footgear. He took on none but the very best workers, and hectored them thoroughly as they worked in his workshop, so that they would follow him and do everything as he ordered. Indeed he succeeded so well that his services were employed not only by all of Gschaid—which had been buying most of its footgear from neighboring valleys—but by the entire valley, and at last there were even people from Millsdorf and other valleys who came to have their footgear made by the shoemaker in Gschaid. His fame spread even to the lowlands, so that people planning to travel in the mountains would have him make the boots for their journey.

He furnished his house beautifully, and in the shop the shoes, low laced boots, and tall boots gleamed on the shelves; and on Sundays, when all the valley dwellers came to town and gathered by the four lindens on the square, they would go to the shoemaker's house and look through the windows into the shop where customers were making purchases and placing orders.

With his love of the mountains, what he still made best was the low laced mountain boots. At the inn he liked to say that no one could show him another man's mountain boot that compared with one of his. "They don't know," he'd continue, "they've never learned in their lives how a boot like that must be, that the starry sky of the hobnails must sit properly on the sole, with all the iron reinforcement required, that the boot must be hard on the outside, so that not a single rock, however jagged, may be felt, yet enfold the foot as softly and gently as a glove."

The shoemaker had a great big book made in which he entered all the articles he manufactured, along with the names of those who had supplied the material and those who purchased the articles, and a brief note on the quality of the product. Footgear of the same kind was given consecutive numbers; and the book was kept in the big chest in his shop.

Though the beautiful dyer's daughter of Millsdorf never left her parents' house, though she visited neither friends nor relations, the shoemaker of Gschaid contrived that she should see him from afar when going to church, when in her garden, and when looking out her window at the mountain meadows. What with all that seeing, the dyer's wife made long ardent tireless appeals for her daughter until the stiff-necked dyer relented, and the shoemaker, having after all changed his ways for the better, took the rich beautiful Millsdorfer back to Gschaid as his wedded wife. But the dyer, all the same, was a man with a mind of his own. An upstanding person, he said, must pursue his trade so that it flourishes and grows, he must feed his wife his children himself and his servants, keep his house and his farm in splendid state, and set plenty of money aside, for only those savings could ensure his honor and reputation in the world; and so the dyer's daughter would receive only a fine trousseau, the rest being a matter for her husband to provide and establish for all the future. The dyeworks in Millsdorf and the farm belonging to his house, said the dyer, were a sizable and respectable business that must be maintained for the sake of his honor, and all that was there must serve as its foundation stone, for which reason he would give away nothing. When he and his wife were dead, the dyeworks and the farm in Millsdorf would belong to their only daughter, the shoemaker's wife in Gschaid, and the shoemaker and his wife could then do with them as they pleased: but all that would happen only if the heirs were worthy of the inheritance; if they were not, it would pass to their children, and if there were no children, it would pass on to other relatives, excepting the statutory share alone. And the shoemaker demanded not a thing, proudly showing that he had been thinking only of the beautiful dyer's daughter of Millsdorf herself, and that he could feed and keep her as she had been fed and kept at home. Not only did he clothe his wife more beautifully than all the women in Gschaid and all the valley, he gave her clothes more beautiful than she had ever worn at home, and her food, drink, and other amenities had to be better and show more thought than the same things she had enjoyed under her father's roof. And to spite his father-in-law, he used his savings to buy more and more property, until he had amassed considerable holdings.

Since the inhabitants of Gschaid so rarely leave their village, seldom even crossing over to Millsdorf, from which customs and mountain ridges sunder them, and furthermore since none of their men has ever been known to leave his valley to move to the next valley (moves to distant places are more common), and finally since no woman or girl likes to migrate from one valley to another, except in the rather rare event that she follows her heart and goes to another valley as a wife to her husband—so it came that the beautiful dyer's daughter of Millsdorf, having become the shoemaker's wife in Gschaid, was still seen as a stranger by the other Gschaiders, and though no one behaved badly toward her, though indeed they loved her for her beauty and her propriety, there was always the appearance of reserve, or, if you will, of deference, preventing the sort of intimacy and camaraderie that Gschaid women felt toward Gschaid women and Gschaid men toward Gschaid men. So it was, it could not be remedied, and was only exacerbated by the better clothing and domestic conveniences that the shoemaker's wife enjoyed.

After the first year she had borne her husband a son, and several years later a daughter. But she thought he did not love the children as she imagined he should and as she was conscious of loving them; most of the time he was grave faced, preoccupied with his work. He rarely dandled or played with the children, and always spoke calmly to them, just as adults are spoken to. As far as food and clothing and other outward things went, he treated the children irreproachably.

In the early days of their marriage the dyer's wife often came to Gschaid, and the young couple visited Millsdorf for parish fairs or other festive occasions. But once the children were born, this changed.

While mothers love their children and yearn for them, the same is often truer still of grandmothers: at times they pine for their grandchildren with a longing that is veritably morbid. The dyer's wife came to Gschaid often to see the children, to bring them presents and stay for a while, departing with well-meant exhortations. But when the age and health of the dyer's wife no longer allowed her to travel as often, and the dyer raised objections, a different solution was thought up; things were turned around, and now the children went to their grandmother. Their mother often brought them herself in a wagon, but more often, while still of a tender age, they were bundled up and sent off with a maidservant who took them over the saddle in a cart. When they were bigger, they went to Millsdorf on foot, either with their mother or with a maid; in fact, when the boy had grown able strong and clever, they let him cross the saddle by himself on the familiar path, and when he asked, and the weather was very fine, his little sister was allowed to accompany him. This is a common thing among the Gschaiders, for they are used to making strenuous journeys on foot, and all the parents especially men such as the shoemaker are pleased to see their children learn to fend for themselves.

So it came that the two children took the path over the saddle more often than all the other villagers together, and as even their mother had always been treated as a kind of stranger in Gschaid, this circumstance made the children strange too, they were hardly Gschaiders at all, and half belonged over in Millsdorf.

The boy Konrad already had his father's earnest character, and the girl, named Susanna after her mother, or Sanna for short, believed greatly in his skills his wisdom and his power, and submitted absolutely to his guidance, just as her mother submitted absolutely to the guidance of their father, whom she credited with all kinds of wisdom and skill.

On fine days you could see the children walk across the valley toward the south, cross the meadow, and reach the place where the forest of the saddle looms over it. They would approach the forest, then take the forest path to climb gradually over the ridge, and before noon they would descend toward Millsdorf through the open pastures of the other side. Konrad showed Sanna the pastures that belonged to their grandfather, and then they walked through his fields, where Konrad explained the different kinds of grain, then they saw the long lengths of cloth that hung from poles under the eaves, twisting in the wind or making droll faces, then they heard his fulling mill and his tanbark mill, which he had built on his brook for the cloth-makers and tanners, then they rounded another corner of the fields and soon passed through the back gate into the garden of the dyeworks, where their grandmother received them. She always sensed when they were coming, looked out of the windows and saw them from afar when Sanna's red shawl shone out in the sun.

Then she took the children through the washing and pressing rooms into the parlor, had them sit down, made them keep on their neckerchiefs and jackets, so as not to catch cold, and had them stay there for lunch. After lunch they could take off their jackets, play, roam the rooms of their grandfather's house, or do whatever else they wanted, so long as it was not unseemly or forbidden. The dyer, who always joined them at lunch, quizzed them about their school subjects, and hammered into their heads the things they had to learn. In the afternoon, long before it was time, their grandmother would start urging them to leave, lest heaven forbid they should be late. Though the dyer had provided no dowry, and had sworn to give away none of his fortune before he died, his wife did not feel so strictly obligated, and not only did she give the children all sorts of things on their visits, often including coins, sometimes worth quite a bit, she always put together two little bundles of things that she thought would be needed, or would give the children pleasure. And even if the shoe-maker's house in Gschaid often boasted the same things, as fine as could be, in the joy of giving the grandmother gave them all the same, and the children carried them home as though they were something special. So it would happen that on Christmas Eve the children would unwittingly carry home, well packed and sealed in boxes, the presents to be bestowed on them that night.

Because the grandmother always urged the children to set out before it was time, so that they would not be late coming home, the result was that the children dawdled on their way, sometimes in one place, sometimes in another. They liked to sit by the hazel grove on the saddle and crack nuts with stones, or, if there were no nuts, play with leaves or sticks or with the soft brown catkins that drop from the branches of the conifers early in the spring. Sometimes Konrad told his little sister stories, or when they came to the red misfortune column he would take her a ways down the side path to the left, toward the heights, and tell her it was the path up the snowy mountain, where the cliffs and rocks are, where chamois leap about and great birds soar. He often led her up past the forest, where they gazed at the barren turf and the little heather shrubs; but then he would take her back, and bring her home before darkness fell, for which he was always praised.

One Christmas Eve, when dawn's first glow had turned to brightness in the valley of Gschaid, the whole sky was covered by a thin dry veil, so that the sun, low and remote in the southeast, was visible only as an indistinct red spot, and that day mild almost balmy air hung motionless throughout the valley and even in the sky, as shown by the clouds' serene and unchanging forms. At that the shoemaker's wife said to her children: "It's such a pleasant day, it hasn't rained for such a long time, and the paths are dry and firm; and your father gave permission yesterday on the condition that today should be a good day; so you may go to Millsdorf to see your grandmother, but you must ask your father first."

The children, still in their nightgowns, went into the next room where their father was speaking with a customer, and asked him to repeat yesterday's permission, this being such a fine day. Permission was given, and they went back to their mother.

Now the shoemaker's wife dressed her children with foresighted care; or rather, put the girl in protective weathertight things; for the boy had begun to dress by himself, and was ready long before his mother had put the girl in order. Having finished, she said, "Konrad, take heed: I'm letting the girl go with you, so you must leave with time to spare, you must not stop anywhere, and as soon as you've had lunch with Grandmother, you must start back, and head home, for the days are short now, and the sun sets very early."

"I know that, Mother," said Konrad.

"And take good care of Sanna, so that she doesn't fall, or get too hot."

"Yes Mother."

"So, God bless you, and now go to your father and tell him that you're leaving."

The boy slung around his shoulders a satchel which his father had skillfully sewn from calfskin, and the children went into the next room to bid their father farewell. They soon emerged and hopped cheerfully out onto the road, blessed by their mother with the sign of the cross.

They walked quickly down the village square, and then along the house-lined lane and finally between the orchards' board fences and out into the open. The sun now hung over the eastward slopes where the forest was woven with milky strands of cloud, and through the crab apple's bare branches its dull reddish image strode onward with the children.

There was no snow in all the valley; in the taller mountains it had gleamed down for many weeks already, and they were now covered with it, while the lower mountains stood snowless and serene in the cloak of their fir woods and the wan red of their bared branches. The ground had not yet frozen, and what with the long rainless spell it would have been completely dry had not the season covered it with a delicate film of moisture, which did not make it slippery but rather firm and resilient, so that they walked along easily and swiftly. What little grass was still seen in the pastures, chiefly along the ditches, was autumnal in appearance. There was no frost and, looking more closely, not even dew, which for country folk would have meant imminent rain.

Near the bounds of the pastures was a mountain stream crossed by a high bridge. The children climbed onto the bridge and looked down. The stream had hardly any water, a fine trickle very blue in color flowed through the dry pebbles, which the lack of rain had turned utterly white, and the small amount and the color of the water showed that in the higher reaches cold must have set in, sealing the ground so that the soil did not cloud the water, and hardening the ice so that it could release only a few clear drops from within.

From the bridge the children passed through the dales and drew closer and closer to the woods.

At last they reached the edge of the forest, and through it they walked onward.

Once they had reached the higher woods on the saddle, the long ruts in the track were no longer soft, as they were down in the valley, but firm, and this was not because they were dry, but rather, as the children soon ascertained, because they were frozen. In some places they were so frozen through that they carried the weight of the children's bodies. As children will, they now spurned the smooth path next to the wagon track and walked along in the ruts instead, trying to see if this or that ridge of mud would carry their weight yet. An hour later, when they had reached the top of the saddle, the ground was so hard that it rang underfoot, and the clods were like stones.

At the place with the baker's red misfortune column, Sanna was first to notice that today it was not there. They went over to the spot and saw the round red-painted pole that held the picture lying in the dry grass, which stood there like thin straw and hid the fallen column from sight. Though they could not tell why the column was lying there, whether it had been pushed over or fallen on its own, they saw that at the place where it lodged in the ground it was rotten, and could have fallen over quite easily; at any rate, now that it had fallen, they were delighted to see the picture and the writing so close, as they never had before. Once they had looked at everything—the basket with the rolls, the baker's pale hands, his closed eyes, his gray coat and the firs all around—once they had read the writing and recited it aloud, they went on their way again.

After yet another hour the dark woods receded on both sides, scattered trees some solitary oaks some birches and clumps of bushes met them and accompanied them on their way, and soon they were walking down the pastures and into the valley of Millsdorf.

Though that valley lies much lower than Gschaid's, and was so much warmer that the harvest always came two weeks earlier, the ground was frozen here as well, and when the children reached their grandfather's tanbark and fulling mills, the path, often spattered with drops from the mill wheels, had pretty little panels of ice, a thing that children delight in.

Their grandmother had seen them coming and went out to meet them, she took Sanna by her frozen little hands and led her into the parlor.

She took off their warmer clothes, put more fuel in the stove, and asked how they had fared on their way over.

Having heard their reply, she said, "That's fine, that's good, I'm very glad you've come again; but today you must leave quite soon, the day is short, and it's growing colder, even just this morning the ground in Millsdorf wasn't yet frozen."

"It was the same in Gschaid," said the boy.

"You see, that's why you'll have to hurry, so you won't be cold come evening," their grandmother replied.

Then she asked what their mother was doing, what their father was doing, and whether anything of interest had happened in Gschaid.

After these questions she concerned herself with lunch, took care that it would be ready earlier than usual, and prepared little treats for the children herself, things she knew would please them. Then the dyer was called, the children had places set for them at the table like grown-up people, eating with Grandfather and Grandmother now, and she served them especially choice bits. After lunch she stroked Sanna's cheeks, which had meanwhile turned quite red.

Then she bustled back and forth, filling the boy's calfskin satchel and putting things in his pockets. She also put all sorts of things in Sanna's little bag. She gave each a piece of bread to eat along the way, and in the satchel, she said, were two loaves of white bread in case they got hungrier.

"I've packed some good roasted coffee for your mother," she said, "and in the flask, which is plugged and well sealed, there's brewed coffee, better than your mother usually makes, she ought to taste what it's like, a real elixir, so strong that just a sip warms the stomach and won't let the body freeze even on the coldest winter days. But take home the other things in the satchel, in the box, and in the paper wrappings, without opening them."

After talking with the children a while longer, she said that they should go.

"Take care, Sanna," she said, "that you don't get a chill, don't overheat yourself; and don't walk up the pastures and under the trees. If the wind rises toward evening, you'll have to walk more slowly. Greet your father and your mother, and wish them the happiest of holidays."

The grandmother kissed both children on the cheeks and thrust them out the door. But then she followed, accompanied them through the garden, let them out the back gate, locked it again, and went back into the house.

The children walked past the panels of ice by their grandfather's mills, they walked through Millsdorf's fields, and turned toward the pastures.

As they climbed the slopes, where, as we said, scattered trees and clumps of bushes stood, single snowflakes began to fall very slowly.

"You see, Sanna," said the boy, "right away I thought we'd have snow; you know, when we left the house we could still see the sun, blood-red as a lamp by the Holy Sepulcher, and now it can't be seen at all, there's nothing but the gray fog up above the treetops. That always means snow."

The children walked on with greater cheer, and Sanna rejoiced when she managed to catch one of the falling flakes on the dark sleeve of her jacket and it stayed a long time without melting. Once they had finally reached the upper edge of the heights over Millsdorf, where the path approaches the dark firs of the saddle, the solid forest wall was daintily dappled by the flakes that were floating down more and more abundantly. Now they entered the dense woods where the greater part of their journey would lie.

From the edge of the forest the path climbs still farther, until you reach the red misfortune column, where, as noted above, the path descends into the valley of Gschaid. In fact, the woods on the Millsdorf side slope so steeply that the path does not climb in a straight line, but rather in very long twists from west to east and east to west. Along the whole length of the path up to the column and down to the meadows of Gschaid stand tall dense uncleared woods, which do not start to thin out until you reach the plain and emerge onto the meadows of the valley of Gschaid. Though a mere small bridge between two great summits, the saddle itself is so high that if placed on the plain it would stand as an eminent mountain ridge.

The first thing the children saw on entering the woods was that the frozen ground looked gray, as though dusted with flour, that the thin stalks of dry grass that stood between the trees and by the path trailed their tassels, weighed down with snowflakes, and the green boughs of the firs and spruces, opening like hands, were covered with white down.

"Is it snowing at home too, where Father is?" asked Sanna.

"Certainly," said the boy, "it's also growing colder, and you'll see, tomorrow the whole pond will be frozen over."

"Yes, Konrad," said the girl.

She nearly doubled the pace of her little steps to keep up with the boy as he strode onward.

They marched stoutly on up the twists of the path, now from west to east, now from east to west. The wind their grandmother had predicted did not come; on the contrary, it was so still that not a branch or a twig stirred; indeed, it even seemed warmer inside the forest, as loose masses, which forests are, tend to be warmer in winter, and the snowflakes kept falling still more abundantly, so that all the ground was already white, the woods were turning gray with the dusting, and snow settled on the hats and clothes of the boy and the girl.

The children's delight was great. They trod on the soft down, their feet sought the places where it seemed to lie more thickly, to step there and pretend they were already wading. They did not shake the snow from their clothing.

A vast hush had descended. Even in the winter woods the birds flit to and fro at times, and on their outward journey the children had even heard a few birds twittering, but they heard them no longer, nor did they see any perched on twigs, or flying; all life in the woods seemed extinct.

Nothing was behind the children but their footprints, and in front of them the snow was clean and unbroken, so it was clear that they were the only ones crossing the saddle today.

They continued in the same direction, sometimes approaching the trees, sometimes drawing farther away, and wherever there was dense underbrush, they could see the snow on the branches.

Still their delight kept growing, for the snowflakes fell more and more thickly, and soon they no longer had to look for snow to wade in; now it lay so thick that they felt it everywhere soft beneath their soles, and felt it already begin to close in on their boots, and now that all was so quiet and secretive, they seemed to hear the snow rustle as it sifted through the needles.

"Will we see the misfortune column today?" the girl asked. "It's toppled over, and the snow will fall on it, and then the red will be white."

"That's why we'll still see it," the boy replied, "even if the snow falls on it, and even if it's white, we'll have to see it lying there, because it's a thick column, and because it has the black iron cross at the top that will always be sticking out."

"Yes Konrad."

Meanwhile, as they walked onward, the snowfall had grown so dense that all they could see was the very closest trees.

The hardness of the path was no longer to be felt, nor even its ridges, the snow made the path evenly soft all over, and it could be made out only as a uniform white band running onward through the forest. A lovely white coat already covered all the branches.

The children walked in the middle of the path now, their little feet furrowing the snow, and they went more slowly as walking grew more difficult. The boy pulled up his jacket at the neck to keep the snow from falling in, and he pulled down his hat to be better protected. And he tightened the shawl that his mother had placed around his sister's shoulders, and pulled it forward to make a roof over her forehead.

The wind their grandmother had predicted still failed to come; instead, bit by bit, the snow fell so thickly that not even the closest trees could be made out, looming in the air like sacks made of fog.

The children kept walking. They ducked their heads more snugly down into their clothes and kept walking.

Sanna put her hand out to the strap of the calfskin satchel slung over Konrad's shoulders, held it tightly, and so they went their way.

Still they had not reached the misfortune column. The boy could not tell the time, because no sun was in the sky, and because it was always uniformly gray.

"Will we come to the misfortune column soon?" asked Sanna.

"I don't know," the boy replied, "I can't see the trees today, and I can't make out the path, because it's so white. It looks as if we won't see the misfortune column at all, because with so much snow lying it'll be covered and nothing will stick out, not a blade of grass or an arm of the black cross. But it doesn't matter. We'll keep walking up the path, the path goes on between the trees, and when it reaches the place where the misfortune column is, it'll go downhill, we'll keep walking along it, and when it comes out of the trees, we'll already be in the meadows of Gschaid, after that comes the bridge, and we won't be far from home then."

"Yes Konrad," said the girl.

They kept walking along their uphill path. The footprints behind them were not visible for long now; the falling snow's tremendous abundance soon covered them and made them vanish. Now the snow no longer rustled in the needles as it fell, it settled, swift and secretive, on the white blanket already lying there. The children drew their clothes still more tightly about them to ward off the perpetual omnipresent infiltration.

They walked very quickly, and the path kept leading uphill.

A long time passed, and still they had not reached the high point where the misfortune column had to be, and where the path had to turn downhill toward Gschaid.

At last the children reached a place where no trees stood.

"I don't see any trees anymore," said Sanna.

"Maybe it's just that the path is too wide and we can't see them in the snowstorm," the boy replied.

"Yes, Konrad," said the girl.

After a while the boy stopped and said, "I can't see any trees either, we must be out of the woods, and the path is still climbing. Let's stop for a while and look around, maybe we'll see something."

But they saw nothing at all. They gazed through a dim space into the sky. Just as, when it hails, dark frayed swaths jut down over the bloated white or greenish clouds, so it was here, and the mute deluge continued. On the ground they saw but a round spot of white and then nothing more.

"You know, Sanna," said the boy, "we're on the dry meadow where I've often taken you in the summer, where we sat and looked at the turf that slopes upward, where the pretty tufts of herbs grow. Soon we'll go downhill to the right!"

"Yes Konrad."

"The day is short, as Grandmother said, and you know it yourself, so we'll have to hurry."

"Yes Konrad," said the girl.

"Wait a moment, I'll fix you up better," the boy returned.

He took off his hat, put it on Sanna's head, and tied the strings under her chin. The shawl she wore gave her too little protection, whereas he had such a mass of thick curls on his head that snow could fall on it for a long time yet before the wet and the cold would seep through. Then he took off his fur jacket and pulled it over his sister's arms. Around his own shoulders and arms, now in shirtsleeves, he tied the smaller shawl Sanna had had over her chest, and the larger one she'd had over her shoulders. That would be enough for him, he thought, if only he walked stoutly, he wouldn't be cold.

He took the girl's hand, and thus they walked onward.

The girl gazed with willing eyes into the gray that reigned all around, and followed him gladly, only her hurrying little feet could not quite keep pace as he strove onward like someone trying to force a decision.

They were walking now with the doggedness and vigor that children and animals have, not knowing how much is granted them, nor when they have exhausted their store.

But as they walked, they could not tell whether they were coming down the mountain or not. They had immediately turned downhill to the right, but ended up back on a course that led uphill, downhill and up again. Often they came to steep places they had to skirt, and a trench they walked along led them around in a curve. They climbed slopes that proved steeper underfoot than expected, and what they thought was downhill was flat, or a hollow, or stretched on and on.

"Where are we, Konrad?" asked the girl.

"I don't know," he replied.

"If only I could see something with these eyes of mine," he went on, "so that I could get my bearings."

But there was nothing around them but blinding whiteness, everywhere that whiteness which itself merely drew a shrinking circle around them, then shifted to a light fog descending in swaths that consumed every other thing, and concealed it, and in the end was nothing other than the insatiably falling snow.

"Wait, Sanna," said the boy, "let's stay where we are for a moment and listen, and see if we can't hear some sign from the valley, perhaps a dog or a bell or the mill, or perhaps a cry will be heard, we must hear something, and then we'll know where we have to go."

Now they stayed where they were, but they heard nothing. They stayed a while longer, but no sign came, not a single sound not the faintest sound could be heard but their breath, indeed in the silence that reigned it was as though they should hear the falling of the snow on their lashes. Their grandmother's prediction remained unfulfilled, the wind had not come, indeed—a rare thing in those regions—not the faintest breath of air stirred throughout the entire sky.

After waiting a long while, they walked onward again.

"It doesn't matter," said the boy, "don't be discouraged, just follow me, I'll take you over the mountain yet. —If only the snow would stop!"

She was not discouraged, she picked up her little feet as best she could, and followed him. He led her onward in the light white restless opaque space.

After a time they saw crags. They loomed up dark and indistinct from the white and opaque light. As the children approached, they nearly ran into them. The crags rose like a wall, completely perpendicular, so that barely a snowflake could cling to their sides.

"Sanna, Sanna," he said, "there are the crags, let's keep walking, let's keep walking."

They kept walking, they had to go into the crags and continue among them. The crags left them no place to turn to the left or to the right, leading them along a narrow passage. After a time they lost the crags again and could see them no longer. Just as they had blundered unexpectedly into their midst, they unexpectedly left them behind. Again there was nothing but whiteness surrounding them, and all around no intervening darkness could be seen. There seemed to be a great wealth of light, yet it was impossible to see three steps ahead; everything was swathed, if this can be said, in one great white darkness, and as there were no shadows, there was no judging the size of things, and the children could not tell whether they were heading uphill or downhill until they were forced to go uphill by stumbling against a steep place.

"My eyes hurt," said Sanna.

"Don't look at the snow," the boy replied, "look at the clouds. Mine have been hurting for a long time; it doesn't matter, though, I have to look at the snow because I have to watch the path. Don't be afraid, I'll lead you down to Gschaid yet."

"Yes, Konrad."

They went on walking; but however they walked, however they turned, there was nowhere to begin descending. On both sides were steep upward slopes like roofs, and they walked on in the middle, but still always uphill. When they left the sloping roofs behind, and headed downhill, it was soon so steep that they had to turn back; often they stumbled upon bumps, or they had to skirt hillocks.

And they found that their feet, sinking deeper through the fresh snow, did not feel the ground beneath them, it was something else, like older frozen snow; but they walked on and on, walked with haste and endurance. When they stopped, all was still, immeasurably still; when they walked, they heard the swish of their feet, nothing else; for the shrouds of the sky fell without a sound, and so profusely that one could see the snow growing. They themselves were so snow-covered that they merged into the universal whiteness, and if a few steps had sundered them, they would have lost sight of each other.

It was a boon that the snow was as dry as sand, so that it easily slipped and sifted from their feet and boots and socks without leaving clumps or moisture.

At last they arrived among objects again.

There lay gigantic great pieces of debris tumbled in great confusion, covered with snow that sifted everywhere into the gaps, and once again the children had nearly stumbled on them before seeing them. They went up close to look at these things.

It was ice—sheer ice.

There lay great slabs, covered with snow, but with their walls showing smooth green-hued ice, hills lay there, like foam pushed together, but with a dull inward glimmer and gleam in their sides, like jumbled bars and rods of gemstones, and there lay rounded spheres too, completely cloaked in snow, there loomed slabs and other shapes aslant or straight like the steeple in Gschaid or like houses. Some were hollowed out by cavities that an arm could pass through, a head, a body, a whole great hay wain. All these fragments had been forced together or upward, and then frozen, often forming roofs or overhangs over whose edges the snow lay, and reached down like long white paws. There was even a great alarmingly black rock, like a house, amid the ice, lifted up to stand on its tip, so that no snow could cling to its sides. And it was not this rock alone—there were other, still larger ones embedded in the ice, which they noticed only later, rocks like a wall of rubble stretching along it.

"There's so much ice, there must have been lots of water once," said Sanna.

"No, that's not from water," her brother replied, "it's the ice of the mountain, that's up there always, because it has been made that way."

"Yes Konrad," said Sanna.

"We've come to the ice now," the boy said, "we're up on the mountain, Sanna, you know, the mountain that's so white in the sunshine when we look out from our garden. Mark my words well. Do you remember how we often sat in the garden in the afternoons, how beautiful it was, how the bees hummed around us, the lindens smelled so sweet, and the sun shone from the sky?"

"Yes, Konrad, I remember."

"We saw the mountain then too. We saw how blue it was, blue as the gentle firmament, we saw the snow that's there on high even when it's summer where we are, when there's great heat, and the grain is ripening."

"Yes, Konrad."

"And down where the snow ends you see all sorts of colors if you look close enough, green, blue, whitish—that's the ice, it only looks so small from below because we're so far away, father says it will never be gone until the end of the world. And I've often seen how the blue color continues downhill from the ice, those must be rocks, I thought, or solid ground and pastures, and then the woods begin, sloping downhill farther and farther, you see all sorts of crags in them, and then come the meadows, already green, and then the green leafy woods, then come our meadows and fields in the valley of Gschaid. Do you see, Sanna? Now we've reached the ice, so we'll go downhill across the blue color, then through the forests where the crags are, then across the meadows, and then through the green leafy woods, and then we'll be in the valley of Gschaid, and we'll easily find our way to the village."

"Yes Konrad," said the girl.

Now the children walked into the ice, wherever they could find a way in.

They were minuscule moving dots amid these monstrous fragments.

Peering in under the overhangs, as though following some instinct to seek shelter, they came into a trench, a broad deep-cut trench that emerged straight from the ice. It looked like the bed of a river, but dried up and filled in with fresh snow. Where it came forth from the ice, it emerged beneath an ice vault beautifully arched above it. The children walked on up the trench, and went into the vault, and went in deeper and deeper. It was quite dry, and beneath their feet the ice was smooth. But the entire cave was blue, as blue as nothing on earth, a blue much deeper and lovelier than the firmament, like sky-blue stained glass with radiance sinking through it. There were arches thick and thin, there were hanging spikes needles and tassels, the passage would have reached back still deeper, they knew not how deep, but they went no farther. The cave would have been a fine place, it was warm, no snow fell, but it was so alarmingly blue that the children were afraid, and went back out again. They walked on for a time along the trench, and then climbed out over its edge.

They walked along the edge of the ice, so far as they could find their way across the debris and between the slabs.

"We'll just cross over that way, and then walk downhill from the ice," said Konrad.

"Yes," said Sanna, and clung to him.

From the ice they struck out downhill through the snow in a way that should have led to the valley. But they did not get far. A new tide of ice, like a gigantic rampart, banked and bulging upward, lay athwart the soft snow, and reached around them like arms to the right and the left. Beneath the white blanket that cloaked it the sides glimmered from within, shades of green and blue and dark and black and even yellow and red. Now they could see broader swathes of it, for the vast tireless snowfall had subsided, falling merely as on any snowy day. With the fortitude of ignorance they clambered into the midst of the ice to cross the tide that thrust across their path, and continue downhill on the other side. They slipped into the gaps, they set their feet on those parts of these shapes that bore white caps of snow, whether rock or ice, they used their hands, crawled where they could not walk, and with their light shapes they worked their way up until they had surmounted the side of the rampart, and stood upon the top.

They meant to climb down the other side.

But there was no other side.

As far as the children could see there was sheer ice. Pinnacles and humps and floes rose up like sheer terrible snow-covered ice. It was not a ridge that one could climb over, that would give way to snow again, as they had thought below; from the bulging surface new walls of ice rose, blasted and clefted, filled with countless snaking blue lines, and behind them were more such walls, and behind those more again, until the falling snow covered the rest with grayness.

"Sanna, we can't walk there," said the boy.

"No," his sister answered.

"Then we'll turn around again, and try to come down somewhere else."

"Yes Konrad."

Now the children tried to come down from the icy rampart at the spot where they had climbed up, but they could find no way to come down. There was nothing but sheer ice, as though they had mistaken the direction they had come from. They turned this way and that, and yet they could not leave the ice, as though it had engulfed them. They climbed downhill, and came upon more ice. At last, as the boy kept going in the direction he thought they had come from, they reached debris that was more thinly scattered, but larger and more formidable than that at the edge of the ice, and the children crawled and clambered their way out of it. At the edge of the ice were enormous rocks, heaped in ways the children had never seen in their lives. Many were cloaked in white, many had sloping undersides that were polished smooth and sleek, as though they had been slid along, many leaned against each other like shanties and roofs, many lay atop each other like great hulking lumps. Not far from the children several rocks stood leaning their heads together, and broad blocks lay balanced upon them like a roof. They formed a little house, open in the front, but protected in the back and on the sides. Inside it was dry, for the snow fell straight down, and not a flake had strayed in. The children were glad indeed that they were in the ice no longer, and were standing on the ground of their earth.

But at the same time it had grown dark at last.

"Sanna," said the boy, "we can't go down now, because night has come, and we could fall, or even slip into a pit. We'll go in there under the rocks, where it's so dry and so warm, and there we'll wait. Soon the sun will rise again, and we'll go down. Don't cry, I beg you, don't cry, I'll give you all the things that Grandmother gave us to eat."

Nor did she cry; when they had gone in under the rocky roof, where they could sit comfortably, and even stand and walk around, she sat close by his side, and was quiet as a mouse.

"Mother won't be angry," said Konrad, "we'll tell her about all the snow that held us up, and she won't say a thing; neither will father. If we get cold, you know, you must slap your hands against your body, the way the woodcutters do, and you'll feel warmer."

"Yes Konrad," said the girl.

Sanna was not as disappointed as he might have thought to hear that they could not go down from the mountain today, and walk home; for the immeasurable exertion, greater than the children had realized, made it seem sweet unspeakably sweet to sit, and they surrendered to it.

But now hunger asserted itself. Almost simultaneously both took the pieces of bread from their bags, and ate them. And they ate the things—little bits of cake almonds nuts and other treats—that their grandmother had put in the satchel.

"But Sanna, now we must brush the snow from our clothes," the boy said, "otherwise we'll get wet."

"Yes, Konrad," Sanna replied.

The children went outside their little house, and first Konrad cleaned his little sister of snow. He took the tail ends of her clothes, shook them, removed the hat he had put on her head, emptied out the snow, and with a cloth he dusted off whatever remained. Then, as best he could, he cleaned off the snow that had settled on him.

By this time the snowfall had utterly ceased. The children felt not a single flake.

They went back into their stone hut and sat down. Standing up had shown them how tired they really were, and they were happy to be sitting. Konrad removed his calfskin satchel. He took out the cloth in which their grandmother had wrapped a box and several paper packages, and put it around his shoulders for greater warmth. He took the two white loaves from the satchel as well, and handed them both to Sanna; the child ate greedily. She ate one of the loaves and part of the second. But she handed the rest to Konrad when she saw that he was not eating. He took it, and ate it.

From then on the children sat and gazed out.

As far as they could see in the twilight, the glimmering snow stretched downward, its distinct tiny wafers beginning here and there to sparkle strangely in the dark, as though by day it had drunk up the light, and now was giving it off.

Night descended with the rapidity typical of high elevations. Soon it was dark all around, only the snow went on shining with its pallid illumination. Not only had the snow stopped falling, the mist that veiled the sky began to thin and part, for the children saw the twinkle of a star. With the snow truly seeming to give off light, and no mist now trailing from the clouds, from the cave the children could see the snowy hills, standing out in lines against the dark sky. Because it was much warmer in the cave than anywhere they had been all day, the children rested, sitting close together, and even forgot to be afraid of the dark. And soon the stars multiplied, appearing now here now there, until there seemed not a cloud left in the sky.

It was the time when the candles are lit in the valleys. First one is lit and set on the table to light the room, or a mere wooden splint burns, or a flame burns in a niche, and all the windows of lived-in rooms turn bright and shine out into the snowy night—but now, on Christmas Eve, still more were lit to light the gifts for the children, on the tables or hanging from the trees, countless candles were lit, for in nearly every house every hut every room there was a child or children whom the Holy Child had brought gifts, and candles had to be placed next to them. The boy had thought they could soon descend from the mountain, yet of all the lights that burned today in the valley, not a single one shone up to them; they saw nothing but the pale snow and the dark sky, all else had sunk away into the invisible distance. In all the valleys at this hour the children were receiving their gifts from the Holy Child; only these two sat up at the edge of the ice, and the exquisite gifts they were supposed to have received today lay sealed in packages in the calfskin bag in the back of the cave.

All around the snow clouds had sunk away behind the mountains, and an utterly dark-blue nearly black vault stretched about the children, filled with thickset blazing stars, and through the midst of these stars was woven a wide shimmering milky band that they had seen before from the valley but never with such clarity. The night drew on. The children did not know that the stars advance westward and move onward, or they could have told the hour of the night by their progress; new ones came and the old ones went, but they thought it was always the same stars. With the glow of the stars it grew brighter around the children; but they saw no valley no country, all around only white—sheer white. Only a dark horn a dark head a dark arm loomed, rising here and there from the shimmer. The moon was nowhere to be seen in the sky, perhaps it had set early with the sun, or it had not yet appeared.

When a long time had passed, the boy said, "Sanna, you mustn't sleep; for you know what Father said, if you sleep in the mountains you'll freeze to death, just as the old hunter, the Eschenjäger, fell asleep and sat dead on a stone for four months, and nobody knew where he was."

"No, I won't sleep," the girl said faintly.

Konrad had tugged at a tail end of her clothing to rouse her to say those words.

Now she was quiet again.

After a while the boy felt a gentle pressure on his arm, weighing heavier and heavier. Sanna had fallen asleep and was leaning against him.

"Sanna, don't sleep, I beg you, don't sleep," he said.

"No"—her speech slurred, sleep-drunk—"I won't sleep."

He moved farther away from her, to make her move, but she fell over, and would have gone on sleeping where she lay on the ground. He took her by the shoulder and shook her. Now that he was moving more vigorously himself, he realized that he was cold, and his arm had grown heavy. Alarmed, he leapt up. He seized his sister, shook her harder, and said, "Sanna, stand up for a bit, let's stand for a while until it gets better."

"I'm not cold, Konrad," she replied.

"Oh, yes, you're cold, Sanna, get up," he cried.

"The fur jacket is warm," she said.

"I'll help you up," he said.

"No," she replied, and was silent.

Now the boy had another idea. The grandmother had said, "Just a sip warms the stomach and won't let the body freeze even on the coldest winter days."

He took the calfskin satchel, opened it, and rummaged until he found the flask of brewed black coffee that their grandmother had intended for their mother. He took out the flask, removed its wrappings, and pulled out the cork with an effort. Then he bent down to Sanna and said, "Here's the coffee Grandmother's sending to Mother, have a little taste, it'll make you warm. Mother would give it to us if she knew what we need it for."

The girl, instinctively yearning for rest, replied, "I'm not cold."

"Just have some," said the boy, "and then you can sleep."

Enticed by the prospect, Sanna mastered herself enough to swallow the drink. Then the boy drank some too.

The strong extract took effect at once, all the more powerfully as the children had never tasted coffee in their lives. Instead of falling asleep, Sanna now grew livelier, and said herself that she was cold, but that on the inside she was quite warm now, and the warmth was moving into her hands and feet. The children even chatted for a while.

And so, despite its bitterness, they had more of the drink whenever its effect began to fade, and worked their innocent nerves into a fever capable of withstanding the weight that dragged them toward slumber.

Midnight had come. Because they were so young, and in joy's urgency always fell asleep very late on Christmas Eve, only when the physical urgency of sleep overcame them, they had never heard the bells' midnight pealing, never heard the church organ when Mass was celebrated, although they lived close to the church. Now, at this moment of this night, all the bells were rung, the bells rang in Mills-dorf, the bells rang in Gschaid, and behind the mountain there was a chapel with three brightly chiming bells that rang. In the distant lands outside there were countless churches and bells, and at this moment all those bells were rung, the wave of sound passed from village to village, indeed, through the leafless boughs one sometimes heard the chiming from one village to the next: but not a sound reached up to the children, here nothing was heard, for here there was nothing to herald. In the valley's folds the lights of the lanterns now passed along the mountain slopes, and many a farm rang its own bell as a reminder to the people; but from up here those things were still less visible and audible; only the stars shone, quietly glowing and glittering on.

Though Konrad fixed his mind on the fate of the hunter who had frozen to death, though the children had nearly emptied the flask of black coffee, stirring their blood to greater activity, yet in so doing caused exhaustion to follow—they could not have vanquished sleep, whose seductive sweetness outweighs all reasons, if nature in its grandeur had not stood by them, summoning within them a force that was able to withstand it.

In the prodigious stillness that prevailed, the stillness in which not the least little crest of snow seemed to stir, the children heard, three times, the cracking of the ice. The sounds were made by the glacier, that thing that seems most unyielding, and yet is most astir and alive. From behind them, three times, they heard the report, appalling, as though the earth had cracked in two, the sound spread-ing throughout the ice in all directions, seeming to course through all its fine veins. The children sat where they were with open eyes, gazing out into the stars.

Now something for their eyes began to unfold. As the children sat there, in the sky before them a pale light blossomed amid the stars, and traced a faint arc between them. It had a green glimmer that drifted gently downward. But the arc grew brighter and brighter, until the stars receded before it and faded. It sent a light to other regions of the sky, spilling glimmergreen gentle and alive among the stars. Then sheaves of variegated light rose like a crown's prongs from the apex of the arc and blazed. The light spilled brightly through the neighboring regions of the sky, it sent out soft showers, and passed through long spaces in gentle tremors. Had the unprecedented snowfall so stretched the sky's thundery electricity that it burst forth in these mute magnificent surges of light, or was it some other cause found in unfathomable nature? Bit by bit it grew fainter and fainter, the sheaves fading first, until gradually and imperceptibly it lessened, and once again there was nothing in the sky but the thousands and thousands of plain stars.

Neither child said a word to the other, they sat on and on, gazing wide-eyed into the sky.

Nothing unusual happened after that. The stars gleamed, sparkled, and quivered, and now and then a meteor shot through them.

At last, after the stars had shone a long while all alone, with not a sliver of moon to be seen in the sky, something else happened. The sky began to brighten, slowly but perceptibly; its color became visible, the palest stars faded, and the others no longer stood so thickly set. At last even the most luminous ones vanished, and the snow below the heights was more clearly to be seen. Finally one part of the sky turned yellow, and a streak of cloud within it ignited to a glowing thread. All things were clear to the eye, and the distant snowy hills were limned sharply in the air.

"Sanna, day is breaking," said the boy.

"Yes, Konrad," the girl replied.

"When it gets just a little brighter, we'll go out of the cave, and walk down the mountain."

It grew brighter, not a star could be seen now across the whole sky, and all objects stood there in the dawn.

"Well we're going now" said the boy.

"Yes, we're going," said Sanna.

The children stood up, and tested their limbs, which only now felt truly tired. Though they had not slept at all, the morning braced them, as it always does. The boy slung the calfskin satchel over his shoulders, and fastened Sanna's fur jacket more tightly. Then he led her out from the cave.

Believing they merely had to walk down the mountain, they did not think of food, and did not look to see if their bags still held white bread or other things to eat.

Now that the sky was clear, Konrad meant to look down from the mountain into the valleys, to make out the valley of Gschaid and head down toward it. But he saw no valleys at all. It was as though they found themselves not on a mountain from which you look down, but in a strange alien region filled with unknown objects. Today, even at a great distance, they saw rising from the snow terrible crags they had not seen yesterday, they saw the ice, they saw hills and snowy slopes staring up, and behind them was the sky, or the blue tip of a very distant mountain looming at the edge of the snow.

At that moment the sun rose.

A gigantic blood-red disk rose into the sky at the snow's rim, and instantly the snow around the children went red as though strewn with millions of roses. The peaks and the horns cast lengthy green-hued shadows along the snow.

"Sanna, we'll keep going forward until we reach the edge of the mountain and look down," the boy said.

They walked out into the snow. It had grown drier still in the clear night, and yielded still more easily to their steps. Vigorously they waded onward. Indeed, as they walked their limbs grew stronger and suppler. But they did not reach an edge, and could not look down. Snowfield unfolded from snowfield, and at the rim of each the sky loomed every time.

All the same they kept on walking.

Then they entered the ice again. They did not know how the ice had come to be there, but they felt the smooth footing, and though it was not the terrible debris at whose edge they had spent the night, they saw nonetheless that they were walking on slick ice, here and there they saw great fragments, then more and more, crowding closer to them, and forcing them to climb again.

But still they were following their course.

Again they clambered up great blocks, and stood on the ice field once more. Today, in the bright sun, for the first time they saw what it was. It was vast, and beyond it more black cliffs loomed, wave rose behind wave, the snow-covered ice was packed, distended, upheaved, as though it were still creeping forward, surging toward the children's chests. In the white they saw countless blue lines snaking their way forward. And between those places, where the ice shapes jutted as though dashed against each other, there were lines like paths, but they were white, strips of firm ice surface, or places where the fragments had not been so shunted about. The children walked into these paths, seeking to cross part of the ice, and reach the edge of the mountain, and look down from it at last. They spoke not a word. The girl followed the boy. But today, too, all was ice, sheer ice. Now that they sought to cross it, it seemed to grow wider and wider. At that, abandoning their course, they turned back. When they could not walk, they clawed their way through the masses of snow, which often broke away before their eyes, showing the intense blue band of an ice crevasse where just now all had been white; but they paid no heed, they worked their way onward until somewhere they emerged from the ice once again.

"Sanna," the boy said, "let's not go into the ice again; we can't make any headway there. And since we can't see down into our valley, we'll go straight down the mountain. We'll have to come to a valley; we'll tell the people there that we come from Gschaid, and they'll give us a guide to take us home."

"Yes, Konrad," the girl said.

And so they began walking downhill in the snow by whichever path offered itself. The boy led the girl by the hand. But once they had gone downhill a while, the slope ended, and the snow rose up again. So the children changed direction, and walked down the length of a hollow. But there they found more ice. They climbed up the side of the hollow to seek a way downhill in a different direction. A slope led them down, but bit by bit it turned so steep that they could hardly find a foothold, and feared they would slip down it. So they climbed up again to seek another downhill path. When they had climbed uphill in the snow for a long while, and then walked along a level ridge, it was the same thing as before; either the snow sloped off so steeply that they would have plunged down, or it rose once again, so that they feared they would reach the top of the mountain. And so it went, on and on.

Then they decided to seek the direction they had come from, and go down to the red misfortune column. Because it was not snowing, and the sky was so bright, they would be sure, thought the boy, to make out the place where the column should be, and from there walk down to Gschaid.

The boy told his little sister his thought, and she followed.

But the way down to the saddle could not be found either.

However crystal-clear the sun shone, however lovely the looming snowy heights and the sprawling snowfields, they could not recognize the places through which they had ascended yesterday. Yesterday all things had been veiled by the terrifying snowfall, so that they could barely see a few feet around them, and all had been one great white and gray chaos. All they had seen were the crags as they walked along them and between them; but today too they had seen many crags that all looked the same as the ones they had seen yesterday. Today they left fresh tracks in the snow; but yesterday the falling snow had covered all their tracks. By appearance alone they could not tell which place led down to the saddle, for all places looked the same. Snow sheer snow. But they walked on and on, and believed they could prevail. They skirted the steep drops, and avoided climbing the steep rises.

Today, too, they often stopped to listen; but today, too, they heard nothing, not the least little sound. And nothing could be seen but the snow, the bright white snow from which, here and there, the black horns and the black rock ribs loomed.

At last the boy thought he saw a fire bobbing on a distant sloping snowfield. It leapt up, it leapt down. Now they saw it, now they didn't. They stopped in their tracks and gazed across at that place. The fire bobbed on and on, and seemed to come closer; for it grew larger and they saw its bobbing motion more clearly. It no longer vanished as often or as long as before. After a time they heard in the still blue air faintly very faintly something like a drawn-out note from a shepherd's horn. Instinctively both children gave a loud shout. After a while they heard the sound again. They shouted again, and stayed where they were. The fire drew nearer. The note came for the third time, and this time more clearly. Again the children replied with loud shouts. After a long while they made out the fire. It was no fire, it was a waving red flag. At the same time the shepherd's horn rang out closer by, and the children answered.

"Sanna," the boy cried, "people from Gschaid are coming, I know the flag, it's the red flag that the strange gentleman who climbed Gars with the young hunter Eschenjäger planted on the summit, so that the pastor could see it with his telescope, as a sign that they'd reached the top, and then the strange gentleman gave the flag to the pastor. You were just a little child then."

"Yes, Konrad."

After a while the children also saw the people with the flag, little black spots that seemed to be moving. The call of the horn came again from time to time, and drew closer and closer. Each time the children answered it.

At last they saw several men climbing down the snowy slope toward them with their sticks, carrying the flag in their midst. As the men drew closer, they saw who they were. It was the shepherd Philipp with his horn, his two sons, the young Eschenjäger, and several people from Gschaid.

"Blessed be the Lord!" cried Philipp, "there you are. There are people all over the mountain. Someone run down to the Sider Alp, and ring the bell, so they'll hear that we've found you, and someone should go up to Crab Rock and plant the flag there so that they'll see it in the valley, and fire the mortars, so that the searchers in the Millsdorf Forest will know, and so that the people in Gschaid will light a fire and send smoke into the air to tell those who are still on the mountain to come down to the Sider Alp. What a Christmas!"

"I'll run down to the alp," said one.

"I'll take the flag to Crab Rock," said another.

"And we'll bring the children down to the Sider Alp, as best we can, with God's help," said Philipp.

One of Philipp's sons struck out downhill, and the other went off with the flag through the snow.

The hunter Eschenjäger took the girl by the hand, the shepherd Philipp took the boy. The others helped as best they could. And so they set out on their way, in switchbacks. Now they went in one direction, now they turned in the other, now they went downhill now uphill. The way was always through the snow, always through the snow, and the surroundings never changed. On very steep slopes they put crampons on their feet and carried the children. At last, after a long while, they heard the sound of a bell rising toward them, gentle and ethereal, the first sign sent up to them again from the lower regions. They must have descended quite far indeed, for they saw a snowy summit rising above them, very high and very blue. The bell they heard was the bell at the Sider Alp, ringing because that was the agreed-on meeting place. And once they had come still farther, they heard, rising faintly in the still air, the mortar shots being fired because the flag had been planted, and they saw thin columns of smoke rise.

After descending for a time across a gentle slope, they saw the hut on the meadow of the Sider Alp. They were walking toward it. A fire was burning in the hut, the children's mother was there, and she sank back in the snow with an awful cry when she saw the children approaching with the hunter Eschenjäger.

Then she ran toward them, examined them all over, wanted to give them food, wanted to warm them, wanted to bed them down in some hay that happened to be there; but soon she persuaded herself that the children's joy made them stronger than she had thought, that they only needed a warm meal, which was given them, and a little rest, which also was granted.

After a while of calm and rest another group of men came down the snowy slope, while the bell of the hut kept chiming, and the children went out with the others to see who it was. It was the shoemaker, the erstwhile alpine climber, with his alpenstock and his crampons, accompanied by his friends and comrades.

"Sebastian, they're here," his wife cried.

But he was mute, he trembled, and ran toward them. Then he moved his lips as though to say something, but he said nothing, he snatched the children up, and held them for a long time. Then he turned to his wife, hugged her close, and cried, "Sanna, Sanna!"

After a while he picked up his hat, which had fallen into the snow, went up to the men, and tried to speak. But all he said was, "Neighbors, friends, I thank you."

After waiting until the children had rested enough to set their minds at ease, he said, "If we're all here now, then we can set out, by God."

"It seems not all are here," said the shepherd Philipp, "but the missing men know from the smoke that we've found the children, and they'll go home sure enough when they find the hut empty."

They prepared to set out.

The Sider Alp hut was not far at all from Gschaid, from whose windows, in summer, one distinctly saw the green meadow where the gray hut stood with its little bell tower; but below it was a perpendicular cliff that dropped for many fathoms, which could be descended in summer only with crampons and in winter not at all. And so they had to take the long way to the saddle to descend to Gschaid from the misfortune column. On their way they crossed the Sider Meadow, still closer to Gschaid, from which one seems to see the windows of the village.

As they crossed this meadow, the bell of the church in Gschaid rang out bright and clear, heralding the Consecration at High Mass.

Because of the general commotion that morning in Gschaid, the pastor had postponed the High Mass, believing the children would reappear. But at last, when no news had come, the sacred ritual had to be performed after all.

When the Consecration bell rang, all the people crossing the Sider Meadow sank to their knees in the snow and prayed. Once the bell had finished ringing, they rose to their feet and walked onward.

For most of the way the shoemaker carried the girl, and had her tell him everything.

Already approaching the woods on the saddle, they came across tracks, and the shoemaker said, "These are not the prints of any boots I made."

The matter was soon cleared up. Another company of men came toward the descending party, probably drawn by all the voices echoing across the area. It was the dyer, ashen with fear, coming down the mountain at the head of his servants his journeymen and several men from Millsdorf.

"They crossed the glacier and the crevasses without knowing it," the shoemaker cried to his father-in-law.

"There they are—there they are—thank the Lord," replied the dyer, "I know they were up on the mountain when your messenger reached us last night, and we searched the whole forest with lights and found nothing—and when dawn broke, by the path that leads up to the left toward the snowy peak from the red misfortune column, I saw that just where it turns away from the column little twigs or branches were bent now and then, as children like to do when they walk along a path—then I knew it—the course left them no escape, because they were walking in the hollow, because they were walking between the crags, and then along the ridge, which falls off so steeply on both sides that they could not descend. They had to go up the mountain. When I realized this I immediately sent a messenger to Gschaid, but the woodcutter Michael, who made the crossing, came back up to meet us when we had nearly reached the ice, and said that you had already found them, so we went back down again."

"Yes," said Michael, "I said so because the red flag was already planted on Crab Rock, and the Gschaider recognized it as the sign that was agreed on. I told you that everyone coming down the mountain must take this path, because you can't go down the cliff."

"And kneel down and thank God on your knees, my son-in-law," the dyer went on, "that no wind was blowing. Another hundred years will pass before so marvelous a snowfall descends, before the snow falls straight as wet strings hanging from a stick. If a wind had been blowing, the children would have been lost."

"Yes, let's thank God, let's thank God," said the shoemaker.

The dyer decided to accompany the people to Gschaid, where he had never been since his daughter's marriage.

As they approached the red misfortune column, where the logging road began, a sleigh was waiting, which the shoemaker had sent just in case. The mother and the children were put in the sleigh, wrapped in the blankets and furs that were stored there, and sent ahead to Gschaid.

The others followed, and arrived in Gschaid that afternoon.

The people who had still been on the mountain, and learned only from the smoke signals that it was time to return, gradually straggled in as well. The last one, who did not arrive till evening, was the son of the shepherd Philipp, who had carried the red flag to Crab Rock and planted it there.

In Gschaid their grandmother was waiting, having driven across.

"Never never," she cried, "never again in their lives must the children cross the saddle in winter."

The children were dazed by all the commotion. They were given more to eat and then put to bed. Later, toward evening, when they had rested somewhat, when friends and neighbors had gathered in the parlor, discussing what had happened, and their mother sat in the bedchamber by Sanna's bed, caressing her, the girl said, "Mother, last night, when we were up on the mountain, I saw the Holy Child."

"Oh, my patient, my dear, my darling child, you," her mother replied, "he's sent you presents too, and soon you'll receive them."

The boxes had been unpacked, the candles had been lit, the door to the parlor was opened, and from their beds the children gazed out at the belated brightly shining inviting Christmas tree. Despite their exhaustion they had to be dressed to go out, receive their gifts, marvel at them, and finally doze off with them.

The inn of Gschaid was livelier that evening than ever before. All who had not been to church were there now, and the others as well. Everyone told what he had seen and heard, what he had done, what advice he had given, and what adventures and dangers he had gone through. But especially they emphasized how everything could have been done differently and better.

The incident marked a new chapter in the history of Gschaid, providing a subject of conversation for a long time to come, and it will be talked of years from now, when people see the mountain with special vividness on clear days, or tell strangers about its idiosyncrasies.

From that day on the children were truly village property, from then on they were no longer viewed as foreigners, but as natives whom the villagers had fetched down from the mountain.

Their mother, Sanna, was now a native of Gschaid as well.

The children, for their part, will never forget the mountain, and will regard it still more gravely from their garden when, as in the past, the sun shines splendidly, the linden tree smells sweet, the bees hum, and the mountain gazes down at them as lovely and blue as the gentle firmament.

CAT-SILVER

In a remote but beautiful part of our fatherland, there stands a stately manor. Perched atop a hillock, it is surrounded on one side by its fields and pastures and on the other by its little wood. One ought really to mention a garden as well, but then that would be the wrong word for it; that high-lying region covered with hills and wooded peaks lacks such gardens as are common throughout the lands, for the winter storms and the frosts of spring and fall wreak havoc on the plants people like to raise in gardens; but by a steep sandy slope whose warm spots reflect the sun's rays hotly, the manor's owner has planted trees upon a beautiful lush lawn, shielded from the west north and east winds, protected from the frost by the elevated, enclosed location, and growing so quickly in their warm place that the shoots grafted onto them have become flourishing branches and each year bear great black cherries, sour cherries pears and red-cheeked apples. Not to mention smaller plants such as currants gooseberries strawberries. Against a wall built along the sandy slope there are even peaches and apricots that ripen when a hot summer comes, and when the protective wrapping of reed mats has not been forgotten on cool spring evenings. The owner keeps his flowers in various hothouses, and on fine days and in the warm summer months he sets them in the windows or on wooden stands outside the house. Even indoors one sees the finest ones standing on special tables. Those fit for the region's air and weather grow in the ground out in the open.

At the end of the climb up the sandy slope, an outcropping rises, lending stability to the mountainside, keeping scree from sliding down to the garden, and helping considerably to augment the warmth.

The manor's owner has built a path with a sturdy railing up the sandy slope and around the outcropping for its fine view of the house the garden and the landscape. In places he has installed little benches for sitting and contemplating things at leisure. Past the crags toward the north comes a stretch of bushes, followed by scattered oaks and birches on the ever-rising ground, then the conifer wood which covers the crest and crowns the tableau.

Around the house, in circles close and far, lie the ubiquitous hills of that countryside, covered with fields and pastures, displaying many a farmhouse many an estate, and each bearing on its crest the wood which, as though by some appointed law, caps each summit in that rolling country. Between the hills, which often drop off unexpectedly to precipitous gorges, there flow streams indeed raging torrents crossed by footbridges, or mere tree trunks in remote parts. There are proper bridges only where the roads cross these streams. The whole country-side rises toward the north, to the great dark far-flung forests that mark the beginning of the Bohemian lands. Toward the south you see the gracious blue chain of the mountains sweep onward against the sky.

Once, as a very young man, the owner of the manor had gone out into the world, and learned many things, and met many people. When he had come to maturity, when his father had died and, along with two bachelor uncles, left him an adequate fortune, he took his inheritance and what he himself had earned, and returned for good to the place of his birth, which before he had visited but rarely, and refurbished the buildings of his father's estate, and added on to them until they formed that charming manor. Then he fetched a lovely girl from the distant capital, and their union was blessed in the little parish church. He preferred the familiar solitude of his native region to a permanent life amid the noise of crowds and strangers in the capital. But when winter came, he returned with his wife to the city of her birth to spend a while there, and to see what projects people had furthered in the meantime, what had happened in the intellectual sphere and what had changed in people's relations. When the sun returned, he went back to his manor.

It was also the home of his mother, who had never left her homeland, knew only the next towns, and had been to the capital of the country but once. She received her new daughter affectionately, and it was charming to see the beautiful young wife stroll alongside the elderly woman in her traditional rural costume. While the couple sojourned in the capital, she looked after the manor and made all the arrangements. When they were due to come she would send a farmhand with the horses to meet them, gazing after him as the carriage rolled off down the hill.

At once her energetic son would resume his interrupted work. Plantings were expanded, new ones were begun, the house was improved and beautified, and agricultural affairs were dealt with. He was seen mingling with his farmhands and his servants.

Once two years had passed, heaven sent an addition to the family; their little daughter Emma arrived. The husband and wife, till then called Son and Daughter, now became Father and Mother, and the mother became Grandmother.

She took the child and instructed her daughter in various aspects of her care.

When the hair began to curl on the little girl's head, tumbling down in a lovely shade of blond, the second, dark, sister Clementia arrived; her head was shadowed even at birth, and soon black ringlets formed upon it.

Now it was not just the father and mother who went off by themselves in the winter, the children did as well, so the grandmother had more worries, she had to fear for four people, and when they came back, they found the rooms for four furnished even more comfortably.

The little girls grew. They had guileless lips red cheeks wide eyes and clear brows, and one's brow was crowned by her father's blond silk-soft curls, the other's by the black curls of her mother.

Grandmother was their playmate; she beckoned them into her chamber, she set up house with them in the garden, in the shady bower by the apple tree's trunk or in the hothouses or on the sandy slope.

Once they were bigger, once their small feet could walk hills and valleys, once their bodies strove upward, slimmer and nimbler, they went with their grandmother up the high nut-hill. When the oats turned pale and ripe, and the wheat and the barley were resting in the barn, the hazelnuts turned color, cheeks brown or rosy.

The children had on wide straw hats, they had dresses whose sleeves left their arms bare, they had white hose, and sturdy shoes so as not to feel the stones of the hill. In one hand each carried a little basket, in the other a pale rod with a hook for bending down the hazel boughs. The rods had themselves been taken from a hazel bush, and then stripped of bark. They walked beneath the fruit trees, they walked up the sandy slope behind the hothouses, they held on to the railing, and they rested on the seats. When they had reached the crags, they sat on a bench or a rock, took a pin from their hatbands or asked their grandmother for the sharp little knife in her bag, and dug out the fine flakes and spangles that were embedded in the rocks, and gleamed and glittered so. They folded them in a piece of paper, and tucked them away in their apron pockets or their grandmother's bag. The grandmother waited for them, or helped them, or told stories. When they climbed still higher, the rocks gave way to soil once more, and on it grew heather and grasses and herbs, and a juniper bush or a birch stump or a thistle. And there they would sit and rest again. They were the only dots of white, around them the hills, gleaming with light stubble from the harvest or glowing brown from plowed fields, or many-colored from the green of the crops planted after the harvest; there lay the valleys the meadows with their second verdure or with glittering waters; the groves climbed the summits of the hills, a gravel pit gleamed, a house or the walls of farmsteads glimmered, and far far beyond stood the blue mountains, with their filmy mosaic of cliffs and their little inlays of snow.

Once, as they sat in the dry grass, the tall stalks swaying, the grandmother told the following story: "Yonder, behind the spiky forest ridge, where the white clouds drift, stands the Hagenbucher House. The Hagenbucher farmer was a harsh man, and no servant could endure him long, and no farmhand and no maidservant could do all the work the big house required. They always left, or he sent them packing. One day a tall maidservant with a brown face and strong arms appeared and said she would serve him, if only he gave her food, and now and then some wool cloth for a skirt and linen for a shirt. The farmer thought it would be worth a try. Now the brown maidservant toiled and kept house like two maids, yet ate for just one, and learned her work better and better. The farmer thought he'd made quite a bargain, and the maid spent years in his house. One day the farmer had two oxen to sell, and put them to the yoke and drove them down through the Gallbrun Woods to the cattle market in Rohrach to sell them. Then he took the yoke upon his shoulders and walked back home through the woods. All at once he heard a voice crying, "Yoke-bearer, yoke-bearer, tell Stura Mura that Rough-Bark is dead—yoke-bearer, yoke-bearer, tell Stura Mura that Rough-Bark is dead." The farmer peered into the trees, but there was nothing to be seen, and he was afraid, and began walking as fast as he could, and by the time he reached home, the sweat was running down his brow. At supper, when he told the story, the tall maid wailed, and ran away, and was never seen again."

Another time the grandmother said, "See, children, where the Gallbrun Woods end there's a pale thing rising up, those are the Karesberg Peaks, and on the grass and in between the rocks are the Karesberg Crofts.

"One day a gnome came to the Karesbergers and said he would tend their goats for them; they should give him no pay, but in the evening, when the goats were in their stall, they must set out a loaf of white bread for him on the hollow stone outside the Karesberg Peaks, and he would fetch it. The Karesbergers agreed, and the gnome became their goatherd. The goats went out in the morning, went out onto the pasture and grazed, they came back at noon with full udders, and went away again, and came back in the evening with full udders, and thrived, and looked finer and finer, and multiplied, white goats and black goats and piebald and brown. The Karesbergers rejoiced, had special white bread baked and laid it on the stone. But then they thought they'd give the goatherd a treat and made him a little red jacket. In the evening, after the goats had returned, they laid the jacket on the stone. The gnome put on the little red jacket and hopped about with it, he hopped about among the gray rocks as though he'd gone crazy with joy; they watched him hop farther and farther downhill like a flame leaping on the greensward, and when the morning had come, and the goats went out to pasture, the gnome was not there, and was never seen again."

Those were tales the grandmother told, and when she had finished, they would get up, and walk along again. They walked past thickets of sloes and alders, surrounded by beetles flies butterflies, hearing the song of the bunting or the twitter of the wren and the kinglet. They saw far in all directions, and saw the goshawks hovering in the air. Then they came to the white birches, with their beautiful trunks that shed thin white skins to show brown smooth bark, and eventually they came to the oaks, with their dark stiff leaves and their gnarled stout branches, and finally they entered the conifer woods, where the pines whisper, the spruces stand with their drooping green tresses, and the firs spread their flat gleaming needles. At the edge of the woods they turned back to look at the house and the garden, tiny below them, the panes of the hothouses gleaming like the flakes they pried from the rock with their pins or the grandmother's little sharp knife.

Then they went into the woods where it was dark, where the berries and the mushrooms grew, the mossy rocks lay, and a bird would flit through the branches and tree trunks. They picked no berries because they had no time, and it was so late in summer that the blueberries were past their prime, the raspberries were finished, the blackberries were not yet ripe, and the strawberries grew on the strawberry hill. They walked along the sandy path, which their father had improved in many places. And after passing the timber that had been felled that summer, and walking a bit longer up the sandy path, they emerged from the woods again.

Now they saw grayish turf before them, with many rocks lying on it, then a valley, and then the high nut-hill loomed.

They walked down the sloping turf, which had a hollow where a little brook flowed. They walked between the gray rocks, on which dry twigs or feathers lay, and the wagtail hopped, beating time with its tail feathers. And once they'd reached the brook, with the gray quick fish darting through and the pretty blue dragonflies flitting about, and once they'd crossed over the wide stone their father had had laid across the brook as a bridge for them, they headed up the high nut-hill.

They climbed the nut-hill, which is round on all sides, has a peak with rocks lying at its foot, is covered with all kinds of bushes—dwarf birch alders ash and all the many hazel shrubs—and gives a sweeping view of fields tilled by strangers, and farther unknown regions.

Grandmother held Black-Locks by the hand. Blond-Locks walked on her own, jumping over the rocks. When they came to the nut-hill, they went in under the fence, the grandmother ducked down, Blond-Locks ducked down, even Black-Locks ducked down, and so they came to the bushes with the nuts. There they were on the hill along with many other things. There were the little reddish mice that eat nuts too, that dig dry tunnels beneath the roots where they bring in the seeds of the hill and other things for their meals, where they bring in grass and hay to make nests for their young, and gnaw the nuts with their teeth to get the sweet hearty kernels—there was the fleeting jay flying through the branches on wings inlaid with little blue-striped panels—there was the squirrel, slipping across the meadow and stopping on a high thick branch to raise its paws to its mouth and busily gnaw away—and who knows what else there was, seeking joy and pleasure on the high nut-hill, things that have wings, or that dart down the sandy hollow like the weasels and the polecats.

The green boughs stretched upward to the blue sky, studded with leaves and nuts, now singly now two now three clustered in great knots, with pale or green- or brown- or red-hued cheeks. The children reached into the branches with their little hands, or they hooked them with their rods and pulled them down to pick the nuts. And when they'd bent down an empty branch by mistake, they released it at once, and looked for another one. So they worked away busily. And when the boughs were too high, or when they were too sturdy and the children could not bend them, the grandmother helped, pulling down the branch and holding it until the children's hands had found the nuts and picked them. She led them to places where the branches were fully laden, studded with nuts upon nuts. When the children had gathered a great many, when their little baskets were filled, when they'd put some in their satchels and even tied them up in their kerchiefs, they stayed on the hill a while longer, walking about, climbing to the top of the summit, and sitting down by a stout old hazel root that looked very inviting, and lingering in the air's resplendent expanse.

The grandmother told them it was here that Little Rooster and Little Hen had gone up the nut-hill, where Little Hen had been so thirsty and Little Rooster had brought her water, and other things had happened as well. Then she showed them the surroundings, and told them the curious names of the mountains, and named various fields that could be seen, and explained the little white dots that were barely visible and signified a house or a village. And when the sky's far reaches were fine and clear and the mountains stood out sharply, she puzzled out the strange peaks that loomed there, and told tales about certain long-stretched ridges, and when faint clouds hung over the mountains, she said they were like real palaces or cities or countries or things that nobody knows. And toward the north they looked out toward the Gallbrun Woods and the Karesberg Peaks and beyond them to the swathe of the Throne Forest, where often a cloud hung, long and dull, lacking the exquisite gleam of the clouds toward the south above the mountains.

And when they'd had plenty of time to gaze out across the land, the grandmother told them of the men who had lived there, of the knights who rode about, of the beautiful women and girls mounted upon palfreys, of the shepherds with their clever sheep, of the fishermen and the hunters.

Then they headed back. They straightened their rumpled dresses, took their baskets and their rods, and went back down the path they'd come up by.

They walked down past the hazel shrubs, they walked across the stones, they walked across the brook with the little gray fish and the blue dragonflies, they walked across the turf, they walked through the woods, they walked down through the crags through the bushes and along the sandy slope, they passed the hothouses and crossed the lawn toward the manor, where their mother often strolled in her fine clothes and with her parasol, coming out to meet them.

Then they were fed, for they were very hungry. They had two nutcrackers; Blond-Locks had a bigger, more solemn one, while Black-Locks had one that was smaller and more comical, with a droll mouth, and a frightful look in his eyes. Into the nutcrackers' mouths they put the nuts they had brought and freed from their green husks, they pressed down the lever and crushed the nuts as the crackers' jaws snapped shut in terrible grimaces. They gave kernels and whole nuts to their father and mother and their grandmother too, who seldom fetched nuts from the high nut-hill, and then just a few, which she always put on the children's table, just as she always returned the nuts which they gave her.

When Blond-Locks was already quite big, and beginning to learn lessons, and Black-Locks was learning too, and a friendly teacher had come from the city and opened beautiful books with them at a table in their nursery and explained the things the books held, a brother was born, Sigismund. And just as Blond-Locks was the father Black-Locks the mother, Sigismund was father and mother, he was Blond-Locks and Black-Locks; for when his hair began to grow, first it was light and then it formed brown ringlets, and his eyes were neither blue nor black, but brown.

Now they could no longer go up the high nut-hill with their grandmother, because she had to stay with their little brother. They were forbidden to go with anyone else, and had to remain near the house. Now they walked about in the garden and looked at the fruit trees, or they went into the hothouses to admire the flowers.

But after their little brother had gone on two winter trips to the city in the big carriage, and two trips back in the summer, he was strong enough to go about with his sisters and his grandmother. They walked through the fields, they went into the woods and exercised their legs. Then they went up the high nut-hill again.

The sisters wore white frocks, they wore yellow straw hats, one of which blended in with Blond-Locks' curls, while the other stood out on Black-Locks' head like a halo, they had red ribbons on their hats and frocks, they carried baskets on their arms and in their hands the pale hooked hazel rods. The boy wore white hose a blue jacket a little straw hat on his brown curls and a smaller rod with a hook. Instead of a basket he had a yellow leather satchel slung from his shoulders on green straps. They walked much more slowly, they rested more often, and the sisters showed their brother many things by the path, things they already knew about, and they showed how fast they could go if they wanted, hopping across the meadow, hopping onto the rocks and running forward and backward. They walked up the sandy slope through the thickets the crags the forest across the gray hollow and up the high nut-hill. They picked the nuts and put them in their baskets, their brother reached up with his little hook too, and all of them helped each other until even his little satchel was filled.

As they sat by the stout old hazel root, the grandmother told another tale. She said: "Near the Throne Forest, on its steep southern slope, there was once another wood, but not a thick one, just birches and maples growing on the meadows. There lived a shepherd who drove his sheep into the woods so that they could graze on the meadow, and give him milk and wool. There came a dark man down from the Throne Forest and said that there was a bloody light in the Hart Cave where the silver flowed. The shepherd didn't know who the man was, or what the silver or the bloody light was, and couldn't ask him, for the man had already gone. He waited for him to come back, though. But the man never came back again. One day, when the shepherd was looking for a lost lamb, he walked up the brook where it flowed down the hill, his eyes on its dancing ripples. He kept hearing the lamb bleating up the hill, and so he walked on and on. He walked so far upstream that the forest grew dense, the stream flowed over slabs and boulders, and rock walls rose on both sides. Then he saw a slab with water flowing from it, falling as though silver bands and fringes were spread across the rock. He climbed up the slab, seeking footholds and handholds on its smooth face. When he came to the top, he saw that the water was flowing from a cave, and the cave was gleaming and hard, like an artfully carved gem. He went into the cave. It grew ever narrower, and ever darker, and the water flowed forth. Then suddenly he saw a gleam in a corner, as though a red bloody droplet were resting there. He went closer, and it went on gleaming. Then it came to him to reach out his hand and take the droplet. He took the droplet, but what he felt in his hand was a cold rough stone, and the stone was so big that his hand could hardly hold it. He carried the stone out into the daylight, and saw that it was an ordinary rock, the sort you find by the thousands, and that a little red eye gazed out from it, as though covered by the lids of the hard rock crust, so that it could merely blink, the color of roses. When the stone was turned, it cast sparks on the things around. The shepherd climbed quickly down the rock slab, walked along the flowing stream and hastened to return to his herd. The lamb that he had lost, and failed to find, was at home, suckling at its mother's teat. He wrapped the stone in a cloth and guarded it closely. Then one day a farmer came, and he sold him the stone for five sheep. And the farmer sold it to a doctor for a horse, and the doctor sold it to a Lombard for a hundred gold pieces, and the Lombard had the gem removed from the rock and cut, and now princes and kings wear it in their crowns, big and brilliant, a carbuncle or some other red stone; they envy each other for it, and when the country is conquered, the stone is carried off with great care, as though carrying a conquered city in a tiny little box."

Another time the grandmother said: "Our streams are brown and gleaming because they carry iron dust from the mountains, but they don't just hold iron, the sand shines as though it were sheer gold, and when you take it, and carefully rinse it, little flakes and grains of true, pure gold are left behind. In early times strange people from far away panned for gold in our streams, and went away rich; then several of our people panned in the streams, and found some themselves; but now it has been forgotten, and no one thinks of the streams except to water their herds. And still more exquisite things can be found there. If you find a shell, and it's the right sort, a pearl will be inside it, so precious that a hole can be drilled through it, and it's strung with other pearls on a string for beautiful women to put around their necks as a dainty adornment, or to wind around pictures of the saints, or to trim holy vessels."

When the children and the grandmother had sat long enough, they got up again, and went home.

But the children went with their grandmother to other places too, they went to the meadows, where the cowslips and the buttercups grew, and above all the forget-me-nots, like fishes' clear little eyes gazing up from the ripples, blossoming a long time on Mother's table in a vessel full of water. They went up the strawberry hill, where the fragrant strawberries grew, smaller but better than those their father grew in beds by the sandy slope. They went into the fields, where the blazing poppies the blue cornflowers and the bright yellow lady's slippers bloomed.

When they were on their own, the children liked to stand by the brook where its flow is gentle and draws all sorts of snaking lines, and gaze at the sand, which really was like gold when the sun struck it through the water, showing gleaming flakes and grains. But when they dug out sand with their little shovels and washed it well, and rinsed it, the flakes were cat-silver, and the grains were snow-white bits of pebbles. Shells were few to be seen, and when they did find one, it was smooth inside, without a pearl.

When Blond-Locks and Black-Locks had grown lovelier and more wondrous, and Sigismund had grown big, and they were sitting once more on the high nut-hill by the stout old hazel root, a strange brown child came out of the bushes. It was a girl, nearly as tall as Blond-Locks and even slimmer, with bare arms that hung down at her sides, and a bare neck, and a green vest and green hose all decked with red ribbons. The eyes of her face were black. She stood there by the hazel bushes, gazing at the grandmother and the children. The grandmother merely went on talking. But the children watched the girl. When the grandmother had finished, she spoke to the girl, saying:

"Who are you?"

The girl did not reply; she sprang into the bushes, and ran off, and they saw the branches swaying.

The grandmother and the children went down from the high nut-hill without seeing or hearing the girl anymore.

Another time when they were sitting by the stout old hazel root, and the grandmother was talking, the brown girl came again, stepped out again from the bushes, stopped and gazed at the children. When they questioned her, she did not run away, like the first time, but withdrew to the bushes so that the leaves covered her bare arms, and watched the children. When they rose to leave, she ran away again down the high nut-hill.

The children asked more and more often to go up the high nut-hill and see the brown girl.

The grandmother went up with them. They went several times without seeing the brown girl, but once, when they had filled their baskets with nuts, and were sitting by the hazel root, the girl came out of the bushes again, stopped again, and gazed at Blond-Locks. Perhaps she stared because she herself had short-cropped black hair instead of long blond curls. When, after a long while, they spoke friendly words to her, she withdrew just a little way, and smiled, showing wonderfully white teeth, but made no reply. The children sat a while longer, the grandmother spoke of many things, and the brown girl stood and watched. When they departed, she did not run away as quickly as the first two times, but walked slowly down the hill as well, on a path close by the children's, and several times they glimpsed her in the bushes. She always wore the same clothes that she had worn the first time.

The father was glad to let the children go up the high nut-hill, merely saying that they should do the strange child no harm. When they reached the top, the girl would come, stop at the edge of the bushes, and watch. She gave a friendly smile when they spoke to her, but did not reply. When they left, she followed as far as the end of the bushes.

Once she appeared with a pale rod stripped of bark, like the children's, and held the rod up high.

Another time, when the children were walking down the hill, and she behind them, and the children slowed a little, she came closer and closer and at last touched Blond-Locks with the rod.

In time she would also lie down in the grass when the grandmother told stories, she propped her brown arm on her elbow, her head on her hand, and fixed her black eyes on the grandmother. She understood the words; the feelings were expressed in her face. The children were very fond of her.

They brought her toys and apples, laying them in the grass near her, and she took them and tucked them away.

When little by little fall had advanced, when no more nuts hung on the boughs, when the boughs were turning yellow, the tilled fields in the distance had taken on the green of winter grain and the days had grown short, so that the time to head home came early, there was such a splendid hot fall day that no one could remember its like. Once more the children sat on the high nut-hill, the brown girl sat in the grass and the grandmother sat on a stone.

They basked in the late warm sun. The old woman's features were lit up, the rocks gleamed, silver threads stretched from jags and knobs, and the brown girl's red ribbons glimmered when the sun caught them, like dangling red-hot bands.

The grandmother was telling stories again, about a beautiful countess who stood on the ramparts to defend herself single-handedly against the peasants in the Peasants' War when they came with pitchforks flails maces and other things to break into the castle and set it on fire, until at last her husband came from distant lands, and smote and destroyed the rebels like a storm wind.

As she spoke, clouds in the sky made a wall, and merged with the mountains, so that all was in a mild haze, and the stubble-fields gleamed and shimmered still brighter.

The children lingered atop the hill. They played games, and had brought pretty things along for the strange girl.

But the clouds grew more and more distinct, and their upper edges were lit by the sun, and gleamed as though molten silver were spilling from them.

The heat grew and grew, and they kept sitting atop the hill, for heat is more wearying in fall than in summer.

The grandmother gazed over at the clouds. Had it been summer, she might have thought a thunderstorm was coming; but at this time of the year it was impossible, it was unthinkable. The brown girl also watched the clouds.

If worst comes to worst and a light fall drizzle comes, thought the grandmother, it's no matter; the children are used to getting wet, and if anything it's good for their health.

But soon she thought differently. From the clouds they heard faint thunder.

They waited a little, and the thunder came again.

Now the grandmother pondered what to do. Between the high nut-hill and her son's manor there was neither house nor hut, and thus no roof to shelter under. In the forest the trees would offer protection from the rain, but would pose a greater risk if lightning struck, and they could not take cover there. It was doubtful that she could reach home with the children before the storm broke. But, she thought, even if the storm did come, it could scarcely be severe this late in the year, the rain would not pour down as in the summer, and so it would easily be weathered.

Meanwhile the shape of the clouds had changed. They formed a dark wall, and at the foot of this wall light whitish flakes were drifting. Already lightning flashed in the clouds, but the claps of thunder that followed were distant as though beyond the mountains. The sun still shone on the high nut-hill and the landscape all around.

The children were not afraid. They had seen the severe thunderstorms that were common in this hill country, and since their father and mother would calmly go on with their business, storms did not terrify them.

The brown girl had been walking back and forth near the place where they were sitting. She peered into certain hazel bushes, looked under tangles of roots and into hollows.

Little by little the clouds had swallowed the sun. All the hazel trees on the hill lay in shadow, the landscape around lay in shadow, and only the stubble fields far to the east were lit up and glimmering.

"Dear children," said the grandmother, "I don't know if it's really true, as my mother often said, that when the Virgin Mary crossed the mountains to see her cousin Elizabeth, she sheltered under a hazel bush, and for that reason lightning never strikes a hazel; but let us seek a dense hazel bush whose branches hang toward the east and form a roof, and whose trunks stand in the west and will hold off the rain from that direction. Let us sit under it as long as the rain lasts, so that it can't harm us and we won't get too wet. Then we'll go home."

"Yes, let's do that, Grandmother," the children cried, "let's do that."

Now they set about finding such a bush.

But the brown girl darted into the thickets and ran away.

After a while she returned with a bundle of brushwood, the kind people make of thin and thick twigs and sticks, which they pile up to dry and take home in the winter to burn for fuel.

Then she ran away again, and brought back two bundles. And so she continued with great speed, until her pale brown cheeks glowed and the sweat ran from her brow.

While the girl was carrying the bundles, and the children and the grandmother were looking for a hazel bush, the clouds, once so slow, had approached much more swiftly, and the thunder rolled clearly and distinctly.

At last the brown girl stopped carrying up bundles, and began to make them into a kind of little house. She looked for a spot that was enclosed to the west by dense hazel bushes, set up bundles as pillars, laid across them rods and sticks taken from the stacks, piled more bundles on top of those, and heaped up more and more bundles so that a cave was formed inside, providing shelter.

When it was finished, the grandmother and the children having meanwhile found a suitable hazel bush and sat down beneath it to wait for the storm, she went to them and said something that they did not understand. Then, because she could not explain in words, she made a sign: she held out her left palm, raised her right hand, made a fist, and slammed it down on the open hand. Then she looked at the grandmother and pointed to the clouds.

The grandmother came out from under the hazel bush and went to stand in a spot where she could see the clouds. They were greenish, luminous almost to whiteness, but despite that light there was a darkness on the hills below them like nightfall. And so they surged closer, and in the stillness of the nut-hill a murmur was heard within them like a thousand cauldrons seething.

"Good heavens, hail!" cried the grandmother.

At once she grasped what the brown girl wanted, she grasped the knowledge and prudence the girl had shown with her bundles of brush; she ran to the hazel bush, dragged the children out, motioned them to follow; the strange girl ran on ahead, the grandmother followed with the children; they came to the bundles, the girl signaled that they should crawl inside; Sigismund was thrust in first, followed by Clementia, then Emma and the grandmother side by side, and finally, on the outermost edge, the brown girl nestled up, holding Emma's blonde curls in her hand.

The children had scarcely managed to lie down beneath the bundles, and were just straining to hear what would happen, when they heard a crash in the hazels like a stone thrown through the leaves. A bit later they heard the same thing again, then nothing more. At last they saw a hailstone, like a gleaming white bullet, fall to the grass outside their house of brush, they saw it bounce high into the air, and fall back down and roll away. The same thing happened nearby with a second hailstone. In that moment the storm came; it seized the bushes and made them rustle, ceased for the space of a breath, so that all was deathly still, and then seized the bushes anew, pushed them over so that the whites of the leaves showed, and hurled the hail upon them like white lightning hurtling down. It beat on the leaves, it beat on the wood, it beat on the earth, the hailstones beat together and made such a roar that though lightning bolts were seen lighting up the nut-hill, the thunder could not be heard. The leaves were beaten down, the twigs were beaten down, the boughs were broken off, the grass was furrowed as though iron spikes had harrowed it. The hailstones were large enough to kill a grown person. They smashed the hazels that stood behind the house, and their falling could be felt on the bundles.

And it came down on the entire hill and on the valleys. Whatever resisted was crushed, whatever was solid was shattered, whatever had life in it was killed. Only soft things withstood, like the earth pounded by the hailstones, and the bundles of brush. In the dark air the ice drove down like white darts to the black earth so that the earth's things were seen no more.

No one knows what the children felt; they did not know themselves. They lay pressed close, and pressed together still closer; the bundles had sagged under the hail and lay upon the children, and the grandmother saw their slight little bodies flinch each time a heavy hailstone struck the bundles. The grandmother prayed. The children were silent, and the brown girl did not stir.

The stumps of the hazel bushes behind the bundles kept the wind from sweeping through them and tossing them apart.

After a long time it let up a little, so that the thunder could be heard again, now as a mild rumble. The hailstones fell more thickly, but they were smaller, and at last came a rain that was a cloudburst. It did not fall in drops or streaks as usual; it seemed whole sheets of water were falling. It filtered down to the children through the bundles' cracks and gaps.

Little by little it abated, the wind grew lighter, and the thunder rumbled farther away. The brown girl crawled out from the bundles, stood up, and peered under them with her black eyes.

The grandmother stood up too, and looked at the sky. The clouds had moved off toward the east; there it was dark, and the falling of the water and ice could be heard. But over the mountains in the west it lightened, lighter gray clouds drifted up, showing that the hail would not return.

Now the grandmother pulled forth Blond-Locks, then Black-Locks, then Brown-Locks.

The wet children came out from under the bundles, their clothes clinging to their bodies. The brown girl's fine dress was spoiled too, clinging wet and besmirched to her body. Her bare right arm was bleeding. Because she had not been able to lie all the way under the brush, a piece of ice had grazed and scratched it. When the children came up to look at it, when the grandmother tried to examine it, she turned away, and made a gesture as though to say that it was not worth troubling with.

They prepared to set out.

The grandmother took the girls' two baskets and the boy's leather satchel, tied everything together with a wet cloth, and carried it herself, so that the children would not be weighed down, so that they could hold on to her as they walked, and pick up their smocks. She kept them close by so that they would not slip and fall on the wet ground and the hailstones. The brown girl went with them.

The children saw how the wind had blown the dry grass the leaves and other things in among the hazel trunks, they saw how no bushes were left standing on the hill, only a mass of stumps, they saw how no grass was left at all, only almost-black earth mixed to slurry with the water. And when the ground could not be seen, it was where white heaps of hailstones lay, like snowbanks lingering in spring after the snow has melted in sunnier places. When the children touched one of the hailstones, it was very cold, and when they looked at it closely, it was as beautiful as a glass globe, with a tiny flake of snow inside. On all sides of the hill the water from the rain ran down.

The grandmother took great care that the children should not slip.

The rain had stopped, and nothing but a damp dust fell from the sky.

They came to the edge of the high nut-hill, and this time the brown girl went with them across the grayish turf.

But it was grayish turf no longer. It had been battered down, and was now black earth, just as the rocks, wet from the rain, looked black. Great white swathes of hail lay there.

When they had come to the brook, there was no brook with little gray fish swimming and dragonflies flitting, it was a great turbid body of water with wood and many many green leaves and grasses floating on it, torn up by the hail. The brook had always been edged by little shrubs that bore red blossoms in summer and grew pretty white catkins once the blossoms fell off. The tips of these shrubs rose out of the water.

The grandmother made for the little stone bridge, but it could not be seen, and it was impossible to tell the place where it had been.

As the grandmother wavered, trying to make out the site of the bridge, the brown girl pointed to a place, and as the others hesitated, she walked up to the water, calm and determined. She walked into it, waded across it, and waded back again, as though to give visible proof that it was possible to go through. As the water reached only to her hips, it was clear to see that she was walking on the bridge.

When she had returned, she bent down toward Sigismund, gently and kindly, and reached her arms out toward him. The boy understood her gesture, he let go of his grandmother's hand and gave himself to the brown girl's safekeeping. She took him in her arms, he wrapped his little arms around her neck, and she carried him to the far bank with firm and confident strides.

Taking Black-Locks in one arm and clasping Blond-Locks tightly by the hand, the grandmother followed the brown girl. Soon she felt the bridge underfoot, and reached the other bank as well.

The strange girl set down Sigismund and the grandmother set down Black-Locks, and then they had to continue on their way. They looked back at the water. The tips of the shrubs could no longer be seen, and the water had grown much wider. It sped along with the wood with the leaves and with the strange black things floating on it.

Now they walked up the meadow toward the woods. They had to skirt the white heaps of hailstones, they had to skirt the water that stood in the hollows, they had to skirt the streams that flowed down all over. Because of them they often had to make headway by leaping from rock to rock, and often had to walk through flowing streamlets. The grandmother surrendered her own garments to the water and the filth of the ground to protect the children's clothes, and help the little ones get along more easily. The brown girl came with them.

When they came near the woods, they saw men emerge from them and hurry across the meadow. As the men approached, they saw that it was their father, leading all his farmhands and manservants. They were carrying poles sticks and dry clothes.

When the father came closer, he cried, "There are the children, thank God, they're alive. Mother, where on earth did you shelter them?"

"Under bundles of dry brush," replied the grandmother.

Black-Locks and Brown-Locks, in their soaking wet clothes, went up to him as they would in the mornings before breakfast, and kissed his hand. Blond-Locks stood where she was, old enough to grasp that that was not proper here.

The father took the children in his arms, kissed them on the cheeks, looked them over, and said, "You poor things!"

The strange girl stood at a distance, just as she always stood at the edge of the hazel bushes, upright and stiff.

"Mother," said the father, "we thought you must have sought shelter in the forest behind a stout trunk or a pile of wood. And so as soon as the hail stopped we went into the forest, taking a bundle of dry clothes to dress the children in, and we looked everywhere along the path, and called your names. When we couldn't find you, and no voice came in reply, I quickly sent a few farmhands for poles and ropes, because I thought you might be on the far side of the brook, which always swells at such times, and we might need those tools to cross the water. When the farmhands had returned, we pressed onward. I was greatly afraid, but I also had great hope in you, dear Mother, that you would have found a place to keep all of you safe."

"I'll tell you shortly how it all happened," his mother said, "but let's keep walking. The children can't change their clothes here, and they mustn't stand around in their wet things. As they walk, they'll warm up, and the damp won't harm them."

"And you're soaked too, dear Mother," their father said.

"I'm a woman of our country's age-old mountains," the grandmother replied, "the damp doesn't harm me. I got wet, my child, when I was just a few years old, I got soaked when I was a little girl, and how often have I worn wet clothes for days on end because I had to work, and you were still small, and your father was already ailing. But send a farmhand at once to run home as fast as he can and reassure your poor wife, who'll be dying of fear for the children."

The father did so at once. The farmhands had gathered in a close circle around the father the children and the grandmother. One man was sent on ahead, and the others set out on their way. The father the children and the grandmother walked in front, and the farmhands followed. The father led Blond-Locks and Brown-Locks by the hand, the grandmother led Black-Locks. Now she told him what had happened on the nut-hill, and how they had come to the place where he had found them.

"But you're all wet yourself," she finished.

"Because we went up into the forest in the cloudburst," he replied, "just as soon as the hail had let up."

Now they entered the forest, and it was a horror to behold.

Just as a mulch is made of fir twigs in years when drought or other misfortunes keep the grain from growing, the entire ground was covered with heaps of pine branches; many a stout bough lay among them, struck and broken in several places, on the trunks rents could be seen in the bark, so that here and there the white wood showed, and a faint scent of resin pervaded the woods, as when conifer wood is sawn or split. The hailstones lay mingled with the litter and covered by it, and here amid the tree trunks they breathed out an inexpressible cold which out in the open had not been felt so keenly. The father and the farmhands had to search for the path, which was covered with litter and could not be seen.

They emerged from the forest back into the open, and walked down to the crags from which the house and the fields could be seen.

The orchard had vanished, only scattered trunks loomed with maimed arms. The green was gone, and the fields beyond the orchard looked as though they had been badly harrowed.

The father and the children walked down the sandy slope.

There they saw that all the panes of the hothouses were destroyed, and inside, where flowers had stood in pots and tubs, lay white heaps of hailstones. The windows of the house that faced westward had been shattered, the tile roofs and the shingle roofs had been smashed, so that in places they looked like sieves, and in places had great breaches through which the underlying timber showed. On the weather side the ornamentation and the plaster had been beaten from the walls, yet the walls did not look new, as they had before they were plastered, but rather as though gouged by hammers.

When they reached the end of the sandy slope they saw a white form hurrying through what once had been the orchard, running through wet grass through hailstones over fallen boughs to meet them at the corner of the hothouses.

It was the mother.

She ran toward the children and stared at them.

The children's cheeks had blossomed with a fine rosy flush from walking, and the hair that fell about their faces was wet and matted but beautiful.

"Father, Father," she cried, "you've brought them back to me."

"Yes, without blemish without harm," he replied.

"My God, my God, how good You are to give them to me. Oh Clementia, oh Emma, oh Sigismund!" the wife cried.

She snatched the children to her, she hugged them, she caressed them, and held all three in her arms.

"Mother, we haven't brought any nuts," the little boy said.

"But you brought yourself, you silly little child," his mother said, "and you're dearer to me than nuts made of gold."

"It was awful and almost magnificent," said Emma.

"Don't let me picture it, Father, I beg you—what might have come to pass!" said the mother.

"They sheltered beneath bundles of brush," replied the father, "but let us go into the house, I'll tell you everything, give them dry clothing and something to eat, so that their blood may return to its regular flow."

"Come then, children," said the mother.

She turned to walk through the orchard to the house. The children followed. She led all three by the hand, as well as she could manage. Then came the grandmother and the father, then the farmhands.

When they had reached the main entrance of the house, the father turned to the farmhands, thanked them, dismissed them, and told them they should put away the clothes they were wearing, change their attire, leave off from their work, and he would send each a glass of wine with his supper.

"And I thank you too," said the mother, who, at her husband's words, had stopped outside the house with the children, and turned around, "I thank you too and shall surely reward you for it."

"There's no need," said the head laborer, "we've done no more than our duty."

Now the farmhands began to disperse.

When the farmhands had gone their separate ways, giving the others a view of the path they had come by, they saw the brown girl standing some distance away in the orchard.

On first seeing the father and greeting him, with the farmhands standing all around, they had lost sight of her; on their way home, with the farmhands walking right behind the father the children and the grandmother, they had not seen her, and had thought that, as was her wont, she must long since have turned back. When the children saw her, they let go of their mother's hands, rejoiced to see the strange child standing in their garden, ran up to her and spoke to her.

But the mother asked, "Why, who is that?"

The father said that it was the brown girl from the high nut-hill, and told what the girl had done that day to protect the grandmother and the children.

Then he turned to the cluster of children, and said, "Come here, dear child, we'll show you every kindness."

At these words the girl slowly drew back from the children, and a little ways off she started to run, she ran back through the orchard, she ran around the hothouses, and a moment later they saw her running up the sandy slope.

The children went back to their parents.

"A pity that the child is so shy, and won't come closer," said the father.

"I'll catch the creature," said a farmhand.

At these words all three children gave a cry of fear and protest.

"Leave be," said the father, "today the girl rendered the greatest of services to my mother and my children. She ought not to be treated roughly at all, and now still less so, as long as she does not prove to be a harmful influence. We'll trace her and find her sure enough, and then she must be treated well, so that she comes to trust us, and we're sure to find a way to reward the child, and perhaps help her to lead a more useful life than she imagines."

Meanwhile the girl, like a stag, had reached the crest of the slope, could be glimpsed amid the crags for a moment, and then vanished.

Already day was turning to evening, and they worried about the child, especially as the grandmother had said that her right arm was bleeding. But the sky was brighter, with a silent haze suspended in it, and there was no threat of rain. The others had to agree with the father that the girl was best off if they let her do as she saw fit, that she was a creature of the woods whom the mountains and the hills could not harm, and that if they had her tracked or watched, she might come to greater grief than otherwise.

Now they went into the house. The mother took the children to an intact and sheltered room on the east side of the house, which, on receiving news from the farmhand who had been sent on ahead, she had even had slightly heated in view of the sudden cold. There the children were undressed, put into a warm bath for a few moments, and then dressed in perfectly dry, warmed clothes. Excited by the events, despite their exhaustion they did not yet go to bed, even once the candles were lit and they had taken their evening meal; when the grandmother had changed her clothes and come back in to join them, they sat around the table with their three nutcrackers and cracked the nuts that they still had on hand or that the grandmother had given them. They spoke of the storm too, and the way they spoke of it, it was clear that they lacked any notion of the danger they had been in. They saw the bundles of brush as something that was self-evident, that was simply there as the warm house was there in winter to keep them from freezing.

When asked if she hadn't seen the storm coming, the grandmother replied, "I didn't think the clouds meant a storm, and when it started to rain, it was too late to reach the woods."

Asked whether she had recognized the clouds as hail clouds, she replied, "I did have a hunch that those clouds might bring hail, but I looked for hazel bushes so dense that ordinary hail wouldn't have gotten through. It was the brown girl who carried up the bundles of brush."

"That image, and the vision of what might have happened had those bundles been brought home sooner, is a thing I shall thrust into the background and far away," said the father to the mother. "Since the children love the high nut-hill so dearly, since their grandmother likes to take them up it and it would be cruel to rob them of this pleasure, I shall buy a small piece of land there, and build a tiny cottage on it to serve as a shelter. Even if it's almost certain that our children will already be grown, might even be old before another hailstorm comes like the one that came today, why, even if, as seems likely, none will come for generations, as no hailstorm this awful was recorded for generations past—all the same, hail clouds shall always loom in your soul and mine each time our children are on the high nut-hill. If they are surprised by one, they can seek safety in the cottage, and if they spy a thunderstorm on their way home, the woods will give them the shelter they need, and we can be reassured when they go by that path, especially when care is taken to watch the clouds and the sky."

"They were watched often," the grandmother returned, "but when God chooses to perform a visible miracle to rescue little angels, so that we may be edified, all human precautions are vain. In my seventy years I've seen all the clouds there are in this land; but if the ones today didn't look just like the haze that rests blue on all the distant woods in the fall, gleaming white at the edges, descending into the valleys and down upon the land toward evening, but vanishing again by morning and letting the bright sun shine—then let me suffer the harshest punishment here and beyond. And this time of the year there've often been thunderstorms. An old proverb says 'The storms come home at the Nativity of Mary,' and today it's six weeks since that holy day. Your old father in his eternal rest will marvel if he learns, or when I come and tell him, that such a great, extraordinary storm came after the Feast of St. Gall, and that it battered the trees and the houses. It's a miracle, how God put the thought into the mind of that wild brown child to notice the clouds, and carry up the bundles."

"You're right, dear mother," the father replied, "what came could not have been expected. No one could have guessed what would happen, and it's fortunate that things took the turn they did. We were in the orchard, with the farmhands working in the neighboring fields, when the thunder came. When the first hailstones fell, the farmhands could only dash into the barn in amazement, and we into the house, and when it came roaring down, smashing the windows the walls and the roof, the children's mother fell into a faint on the carpet."

"Man is a flower," said the grandmother, "first he is a violet then a rose then a carnation, until at last he is an immortelle. And one who's meant to be an immortelle cannot perish as a violet, that is why the dark flower was there, so that the bright ones might live."

"Only the belief that you had almost certainly sought shelter in the dense woods, and hidden behind a stout trunk," said the father, "was able to comfort their mother and me, and stave off our despair."

"The dense hazel bushes would have sufficed," his mother replied, "but because they did not suffice, the bundles were there, and the hand that cut them was ordained long ago."

"When we called you in the woods to no avail," said the father, "I, too, was seized by horror."

"I say to you," his mother rejoined, "the hand was ordained to carry the bundles, just as the feet were once ordained to walk through the woods between Jericho and Jerusalem so that the beaten, wounded man who lay there could be tended to and healed."

"Amen, dear mother-in-law," the wife said, "that's a faith that comforts and eases the heart."

"Surrender yourself to it, and you shall fare well all your life," the old woman replied.

Meanwhile the children had continued their chatter, saying all sorts of things to the adults and among themselves, and understanding nothing of the earnest conversation that had been had on their account.

When it had grown late, when sleep dust began to gather in the pretty eyes, they were taken off to bed. Blond-Locks' bedroom was next to her parents', Brown-Locks' was on the opposite side, and Black-Locks could not yet bear to part from her grandmother; she slept in the old woman's bedroom, drifting off before the eyes that watched over her bed, and waking as those same eyes gazed at her eyelids, waiting for them to open. The first two children were taken to their bedchambers, the grandmother took Black-Locks in her arms, and, after all had said good night, carried her down the hall to their bedroom. What prayers the parents offered before the image of Christ on the cross, no one knows; when they pour out their joy or pain before God, it remains a marital secret.

The next morning a cool day dawned. Cloudbanks drifted steadily from where the sun sets to where it rises, and it often seemed that the sun would soon break through, that the clouds would part and give way to the blue sky, but once again new clouds formed, covered the patches that had thinned, and drifted off toward the east. Yet no rain fell. The vast quantities of hailstones that had descended on the region consumed warmth, and so the cold steadily condensed the vapors in the air and gave rise to the never-ending clouds.

The first thing the father undertook in the morning was to have the hothouses cleaned out. The hailstones were shoveled into wheelbarrows and taken to an old quarry which the father was trying to fill by using it as a dump for all the solid refuse from the house, such as broken dishes, or from the fields, such as cleared-away stones. The hailstones were taken there because there was no good place for them anywhere. The plants they hoped to salvage were set to one side, while the others, along with the potsherds, were taken to the quarry. Farmhands were sent to the attic to inspect the damage there, while others, together with the maids, cleared the orchards of the branches that had fallen from the battered fruit trees. A messenger was sent for the glazier. The father examined the trees to see whether any could be saved. If they could, it must be done soon, before autumn had advanced too far and the cold thwarted the trees' revitalizing powers.

The children went out into the cool air with their grandmother. The vast numbers of little glass wafers that lay on the west side of the house were like the tiny sparkling wafers they liked to pry from the rocks on the sandy slope and elsewhere. They did not recognize the trees of the orchard from their stumps, and could not remember what fruits the trunks had borne. In the open fields they saw people busy removing the heaps of hailstones that still lay here and there in the hollows. At the brook through the meadows, which had receded, though its waters had not yet cleared, they saw that the willow twigs had been beaten down and washed away, that rocks and mud lined the edges of the meadow, and that dead fish lay there with their white bellies turned up.

The day before had been like summer; now the depths of fall had come.

In the afternoon the father went to the parson who lived half an hour away in the parsonage by the little parish church, and asked him about the brown girl.

The parson knew nothing. No such thing had been described in the parish register or the school books, nor seen among the children of the parish.

Now the father went to the huntsman, who often roamed the fields woods and meadows, and ought to know all the things that were there.

But he knew nothing either.

There had been bands of people, he said, but always in the higher-lying forests that stretch across to Bavaria, wandering through the lands along the forest edge. And he said the next huntsman from the regions beyond did not know anything either.

The father returned home empty-handed.

The days that followed were just as cold and sullen. Clouds kept coming, glimpses of sun were rare, and the wind, though not strong, was raw. On the roofs the workers hammered the laths and shingles into place, or inserted the tiles. Finally the glaziers came, having at first been delayed by all the work to be done, and the great hall was given over to them as a workshop for producing all the windows for the house and the hothouses. The masons worked on the outside of the house so that all would be in perfect repair before the cold season came and most of the inhabitants departed. The father was busy aiding the workers, binding up the injured trees, or painting coatings on their trunks. The maids had to tidy the areas in front of the house.

At last, after the storm's lingering afterthroes, deep in the fall came better days that might be called quite warm for the season.

The father himself urged the children to go up the high nut-hill. He said he would come along in the hopes of seeing the brown girl. He wanted to show her his gratitude.

The children went with their grandmother up the high nut-hill as always. Their father accompanied them.

They walked up through the swath of stumps that stood there pathetically and would stay like that all winter.

They did not see the brown girl.

They went up to the peak, they went to the stout old hazel root, at last they went to the place where they had sheltered from the hail. The bundles of brush were still lying there. The father proposed that together they should carry the bundles back to the place they had been taken from. He found the place after some searching, and they put the bundles back on the pile. Blond-Locks could carry one all by herself, and Black-Locks and Brown-Locks carried one together, with the grandmother helping. When all that was done, they stayed on the hill a long while, going to this place and that, and waiting. But the brown girl did not come. Then they went home.

The father went with the children up the high nut-hill a second time, showed them the place where he planned to build the cottage, and waited; but the brown girl did not come this time either.

And so he went several times; but the brown girl was nowhere to be seen.

Then the children went up the high nut-hill alone, and their grandmother went with them.

The sun shone warmly, the sky was blue, the brook through the heath was clear, with the gray quick fish at play, and when the children reached the fence, the brown girl ran up between the leaf- and branch-less stumps of the hazels birches and ash trees, and came to join them. They all gazed at each other with joy in their eyes, and when the children went up and touched the brown girl's arm and her ribbons, she took Blond-Locks' hair in both hands, and held it tight, and then took Black-Locks' curls, and held them. Brown-Locks, bolder, because the brown girl had once carried him, took her finger, and held it, and the brown girl let him; he took her hand, and she let him do that too. She went with them up the high nut-hill, and they gazed far and wide, and the grandmother told stories. The brown girl spoke words, and the children understood them. They gave her cake bread and the other things they had brought. The girl had nothing to give them, and held out her empty hands.

The brown girl wore the same outfit she had always worn, but it had been ruined in the storm, it was dirty and wrinkled.

The grandmother told them of the trees that had fallen down the hill, yet had not ceased to live—then she told them of the kings with the three thrones—then of the wheat that failed to bloom—then she spoke of the distant lands whose high mountains were completely out of sight—and at last of the carts and tools made without metal, which had been used to till the fields long ago.

Then they started on their way back home.

The sun still shone warmly as they walked down the hill, the sky was blue, the shadows were long, for it was deep fall by now, the grass was turning yellow, and the gray quick fish in the clear brook in the hollow played as merrily as in summer.

The brown girl had gone with them. She had gone with them down the high nut-hill, she had gone with them across the brook in the hollow, and went with them across the grayish turf through the woods through the crags and down the sandy slope. And when they had come to the hothouses in the garden, she said a few sweet words, and ran back up the sandy slope, and was seen no more.

The children told their parents that this time the brown girl had come, and gone with them.

Now they went as often as they could up the high nut-hill, and

the strange girl always came, and they played and cuddled. They
brought the brown girl pretty things. And the brown girl brought
them motley stones, she brought them late blackberries, in her vest
she carried hazelnuts she'd gathered in the summer, or brought them
a mottled feather from a vulture or a black one from a raven.

When the children went home, the brown girl always went with
them as far as the hothouses, and they held hands and bantered. At
the hothouses they would embrace and caress, and the brown girl
would run back up the sandy slope.

When it was night, and the children sat at the table by candlelight,
they spoke of the strange girl, and argued over who loved her best.

The grandmother told the parents about the strange girl, and the
father and mother heeded what she said, and noted it well in their
own way.

The season grew later and later. The fine threads spun on the turf
and between the junipers had vanished, the berries of the moors that
had gleamed so red and white in the fen-sedge and alongside the black
earth were finished, the late lingonberries spared from the hail in the
lee of a rock or a tree were gone, their bushes and the stout blueberry
shrubs were withered and weedy, the woods had turned transparent,
the mountains were red, in the morning white frost covered the surroundings, or the long fog came, and the sun, rising late, could barely
disperse it to give a glimpse of the hilltops before setting; or the frosty
clouds came, pouring the rain down in little drops, and when they
passed, the high far forest was dusted with white.

Then one day the big carriage was rolled out and packed, all the
necessities were stowed away in it, and the father and the mother got
in, wrapped in cloaks and warm clothes, the children got in, and they
all drove away.

The children wept as though great pain and great sorrow had been
inflicted on them.

When they had gone a long way, when they had passed through
villages market towns and cities, and seen forests and rivers, their
grief at last subsided, and they spoke and chatted until they entered
the big city, the tall houses loomed with their sparkling windows,

throngs of people walked about in fine clothes, and exquisite wares and precious trinkets glittered under panes of glass fronting the shops.

When the white shrouds had passed from the mountains and valleys and the sky was blue and smiling again more often than it was somber and clouded, when the sun was already rising higher, and shining down more strongly, the carriage came driving back up to the manor in the hill country, and the father and mother and children got out.

There was not the least blade of grass yet, there was not the least leaf; the fields were bare, only the winter grain, already stirring, laid out green panels on the brown earth; and some mornings there was still a slight frost, so that the path seized up, and spikes of ice gleamed at the edge of the puddles: but the sun shone quite cheerfully, triumphing a bit more each day, and each day it filled the children's and grandmother's rooms at the country manor more beautifully with light and warmth.

Once the city clothes had been put away, and the country clothes taken out of the wardrobes, it was found that things had to be altered. The hems of the girls' dresses had to be let down to make them longer, Brown-Locks' jackets had to be let out, and Blond-Locks' Black-Locks' and Brown-Locks' straw hats had to be put away and new ones had to be ordered.

When the sun was already shining quite warmly, when the summer grain was being sowed in the harrowed ground, when it was dry, and the sheen of rocks and fields sparkled in the spring sun, the children clamored to go up the high nut-hill. The grandmother dressed them in warmer clothes than they had worn in the summer, put on warmer things herself, and took them up the high nut-hill. They did not take along their hazel rods with the hooks, for they never took them except when the nuts were ripe. All they carried were the little baskets on their arms. They walked up the sandy slope, they walked through the crags and the forest. As they crossed the gray heath, the brown girl came walking toward them from afar. They rejoiced, they exulted, they caressed, and Brown-Locks wrapped his little arms around the brown girl's neck and held her tight.

But it was not just the children who had changed while they were gone, a change had occurred in the brown girl as well. Just as the hems of their clothes had had to be let down so that they would fit again, the brown girl's green hose were now too short; she had grown taller and more slender, and held her bare arms close to her body. Her abundant black hair had always been cut short before, but she no longer wore it that way; now she, too, had curls that hung down her neck, just as the children had.

They climbed up the nut-hill, they roamed far and wide, they saw every place they had there, and gazed out at the hills of the countryside.

There was no new grass on the ground, but it was dry; there was not a single leaf on the battered branches, but the pure air played about them, and the sun shone down on them kindly.

When the children went home, the brown girl went with them as far as the hothouses, and then she ran back.

Now, as always, the children climbed the high nut-hill often, and often the strange girl came.

Little by little the sun coaxed green color onto the earth. The meadows turned green, mingled with myriads of yellow white red blue flowers. The fields turned green as the new seed sprouted, showing its light-green hue, and the winter grain went on growing, adding its dark green. The father had sent for many plants and shrubs, which now stood in the hothouses alongside those that had survived, and it was as though no damage had ever been done. From the mutilated trees many branchlets grew forth, as beautiful and vigorous as though the stripping of the boughs had been no misfortune, but rather as though a wise gardener had pruned them so that now they would burgeon all the better. The father had grafted twigs onto many of the severed branches, and each sported two or four big leaves. In the forest in the thickets above the sandy slope and even in the gray heathy hollow everything was stirring. The branches sprouted forth as though to make up for lost time, jostling and striving upward. At last, when the earth was green all around, and the branches had grown longer, blossoms came too, later and sparser than in other years, but they were there, almost sweeter and more trusting than in earlier times.

One day in the fullness of spring, when all was blooming and fragrant, and human hearts rejoiced, as the children were coming home from the high nut-hill, accompanied by the brown girl, and had come as far as the hothouses, Blond-Locks seized the brown girl's hand with a grave look in her eyes. Brown-Locks took her by the arm. Blond-Locks looked the brown girl in the face and said, "Come with us, come with us."

Brown-Locks joined in, "Come with us, come with us."

The brown girl looked at the children and took a step forward.

Brown-Locks was overjoyed; he went on a step ahead and said coaxingly, "Come with us, come with us."

The brown girl followed hesitantly. She went from the hothouses on toward the trees, she went along the gravel path through the green of the garden, she went across the sandy yard by the house, she went up the stairs, and stood on the carpet in the room where guests were received.

There was no one there. As soon as they had come up the stairs the grandmother had gone into another room.

The strange girl stood there, and opened her big eyes still wider, and gazed at the mirror on the wall at the clock at the cabinet, where beautiful vessels stood, at the tables and chairs and armchairs and at the marvelous carpet.

The children ran to fetch sweet milk in a bowl, and fine wheaten bread and little silver spoons. The strange child drank the milk from the bowl, picked up a piece of bread, took a bite, and ate it that way.

The children brought their toys and showed them. The brown girl did not know what to make of them. The children brought their nutcrackers too, their good clothes, and their ribbons.

At last the mother came too, in a fine white dress, bringing candied fruits on a tray, and offered them to the strange girl.

The brown girl shrank away to stand straight-backed against the wall. She did not move a hand, she stared at the fruits and left her arms dangling at her sides.

At that the mother turned around again and left the room without another word.

The children went up to the strange girl and caressed her, and she returned their caresses, and after this had gone on for a while, after the children had spoken, after the strange girl had replied, and kept her eyes fixed on the door, they all ran through the door, ran down the stairs, ran through the garden, and behind the hothouses the strange girl ran up the sandy slope by herself.

What happened that day happened again another day. When the children had been on the nut-hill, when the strange girl had come to them, when they had gone homeward as far as the hothouses, Brown-Locks held the strange girl by the arm, tugged her after him, and begged her to come with them. The brown girl let herself be tugged, she followed the boy willingly, they went through the garden, they went up the stairs, and this time they went into the children's play-room. There the brown girl was even persuaded to sit down. She sat at the boy's side, she let him give her cake prunes milk butter and honey. Once they had eaten, once they had shown their spinning top, once they had tried out a shuttlecock and opened up a picture book, they went back out again, the children accompanied the brown girl to the hothouses, where they kissed and hugged her as always, took their leave, and let her run up the sandy slope.

By now the summer was well underway. The high nut-hill was covered all over with green branches. What had happened in the father's orchard had also happened here. The battered trunks of the hazels the birches the ash trees the alders sought to replace their lost limbs by sending up their sap, and sprouted twigs that grew quickly, turned stout, and bore leaves whose size and dark color had never been seen on the nut-hill before. The few branches left from before covered themselves in nuts that clustered densely in fat bunches on the twigs, as though they had to shoulder the duty of those that had been lost, and bring into the world as many nuts as they possibly could. These nuts were still greenish and whitish, but already they were taking on a faint blush of red.

At the same time the father finished building his shelter. He had bought a piece of land on the east side of the mountain, where storms most seldom came. He had built the cottage to have windows with iron shutters toward the south and the west, and the door toward the east. Inside, a bench stood by the wall on the north side, with a little table in front of it. And the house had chairs and footstools as well.

When they were up on the nut-hill, the children had often gone to the building site to watch the men at work. The brown girl stood by too, and observed what was taking form there.

It had not been painted or plastered on the outside; it looked like the boulders or the heaps of rocks that lie up on the nut-hill. The roof was painted dark brown. Inside the father had had it done in a beautiful green, with a nosegay of wild roses of chamomile and cornflowers painted in each corner. When it was finished, the father accompanied the children to the top of the nut-hill to dedicate the cottage. They stepped inside. The children were overjoyed to see the nice little room and all the nice things. The grandmother had brought in her bag a bottle of milk cake in a tin butter and other things along with dishes and silverware. As the kind little crone in the fairy tale had done for Roland's squires, she spread over the table a white cloth that gleamed like the blossoms of the cherry tree, at each place she set a little plate on the table, laid a little white napkin on each plate, and laid a little spoon knife and fork alongside. Then she poured milk from the bottle into a little jug, and laid a silver ladle alongside it, then she put pure honey in the white cups, so that it pooled in them like gold, then she put butter on a plate and set a fine white loaf at each place. Now the children dined in their house, and the father was their guest. When they had finished eating, the leftovers were cleared away and packed up. The children were well pleased with this afternoon tea. The brown girl had not come today, and the father wondered why the girl always failed to come when he was on the high nut-hill.

Now the children went up the hill for the sake of the little cottage. They were in it always, and when the brown girl came, she had to come along inside, sit on a little chair, and dine with them. Meanwhile the strawberries had ripened, and once the children had gathered them in their birch-bark baskets in the woods on the forest edge and up above the sandy slope, back in the cottage the grandmother put them on one of the plates that were kept in the table drawer, and they ate their afternoon meal with pleasure.

But gradually their delight in the little cottage waned. They went inside less and less often, and after some time had passed it was as though it were no longer there. Once again they sat by their old stout hazel root, and when they were not sitting there, they walked about, went into the bushes, collected various things and little stones, and talked with their grandmother.

When the brown girl came, they would go home earlier than usual because the girl would come along, would go with the children to their room, and stay there with them, and eat and talk, and go away again when evening came.

On these occasions the mother often passed through the room, but did not approach the brown girl, and did not speak to her. She dressed in a pale frock, such as Black-Locks wore, her curls were combed back, as Black-Locks had hers, so that she resembled her in all things, a grown-up Black-Locks. Like this she once brought in a plate with many fine large strawberries, not ones that grew in the woods or on the heath, but that were raised by the father in his own beds, which were covered with glass in the spring. The mother had had little plates set at all the children's places. She went to Blond-Locks' plate, put strawberries on it with a spoon, and Blond-Locks began to eat. She went to Black-Locks' plate, put strawberries on it, and Black-Locks began to eat. She went to Brown-Locks' plate, put strawberries on it, and Brown-Locks ate. She went to the brown girl's plate, put strawberries on it, and the brown girl began to eat. Then she went back out the door. Another time she came again, once again a Black-Locks, bringing all sorts of things, and mingled with the children. Now she did this more often, until the brown girl spoke with her too, grew more and more used to the house, played with the children in their room, and went with them into the orchard. Then the mother gave her a dress that was like her old one, only much finer, and with sleeves that came down to her elbows.

Now the father resumed his inquiries into the brown girl's origins. He asked neighbors and acquaintances, but they knew nothing about her at all. Then he resolved to ask the country folk the poor cottagers the pitch burners the wood dwellers. And so he climbed the maple hill that rose beyond the edge of his property, where two old people lived in a hut with a young son who made casks and barrels and was often in the woods. They knew nothing. He walked uphill along the stone wall and inquired at the stone-breakers' huts. The child must come from farther up, they replied. He went farther up, and asked. The girl might belong to the heath people, they said. He asked on the heath, and they said the girl might have come down from the moor huts. He asked on the moors. They knew nothing there. Now he came to the high forests. The woodcutters and pitch burners said that there were all sorts of people. When he described the girl, they all said that they'd seen her before, and when they described the girl, one described her one way, one another way, each in his own fashion. The father went back home again.

When the mother gently asked the girl herself, she was still, and said nothing. The children never asked. And so the time passed.

Sometimes the girl came to the house by herself now. When they opened the shutters in the morning, she would be standing wet in the orchard's dewy grass and waiting.

When the children had their lessons, she stood by and watched. One day she could suddenly recite the letters, and then she could read. More often now she was questioned on what she had learned, and encouraged to keep on learning.

When the grandmother went out with the children, she clung to her apron just like the others, and went along. But she could never be persuaded to spend the night in the house and sleep in a little bed.

And when the summer drew on, when the grain ripened and was gathered in the barns, when the oats stood golden, their filaments trembling, and their husks opening white beaks, which is always the time when the hazelnuts ripen, the children would climb the high nut-hill in the sunshine carrying their hazel rods. They would go in the afternoon, when they had learned their lessons and written their exercises. The brown girl had a long rod with a well-made hook attached. They went up the sandy slope, they went through the crags through the thickets and brush, they went through the woods across the gray heath and through the gray stones, where the brook was as gentle again as it had always been, where the little fish played, the dragonflies darted, and the red flowers grew, ones that would form seed capsules filled with white wool, they went across the talus slope into the hazelnut preserve. Now they had to look hard to find the few places with nuts, and they called to each other when they found them, and reached for the nut-covered branches with their hooks, and the brown girl swung herself up to pull down the highest branches with her rod so that Brown-Locks could gather the nuts and put them in his leather satchel. Then they looked for their favorite spots on the nut-hill, where there were all sorts of things in the stones in the sand and in the bushes, and sat for a while by the old root as usual.

And when the oats had vanished at last from the fields, when the hazel bushes lost their color, and the leaves wrinkled and rolled up, when the white patches of stubble on the hills turned brown, when nothing was left in the fields but potatoes cabbage and turnips, when not an apple or a pear was left in the branches of the trees, when even the leaves of those trees were falling, when the flowers that the father had in pots outside the house were taken back into the hothouses, when the blue juniper berries turned bluer and bluer on their bushes, and the green ones swelled and took on a dewy film, when the gossamer spun out again, and the grandmother grew sadder and sadder, and stroked all the children's curls more and more tenderly—they knew that it was time, that they must soon part, gloomy autumn and fog would cover the surroundings, snow and cold would come, and it would be a long time before they could be together.

When this time had come, and the last day had passed when they could be together still, they bade the brown girl farewell when she left them, they embraced her, and wept, and Brown-Locks gave the strange girl his picture books, and his trumpet.

And they drove off again, the grandmother standing grief-filled by the carriage, the farmhands and maids standing by the carriage, the father with tearful eyes kissing the grandmother's wrinkled cheeks, kissing her hand, as he still did as a grown man, and climbing into the carriage before the horses set the wheels in motion.

The long winter passed, and the snows ceased that had covered the house the garden the hothouses the sandy slope the woods the fields the high nut-hill all the hills and all human habitations, the sun returned, the harsh winds gave way to milder breezes, and the father the mother and the children returned to their house in the country.

They found all as they had left it. The grandmother was healthy, all the farmhands and maids were healthy, and all the manor's animals were alive and frisky.

The brown girl had grown still taller, and her beautiful black hair fell even more abundantly and thickly down her neck. The children ran toward her when she came into the house, they greeted her and gave her all the things they had brought her from the city.

Now country life commenced again, they were together, they learned their lessons, they worked, and when, as in the past year, the grass sprang up in the meadows and on the marges, when the swallows came, with their brown throats and white breasts, and darted low along the path, and shot back up into the air, when the robin perched in the bushes, bobbing its upper body and warbling out its voice, when all the trees were covered with blossoms and little tufts of leaves, and no sign was left of the catastrophic hailstorm, when the fields were green, and the white clouds shone down upon them—then they walked about again, and amused themselves as they had done in previous times.

Now even when the father joined the children the brown girl was not shy, and she did not shrink away from the farmhands and the maids who walked about and worked in the house the garden and the fields.

When, in this way, the summer had drawn far along, one day when the sun was starting to set, when the children had returned from their walk and had their afternoon tea, when the strange girl had gone, and the children and their mother sat by themselves in the room facing the garden, with the father away on a journey—Blond-Locks kept saying that something smelled bad, as though nasty things were being burned. The whole house was searched. There was no fire upon the hearth, nor in the fireplaces either, none being needed in the heat of high summer. Nor was any fire burning in the maids' fireplaces to heat irons for ironing or to boil washing or anything of the sort. When they looked out the windows, all was calm and peaceful, from chimneys near and far not a wisp of smoke was rising.

The mother discussed the matter with the children, and they wondered how anyone could imagine such things, Blond-Locks defended herself, others attacked her, and as they were arguing, a cry came from outside, then several at once, and when they all ran to the window to see what had happened, a dense fuming knot of smoke was rising from the barn roof as a murky black column; it whirled swiftly, and a moment later flashing fire shot up within it, and as the children and their mother watched, it ran in bright little flames, busy and crackling as though the summer heat had made everything ready, from the barn along the roof ridge above the stables and wagon sheds toward the house; all at once there was a burst as when a sheet of paper laid on burning coals suddenly catches fire across its whole surface, and from the entire roof of the stables and wagon sheds one great broad flame rose upward, while the barn roof was a body of embers and flame. The farmhands and maids ran about below, screaming, and the spruce wood of the rafters and the laths cracked hideously in the fire.

"Children! Come to me!" cried the mother.

"Mother, Mother, Grandmother, Sigismund, Clementia, Emma!" cried the children.

They darted back into the room, they snatched things to rescue and knew not what they did. They took a doll, a rag, or whatever else fell into their hands, whether it had any value or not. The mother quickly unlocked a desk that stood in the next room, took out a little box, rushed back into the room, bundled the children together, laden with various things, and led them down the front stairs, which faced away from the fire, and out into the open. Having passed through the front door, now they really heard the roaring rushing and crashing of the terrible power on the far side of the house behind them, raging in their property. The still air pressed down the smoke, which settled on the west side of the house, and the setting sun shone through like a bloody disk. Many people, whether from the manor or already come running from elsewhere, it was impossible to tell, hustled about helter-skelter.

The mother led the children to the east side of the garden. As the heat had caused a rising wind, and the wind tossed up fiery scraps of burning shingles of straw hay or the people's linens and garments, like wicked spirits whirling in the air and scattering, the mother had to shelter her children from the falling flames so that their clothes would not catch fire. Thus she led them away under cover of dense trees and bushes. She took them to the outermost arbor on the east side of the garden, where two luxuriant lindens stood, warding off every spark that might fall in that direction.

"Children, stay here now, don't leave," said the mother, "whatever things you may hear. Nothing can happen to you here, I must go now, but I'll come back soon. Take care of this box while I'm gone."

"Yes," said the children, "we'll stay here."

At these words the mother left the arbor and strode straight to the manor yard; and as her husband was not there, she took his place, urging the farmhands, who were nearly out of their minds, to go into the stables and bring out the horses, so that they would not be smothered, and tether them to trees so that they would not run back into the fire. Some of the people had already done the same for the cattle. Horse after horse was rescued from the burning stable, the mother conducted the operation, and told them where to tether the horses. Someone had loosed the dog. He came to the wife in great bounds, surged up against her, and showed his delight, as though he knew there had been great danger and the wife had escaped unharmed.

When there was a moment to spare the wife ran into the garden to look for the children, and when she had made sure they were in the arbor, she went back to the fire.

At last she found a maid she could send to the children, to stay with them in the arbor.

Meanwhile the farmhands had rescued all the animals.

The doves zigzagged through the air, and like gnats flitting around a candle they fell, wings singed, into the flames.

The wagon sheds abutted the woodshed, where huge supplies of wood were piled up for the winter and for cooking. If that wood caught fire, the carriages would be lost along with the sheds. And so the wife had the carriages dragged out from their sheds and brought to safety under the trees in the garden.

While the people were busy with that, a sudden new crashing and crackling was heard high above, and looking up they saw the roof of the living quarters in flames. There was a fire-squirt in the house, there was water available, partly in the house and partly in the nearby brook; the squirt had been trained on the house roof all the while, and the manor staff and the neighbors who had hurried up in time had kept up an adequate water supply: but the heat of the summer had dried out the timbers, the blaze on the adjoining roofs was too powerful, the jet of water nearly evaporated in the air, the drops that reached the roof were powerless, and once the timbers caught fire, the whole roof was soon a rushing crackling seething volcano. Now it was useless to spray water into the flames; indeed, it only enlivened them. And so the wife ordered that the fire-hooks, of which there were plenty in the house, be used to tear down as many burning rafters as possible.

The wife had little fear for the rooms below, for their ceilings were coated with very thick plaster, and the embers that fell onto it from the burning roof could be removed with the hooks, and later with shovels, before the plaster became so hot that the girders would be seized, catch fire, and cause the ceiling to collapse. Thus she had not ordered things to be removed from the rooms, except what the maids had carried out on their own out of unbidden zeal.

Now that the men had put the fire-hooks in position, and stood ready to tear down the rafters as soon as the fire began to expose them, the wife felt that she could take a moment for herself, as no part of the house could be seized by the flames now, and she went off to see to her children in the arbor.

As she approached the arbor, Emma and Clementina came running toward her, crying, "Mother, we didn't leave, and we took care of the box."

"Where is Sigismund?" the mother cried.

"He must be with Grandmother," said Emma.

"Was Grandmother here with you in the arbor?" the mother asked.

"No," said the children.

"Wasn't Grandmother here with you in the arbor, didn't she go off and take Sigismund with her?" the mother asked again.

"Mother, you didn't take Sigismund downstairs with us," the two girls cried as one.

"Then he must be with Grandmother," the mother said, and called out into the garden, "Grandmother, Grandmother!"

At the very moment she was called, the grandmother came toward the arbor; either she had heard the call, or she had already been coming to join the children.

"Where is Sigismund?" the mother called out to her.

"Isn't he with you?" the grandmother replied.

"No," said the mother.

"I heard him when someone shouted 'Fire!'" said the grandmother, "I heard him call for me outside my room, and at the same time I heard your voice too, calling the children, and I heard you go down the front stairs with them, so I thought he was with you; I locked the door to the passage that leads from the children's room to mine, went out the other door, locked it behind me, and went down the back stairs."

A jolt flashed through the mother.

From the children's room one door opened onto a passage that led nowhere but the grandmother's room. The door from the children's room to the passage tended to latch shut, and Sigismund's small strength was not enough to open it. Probably he had hurried from the children's room to the grandmother's room to warn her that the door had latched shut behind him, had found the grandmother's room locked, had tried to go back, could not get into the children's room, and was now trapped in the passage.

As these thoughts shot through the mother's mind, she cried, "Oh holy heavenly mercy, then he went down the passage to your room to help you, the door latched shut behind him, he couldn't get into your room, and now he's trapped in the passage. All the children were laden down with their odds and ends, and I took them down the stairs without noticing whether there were two or three of them. He might suffocate, the plaster might burn through. The key is in the lock inside the children's room, I must go up and let him out."

Having cried out these words, she ran toward the burning house without heeding the other children. She ran straight through all the plants and amid the rain of sparks. The grandmother followed her. The maid could not hold the children back; they ran toward the fire too, and the maid ran with them.

By the time the mother reached the fire, the rooms were in far greater danger than she had thought. The roof truss was nearly consumed, or at least had already collapsed. An awful mound of embers, its heat rippling the air, rested on the ceiling of the rooms. There was nothing but a layer of plaster between these embers and the girders; they could easily heat up, and burn, and the roof could collapse. The men with the fire-hooks had done extraordinary work. They had torn down a great many of the rafters, and the debris lay about the house, burning and smoking; but some hung on up above as their joints still held, and it was impossible to extricate them. By now night had fallen, and in the murky darkness the glare of the fire and the smoke the glow of the jutting beams and the gleam of the surrounding trees were doubly eerie.

The mother ran straight to the door behind which the stairs led up to the children's room. She meant to go up to the room, turn the key in the door to the passage, and let the boy out. But when she reached the door, a pile of torn-down beams was lying in front of it, burning.

It was impossible to get through.

"Drag the wood away, Sigismund is in the house!" she shouted to the men nearby.

The men understood. They came up to the flaming heap, sunk in their hooks, and tried to pull the beams away. But it was in vain. Some of the beams were still joined, and some had become snagged with others that had fallen, so that even with the greatest efforts the men would not have managed to drag away the conjoined mass any sooner than its entanglements would come loose on their own as it burned on.

"That won't do," cried the mother, "we'll have to go up the back stairs to your room, Grandmother, and get into the passage from there. Where do you have the keys?"

"I don't know, they must be in my handbag, I might have left it in the hothouses," the grandmother replied, "I'll go and get them."

"For heaven's sake, why did you lock the door?" cried the mother.

"To keep out the thieves," the grandmother cried, and hurried away with a farmhand.

There was still time; for all the windows of the house were still black, showing that the fire raging above had not yet broken into the rooms.

But the farmhand came running up and said that the grand-mother's keys were nowhere to be found.

The mother changed her plan. She went around the corner of the house to a side that faced the garden, covered with vine trellises, where there was an open window to the children's room. She pointed up at the window and cried, "A ladder, a ladder, so that someone can climb into the children's room!"

The farmhands ran to fetch a ladder. Others joined them. The ladders hung from a special frame under a little oaken roof near the wagon sheds. But there, in one ghastly serene flame that rose majestically into the air, the manor's entire supply of firewood was ablaze. It was impossible to come near. A man attempted it wrapped in a wet blanket, but he was hurled down by the blast of heat, and they had to rescue him with a fire-hook, dragging him back out from the hot air. A moment later the little roof over the ladders caught fire, and it and the ladders began burning.

The farmhands came back, and reported this to the mother.

At that she fell to her knees, spread out her arms and cried, "Then You rescue him, You who have the power and the fulfillment, and who cannot destroy an innocent life!"

In that instant a shrill cry rang out: "Brown-Locks, Brown-Locks!"

And before they knew it a dark figure had darted toward the house, scrambled up the vine trellises like a squirrel, and a moment later vanished through the window.

Everyone forgot what they were doing, or whatever they had in their hearts, and fixed their eyes on the window.

It was not long before two figures appeared at the window. Burning beams jutting out over the wall of the house above lit them up like torches. It was the brown girl and Sigismund.

At the sight all the bystanders cried out as one.

Emma and Clementia shrieked with horror and with joy.

But the children could not get down. The brown girl could have, but she could not get the boy down onto the vine trellises. Like a nocturnal scene that an artist has limned and lit by the glow from outside, they stood within the window's black frame.

"Sheets, sheets, tie sheets together!" several voices called up.

"There's a ladder," a cry was heard from below, "the ladder will do, it'll hold, it's sure to hold for children."

At that moment the head laborer and the groom pushed their way through the huddle of people, carrying up a ladder. It came from the wagons that had been saved through God's care and the wife's will, two lashed-together ladders from a harvest wagon.

It was leaned against the wall, and reached to the window.

First the brown girl climbed out of the window. She found a firm foothold on the rungs, and then she helped the boy out. Now the two children climbed quickly and nimbly down the ladder.

When they reached the grass, the brown girl knelt down in front of the boy, crouched back on her heels, and looked at him with her black eyes.

In the dark night and in the glow of the fire one would have seen those eyes sparkling with joy at his rescue.

The boy could not speak, he reeled, and looked as though he would fall.

The mother rushed up, took him in her arms, wiped his brow, and tried to comfort him.

At that moment the grandmother came too, running as fast as she could at her age, clothes disordered by her haste, holding the keys in her hand.

Seeing that the boy had been rescued, she joined the mother in ministering to him. The other children stood by, and many people came crowding up.

As the child was still half unconscious, the mother and grandmother lifted him up, brought him to the well in the garden, and laved his brow and temples with fresh water.

At this the boy recovered, and they brought him into the arbor where the children had been at the start of the fire.

While the mother was busy with the boy, examining him to see if he had suffered any injury, questioning him and calming him down, the old woman could be seen kneeling by the trunk of a fruit tree and praying with folded hands.

Little by little the child was soothed. The mother straightened his clothes and stroked his cheeks and his hair. The two sisters also stroked his curls and his cheeks, and caressed him.

The boy really had gone unharmed. He had indeed hurried from the children's room into the passage leading to the grandmother's room to go and tell her that there was a fire in the house and she must flee. As he often did, he had slammed the passage door behind him, and the latch had fallen into place. Unable to open the grandmother's door, unable to summon her with his cries, he went back. But then he saw to his horror that he had latched the door shut. With all his strength he tried to pull back the bolt, but the spring was too strong, and it was no use. At that he pounded his fists on the door to the children's room then the grandmother's door. He cried with all his might to be heard. But having done that for a while, with no one hearing, he sat down on the floor of the corridor and waited in the hope that someone would come and open the door for him.

He heard the roaring and rushing of the fire above him.

Then the brown girl came, led him away, and climbed down the ladder with him.

When he had fully recovered from his fright, the mother left him to the grandmother and the maids in the arbor and went off again to attend to the fire.

The men were tearing down the last of the beams. All the spraying with water was to no avail, and the embers heaped over the rooms of the master and his family would have burned through the ceiling; but while the mother was in the arbor, the pastor had come with the church ladders. Their iron hooks were fastened over the walls of the burning house, and the men climbed up and began using pokers to throw down the embers. They took turns working. As the embers diminished, the water that was sprayed up became more and more effective, in part smothering the blaze, in part restoring moisture to the dried-out, fissured plaster, so that it stopped transmitting so much heat to damage the girders. In this way the rooms were saved.

As the servants' rooms could not simultaneously receive the same attention, several of them were in fact gutted by the flames. But once it was clear that the master's rooms were safe, efforts were shifted to the servants' rooms, preventing the fire from spreading.

Then the beams and rafters that lay scattered around the house, burning, were dragged away and extinguished. And before midnight had come, the worst of it was over. Only the store of firewood burned on, a conflagration quiet but fierce. The fire-squirt merely fed the blaze, as the water turned to vapor and made the flames burn hotter. Dirt might have been shoveled onto the fire, but the heat prevented anyone from coming within throwing range. And so there was no choice but to set a watch around the fire, let it burn down, and merely take care that it should not spread anew. Watchmen were posted outside all the parts of the house as well, to make sure that no spark should be rekindled or carried onward. The stack of hay that stood smoldering in the burned-down barn could not be extinguished, but the fire-squirt kept the fire contained so that it did not revive, and was finally smothered in its ash.

Now that everything had thus far been calmed, and set to rights, the mother thought to put the children to bed. She went to the arbor, took her little box, took the children by the hand and led them behind the house to the hothouses. She had chosen the hothouses because no one knew the state of the rooms the fire had left unscathed. As it was summer, and some of the plants stood outside, one of the hothouses had room to spare. The mother had the maids fetch bedding blankets and all that was needed from the rooms. They even brought little tables chairs and footstools.

As they did, they also looked for the brown girl. In the confusion and fright and with the further efforts the fire had demanded of the mother, the girl had been forgotten. And now she was nowhere to be found. But they did not worry, thinking that she must have gone off again, as she had never before spent the night in the house.

Now the beds were made some on the hothouse benches some on the ground, and after the children had said their prayers, they were tucked away under their blankets, and watched the blaze from the heap of firewood gleaming in the panes of the hothouse before dozing off, peaceful and reassured.

The mother and grandmother sought a brief spell of rest as well.

At dawn the brown girl stood waiting in the garden. The children went out to her, and the grandmother and mother joined them. They went to all the parts of the grounds. The garden was a stable: horses oxen cows and calves had been tethered to the trees, with hay in front of them, for even before daybreak neighbors and other people had come with carts bringing hay straw and provisions; frightened chickens ran about amid the flowers and shrubs, and pigs rooted in the lawn. The walls of the house were black and begrimed, the sandy yard and the lawn in front of the house were black as a charcoal pile, the firewood shed was a heap of wet coal and ash, and faint, foul-smelling smoke was still rising from the hay.

When the children had seen everything, the mother went with them to the meadow where the carts that had brought donations were standing, along with the people who had driven them. The mother thanked them all from the bottom of her heart.

Then she instructed her people, and those who had gladly come to help, in the things that had to be done.

The children set up house in the hothouse, and a few things that had not been needed yesterday were brought there.

That afternoon the father came. He had seen the red of the fire in the sky that night. Thinking that it might be his home, he had authorized another man to handle his business, and set out. When he was almost there, he had learned that his manor had burned down, and he hired a horse to ride home, taking a shortcut along footpaths and farm roads.

When he saw his mother his wife and the children, when he learned that no one had perished in the fire, he was overjoyed, and did not ask what else he might have lost.

Now he set about repairing the damage.

First the ceilings of the rooms had to be examined. The girders proved to be good, and it turned out that they had not been damaged by the heat and the cracked plaster, nor had they suffered from the damp, so the mother the children and the grandmother moved back into their rooms. The next day a makeshift roof of boards was erected over the house for the interim.

Then the ground all around the house was cleared, to remove the sight of the filth and disorder. The animals were returned to their stalls, which had survived with their sturdy vaults and been aired to free them from the smoke and the stench. He had the hay completely extinguished, and then piled in a secluded spot to turn into compost. He also proceeded at once to have new panes cut for the broken windows, and he amply replaced the losses his servants had suffered, because they had taken such pains to save his house.

After all that had been done, they began to build.

Rafters were put up atop the house, and on the rafters carpenters hammered the laths into place, and tilers laid the roof tiles. The father had a masonry vault put in the barn, and equipped its roof hatches and other openings with iron shutters, so that in case of fire they could be closed, along with the barn doors, and the fire could be stifled. The outer walls were cleaned, freshly plastered, and whitewashed. The vine trellis, which the father had often meant to take down, because vines do not bear grapes in those regions, and the vine leaves are not the adornment they are in other lands, was not taken down, but rather made sturdier and more attractive, with the firm resolution to tend the vines properly. The lock on the door from the children's room to the corridor was replaced with a new one whose latch could not catch. The woodshed was also given a vault that could be closed on all sides with iron doors and shutters. The ladder shed was built within easy reach in the garden, its roof was painted red, and beneath it new ladders hung horizontally in all different lengths.

The whole summer was spent rebuilding, and once autumn had come, the house stood more beautiful and more imposing than ever before.

The cause of the fire could not be determined. As it had broken out in the barn, it had probably been due to some carelessness.

They went to the city earlier that year, because there were many things to take care of, and they went more anxiously than in previous times.

But none of their anxieties was borne out. When the spring breezes blew, they returned once more, and found everything safe and sound.

The mother had brought the brown girl fabric for pretty clothes, and handed it to her with a loving, tender gaze.

The father and the mother had decided to raise the brown girl, and guide her to whatever happiness she was capable of. They were very careful not to frighten her off, and let her do as she pleased, so that she would become more trusting.

She came often with the children, she came on her own, and once she had her new clothes, which were cut just like the old ones, she sometimes stayed overnight, in a little bed made up especially for her.

They presumed the girl's parents would offer no resistance, seeing how little care they took of her, seeing how they let her wander about, seeing how they never came forward, though they had to know that the child was often in the house, and they had to notice the new clothes she had been given.

They hoped to bind her to the house by exerting, as they always had, the gentle ties of indulgence and love, until such time as her soul would dwell in the house of its own accord, until she would never go away again, and yield her heart unreservedly.

Already the girl had joined in many of the children's lessons, and she had been questioned and drawn into the discussion without her noticing their intent, and the things she learned had been ordered and enlarged on. Now they made arrangements that the young priest who instructed the children in religion should come twice a week from the parsonage to introduce the girl to God and the practices of our sacred religion. The mother repeated his teachings, and spoke of sacred things to the child.

The girl learned with great passion, and just as she surpassed the children in physical skills and dexterity, and they emulated her, especially Sigismund, she learned different things from them when they were busy in their rooms, or when they were with their mother, or with the grandmother, or wandering about with her outside.

In this way several years passed. The brown girl grew more and more used to the house, she stayed there always, and hardly went away at all. She learned all sorts of crafts such as the other girls pursued, and engaged in the same activities as they.

She could not be persuaded to go with them to the city. In the winter she always stayed with the grandmother.

At last she was induced to wear girls' clothes. The mother bought the fabric for them, the fabric was made into dresses and decorated with ribbons according to her custom.

Now that she wore girls' clothes, she was shyer, and took shorter steps.

Little by little the children grew to be as tall as their parents. Now there were three Black-Locks. The mother, who had kept her beautiful, lustrous dark hair, was one; Clementia was the second and the brown girl the third. The father and Emma were Blond-Locks. The only Brown-Locks was Sigismund. And there was a White-Locks in the children's midst—the grandmother. Her gray hair had finally turned so white that when a curl chanced to peep out beside the white bonnet's ruffle, it could not be told apart from it.

Emma was now a beautiful maiden with an earnest gaze, with blue eyes in a head carried calmly, and an abundance of blond hair that she let dangle down her neck; she resembled a medieval portrait. Clementia was delicate and rosy, and beneath her black hair the sweet fire of her black eyes gazed straight from the soul. Sigismund was bold blithe and free, true to the meaning of his name, a mouth of triumph; for when his voice rang out, he captured hearts.

People came from the neighborhood, youths and maidens, friends even came from the distant capital to visit them in their remote manor. All were merry but the brown girl. Her cheeks looked as though she was ill, and her gaze was mournful. When all the others were merry, she sat in the garden and looked about with lonesome eyes.

One summer, on a very fine day when strangers were there, when they were engaged in dancing piano-playing games of forfeit and city pleasures in the manor's big parlor, the father and mother strolled off toward the sandy slope. There on a pile of sand in her pretty clothes lay the brown girl, teary eyes staring at the ground. The mother went closer and asked, "What is the matter?"

The girl straightened up a little; the father and mother had taken seats on a little bench by the sand pile, and it was as though she was sitting at their feet.

"Dear, precious girl," said the mother, "don't be sad, all will be well, we love you, we'll give you all your heart desires. You're our child, our dear child. Or if you still have a father and a mother, then tell us, so that we can do our best for them as well."

"Stura Mura is dead, and the high crag is dead," said the girl.

"Then stay with us," the mother went on, "here is your mother, here is your father, we'll share with you all we have, we'll share our heart with you."

At these words the girl burst into sobs so violent that they convulsed her, and it seemed that her heart would be crushed. Suddenly she fell face down in the sand, with her hands she balled together part of the hem of the wife's dress, and pressed this ball to her lips. Feeling, after a while, the wife's hand on her dense dark lovely locks, resting there with friendly pressure, she jumped up, lifted her arms, no longer so full and sleek, wrapped them tight around the wife's neck, kissed her on the cheek as though to mark it with lips and teeth, and went on weeping, so that the tears flowed down the woman's cheek and bedewed her dress. When gradually the outburst ebbed, when the girl leaned her head back and looked at the father, when she saw that he was holding her hand, but could not speak because his eyes swam with tears—then she, too, could speak no more, her lips trembled, her heart heaved in short spasms, and she withdrew behind the hothouses.

The father and mother did not follow the girl, so that she could calm herself on her own. They thought it would all work out in the end.

But it did not work out. They saw the girl walk up the sandy slope, and they never saw her again.

When some time had passed without the brown girl appearing, the parents and children thought she had merely gone off and stayed away longer than expected; but as her absence grew more worrying, the father made inquiries, and when the girl still failed to come, these inquiries were pursued by all possible means. But like the earlier inquiries, they bore no fruit. In the vicinity she was known as a girl who had always visited the children in the manor, and was almost regarded as a member of the family; farther away no one knew of her at all. All the people of the manor father mother children grandmother grieved, and the wound burned hotter and hotter.

But as the months and the years passed, the pain abated, and her figure, like others, sank deeper into the realm of the past.

But the girl could never be forgotten. All especially the children often spoke of her, and once many years had passed, once the grandmother had died, once the father had died, once the mother was a grandmother, once the sisters were wives in faraway places—when Sigismund stood there in the heights, where the brook with the gray fish now seemed quite small, where the high nut-hill seemed quite small, he seemed to sense the brown girl's shadow slip past him, he felt a deep ache in his heart, and thought: How often must she have come here, how often must she have waited all alone for her playmates to come, and how she bore back to her old world the pain that had stricken her in the new one. He thought: Only let her be granted much much good in this world.

ROCK MILK

IN OUR fatherland there stands a castle, of the sort in which certain regions abound, surrounded by a broad moat, so that in fact it seems to be standing on an island in a pond. Castles on flat ground tend to have such defenses surrounding them; having, that is, the defense of water, but lacking the kind possessed by their proud sisters atop lofty mountains and rugged cliffs. And the lesser security provided by a moat must be purchased with damp air croaking frogs and plagues of flies, while their exalted sisters enjoy not only the greater protection of the lofty cliffs, but the pure air and the view as well. Then again, the former can burrow into a whole bed of trees to shelter from winter storms, while the latter are abandoned to the onslaught of the winds like a pebble in the river to the water's endless smoothing. But since our fellow men have gradually shed their armor, since the invention of gunpowder, against which moats and lofty cliffs are useless, the mightiest are moving from the mountains and out of the ponds, leaving the ruins behind like torn discarded garments. Those who are not so rich and mighty, though, must inhabit their old dwellings, seeking as best they can to ward off adverse influences. And so one sees many an inhabited castle still standing in its pond like a chronological error, and many a castle staring down from its cliff with windows and shutters closed tight. The moat of the one turns into a marsh, while the other's weather side is abandoned to the elements, and the inhabited rooms withdraw inward.

Our moated castle, the one mentioned at the start, is called Ax. In recent years the owners have made efforts to improve its situation.

The old arched bridge, which always needed repairs, and which culminated, at the castle gate, in an actual drawbridge that constantly caused delays, was replaced with a big, solid stone causeway atop which ran a road paved with round pebbles and edged by parapets, so that one can sally forth straight from the castle in a spacious carriage or on horseback, whereas previously even a wheelbarrow had to be pushed gingerly so as not to damage the drawbridge and the arches. The latest owner's grandfather even brought up thousands of loads of rocks and dirt from his holdings in the Ax Woods and filled in the pond behind his abode, heaped up soil, planted trees, and thus brought the house garden right up to the building. This in no way diminished the castle's defenses, should it have need of such; for the garden is surrounded by a very high very old very thick wall of stone, with a stout cast-iron gate leading out into the fields.

His successor did nothing, and the latest owner—who remained a bachelor, and had no relatives at all, so that he did not even know to whom to bequeath his estate—felt no inclination whatsoever to alter his ancestors' legacy. And so the building stood as it had stood in his grandfather's day, outside its windows the water from the age of chivalry and from the Peasants' War, and it breathed the marsh miasma, and suffered the croaking frogs and the mosquito bites just as they were suffered by the knights and peasants who once lived and fought there.

The castle had all sorts of protrusions parapets thick walls arrow slits and things we no longer comprehend that once made such buildings quite secure, and today lend them a most strange and mysterious aspect, especially in young people's eyes, and above all when a vambrace or a helmet turns up in some corner of the house. But what gives our castle an especially striking appearance is a very stout very high round tower, with no windows at all and hence nothing but pitch-black rooms inside, with no proper roof, but cobbled with stones that form a gutter in one place to drain off the rainwater, and surrounded by a parapet four to five feet high. As the castle stands on a plain, the tower likely served as a lookout and for defense in case of siege. Now its interior rooms, which the thickness of the walls keeps quite cool, store all sorts of vegetables potatoes turnips greens even wine and beer, and can be aired on cool days by opening hatches. The top of the tower now serves solely as an observation deck, though sadly the only prospect is of a wide fertile plain.

The latest owner, as we said, never married. He was his father's only son his mother had indulged him and nature had given him contradictory endowments. For while he had a wonderfully fine face and a well-formed head, the rest of his body was left stunted, as though it belonged to someone else entirely. In his father's house he was called the little one, though there was none bigger, as he was the only one. But he went on being the little one even when he was thirty and no one could think now that he might go on growing. At Latin school and at the university he had also been called the little one. The contradiction in his body parts was joined by one in the powers of his mind. He had so pure a heart, in old age almost as pure as a boy's, that he could have gained the love and veneration of the noblest souls; he had a lucid unerring intellect that struck the mark with acumen, and would have inspired respect in the cleverest people—but his imagination was so nimble and lively, so far surpassing his other mental forces, that it constantly spoiled the expression of his mind's other pursuits, venting itself in shaggy tangled spiky notions. Had his imagination been constructive he would have been an artist; but it remained digressive fractured and erratic, and so he said things that no one understood, he was witty, then ridiculous, and had so many plans that he never got around to taking action. In consequence his life was all beginnings with no sequels, and sequels with no beginnings.

Once, after his father and mother had died, he was the object of a girl's great affection. He loved the girl so dearly, no other creature on earth could have inspired the same fondness or anything approaching it. And so all the conditions for a happy union seemed at hand. But once, in front of many people, he so embarrassed himself with his disquisitions and rhetorical capers that the girl sat there flushed with burning shame. The next day he wrote to his betrothed that he was unworthy of her, and could not bring himself to make her unhappy. All his friends' exhortations were for naught, the girl bitterly lamented his feelings and bewept the fateful day: but it was all in vain, and their union was severed for good.

And so he never came to use his gifts especially his heart, and lived on toward old age by himself.

Having resolved never to marry, he set about seeking his future heir. The estate, which apart from the castle consisted in landed property mainly forests, and drew the usual income, had once been a princely fief, but due to an ancestor's great services it had passed into his ownership, with distant claimants being compensated. Thus the lord of the castle, as they called him throughout the area, could freely dispose of the estate in his will. But he wished to adhere to the legal succession, to bequeath his property to the heir who would legally succeed him if he died intestate; only he wanted to meet the heir beforehand to see if he was worthy of the inheritance.

And so he opened the book of his ancestry. Descendants of his own were naturally lacking. On to the siblings, then. They, too, were lacking. On to the forebears. Father and mother were dead, neither had siblings. On to the grandparents. One grandfather, on his father's side, had one brother, but his line had gone extinct. On to the great-grandparents. All the lines descending from them that he found recorded in the book, and investigated throughout the lands, petered out before the present. Their extinction was officially documented. He went one level higher; the matter grew more and more vexed. But all lines descending from all levels, however high, terminated, their termination was attested, and at last he reached the point where no more can be known, and no lineage sheds any more light, nor can be proven. After making so many journeys, after spending a good portion of his life in the process, after going so far as to publish an announcement in the newspapers asking any relations to come forward, and after some people had come, but had not been able to offer any proof, he arrived at the sad discovery that he had no heirs whatsoever.

And so, wishing at least to provide for the event that he should be taken from this world quickly and unexpectedly, out of patriotism he appointed the emperor to be his heir. He put his will in the drawer of his desk.

Though he had forsaken the notion of bestowing his heart on a woman, with friends it was another matter. He had always had friends, and as he grew old, he acquired still more. Indeed, even the women now grew fonder of him, though not in the sense of wishing to marry him; as he grew older his eccentricities, though still greater, were no longer so striking, indeed, backed as they were by wit and imagination they became the sprightliness that most graces an old man, and everyone said how lovable he was. His dissonance of body vanished as well, for none sought beauty and harmony in an old man.

Of his friends, the first and dearest was his own steward. Even in his youth—and he came into his fortune very early—he saw how his imagination tempted him to experiment constantly tinker with or even neglect his properties, which especially in the agricultural sphere always leads to poor results. So he looked about for a young man who could administer his estate, and as his intellect made him an excellent judge of other people's qualities, he succeeded in finding a very capable one. He hired him as the manager of his estates with a very respectable salary and under the condition that the manager should tolerate interference from no one, least of all from himself. The contract was signed, and the men got on beautifully. The steward had an excellent grasp of his duties, gradually improved the estate, fell in love with it, and finally regarded it and treated it as his very own, making a habit of telling his master not to interfere in things that did not concern him; but they kept the money and financial papers in a separate coffer to which each had a key, treating the money like that of a third party, and paying themselves their earnings from it. The steward had his eccentricities too, and particularly embraced his master's books and political views, so that they came to love each other, the lord of the castle stayed in his castle always, and the steward sought no better post. It seemed that both had drawn the same lot of unmarried life.

But, so mutable are men's fates, late in life the steward fell into the snares of a girl, and married her.

Now a very strange state came over the lord of the castle. Just as the steward saw himself as the owner of the estate, and dealt with it accordingly, the lord of the castle saw himself as married. His steward was always in the fields meadows woods, saying: my oats my trees, my wood, my newly purchased field; he meanwhile was always in the castle, saying: our cupboards, our view, our new furniture, our children.

Just as previously the steward and the lord of the castle had always dined at one table, so it now continued, and the lord of the castle dined with the steward's family. The arrival of children showed how well family life would have suited the lord; for he loved children, and the children sensed it early on, and it was discovered that all four of them called the lord by his first name; no amount of severity could break their habit, and he was glad of it, and if it could have been broken he would have been saddened. The castle's denizens all lived together in the same wing, and if a stranger had come without knowing their relations, he would have taken the lord for an old relative spending his waning days amid his kinfolk.

The first child born to the steward was a girl. She was given the name Ludmilla. The lord of the castle refused to call her that, and always called her by the nickname Lulu.

The second child was a boy, Alfred; the third was a girl, Clara; and the fourth was a boy, Julius.

With that their ranks were complete; no more children came.

Lulu grew. She came to have her father's wise calm brown eyes and her mother's dainty mouth. And like her, all the children were in one way or another a mixture of their parents.

They all began to grow, the lord of the castle escorted them everywhere, took pride in them, always sided with them against their parents, and, had not other excellent qualities and circumstances intervened, would have spoiled them utterly.

One circumstance was the mother herself. She was a calm prudent housewife with a generous heart. She presided over the house with cleanliness order and virtue, and managed to instill some degree of these qualities into her servants and thus her children as well. She never scolded; nor, though, did she tire of giving the same order and having it carried out until it came easily and habitually to the person who was tasked with it. The equanimity and cheer of her nature brought equanimity and cheer to the children, the absence of all that was harsh crude and unseemly made them sensitive and decent, and the shame of doing wrong was what aided them especially, even a blush being harsh punishment, for their mother herself, with great earnest, avoided all unbecoming behavior.

The second circumstance was the father. The consummate rectitude and honesty of his nature made a great impression on the children, even when they were very small. For them he was the image of perfection and knowledge, and when they were told of their Father in Heaven, they imagined him just as their father on earth, only older. They had more fear and awe of their amiable father, who never gave them a reprimand, at most a word of counsel, than of their mother who often chided and warned them.

The third circumstance was the children's tutor. Just as the lord of the castle had judiciously chosen a steward, so the steward judiciously chose a tutor. He brought to the house a man somewhat advanced in years calm and serious, who the steward knew would soon love the children dearly. He drew a modest annuity from a previous tutoring position, from which, as a bachelor, he might have lived, but tutoring had become such a part of his nature that he was delighted at the steward's proposal, and took up the burden as though it were a gift.

The man was in such accord with the other two, in fine and foolish notions, that people said half in earnest half in jest, "Now, he was all they needed."

After a short while he said just like the other two, "My household, my children."

The children loved him dearly, but they never teased him, as they often teased the lord of the castle. To varying degrees all the men had their oddities, but the children noticed it only in the most distinctively odd of them the lord of the castle. The mother alone was always clear and simple.

When Lulu began to grow up, when she showed promise of becoming quite lovely and sweet, when she began humbly to cast down her wide eyes, slanting her lashes down over them, and no longer glanced up pertly as often as she once had, when finally one last thing

transpired, a penchant for hot blushes with no reason whatsoever—
one day the master of the castle crept quietly to his room, bolted the
door behind him, went stealthily to the drawer of his desk, opened
it, took out the will that made the emperor his heir, and crossed all
of it out. Then he busied himself writing a new one, and set down
Lulu's name. He set aside legacies for the other children that Lulu
would have to pay out, putting them closer to Lulu without quite
matching her. When he had done this, he went out into the garden
with his face aglow as though he'd played a prank and looked forward
to its discovery. To prevent any fuss, and avoid speculation and gossip,
he did not have the will signed by witnesses, instead satisfying our
laws, which he knew well, by writing at the outset: "Written and
signed by my own hand."

Yet there was a moment when Lulu would have utterly forfeited
his favor and probably the inheritance, of which she knew nothing,
had she not—unwittingly—already subjugated him so completely
that he was unable to free himself from his enslavement.

Those sad days had come when a foreign foe trod the soil of our
fatherland, lingering long and often, and ravaging it with battles,
until the praiseworthy struggles of great men, in which our fatherland
had a glorious part, drove him forth from all the lands where the
German tongue is spoken.

The very onset of the French wars threw the three men into great
agitation. All of them were zealous patriots; they would not hear a
single good word about the French, wishing only that they might
soon be beaten destroyed extirpated and laid low. The lord of the
castle went the furthest, regarding the attack upon our country as
the most unforgivable act of moral turpitude, a view explained by his
attachment to his ancestral soil and the fact that, before his heart
persuaded him differently, he could think of no worthier heir to his
fortune than the emperor. He held that the French were plain robbers
and murderers, they should be exterminated like vermin, and each
and every one of them, wherever he might show his face, should be
slain as a wolf is slain if it comes charging through the fields and into
the yard. Not even in heaven would he grant them a place; all of them

belonged in hell. Whether he would have done any slaying in earnest, had it come to that, we do not know, for so far he had found no opportunity to work his disposition into a state of active fury.

As the French advanced, it grew worse and worse, the men spoke of nothing but newspapers dispatches and so on, and let brutal words pass their lips. The children knew nothing, their only obligation at that time was to grow, and they were the only ones who went untouched by the events.

The mother found herself in an agonizing position. She could not share the men's lofty joy at each advantage achieved by our side, she only sensed the wounds that were dealt, even if they were dealt to the foe, and however much she wished that peace would come, and our lands would be liberated from the foe, she wished it to come not by slaying all enemies, but merely by expelling them, and could not hide from herself how repugnant she found it that rational creatures could not settle their disputes reasonably and equitably, but did so instead by killing each other; and she decried the fierceness of these three men, who, she said, no longer saw the facts right and left, but kept their eyes trained on the foe, longing to charge him blindly.

And so things had reached the point at which our troops, beaten on our soil, were retreating to the north, there to suffer still deeper and more painful wounds, until the cup was full to the brim, and the reckoning came, and presumption and tyranny were cast back within their borders, indeed were harshly punished there.

Back when our troops were retreating before the victor, it happened for the first time that a large division of our forces entered the region where the castle stood. All day long troops had marched, judges civil servants town councilors were busy, horse teams and guides had to be provided, and each household gave what it was able to. The inhabitants of the surrounding area had brought whatever they could, and piled it up upon the village square.

Toward evening a Russian division arrived. It seemed that rather than go farther, they meant to rest here for the night. But they did not seem very sure of themselves, and began taking extensive precautionary measures. They did not disperse, they were not quartered in the houses, and remained in fighting formation. Straw had to be brought from the surrounding area to bed the soldiers such that each man could leap up from his slumbers and instantly be standing in position. The men on watch were sent out to reconnoiter and posted to give warning. Several units halted farther back in the fields, all spaced out in a certain arrangement. The villagers had to fetch provisions fuel and other things and deliver them to certain locations. But they were not allowed to walk about among the ranks or intrude on the military arrangements, for fear that they might cause disorder. They had orders not to leave their homes after darkness fell.

As might be imagined, all this caused the utmost excitement among the villagers. They were glad to contribute their share, they would have given everything to bring our side the victory; but they worried what the night what the coming day might bring. Understandably, not one of them thought of resting.

The lord of the castle had thrown open his pantry his store room his kitchen and his cellar, he gave more than was demanded, and while it was still day he sent servants with carts to remote parts of his estate where he had barns and granaries to fetch supplies in case more should be needed on the morrow.

In the meantime night had fallen. It was dark, being late in fall, the sky covered by low-hanging clouds.

Lights burned in the houses of the village, as people were staying up. It was still, the silence broken only by an occasional muffled cry from the guards or the clatter and thud of a weapon.

The entire family of the castle, including the servants, had taken shelter in the garden hall, a large chamber that got its name because it looks back out on the garden. It is vaulted, with very strong thick stone walls, the windows have iron bars, and the furniture is very old and very sturdy. It was a favorite retreat in summer because of the cool of the room, and the graceful play of the green boughs at the windows. In the winter, as it was easy to heat, the maids often sat there on long evenings, spinning or doing other work, and often the steward's family the lord of the castle and the tutor would come down, they would gather by the heating stove and fall to telling stories and fairy tales.

It was the father's doing that they had chosen this chamber to shelter in today. If something should happen, and bullets should fly, they would be safest here when it began. Toward the village and the pond they were shielded by the full breadth of the castle, toward each side they were protected by half the castle's length, as the chamber lay in the middle, and on the garden side by the garden itself, whose great length could thwart a bullet's flight, and whose stoutest, closest-set trees, standing by the windows of the chamber, could intercept it. The decision had been made to spend the whole night there. There was no light anywhere else in the castle. Only a few farmhands in the dairy had a light in their room, but it was soon extinguished when they went to bed. The maids were all in the garden hall, spinning.

When all had made themselves comfortable, when the two youngest children had fallen asleep, and the two oldest had huddled together near their mother by the stove, and the spinning wheels were purring, they fell to telling tales again, but today with great zeal they told tales of the war, each in the hues lent by their separate passions.

After the tutor had related an episode from ancient history by way of comparison, the lord of the castle said, "The Tyrolese did that better and more fiercely; when the Frenchies marched down the valley of the Gleres, there wasn't a soul in the village. The men, with their carbines, had gone up into the crags that loom on both sides of the road, and the women and children had been taken up still farther, into the woods, even up toward the snow. No one was left in the village but an eighty-year-old carpenter with no friends and no enemies. He stood behind his barn, and his carbine was loaded. When the snow-white cloaks came—for the French cavalry had white cloaks, and formed the advance guard—he held his breath, and used his eyes. The finest helmet plumes waving in their midst seemed to belong to the man of highest rank, for the others treated him with reverence. The carpenter leapt out from behind the barn, leveled his gun— smoke—a flash—a crack—the plumes had vanished, and the rider lay dead beneath his horse. A moment later they cut the carpenter down; he laughed to himself, and let them. Now they galloped into the village, searched everything, found no people, found no treasure, and, once their comrades the foot soldiers had followed, they set fires all over the village, and marched on. The going was good, they marched on in the silence of the mountains until the valley narrowed, and the Gleres flowed alongside the road. Then the cliffs came to life, smoke and flashing and cracking everywhere, and at each shot a man fell, and again the guns were loaded, and again and again it cracked as though thousands of people were up there; and when the soldiers shot upward they hit no one because they saw no one, and when they tried to climb upward, they could not, because the crags were too steep, and because they were being shot down. And when they made haste, moving onward at a run to escape the awful road, and reached its final stretch, where it leads out through the narrowest ravines, countless boulders leapt down from the mountains, logs that had been lodged there rolled down, smashing everything in their path, forming a barricade in the narrows, the Frenchmen could go no farther, they had to go back, they fled, they ran—but below them was the burning village, which they themselves had set on fire, the wooden houses were all ablaze, so that no one could pass through them. Now they were hard-pressed, many snow-white cloaks turned red, many drifted in the Gleres, many a horse had a white cloak laid across its blanket though the rider was nowhere to be seen, many men lay on the road, many burned to death, and only a few came through on lonely paths to tell the outside world what had befallen them, or to be captured and killed by peasants as they wandered."

A silence followed his story; then he said, "We should do the same, we may lack mountains and narrow valleys where we could ambush them, like the Tyrolese; but we should band together as they did, we should carry weapons, drill, scheme, collect intelligence, and if we learn that a troop we're equal to is marching through woods or bushes or a defile, we should ambush it, and shoot all its men. Up in the foothills, in a remote village, I can't recall the name, I was told the tale by someone else, twelve French horsemen arrived to sack the place. But the peasants took exception to that, and attacked them as they caroused in a lonely inn, and slew them all at once. Their horses were tethered in the yard, and they drove them all the way to Hungary, and sold them; they burned the saddles the clothes the white cloaks and the guns in a bonfire. And so many a foe may have strayed from his division, and never come back, and no one knows what became of them."

"But," said the mother, "if it has been agreed between the peoples that wars should be fought by armies, the civilian populations should stay peaceful, and put the matter in the army's hands. To kill an individual foe who approaches unoffending seems to me a sinful murder."

"But they aren't approaching unoffending," said the lord of the castle, "look how they kept their own house, they hanged drowned shot guillotined their countrymen because they seemed suspect, or loved the king, and then they went out and sought to do the same in our lands. We were to be set against each other, plunging the country into discord from which it might hardly escape. And so we should persecute, extirpate, exterminate them in whatever way we can; and if this incurs their wrath and makes them run riot, all the better, for then the people will cease to endure it, they'll band together and chase them from the country, so that we shall see not a hoof nor a plume of theirs. When the French come tomorrow things may happen—what might happen, who can know?"

He spoke these words, and the servants listened, the maids' spinning wheels stood still, the farmhands watched him, and the steward and the tutor stared into space. By now it had grown so dark that the windows of the room were like black panels, and not the slightest thing could be heard from outside, only the monotonous tick of the clock on the wall. The two youngest children slept soundly, Alfred huddled next to his mother, afraid, Lulu stood beside him and helped him be afraid.

At that moment the door handle made a soft noise, the door opened, and in strode a man with a gleaming helmet, wrapped in a long white cloak.

Everyone stared at him.

"I saw light shining through these windows," he said in good German, "and have come to make a request."

"What request?" the steward and the lord of the castle asked in unison.

"You will, if you please, follow me to the top of the big tower," the stranger said, pointing at the steward.

As he spoke he raised one arm, parting his cloak, and they saw that his other hand held a double-barreled pistol.

"Who can demand that? I am the master here," cried the lord of the castle.

"So, you are the master?" said the strange man. "Then you shall come too."

At that he reached for the pistol with his free hand, and cocked both hammers with an audible click.

"You'll take a lantern up the stairs, and go on ahead of me," he continued, "not a hair of your heads will be hurt if all is done smoothly and quietly. But if I sense treachery, I'll have to use my weapons, happen what may. Sit quietly where you are, the rest of you, until they return."

He stood there with his back to the doorjamb and the pistol in his hand, gazing at them all.

"It's no matter, don't worry, and you follow us, sir," said the steward, taking the lord of the castle by the hand, "and until we return none of you must leave the room."

With these words he reached for the lantern that hung by the holy water stoup, opened it, lit the candle stump inside, closed it tightly, strode farther into the room and said, "If you please."

The strange man stepped aside to let the steward and the lord of the castle through the door, and then followed them, sidling so that he could keep an eye on the room and the men ahead of him at the same time.

Those left behind had said not a word; for one thing it had all happened so quickly, and for another the steward's calm had reassured them.

With the lantern the two men walked down the passageway to

the tower, the stranger following, so that they always heard the jingle of the spurs on his feet.

They reached the stairs, and climbed them. When the stranger saw that they had nearly reached the top, he ordered them to stand still, to set the lantern on a step, open it, and go up several more steps.

Once they had done so, he went up to the lantern, took a tiny lantern out of his cloak pocket, lit a light inside it that barely shone, left the other lantern standing on the step, climbed toward the waiting men, and ordered them to go on.

When they had emerged onto the stone paving of the tower, which, as noted above, made up its roof, he had the men stand by the parapet where he could see them, while he himself went to a different part of the parapet, set his tiny lantern atop it, laying his pistol alongside, took out a notecase and began to write or draw in the light of his lamp. The night was so dark that nothing was visible but one great black space in which the lights and watchfires stood out like red stars. All that could be seen of the village was the outline of a few roofs and the church. Part of the square was lit up by the troops' fires.

Once the stranger had spent a while drawing or writing, he put his notecase away again, took his lantern in one hand his pistol in the other, and ordered the men to go down the stairs ahead of him.

When they had come to the place where the lantern stood, they had to take it and lead the man back down the way they had come.

When they reached the door of the garden hall, the stranger said that the two men must now take him through the garden to the cast-iron gate leading out into the fields. Once he was outside the iron gate, they could return. They would have to leave the lantern in the passage that led past the hall to the main castle gate.

And so the lord of the castle and his steward walked through the dark garden ahead of the stranger.

Not far from the castle they found a horse tethered to a tree. The stranger untied it, wrapped the reins around his arm, and led it along behind him. He did not lead it along the garden path, where his two guides walked, but through the grass beside it, so that its hooves would not be heard.

When they drew near the cast-iron gate, dark figures appeared outside it. The stranger suddenly came up behind the two men in front of him and whispered, "Halt."

Then he watched the figures for a long time with evident intentness.

At last he said very softly that they should lead him back to the hall.

They did so, and he led his horse along behind him.

When they had reached the hall, he ordered them to open the gate at the end of the passage next to it, which was the main gate of the castle.

The steward went to fetch the key, while the lord of the castle had to remain in the stranger's power, and when the steward emerged from the garden hall, where the key was kept, the people in the hall followed him, curious. The stranger held on to his horse, with his eyes on the lord of the castle and the pistol in his hand. The steward and a servant unlocked the gate, removed the great oaken crossbar in the light of the lamp, opened both wings—and they looked out into black space.

"Put the lantern away," said the stranger.

When they had done so, he stared through the gate for a while, but kept glancing back at the lord of the castle so that he could not escape. Then, as far as could be told by the light of the lantern, he adjusted something on his horse, inspected something else, and when he was satisfied, swung himself into the saddle. Once on his horse, there was a brief moment in which he seemed to plant himself in his seat, then he dug in the spurs, gave a shout, and with such terrible swiftness that the eyes could barely see and the sparks flew in showers, he sped out down the causeway. When he reached the other side, as they could tell from the fainter sound of the hooves, he shot his pistol to the right and to the left, at which flashes appeared behind him, shots cracked, cries rang out and receded into the distance.

"Now that's a man," Lulu exulted.

"You beast, you little monster," cried the lord of the castle, "your admiration is driving you to our foes."

"He's no Frenchman," Lulu replied, "he speaks such beautiful German."

"That makes him all the worse, a thousand times worse," said the lord of the castle, "as a German he should go to the ends of the earth and live as a beggar sooner than ally himself with our archfoe, indeed he should sooner suffer death. Instead he's recorded the position of the coalition troops from our tower, betraying them, as we'll see to-morrow morning, if they haven't shot him down or captured him."

"He's running his horse up against a house, he'll dash himself and the beast to pieces," said a maid.

"He won't run up against it," a manservant rejoined, "he's got eyes like a hawk, he knows what he's doing."

"He's a man after all, even if he's an enemy," said Lulu.

"Why didn't you slay him? He was wearing a white cloak," Alfred asked the lord of the castle.

The lord looked at his questioner and had no reply.

"Children, everyone, we'll soon have a different drama on our hands," said the steward, "whether or not that audacious man was killed, he is an enemy, as his actions showed; he galloped out from our castle into our allies' midst, and soon they will come and demand an accounting. Let everyone be sure to take close note of what they witnessed, so that they can profess the truth, and so that there shall be no contradictions that might have evil consequences for us. The soldiers out there in the village are in retreat, and embittered. Let us close the gate again, but open it quickly and readily at the first knock. Until then let us go back to the garden hall."

The manservants shut the gate, barred it with the oaken beam, gave the key to the steward, and carrying the lantern they returned to the hall.

They had not been there long when blows were heard on the door.

The mother gave a faint cry and moved in the father's direction. He soothed her, ordered the door to be opened, and himself went forward with a light to greet the intruders. They were two senior officers accompanied by soldiers. Soldiers stood all along the causeway.

"Are there some enemies still here?" one of the senior officers asked in quite intelligible German.

"There was only the one who just rode out," replied the steward.

At once the officer sent men to guard all the stairs all the doors and the exits into the garden. The inhabitants were put under guard in the hall, and the lord of the castle and his steward had to go under escort into all the castle's rooms so that they could be searched. The lord of the castle was much more genial talkative and amiable toward all the armed soldiers accompanying him now than he had been toward the single one before. After finding nothing suspicious anywhere, they returned to the garden hall. The garden was not searched, but the exits from the castle to the garden were barricaded so that if there were an enemy in the garden, that alone would hold him captive.

Then the interrogation began. The steward related the events as they had taken place. He conjectured that the stranger must have come through the garden, because the gate leading out to the village had been locked, and because the allied troops were in the village. At any rate the stranger had meant to escape through the garden, as would clearly be shown by the footprints and especially the hoof prints in the grass, if they investigated tomorrow by daylight.

"The matter will be investigated," the officer said.

After that the lord of the castle was interrogated separately, and then all the others, including the children.

When that was over, the men were led to a vault in the tower, locked in and guarded. The women and children were allowed to remain in the garden hall, but they, too, were locked in and guarded.

From then on the time passed quietly, apart from the fear and the worry. Not a sound could be heard but the occasional footstep of a guard outside the door the jangle of a gun or the thud of a rifle butt. Not a breeze passed through the sky, the clouds seemed suspended, motionless, and the treetops in the garden never stirred. The captives in the garden hall spent the night amid these impressions. Understandably, sleep never touched their eyes. They did not know where the men had been taken.

When day broke at last, they heard a muddled din as of rolling riding running shouting, finally they heard horns trumpets and drums, but all muffled, coming from the far side of the castle. Nothing could be seen, for the door was locked, and outside the windows were only the trees of the garden, their dark tops standing out more and more clearly against the gray brightening sky.

Finally there came a blast, dull and distant, but so strong that it almost shivered the air. A moment later a second blast. Now they came more quickly, and it was almost like faraway thunder, so deep a sound that now and then the windows jittered. The trumpet calls the blowing of horns the rolling of drums swelled nearby.

The day waxed further and further toward morning.

The rumbling thunder drew nearer, giving way to cracking, and white smoke rose behind the treetops. At last there came a cracking quite near the castle, none could tell where from, now on the right now on the left, now in front now in back, now more now less, but the terrible thing was that the room seemed to move; and when the slightest pause came, a sound was heard like countless sticks striking together, which was the shots from the smaller guns. Even the drums could sometimes be heard.

At last so much smoke had crept into the garden that it hung in the trees like a fog. It increased and condensed until the closest tree trunks could barely be seen. A foul smell filled the room.

After this had gone on a long while, the thunder receded into the distance in the opposite direction, the rumbling grew duller, isolated blasts could still be heard nearby, but mostly cries roaring and confused commotion. At last that, too, grew fainter and fainter, nothing more could be heard, slowly the smoke withdrew from the trees, the noise had chased off the clouds, as it were, and the sun, which had loomed at first as a red disk in the smoke, finally shone down kindly upon the garden.

The women in the hall waited a long time. But when not a sound could be heard, not even a noise from the guards outside the door, they called out to them. They got no reply. They called again, louder, but again got no reply. At that they rattled at the door and the lock. No sign and no resistance came from outside. Now, using axes and crowbars, tools that were always at hand in the garden hall, they actually pried out the lock, and opened the door. Not a soul was outside. The gate stood wide open. In the village charred straw was still smoking, and smoke rose from a hut that blazed in the distance. Otherwise they saw no damage, but neither did they see any people in the village. An iron ball lay beneath the arch of the gate, and another was embedded in the wall of the castle.

Even as they looked about, they suddenly heard the rattle and clatter of galloping horses, and at that same moment a host of white riders came around the houses, turned toward the castle, and rode up across the causeway. Lulu nearly cried out with joy to see them headed by the man in the white cloak who had been in the castle that night. They hoped at least to be freed from their uncertainty, and perhaps from their fear and anxiety too.

The man rode up to the assembled women. Now, by daylight, they saw that he was very young, with a bloom on his face. He dismounted at once and said, "I have very little time, yesterday I subjected you to terror and violence so that today we might reap the fruits. We have reaped them, and are advancing. But I have come for one moment to ask forgiveness for making use of a harsh law of war, and I have also come to release the occupants from any unpleasant consequences my actions may have caused them. Where are the men?"

"We don't know, just this moment we freed ourselves from our captivity in the garden hall, they were taken away as prisoners last night," the mother said.

"Then we must search for them," the stranger replied, "perhaps they're in the house."

As a precaution he took several armed troopers with him, and, knowing the ways of war, headed at once toward the tower. All the women followed him. The key was in the lock of the door to the vault where the men had been taken. The key was turned, and the captives were found and released.

Once all had reassured themselves that their kin had not been harmed, and once the commotion of questions and answers had quieted, the stranger went up to the men and said, "We have won the day, and, so I hope, this was due in some small part to the observations I made yesterday. I have come, esteemed gentlemen, to make use of what time I have to ask forgiveness for my behavior toward you last night. Here is a card with my name and title; you may demand satisfaction from my person and my fortune if you see fit to seek it."

As he spoke he handed a piece of paper to the lord of the castle.

"Of course," he went on, "I can give no satisfaction to the women for all their fear and terror, and so I am all the more in need of their forgiveness, and beg it of them all the more fervently."

"The best satisfaction," said the lord of the castle, "would be if you were not on the side you are on."

"My lord," the stranger rejoined, "if you can persuade my king of this view, I shall perform such deeds as I did last night with a lighter heart than I did then. But a soldier must obey. Now fare you well, my time is very short."

He gave his hand to the lord of the castle, who took it.

"Have you suffered no injuries?" asked the steward.

"Not one," replied the young man.

"Then fare you well," said the steward, "and may your deeds soon be attended by lighter thoughts."

"Amen," said the young man.

He bowed to the men, but lower still to the women and even to the maids, his escort swung about, and he went away with them.

The others gazed after them, glimpsed them mounted on their horses beneath the arch of the gate and riding out down the causeway.

Now there were no more soldiers to be seen.

After the steward and the lord of the castle had, as far as possible, inspected the disorder in their own house, deploring the bullet damage to several fine trees in the garden, they betook themselves to the village to assist the people there and in the surrounding area in the measures required in the wake of the battle. The first was to accommodate the wounded who had been found or were straggling in, friend or foe. The doctor set up a hospital in the castle, and the steward's wife cooked for friends and foes. The second was to bury the dead. At last they went about gathering and storing away the weapons and implements of war, and gradually repairing the damage to their own houses and buildings.

In these days many a wounded man tended his more severely wounded fellow. Many a man carried up a foe to be tended, and on the third day word spread that a horse was standing motionless by its dead rider in the cabbage patch on the hill, and elsewhere a spitz dog refused to leave its master's grave.

At first many more enemy divisions passed through in pursuit of the fleeing troops, but then this ceased, nothing more came, and until the advent of peace the castle and the village saw no more soldiers, be they friends or foes. ⸺

Years had passed since that incident. The enemies who had then been victorious were now utterly defeated, their capital occupied, their world-famous leader exiled to Elba and then, following his escape, all the way to St. Helena, and peace blessed all the lands that had so long been ravaged. The people who had known war fully recognized its horror, and saw that whoever wantonly ignites it, though later, deluded times may venerate him as a hero and a demigod, is a despicable murderer and a scourge of humanity, and they believed that humanity had come to its senses and that the times for such doings were over: but they forgot that other times would come and other people who did not know war, who would let their passions rule, and in their wantonness would again call forth that thing that is so terrible.

Autumn had returned to our castle, but such a mild autumn that most of the time could be spent outdoors, and the castle dwellers took long walks each day to enjoy nature's last tranquil smiles before the storms and the frosts should come.

And so one afternoon they all sat atop a hill that had been raised up in the garden near the cast-iron gate leading out to the fields. For Alfred and Julius had spent all their university holidays using their own hands and little wheelbarrows to pile up a hill and build atop it a columned folly that could seat all the castle dwellers. The lord of the castle and his steward had indulged the boys, thinking it better for them to build, albeit something as hulking as a hill, than to destroy things by hunting or catching birds. Because the sun was shining so mildly, they had decided to take their afternoon coffee in the folly. The table was set and they were waiting to pour the coffee, toying with the yellow leaves that lay about, or with the strands of gossamer that drifted in particular abundance today, clinging to the folly's columns and the clothing of the party.

Suddenly Lulu, now a grown maiden, and, we must say, a very lovely one, let out a cry.

"Were you startled by a spider?" the others asked.

"No a white cloak," she replied, and pointed where she had been gazing when she uttered her cry.

All of them looked over.

Outside the cast-iron gate, on the cart track that passed around the garden, there stood a carriage, and in it sat a lone man with a white cloak around his shoulders, gazing in at their party.

"Run, Julius," said the father, "and ask him if there's something he wishes."

The boy ran over, spoke with the man, returned, and said, "He wishes to be admitted, he says he is not entirely a stranger."

The boy was given the key, which, for the sake of convenience, they always took with them on walks, he opened the gate, the stranger entered, came up the hill, and presented himself to the party.

They recognized him at once. It was the young man from that terrible night in the war. Now he was no longer a youth, but an amiable man with such a kind gaze that no one could have believed he was the same one who had played the terrible game of life and death back then.

"Forgive my coming, sirs and madams," he said, "I am no stranger to you, you have no cause to think well of me in any way; but it seems you do not hate me, as I must conclude from the fact that in all these years no satisfaction has been demanded for that night."

"No, no, nor shall it be demanded," they cried, and urged him to sit.

He did so, and said, "Let me continue for a moment. Every person has some point of yearning in his life toward which he is always drawn, and which he must reach if he wishes to be at peace. My yearning is that cast-iron gate there. Ever since I forced its lock that night to climb the tower and sketch the position of the enemy's fires, since the moment when, returning, I found it guarded by the enemy, and was left with the prospect of being captured as a spy and ignominiously hanged, or else galloping rashly forth into the enemy's midst and surprising them, so as to fall honorably, or break through thanks to the startling stunt—I could not have galloped out the back way because of the plowed ground and other obstacles—since that moment I have always felt the pull of the gate, and I thought to myself that I must see it again after all. And so I came here, and rode around the garden on the path to the gate. And let me speak candidly, what played no less a part in my coming was the thought of seeing all of you again, obtaining your full forgiveness for the wrong that I did you and that has always perturbed me, and winning your esteem; for afterward I fought in many battles with the light heart that this gentleman wished me back then."

At that he pointed to the steward.

"I like you much better like this, young man, than I did that night," said the lord of the castle, red face and white hair resplendent.

"Yes, dear sir," the stranger rejoined, "I know no happier feeling than to ride out, with an unburdened breast, alongside members of my people and speakers of my tongue, to meet an arrogant and insolent foe of the fatherland. I have been granted this feeling, I have sought to heal the wound which, that night, my official duty may have dealt to the common cause, and may all the heavens grant that the German people, so noble-hearted profound in thought and feeling, shall never again revert to its hoary error and take arms against itself."

"Yes God willing, God willing," said the men.

Meanwhile the coffee had been poured, and the mistress of the house gave the first cup to the stranger. The steward had the carriage brought around the garden wall into the castle, and the master of the castle and all the others invited the stranger to stay at his leisure, and look at the cast-iron gate as often as he pleased.

The invitation was accepted.

Now the stranger stayed in the castle. He could contemplate the cast-iron gate the tower the garden and the surroundings as much as ever he wished. But fate had quite a different aim in store for his journey. Everyone grew fond of him. Relations between Lulu and himself had been utterly reversed. Just as she had admired him that night, now he for his part could find no end nor bounds to admiring the girl. And as even that night he had appealed to the child, and now he was so good and amiable besides, it could not be otherwise, the maiden soon loved him beyond measure, and the adoration was fully mutual.

As he lingered longer and longer in the castle at everyone's wish, having formed friendly bonds with all of them; as he possessed rank and fortune, and finally even purchased a neighboring estate that had come up for sale, so as to settle down in the region, there were no obstacles to the union, and in the village church the two young people received the sacrament of marriage.

And from now on a quiet peaceful happy life commenced. Often, in future, when the couple sat by themselves, when he called Lulu his joy and his greatest bliss on this earth, she said, "With your heart you have granted the finest satisfaction you could grant."

"It's a good thing I didn't slay him after all," the lord of the castle kept repeating for a long time to come, ancient and seeming to dwindle and dwindle.

Lulu always smiled at these words, later Alfred and Julius also smiled, and at last all of them did, down to the gray-haired tutor, now merely the lord's companion for walks or chess games.

For a long time the white cloaks played a role in the family. Not only did Alfred and Julius, who served in the emperor's army, wear white cloaks; little Alfred and little Julius, Lulu's boys, wore white cloaks in winter when they rode across the plain in their sleigh, cut from the one their father had worn on his quest to find the old cast-iron gate. Their father had shed his white cloaks along with his weapons, and now wore distinguished dark furs in the winter.

TITLES IN SERIES

For a complete list of titles, visit www.nyrb.com or write to:
Catalog Requests, NYRB, 435 Hudson Street, New York, NY 10014

J.R. ACKERLEY Hindoo Holiday
J.R. ACKERLEY My Dog Tulip
J.R. ACKERLEY My Father and Myself
J.R. ACKERLEY We Think the World of You
HENRY ADAMS The Jeffersonian Transformation
RENATA ADLER Pitch Dark
RENATA ADLER Speedboat
AESCHYLUS Prometheus Bound; translated by Joel Agee
ROBERT AICKMAN Compulsory Games
LEOPOLDO ALAS His Only Son *with* Doña Berta
CÉLESTE ALBARET Monsieur Proust
DANTE ALIGHIERI The Inferno
JEAN AMÉRY Charles Bovary, Country Doctor: Portrait of a Simple Man
KINGSLEY AMIS The Alteration
KINGSLEY AMIS Dear Illusion: Collected Stories
KINGSLEY AMIS Ending Up
KINGSLEY AMIS Girl, 20
KINGSLEY AMIS The Green Man
KINGSLEY AMIS Lucky Jim
KINGSLEY AMIS The Old Devils
KINGSLEY AMIS One Fat Englishman
KINGSLEY AMIS Take a Girl Like You
ROBERTO ARLT The Seven Madmen
U.R. ANANTHAMURTHY Samskara: A Rite for a Dead Man
IVO ANDRIĆ Omer Pasha Latas
WILLIAM ATTAWAY Blood on the Forge
W.H. AUDEN (EDITOR) The Living Thoughts of Kierkegaard
W.H. AUDEN W. H. Auden's Book of Light Verse
ERICH AUERBACH Dante: Poet of the Secular World
EVE BABITZ Eve's Hollywood
EVE BABITZ I Used to Be Charming: The Rest of Eve Babitz
EVE BABITZ Slow Days, Fast Company: The World, the Flesh, and L.A.
DOROTHY BAKER Cassandra at the Wedding
DOROTHY BAKER Young Man with a Horn
J.A. BAKER The Peregrine
S. JOSEPHINE BAKER Fighting for Life
HONORÉ DE BALZAC The Human Comedy: Selected Stories
HONORÉ DE BALZAC The Memoirs of Two Young Wives
HONORÉ DE BALZAC The Unknown Masterpiece *and* Gambara
VICKI BAUM Grand Hotel
SYBILLE BEDFORD A Favorite of the Gods *and* A Compass Error
SYBILLE BEDFORD Jigsaw
SYBILLE BEDFORD A Legacy
SYBILLE BEDFORD A Visit to Don Otavio: A Mexican Journey
MAX BEERBOHM The Prince of Minor Writers: The Selected Essays of Max Beerbohm
MAX BEERBOHM Seven Men
STEPHEN BENATAR Wish Her Safe at Home
FRANS G. BENGTSSON The Long Ships
WALTER BENJAMIN The Storyteller Essays
ALEXANDER BERKMAN Prison Memoirs of an Anarchist

GEORGES BERNANOS Mouchette

MIRON BIAŁOSZEWSKI A Memoir of the Warsaw Uprising

ROBERT MONTGOMERY BIRD Sheppard Lee, Written by Himself

ADOLFO BIOY CASARES Asleep in the Sun

ADOLFO BIOY CASARES The Invention of Morel

PAUL BLACKBURN (TRANSLATOR) Proensa

CAROLINE BLACKWOOD Corrigan

CAROLINE BLACKWOOD Great Granny Webster

LESLEY BLANCH Journey into the Mind's Eye: Fragments of an Autobiography

RONALD BLYTHE Akenfield: Portrait of an English Village

HENRI BOSCO Malicroix

NICOLAS BOUVIER The Way of the World

EMMANUEL BOVE Henri Duchemin and His Shadows

EMMANUEL BOVE My Friends

MALCOLM BRALY On the Yard

MILLEN BRAND The Outward Room

ROBERT BRESSON Notes on the Cinematograph

DAVID BROMWICH (EDITOR) Writing Politics: An Anthology

SIR THOMAS BROWNE Religio Medici and Urne-Buriall

DAVID R. BUNCH Moderan

JOHN HORNE BURNS The Gallery

ROBERT BURTON The Anatomy of Melancholy

DINO BUZZATI Poem Strip

INÈS CAGNATI Free Day

MATEI CALINESCU The Life and Opinions of Zacharias Lichter

CAMARA LAYE The Radiance of the King

GIROLAMO CARDANO The Book of My Life

DON CARPENTER Hard Rain Falling

J.L. CARR A Month in the Country

LEONORA CARRINGTON Down Below

LEONORA CARRINGTON The Hearing Trumpet

BLAISE CENDRARS Moravagine

EILEEN CHANG Little Reunions

EILEEN CHANG Love in a Fallen City

EILEEN CHANG Naked Earth

JOAN CHASE During the Reign of the Queen of Persia

UPAMANYU CHATTERJEE English, August: An Indian Story

FRANÇOIS-RENÉ DE CHATEAUBRIAND Memoirs from Beyond the Grave, 1768–1800

NIRAD C. CHAUDHURI The Autobiography of an Unknown Indian

ELLIOTT CHAZE Black Wings Has My Angel

ANTON CHEKHOV Peasants and Other Stories

ANTON CHEKHOV The Prank: The Best of Young Chekhov

GABRIEL CHEVALLIER Fear: A Novel of World War I

DRISS CHRAÏBI The Simple Past

JEAN-PAUL CLÉBERT Paris Vagabond

RICHARD COBB Paris and Elsewhere

COLETTE The Pure and the Impure

JOHN COLLIER Fancies and Goodnights

CARLO COLLODI The Adventures of Pinocchio

D.G. COMPTON The Continuous Katherine Mortenhoe

IVY COMPTON-BURNETT A House and Its Head

IVY COMPTON-BURNETT Manservant and Maidservant

BARBARA COMYNS The Juniper Tree

BARBARA COMYNS Our Spoons Came from Woolworths

BARBARA COMYNS The Vet's Daughter

ALBERT COSSERY Proud Beggars

ALBERT COSSERY The Jokers

HAROLD W. CRUSE The Crisis of the Negro Intellectual

ASTOLPHE DE CUSTINE Letters from Russia

JÓZEF CZAPSKI Inhuman Land: Searching for the Truth in Soviet Russia, 1941–1942

JÓZEF CZAPSKI Lost Time: Lectures on Proust in a Soviet Prison Camp

LORENZO DA PONTE Memoirs

ELIZABETH DAVID A Book of Mediterranean Food

ELIZABETH DAVID Summer Cooking

L.J. DAVIS A Meaningful Life

AGNES DE MILLE Dance to the Piper

VIVANT DENON No Tomorrow/Point de lendemain

MARIA DERMOÛT The Ten Thousand Things

DER NISTER The Family Mashber

TIBOR DÉRY Niki: The Story of a Dog

G.V. DESANI All About H. Hatterr

ANTONIO DI BENEDETTO Zama

ALFRED DÖBLIN Berlin Alexanderplatz

ALFRED DÖBLIN Bright Magic: Stories

JEAN D'ORMESSON The Glory of the Empire: A Novel, A History

ARTHUR CONAN DOYLE The Exploits and Adventures of Brigadier Gerard

CHARLES DUFF A Handbook on Hanging

BRUCE DUFFY The World As I Found It

DAPHNE DU MAURIER Don't Look Now: Stories

ELAINE DUNDY The Dud Avocado

ELAINE DUNDY The Old Man and Me

G.B. EDWARDS The Book of Ebenezer Le Page

JOHN EHLE The Land Breakers

CYPRIAN EKWENSI People of the City

MARCELLUS EMANTS A Posthumous Confession

EURIPIDES Grief Lessons: Four Plays; translated by Anne Carson

J.G. FARRELL Troubles

J.G. FARRELL The Siege of Krishnapur

J.G. FARRELL The Singapore Grip

ELIZA FAY Original Letters from India

KENNETH FEARING The Big Clock

KENNETH FEARING Clark Gifford's Body

FÉLIX FÉNÉON Novels in Three Lines

M.I. FINLEY The World of Odysseus

THOMAS FLANAGAN The Year of the French

BENJAMIN FONDANE Existential Monday: Philosophical Essays

SANFORD FRIEDMAN Conversations with Beethoven

SANFORD FRIEDMAN Totempole

MARC FUMAROLI When the World Spoke French

CARLO EMILIO GADDA That Awful Mess on the Via Merulana

WILLIAM GADDIS J R

WILLIAM GADDIS The Recognitions

BENITO PÉREZ GÁLDOS Tristana

MAVIS GALLANT The Cost of Living: Early and Uncollected Stories

MAVIS GALLANT Paris Stories

MAVIS GALLANT A Fairly Good Time *with* Green Water, Green Sky

MAVIS GALLANT Varieties of Exile

GABRIEL GARCÍA MÁRQUEZ Clandestine in Chile: The Adventures of Miguel Littín

LEONARD GARDNER Fat City

WILLIAM H. GASS In the Heart of the Heart of the Country and Other Stories

WILLIAM H. GASS On Being Blue: A Philosophical Inquiry

THÉOPHILE GAUTIER My Fantoms

GE FEI The Invisibility Cloak

GE FEI Peach Blossom Paradise

JEAN GENET The Criminal Child: Selected Essays

JEAN GENET Prisoner of Love

ANDRÉ GIDE Marshlands

ÉLISABETH GILLE The Mirador: Dreamed Memories of Irène Némirovsky by Her Daughter

FRANÇOISE GILOT Life with Picasso

NATALIA GINZBURG Family *and* Borghesia

NATALIA GINZBURG Family Lexicon

NATALIA GINZBURG Valentino *and* Sagittarius

JEAN GIONO Hill

JEAN GIONO A King Alone

JEAN GIONO Melville: A Novel

JOHN GLASSCO Memoirs of Montparnasse

P.V. GLOB The Bog People: Iron-Age Man Preserved

ROBERT GLÜCK Margery Kempe

NIKOLAI GOGOL Dead Souls

EDMOND AND JULES DE GONCOURT Pages from the Goncourt Journals

ALICE GOODMAN History Is Our Mother: Three Libretti

PAUL GOODMAN Growing Up Absurd: Problems of Youth in the Organized Society

EDWARD GOREY (EDITOR) The Haunted Looking Glass

JEREMIAS GOTTHELF The Black Spider

A.C. GRAHAM Poems of the Late T'ang

JULIEN GRACQ Balcony in the Forest

HENRY GREEN Back

HENRY GREEN Blindness

HENRY GREEN Caught

HENRY GREEN Doting

HENRY GREEN Living

HENRY GREEN Loving

HENRY GREEN Nothing

HENRY GREEN Party Going

HENRY GREEN Surviving

WILLIAM LINDSAY GRESHAM Nightmare Alley

HANS HERBERT GRIMM Schlump

EMMETT GROGAN Ringolevio: A Life Played for Keeps

VASILY GROSSMAN An Armenian Sketchbook

VASILY GROSSMAN Everything Flows

VASILY GROSSMAN Life and Fate

VASILY GROSSMAN The Road

VASILY GROSSMAN Stalingrad

LOUIS GUILLOUX Blood Dark

OAKLEY HALL Warlock

PATRICK HAMILTON The Slaves of Solitude

PATRICK HAMILTON Twenty Thousand Streets Under the Sky

PETER HANDKE Short Letter, Long Farewell

PETER HANDKE Slow Homecoming

THORKILD HANSEN Arabia Felix: The Danish Expedition of 1761–1767

ELIZABETH HARDWICK The Collected Essays of Elizabeth Hardwick

ELIZABETH HARDWICK The New York Stories of Elizabeth Hardwick

ELIZABETH HARDWICK Seduction and Betrayal

ELIZABETH HARDWICK Sleepless Nights

L.P. HARTLEY Eustace and Hilda: A Trilogy

L.P. HARTLEY The Go-Between

NATHANIEL HAWTHORNE Twenty Days with Julian & Little Bunny by Papa

ALFRED HAYES The End of Me

ALFRED HAYES In Love

ALFRED HAYES My Face for the World to See

PAUL HAZARD The Crisis of the European Mind: 1680–1715

ALICE HERDAN-ZUCKMAYER The Farm in the Green Mountains

WOLFGANG HERRNDORF Sand

GILBERT HIGHET Poets in a Landscape

RUSSELL HOBAN Turtle Diary

JANET HOBHOUSE The Furies

YOEL HOFFMANN The Sound of the One Hand: 281 Zen Koans with Answers

HUGO VON HOFMANNSTHAL The Lord Chandos Letter

JAMES HOGG The Private Memoirs and Confessions of a Justified Sinner

RICHARD HOLMES Shelley: The Pursuit

ALISTAIR HORNE A Savage War of Peace: Algeria 1954–1962

GEOFFREY HOUSEHOLD Rogue Male

WILLIAM DEAN HOWELLS Indian Summer

BOHUMIL HRABAL Dancing Lessons for the Advanced in Age

BOHUMIL HRABAL The Little Town Where Time Stood Still

DOROTHY B. HUGHES The Expendable Man

DOROTHY B. HUGHES In a Lonely Place

RICHARD HUGHES A High Wind in Jamaica

RICHARD HUGHES In Hazard

RICHARD HUGHES The Fox in the Attic (The Human Predicament, Vol. 1)

RICHARD HUGHES The Wooden Shepherdess (The Human Predicament, Vol. 2)

INTIZAR HUSAIN Basti

MAUDE HUTCHINS Victorine

YASUSHI INOUE Tun-huang

DARIUS JAMES Negrophobia: An Urban Parable

HENRY JAMES The Ivory Tower

HENRY JAMES The New York Stories of Henry James

HENRY JAMES The Other House

HENRY JAMES The Outcry

TOVE JANSSON Fair Play

TOVE JANSSON The Summer Book

TOVE JANSSON The True Deceiver

TOVE JANSSON The Woman Who Borrowed Memories: Selected Stories

RANDALL JARRELL (EDITOR) Randall Jarrell's Book of Stories

DIANE JOHNSON The True History of the First Mrs. Meredith and Other Lesser Lives

UWE JOHNSON Anniversaries

DAVID JONES In Parenthesis

JOSEPH JOUBERT The Notebooks of Joseph Joubert; translated by Paul Auster

ERNST JÜNGER The Glass Bees

KABIR Songs of Kabir; translated by Arvind Krishna Mehrotra

FRIGYES KARINTHY A Journey Round My Skull

ERICH KÄSTNER Going to the Dogs: The Story of a Moralist

ANNA KAVAN Machines in the Head: Selected Stories

HELEN KELLER The World I Live In

YASHAR KEMAL Memed, My Hawk

YASHAR KEMAL They Burn the Thistles

WALTER KEMPOWSKI All for Nothing

WALTER KEMPOWSKI Marrow and Bone

MURRAY KEMPTON Part of Our Time: Some Ruins and Monuments of the Thirties

RAYMOND KENNEDY Ride a Cockhorse

DAVID KIDD Peking Story

ROBERT KIRK The Secret Commonwealth of Elves, Fauns, and Fairies

ARUN KOLATKAR Jejuri

DEZSŐ KOSZTOLÁNYI Skylark

TÉTÉ-MICHEL KPOMASSIE An African in Greenland

TOM KRISTENSEN Havoc

GYULA KRÚDY The Adventures of Sindbad

GYULA KRÚDY Sunflower

SIGIZMUND KRZHIZHANOVSKY Autobiography of a Corpse

SIGIZMUND KRZHIZHANOVSKY The Letter Killers Club

SIGIZMUND KRZHIZHANOVSKY Memories of the Future

SIGIZMUND KRZHIZHANOVSKY The Return of Munchausen

SIGIZMUND KRZHIZHANOVSKY Unwitting Street

K'UNG SHANG-JEN The Peach Blossom Fan

GIUSEPPE TOMASI DI LAMPEDUSA The Professor and the Siren

D.H. LAWRENCE The Bad Side of Books: Selected Essays

GERT LEDIG The Stalin Front

MARGARET LEECH Reveille in Washington: 1860–1865

PATRICK LEIGH FERMOR Between the Woods and the Water

PATRICK LEIGH FERMOR The Broken Road

PATRICK LEIGH FERMOR Mani: Travels in the Southern Peloponnese

PATRICK LEIGH FERMOR Roumeli: Travels in Northern Greece

PATRICK LEIGH FERMOR A Time of Gifts

PATRICK LEIGH FERMOR A Time to Keep Silence

PATRICK LEIGH FERMOR The Traveller's Tree

PATRICK LEIGH FERMOR The Violins of Saint-Jacques

NIKOLAI LESKOV Lady Macbeth of Mtsensk: Selected Stories of Nikolai Leskov

D.B. WYNDHAM LEWIS AND CHARLES LEE (EDITORS) The Stuffed Owl

SIMON LEYS The Death of Napoleon

SIMON LEYS The Hall of Uselessness: Collected Essays

MARGARITA LIBERAKI Three Summers

GEORG CHRISTOPH LICHTENBERG The Waste Books

JAKOV LIND Soul of Wood and Other Stories

H.P. LOVECRAFT AND OTHERS Shadows of Carcosa: Tales of Cosmic Horror

DWIGHT MACDONALD Masscult and Midcult: Essays Against the American Grain

CURZIO MALAPARTE Diary of a Foreigner in Paris

CURZIO MALAPARTE Kaputt

CURZIO MALAPARTE The Kremlin Ball

CURZIO MALAPARTE The Skin

JANET MALCOLM In the Freud Archives

JEAN-PATRICK MANCHETTE Fatale

JEAN-PATRICK MANCHETTE Ivory Pearl

JEAN-PATRICK MANCHETTE The Mad and the Bad

JEAN-PATRICK MANCHETTE Nada

JEAN-PATRICK MANCHETTE No Room at the Morgue

OSIP MANDELSTAM The Selected Poems of Osip Mandelstam

OLIVIA MANNING Fortunes of War: The Balkan Trilogy

OLIVIA MANNING Fortunes of War: The Levant Trilogy

OLIVIA MANNING School for Love

JAMES VANCE MARSHALL Walkabout

GUY DE MAUPASSANT Afloat

GUY DE MAUPASSANT Alien Hearts

GUY DE MAUPASSANT Like Death

JAMES McCOURT Mawrdew Czgowchwz

WILLIAM McPHERSON Testing the Current

DAVID MENDEL Proper Doctoring: A Book for Patients and their Doctors

W.S. MERWIN (TRANSLATOR) The Life of Lazarillo de Tormes

MEZZ MEZZROW AND BERNARD WOLFE Really the Blues

HENRI MICHAUX Miserable Miracle

JESSICA MITFORD Hons and Rebels

JESSICA MITFORD Poison Penmanship

NANCY MITFORD Frederick the Great

NANCY MITFORD Madame de Pompadour

NANCY MITFORD The Sun King

NANCY MITFORD Voltaire in Love

KENJI MIYAZAWA Once and Forever: The Tales of Kenji Miyazawa

PATRICK MODIANO In the Café of Lost Youth

PATRICK MODIANO Young Once

FREYA AND HELMUTH JAMES VON MOLTKE Last Letters: The Prison Correspondence

MICHEL DE MONTAIGNE Shakespeare's Montaigne; translated by John Florio

HENRY DE MONTHERLANT Chaos and Night

BRIAN MOORE The Lonely Passion of Judith Hearne

BRIAN MOORE The Mangan Inheritance

ALBERTO MORAVIA Agostino

ALBERTO MORAVIA Boredom

ALBERTO MORAVIA Contempt

JAN MORRIS Conundrum

JAN MORRIS Hav

GUIDO MORSELLI The Communist

GUIDO MORSELLI Dissipatio H.G.

PENELOPE MORTIMER The Pumpkin Eater

MULTATULI Max Havelaar, or the Coffee Auctions of the Dutch Trading Company

ROBERT MUSIL Agathe; or, The Forgotten Sister

ÁLVARO MUTIS The Adventures and Misadventures of Maqroll

L.H. MYERS The Root and the Flower

NESCIO Amsterdam Stories

FRIEDRICH NIETZSCHE Anti-Education: On the Future of Our Educational Institutions

DARCY O'BRIEN A Way of Life, Like Any Other

SILVINA OCAMPO Thus Were Their Faces

YURI OLESHA Envy

IONA AND PETER OPIE The Lore and Language of Schoolchildren

IRIS ORIGO A Chill in the Air: An Italian War Diary, 1939–1940

IRIS ORIGO Images and Shadows: Part of a Life

IRIS ORIGO The Merchant of Prato: Francesco di Marco Datini, 1335–1410

IRIS ORIGO War in Val d'Orcia: An Italian War Diary, 1943–1944

MAXIM OSIPOV Rock, Paper, Scissors and Other Stories

IRIS OWENS After Claude

LEV OZEROV Portraits Without Frames

RUSSELL PAGE The Education of a Gardener

ALEXANDROS PAPADIAMANTIS The Murderess

BORIS PASTERNAK, MARINA TSVETAYEVA, AND RAINER MARIA RILKE Letters, Summer 1926

CESARE PAVESE The Moon and the Bonfires

CESARE PAVESE The Selected Works of Cesare Pavese

BORISLAV PEKIĆ Houses

ELEANOR PERÉNYI More Was Lost: A Memoir

LUIGI PIRANDELLO The Late Mattia Pascal

JOSEP PLA The Gray Notebook

DAVID PLANTE Difficult Women: A Memoir of Three

ANDREY PLATONOV The Foundation Pit

ANDREY PLATONOV Happy Moscow

ANDREY PLATONOV Soul and Other Stories

NORMAN PODHORETZ Making It

J.F. POWERS Morte d'Urban

J.F. POWERS The Stories of J.F. Powers

J.F. POWERS Wheat That Springeth Green

CHRISTOPHER PRIEST Inverted World

BOLESŁAW PRUS The Doll

GEORGE PSYCHOUNDAKIS The Cretan Runner: His Story of the German Occupation

ALEXANDER PUSHKIN The Captain's Daughter

QIU MIAOJIN Last Words from Montmartre

QIU MIAOJIN Notes of a Crocodile

RAYMOND QUENEAU We Always Treat Women Too Well

RAYMOND QUENEAU Witch Grass

RAYMOND RADIGUET Count d'Orgel's Ball

PAUL RADIN Primitive Man as Philosopher

GRACILIANO RAMOS São Bernardo

FRIEDRICH RECK Diary of a Man in Despair

JULES RENARD Nature Stories

JEAN RENOIR Renoir, My Father

GREGOR VON REZZORI Abel and Cain

GREGOR VON REZZORI An Ermine in Czernopol

GREGOR VON REZZORI Memoirs of an Anti-Semite

GREGOR VON REZZORI The Snows of Yesteryear: Portraits for an Autobiography

JULIO RAMÓN RIBEYRO The Word of the Speechless: Selected Stories

TIM ROBINSON Stones of Aran: Labyrinth

TIM ROBINSON Stones of Aran: Pilgrimage

MAXIME RODINSON Muḥammad

MILTON ROKEACH The Three Christs of Ypsilanti

FR. ROLFE Hadrian the Seventh

GILLIAN ROSE Love's Work

LINDA ROSENKRANTZ Talk

LILLIAN ROSS Picture

WILLIAM ROUGHEAD Classic Crimes

CONSTANCE ROURKE American Humor: A Study of the National Character

SAKI The Unrest-Cure and Other Stories; illustrated by Edward Gorey

UMBERTO SABA Ernesto

JOAN SALES Uncertain Glory

TAYEB SALIH Season of Migration to the North

TAYEB SALIH The Wedding of Zein

JEAN-PAUL SARTRE We Have Only This Life to Live: Selected Essays. 1939–1975

ARTHUR SCHNITZLER Late Fame

GERSHOM SCHOLEM Walter Benjamin: The Story of a Friendship
DANIEL PAUL SCHREBER Memoirs of My Nervous Illness
JAMES SCHUYLER Alfred and Guinevere
JAMES SCHUYLER What's for Dinner?
SIMONE SCHWARZ-BART The Bridge of Beyond
LEONARDO SCIASCIA The Day of the Owl
LEONARDO SCIASCIA Equal Danger
LEONARDO SCIASCIA The Moro Affair
LEONARDO SCIASCIA To Each His Own
LEONARDO SCIASCIA The Wine-Dark Sea
VICTOR SEGALEN René Leys
ANNA SEGHERS The Seventh Cross
ANNA SEGHERS Transit
PHILIPE-PAUL DE SÉGUR Defeat: Napoleon's Russian Campaign
GILBERT SELDES The Stammering Century
VICTOR SERGE The Case of Comrade Tulayev
VICTOR SERGE Conquered City
VICTOR SERGE Memoirs of a Revolutionary
VICTOR SERGE Midnight in the Century
VICTOR SERGE Notebooks, 1936–1947
VICTOR SERGE Unforgiving Years
VARLAM SHALAMOV Kolyma Stories
VARLAM SHALAMOV Sketches of the Criminal World: Further Kolyma Stories
SHCHEDRIN The Golovlyov Family
ROBERT SHECKLEY Store of the Worlds: The Stories of Robert Sheckley
CHARLES SIMIC Dime-Store Alchemy: The Art of Joseph Cornell
MAY SINCLAIR Mary Olivier: A Life
TESS SLESINGER The Unpossessed
WILLIAM SLOANE The Rim of Morning: Two Tales of Cosmic Horror
SASHA SOKOLOV A School for Fools
BEN SONNENBERG Lost Property: Memoirs and Confessions of a Bad Boy
VLADIMIR SOROKIN Ice Trilogy
VLADIMIR SOROKIN The Queue
NATSUME SŌSEKI The Gate
DAVID STACTON The Judges of the Secret Court
JEAN STAFFORD The Mountain Lion
FRANCIS STEEGMULLER Flaubert and Madame Bovary: A Double Portrait
RICHARD STERN Other Men's Daughters
GEORGE R. STEWART Names on the Land
STENDHAL The Life of Henry Brulard
ADALBERT STIFTER Motley Stones
ADALBERT STIFTER Rock Crystal
THEODOR STORM The Rider on the White Horse
JEAN STROUSE Alice James: A Biography
HOWARD STURGIS Belchamber
ITALO SVEVO As a Man Grows Older
HARVEY SWADOS Nights in the Gardens of Brooklyn
A.J.A. SYMONS The Quest for Corvo
MAGDA SZABÓ Abigail
MAGDA SZABÓ The Door
MAGDA SZABÓ Iza's Ballad
MAGDA SZABÓ Katalin Street
JÁNOS SZÉKELY Temptation

ANTAL SZERB Journey by Moonlight

SUSAN TAUBES Divorcing

ELIZABETH TAYLOR Angel

ELIZABETH TAYLOR A Game of Hide and Seek

ELIZABETH TAYLOR A View of the Harbour

ELIZABETH TAYLOR You'll Enjoy It When You Get There: The Stories of Elizabeth Taylor

TEFFI Memories: From Moscow to the Black Sea

TEFFI Other Worlds: Peasants, Pilgrims, Spirits, Saints

TEFFI Tolstoy, Rasputin, Others, and Me: The Best of Teffi

GABRIELE TERGIT Käsebier Takes Berlin

HENRY DAVID THOREAU The Journal: 1837–1861

ALEKSANDAR TIŠMA The Book of Blam

ALEKSANDAR TIŠMA The Use of Man

TATYANA TOLSTAYA The Slynx

TATYANA TOLSTAYA White Walls: Collected Stories

EDWARD JOHN TRELAWNY Records of Shelley, Byron, and the Author

LIONEL TRILLING The Liberal Imagination

LIONEL TRILLING The Middle of the Journey

THOMAS TRYON The Other

MARINA TSVETAEVA Earthly Signs: Moscow Diaries, 1917–1922

KURT TUCHOLSKY Castle Gripsholm

IVAN TURGENEV Virgin Soil

JULES VALLÈS The Child

RAMÓN DEL VALLE-INCLÁN Tyrant Banderas

MARK VAN DOREN Shakespeare

CARL VAN VECHTEN The Tiger in the House

SALKA VIERTEL The Kindness of Strangers

ELIZABETH VON ARNIM The Enchanted April

EDWARD LEWIS WALLANT The Tenants of Moonbloom

ROBERT WALSER Berlin Stories

ROBERT WALSER Girlfriends, Ghosts, and Other Stories

ROBERT WALSER Jakob von Gunten

ROBERT WALSER Little Snow Landscape

ROBERT WALSER A Schoolboy's Diary and Other Stories

MICHAEL WALZER Political Action: A Practical Guide to Movement Politics

REX WARNER Men and Gods

SYLVIA TOWNSEND WARNER The Corner That Held Them

SYLVIA TOWNSEND WARNER Lolly Willowes

SYLVIA TOWNSEND WARNER Mr. Fortune

SYLVIA TOWNSEND WARNER Summer Will Show

JAKOB WASSERMANN My Marriage

ALEKSANDER WAT My Century

LYALL WATSON Heaven's Breath: A Natural History of the Wind

MAX WEBER Charisma and Disenchantment: The Vocation Lectures

C.V. WEDGWOOD The Thirty Years War

SIMONE WEIL On the Abolition of All Political Parties

SIMONE WEIL AND RACHEL BESPALOFF War and the Iliad

HELEN WEINZWEIG Basic Black with Pearls

GLENWAY WESCOTT Apartment in Athens

GLENWAY WESCOTT The Pilgrim Hawk

REBECCA WEST The Fountain Overflows

EDITH WHARTON The New York Stories of Edith Wharton

KATHARINE S. WHITE Onward and Upward in the Garden

PATRICK WHITE Riders in the Chariot

T.H. WHITE The Goshawk

JOHN WILLIAMS Augustus

JOHN WILLIAMS Butcher's Crossing

JOHN WILLIAMS (EDITOR) English Renaissance Poetry: A Collection of Shorter Poems

JOHN WILLIAMS Nothing but the Night

JOHN WILLIAMS Stoner

HENRY WILLIAMSON Tarka the Otter

ANGUS WILSON Anglo-Saxon Attitudes

EDMUND WILSON Memoirs of Hecate County

RUDOLF AND MARGARET WITTKOWER Born Under Saturn

GEOFFREY WOLFF Black Sun

RICHARD WOLLHEIM Germs: A Memoir of Childhood

FRANCIS WYNDHAM The Complete Fiction

JOHN WYNDHAM Chocky

JOHN WYNDHAM The Chrysalids

BÉLA ZOMBORY-MOLDOVÁN The Burning of the World: A Memoir of 1914

STEFAN ZWEIG Beware of Pity

STEFAN ZWEIG Chess Story

STEFAN ZWEIG Confusion

STEFAN ZWEIG Journey Into the Past

STEFAN ZWEIG The Post-Office Girl